The Seven

by Simon Leighton-Porter

Mauve
Square
Publishing

This book is dedicated to my dear wife, Wendy.

Chapter One

Patras, Greece. AD 60

Gasping for breath, the Galilean dashed between the market stalls, pulling down awnings, lines of washing and baskets of produce as he ran. Anything to buy time, anything to slow them down. To the left a narrow opening between the mud-brick walls, partially hidden by a curtain: he pulled it aside, moving from bright sunshine into the cool depths of the passageway beyond. Now in his fifties and overweight, he knew he couldn't out-run them; he would just have to try and lose them in the warren of lanes and alleys surrounding the port. As he ran, lungs bursting, he heard once more the sound of pursuit closing in: they had seen him. A bend in the passage hid him from sight and at the end, emerging into the sunlight once more, he turned right and forced his unwilling legs uphill towards the acropolis. It would take him away from the port, in completely the wrong direction, but perhaps they might not expect him to head that way. Perhaps.

Glancing behind, he never saw the outstretched arm which caught him across the throat like a rope, slamming him down onto his back. Winded and in pain, he tried to ward off the kicks that seemed to be coming from all directions: a vicious blow to the ribs and then rough hands pulling him upright. 'Not planning on leaving us so soon, Andreas?' said a short, wiry young man who had pushed himself to the front of the crowd. 'Aegeas would like a little word with you first.' A fist caught him flush on the side of the head.

He struggled but there were too many of them; thirty or more, the usual band of dockside toughs, marshalled by five Roman soldiers who looked on in contempt as more blows rained down.

The soldiers dragged him, bloodied and groaning, into the presence of Aegeas. Tertiary syphilis had rendered the Roman governor of Achaea's face a hideous mask and had twisted his mouth into a permanent rictus grin. He stood up from behind his desk and, using his cane for support, hobbled round to Andreas. 'Release him,' he said.

The soldiers obeyed but the Galilean's feet went from under him and he slumped down onto the cold marble floor. He looked up at Aegeas in supplication and through lips swollen from his beating, tried to speak. 'I can explain –'

The Roman moved closer and one of the soldiers bent to pick

1

Andreas up. 'Leave him,' said Aegeas, gesturing them away. They stepped back at once: Obedience to Aegeas was instinctive; a life-preserving reaction. For a moment he stood over Andreas, saying nothing and then struck him across the face with the heavy cane, causing his victim's hands to come up in an effort to protect himself. After ten, maybe a dozen blows he stopped, caught his breath and then spoke as though they were discussing the price of olive oil.

'If there's one thing I cannot abide, it's disrespect, Andreas.'

'Please sir, let me explain –'

'No, please, kindly allow me. Interrupt again, Andreas,' he said without a trace of emotion, 'and I'll have your tongue cut out. Now, talking of tongues, it's your stupid tongue that's landed you in this mess, isn't it? Answer me, man.' As his voice rose, his disfigurement caused the words to run into a menacing cobra's hiss.

'Yes, sir, it has.' Andreas spoke as though every word was an agony.

'Yes.' Another venom-laden hiss. 'I very politely asked you to stop preaching sedition. Nero himself has made it clear that filling the plebeians' heads with nonsense about your imaginary Jewish god and about Christ and his stupid conjuring tricks, is punishable by death. I've been lenient with you, Andreas, I could've had you crucified but I gave you a chance, didn't I?'

Andreas tried to shift position, but the pain from a broken rib caused him to cry out. 'But you don't understand, sir. I serve a higher authority – '

'A loose tongue and a disrespectful one. You disobeyed an order from the Emperor, you turned down a polite invitation to come and speak to me and then had the discourtesy to try and leave my province without permission. And then when you are brought before me, you fail to remain standing in my presence.' He gestured once more to the guards. 'Pick him up. I want to make sure he hears this.' They heaved Andreas to his feet and Aegeas hobbled towards him, so close that the Galilean could almost taste the foul odour from the governor's rotting gums. 'Together with your friends, the boatmen, you will be scourged and crucified tomorrow on the beach. For you, however, we have a little treat. No nails, just ropes. And before you thank me, understand that it will take you twice as long to die. Get him out of my sight.'

Expressionless, Aegeas watched the soldiers drag him away, his pleas for mercy echoing down the corridor. Once they were out of sight he returned to his desk and picked up a folding bronze frame no bigger than a man's hand. On each interior face was a layer of hardened beeswax. With a stylus he carved two simple figures: A.X. Pulling the leather strap tight around the frame, he applied his wax seal and shouted for his personal slave. 'Tell the captain of the guard,' said Aegeas, 'that he is to deliver this into the hand of the emperor himself. He will be expecting it.'

The slave disappeared at a trot down the same corridor, closing the door at the end. A few moments later, Aegeas was joined by the young man who had spoken to Andreas from the crowd. The governor turned to greet the new arrival. 'You did well, Josephus.' he said. 'The emperor will be most grateful.'

'A pleasure as always, sir.' he replied, his slightly accented Latin betraying his Judean origins.

Andreas' fate was sealed and with his execution, the newly-fledged Christian church would have its first martyr – Saint Andrew. Few but Josephus knew the crimes of which Andreas was guilty: and for Josephus this was personal.

Chapter Two

Oxford University, the present day.

Flora Kemble glared at the ringing telephone. The evening out with her girlfriends had already been organised so this had to mean work and more delays. Who else but a fellow academic – and probably one of the many at the university without a social life – would call at six o'clock on a Friday?

At twenty seven she was the youngest member of the department and Friday had been an eternity in coming. After a long week teaching a summer school class whose members made up for their lack of knowledge by an overdose of enthusiasm, she was tired, hot and wanted to go home. With a sigh she put down her briefcase, pulling her long dark hair away from her face, first into a pony-tail then away from her left shoulder as she put the receiver to her ear. 'Department of palaeography, Dr Kemble.' In response, a man's voice greeted her in Italian, a language she spoke fluently, but none the less, it took her a few seconds to work out who was speaking. Then she recognised the voice and a tiny but palpable frisson ran through her, something she couldn't define, a spontaneous warmth that caused her attractive, heart-shaped face to break into a smile. Flora hadn't spoken to Dr Francesco Moretti for nearly a year and the pleasure at hearing the handsome archaeologist's voice put aside all thoughts of leaving the office. 'What a lovely surprise, Francesco. Not like you to be working so late on a Friday,' she said, gently teasing.

'That's why I'm calling. It's so good I don't want to go home.'

Flora smiled again and looked at her watch: six o'clock in the UK meant seven in Naples. 'For you to be at work at this hour on a Friday, it must be good. What have you found?'

'Well, it's not 100% certain, but we've found a villa at Pompeii….a villa that looks like it belonged to Josephus.'

'Josephus!' Flora sat upright and almost dropped the phone in shock. 'There's no evidence of his ever having set foot in Pompeii. Are you sure?' she asked, her hands trembling with excitement.

'Pretty sure, but we're going to need your help,' said Moretti. 'How quickly can you get here?'

'Well, I'll have to check with the Dean but tell me what you've got

4

and I'll call him.'

'What we've got is the ground floor and cellar of a villa, about three hundred metres south of the main site, just off the Via Tenente Ravallese. They're redeveloping some flats and the guys putting in the foundations hit archaeology.'

'Hardly surprising.'

'No, and we thought it was going to be a routine conservation job too. But then we found a lintel with "*T. Fl. Ios fecit.*" on it.'

'Come on, Francesco, don't tease. That's not conclusive, you know as well as I do. What else have you got?'

She heard him laughing down the line at her impatience. 'Are you sitting down, Flora?' he said.

'Yes, I'm in my office. Come on, this isn't fair,' she laughed. 'What've you got? Tell me.'

He paused for effect. 'A largely intact codex on parchment of *The Wars of the Jews* and plenty of fragments from *The Antiquities of the Jews*: we may even have enough to put together a full copy, we're keeping our fingers crossed.' A piercing squeal of excitement forced him to hold the phone away from his ear.

Flora could barely contain herself. 'But that means –'

'Yes,' continued Moretti, 'They predate the Martial codex by at least twenty years, maybe more, because although most of them are in Greek, some are written in Aramaic.' Once again, he moved the phone away a few inches. It was a wise precaution.

'But that's unbelievable,' said Flora, unable to control her excitement. 'Has anyone made a start on translating them? Any textual validation?'

'Yes. I was waiting for the results before I called you. They've just come in. Donald Sumter got here three weeks ago and he's positive about the date – he says they were written within ten years of the eruption – but he's still hedging his bets on the authorship.' The line went quiet. 'Flora, are you still there?'

'Yes. I'm here,' she said, all the enthusiasm gone from her voice. Donald Sumter, professor of ancient history at William Sunday University, Alabama: world authority on ancient Aramaic and Coptic, Bible scholar, TV evangelist and full-time pain in the neck: that's all I bloody need, she thought. 'Nothing like Donald to take the shine off things, is there?'

'Look, I know you two don't get on –'

'Don't get on?' said Flora. 'The man's a bigot, a misogynist and a

5

religious maniac. Why on earth did you use him of all people?'

'Because he was available at short notice, he self-funds and he's good.'

'Does he know I'm coming?' she heard Moretti's voice catch and pause. 'Well? Does he know or not?'

'Yes.'

'And what did he say?'

'Look, Flora, we can talk about that once you're here.'

Flora sighed. 'OK, Francesco, it's your dig, I'm sorry. I didn't mean to be rude. Now, come on, this is better than Christmas: tell me what else you've found.'

'It's simple,' he replied. 'As well as a domestic occupation layer we've got a scriptorium. Nearly everything in it looks like original texts by Josephus: some in Aramaic, others in Greek and a big heap of letters in Latin, but those are on papyrus and in a pretty poor state so the conservators are nervous about letting us near them yet.'

'That's brilliant,' she said, all thoughts of the odious Sumter banished from her mind. The questions tumbled out. 'What about the other finds, the codices, what's the state of conservation like?'

'Much of it's in poor condition but some of the parchments are fabulously preserved – almost up to Egyptian standards. The roof of the building stayed in one piece when it came down. It obviously gave way early on during the eruption and there was a good thick layer of dry, compacted pumice and ash around everything. The pyroclastic surge doesn't seem to have had much effect on the finds: too much insulation and too little oxygen at a guess, and the concretion layer has done an excellent job of keeping the humidity constant.'

'Francesco, I'll be there,' she said. 'Even if I have to pay my own way, I'll come. Let me call the Dean.'

When at last she tracked him down, the Dean of the faculty agreed to the trip at once such was the importance of finding new work by one of the few known eye-witnesses to the tumultuous history of first century Galilee and Judea.

She phoned around her friends to let them know she wouldn't be coming out that evening. But despite her excitement over the coming trip to Italy, she couldn't help having slightly mixed feelings on what she would be missing. One of her old girlfriends from undergraduate days, who, after a long period of singledom, punctuated only by a succession of unsuitable men, had finally found what promised to be "the one" and so Flora and the rest of the gang were going along to give him the once-over. Herself recently single, at least she could savour the vicarious enjoyment of seeing a dear friend happily paired off. But instead, she was packing for at least two weeks in Italy, jumping up and down on her suitcase, trying to get the lid down on a several "just in case" items she knew she'd never need but would feel lost without.

Next, she phoned her parents and then set off in search of the cat which was sunning himself in the small courtyard garden at the back of her two-up, two-down Victorian cottage just off the Iffley Road. It was her little refuge against the world: safe behind its shiny blue front door, she felt nothing unpleasant could ever reach her, and to leave it, even for something that promised to be the highlight of her professional year, was still a wrench.

She bundled the protesting cat into his carrying box and put it into the back of her elderly Toyota before heading out of town towards her parents' house which stood at the head of a wooded valley just outside the Oxfordshire village of Shipton-under-Wychwood. Despite her good intentions to return to Oxford straight away and spend the evening finishing off all the loose odds and ends of work, the prospect of cold poached salmon with her mother's home-made mayonnaise for supper was just too tempting. She put up a brave fight, but then when her father brought her one of his eye-wateringly strong gin-and-tonics for "sundowners" she realised that resistance was futile and she'd be spending the night in her old bed.

The main course was nearing its end when Flora's father got up from the table. 'I don't know what it is about Chablis, but one bottle between three is never enough.' Her mother pretended to disapprove but did nothing to prevent him reappearing with the slim green bottle, its sides dripping with condensation.

'So what's the hurry?' her mother asked as the cork popped open. 'You said you had to go to Pompeii, but why?'

Flora took a sip of the cool, golden-green wine. 'Well, I still can't bring myself to believe it, but Francesco Moretti – I've told you about him before haven't I –?'

'I think so, dear,' said her mother absent-mindedly.

'Anyway, Francesco's people have uncovered a villa that looks as though it belonged to Josephus.'

'Is that good?' her father asked.

'Good? It's better than that. Josephus is one of the only reliable – well reliable-ish – eye-witnesses to what happened in Israel during the second half of the first century. He was a Jewish priest who was very

7

pally with Nero at one stage but then ended up as a rebel commander during the war against Rome in AD 66.'

'So what did they do? Feed him to the lions?'

'No, that's the funny thing. They captured him in AD 67 and somehow he talked Vespasian round into believing that he, Vespasian that is, would fulfil a religious prophecy by becoming a great leader and in the end they let him go.'

Her father shook his head in disbelief. 'Amazing what people will believe. Nothing changes, does it?'

'It gets better,' said Flora. 'A few years later he went to Rome and became a protégé of the Flavians – that's Vespasian, Titus and Domitian – and he didn't do badly out of it financially either. And if Francesco's right, at some stage he was given a house at Pompeii. Up till today there's no record of his ever going there. What we do know, or thought we knew, is that he did most of his writing in Rome for a Roman audience, trying to spin the history of the Jews to make them seem a more significant civilization.'

'He seems to have had a happy knack of changing sides when it suited him,' her father said. 'He'd have made a good spin-doctor.'

'Let's put it this way,' said Flora. 'History hasn't been very kind to him and he doesn't get a good press. But to answer your question, mum, the reason they've asked me to go is that they've found what look like original writings by him. Isn't that wonderful?'

Her mother's eyebrows rose. 'Well I hope it keeps fine for them, but if these bits of paper –'

'Papyrus and parchment actually, mum.'

'Well whatever they are, if they've been in the ground since Vesuvius erupted, why the rush?'

The logic was inescapable and Flora smiled. Good old mum, she thought, sensible to the last: good job one of us is. 'Well it's a rush for us. It may not sound much, but for me it's a bit like finding the Holy Grail. You see, not only is it some of the earliest ever surviving writing on parchment – it has to be AD 79 or before because that's when Pompeii was buried – but it throws the chronology of Josephus' writing up in the air. Plus there are some unidentified works which I'm hoping might give us some clues about *The Seven Stars*.'

'And what's that?' asked her father.

'It's a work attributed to Josephus that's mentioned in passing by Suetonius, the Roman historian. Supposedly it's a major demolition job on the early Christian Church but no copies survive.'

'So what happened to it?'

'The smoking gun suggests it was suppressed by Eusebius, one of the church fathers who edited the Bible to suit the status quo of the time.'

'I think we did something about him at school – can't remember much about it though, rather a long time ago.'

Flora smiled at him indulgently: playing the old buffer again. She continued. 'A few of the writings that got kicked out of what became the New Testament have turned up in places like Qumran and Nag Hammadi, some have been lost forever. Other works Eusebius and his chums didn't like got the chop too.'

'Like *The Seven Stars*, you mean?' said her father, taking a sip of his wine and settling back in his seat with a contented sigh.

'Precisely. And if Francesco's people have found even a fragment from it, well,' she paused. 'It would be too wonderful for words.'

'Well I think that sounds like cause for celebration,' he said, pouring the last of the wine into their glasses. 'I'll open another bottle.'

Flora's mother turned a beady eye on him. 'No you won't,' she said. 'Flora's got things to do tomorrow and besides, it'll make you snore.'

***

And so the following Monday, with most of her last-minute good intentions for the weekend still pending, Dr Flora Kemble, head of Oxford University's palaeography department, set off to catch the 10:55 flight from Heathrow to Naples.

As the door swung open and Flora stepped onto the air-bridge the heat at Capodichino airport hit her like the blast from a jet engine. From the controlled chaos of Naples station she took a Circumvesuviana train to *Pompei Santuario*.

By the time she arrived her t-shirt was clinging to her back and she could feel beads of sweat gathering under her thick hair starting to trickle down her back. The reality of seeing modern Pompeii for the first time came as a shock. Even on a hot summer's afternoon the dirty streets wore a sombre air of menace: two prostitutes lounged semi-naked on a bench under a tree, indifferent to the disapproving looks of an elderly *nonna* who scuttled past like a black beetle; stray dogs squabbled over the contents of shredded bin-bags in the streets which were criss-crossed by a web of wires providing illegal electrical connections to the tenements on either side.

Pulling the bag behind her, she trudged the few hundred metres to the hotel Sorrento which was in a side-street just off the Via Sacra. After what seemed like an eternity, her ring on the reception counter bell

9

produced a surly young woman whose tousled appearance suggested she'd just got out of bed. On hearing Flora's fluent Italian, she became more welcoming and even offered a better room at no additional charge. The room itself was clean, basic and to her surprise, not only did the air conditioning work but the small en-suite bathroom looked as though it had been refurbished by someone fully-sighted and was devoid of live bare wires.

The following morning dawned cloudless and, fortified by almost ten hours' sleep and an industrial-strength coffee with breakfast, Flora, clad in shorts and t-shirt, a pair of stout boots and wearing a broad-brimmed hat to keep off the sun, slung her bag over her shoulder and set off to walk the few hundred metres to the dig site. The local policeman at the entrance was reluctant to let her in, but over his shoulder, she saw a familiar tall, angular figure striding towards her, arms outstretched. His, angular, high-cheekboned face creased into a boyish, lop-sided grin. She subconsciously rebuked herself for the reaction it caused: unbidden and unexpected, that same indefinable sensation that she'd felt when he had phoned her in Oxford was back.

Moretti greeted her with a hug and a smacking kiss on both cheeks: the policeman shrugged and without further comment let her pass. Moretti's words tumbled out in an excited rush as they walked across the sun-baked patch of waste-ground that had once been the communal gardens of the flats. 'We've found more this morning,' he said. 'It just keeps coming.'

'No problems with the *Soprintendenza Archaeologica* wanting you to conserve rather than dig?' she asked. The administrative body charged with overseeing Herculaneum, Pompeii and the other Roman sites in the shadow of Vesuvius, had decided a few years earlier to concentrate on conserving and protecting what had already been found, rather than adding to the problem by allowing new excavations. As they neared the dig site, Flora recognized several familiar faces from the *Soprintendenza Archaeologica di Pompei* and from the National Archaeological Museum in Naples, for whom Francesco Moretti worked.

'They were as keen as we were to dig this site and to get it as much publicity as possible,' he said, stopping a few paces short of the trench.

'That's not like them,' said Flora. 'Pompeii's falling apart faster than they can conserve it.'

'Local politics,' said Moretti, with a shrug.

'But I thought you were part of the Ministry of Culture, what's local politics got to do with it?'

'The land has been bought by local businessmen, the building company is owned by local businessmen, the same local businessmen who also own the demolition company and same ones whose company is putting in the drains. Now do you understand?'

'The Mafia, you mean?' asked Flora.

'Shh, not so loud. Anyway, they're called the *Camorra* round here. But yes, them. They usually have no cause to bother us but it's easier to stay on good terms.'

'What? Even the *Soprintendenza?*' she asked.

He gestured for her to follow him, away from where the diggers were working. 'You don't know how this place works, and it's not just Pompeii and Naples, it's the whole Campania region.'

'What is?'

'The Camorra. Everything that moves, anything that's sold, every contract that's signed, they're involved. If we upset them over this dig another Roman pillar will just happen to fall down at the ruins or another restored building will catch fire. Tomorrow I'll show you all the illegal restaurants and souvenir stalls – in fact on second thoughts, I'll show you the legal ones, there are fewer of them.'

Flora looked at him aghast. 'D'you really mean they'd damage Roman Pompeii itself? Surely, not even the Mafia –'

'Camorra. Yes, they do when it suits them or they've got a bone to pick. To them, it's theirs, their livelihood to exploit as they see fit: the *Soprintendenza* is nothing more than a minor irritation if they feel like digging up something valuable and clearing off with it. Just remember, Flora, they're everywhere.'

'It just seems so unfair,' she said.

'I sometimes think God has a sick sense of humour,' said Moretti. 'Look at the countries that've got all the oil and if that wasn't bad enough look where he left Pompeii for us to find: Campania. Great eh? So please, for my sake, watch what you say and who you say it to.'

She nodded. 'Understood. Can we take a look? I'm dying to get started.' Donning a hard hat, she accepted the invitation of Moretti's archaeologists and climbed down the ladder into their trench. Patiently and with the finesse of a watch-maker, one of the diggers, a young woman about the same age as Flora, was using a dental pick and an artist's brush to remove two-thousand-year-old solidified ash from around what had once been a wooden box.

'It's a difficult balance,' she explained to Flora. 'We have to work quickly because the wood has already started to deteriorate in contact with the atmosphere, but if we go too fast, we risk destroying the archaeology.'

'Is the wood carbonised?' Flora asked.

'Amazingly enough, no. There was enough depth of pumice to protect it.'

'Any idea what's likely to be inside?'

'More of the same at a guess. Parchment, papyrus, writing tablets.'

'Any dating evidence?' asked Flora, eyes wide with excitement.

'Not yet. I don't know whether Francesco told you but we found a box like this containing letters, but they're too delicate for us to handle.' She stopped scraping at the concretion for a moment and turned to Flora. 'I suppose that's why you're here, isn't it?' she said with a smile.

'It is. And I can't wait to get started,' she replied, getting to her feet and brushing the grit from her knees.

'Oh, I nearly forgot,' said the digger. 'There were some other finds and they've been taken back to the Applied Research Laboratory: an astrolabe and several sheets of what we think is copper, but nothing datable. They're covered in some sort of grid and there are a few letters: it looks like some kind of board game.'

'Like you said, that's why I'm here. And thanks for letting me look in your trench.' Flora climbed the ladder back up to ground level and exchanged hard hat for sun-hat.

She found Moretti, chatting to another group of archaeologists working on a section of painted Roman wall plaster. He broke off to join her. 'Exciting, isn't it?' he said.

'It's great, but I won't be happy until I've seen the documents themselves.'

Moretti laughed. 'Come on, I'll drive you over to the lab and you can take a look. You can say hello to your old friend, professor Sumter, too.'

Flora pulled a face at him. 'Yeah, great. I can hardly wait.'

They pulled up outside the modern, single-storey building and Moretti led the way into the air-conditioned cool of the conservation lab. The clinical silence together with the white coats of the technicians gave it the air of a medical facility rather than anything connected to archaeology. He introduced Flora to his staff and then took her to a smaller room where a tweed-coated back greeted them as they opened the door. Even at the height of summer, Professor Donald Sumter always wore a jacket and tie. He looked up from a series of fragments of *The Wars of the Jews* codex, turned and rose to greet them. Although he was in his mid sixties, the American academic looked younger: a full head of snow-white hair topped a suntanned and artificially lifted face. He flashed them his well-practised and artificially whitened TV evangelist's smile. 'Good morning, Francesco, and good morning, Flora. How nice to see you again.' He took off one of his white cotton gloves and extended a hand which she shook, doing her best to return the smile. She already felt ill-at-ease in his presence and was aware of how scruffy she looked in her digging clothes.

'So you've come to help me out?' he asked. The smile had already been turned off and with his back turned once more; the question was addressed to the window opposite. She assumed it was meant for her.

Flora searched for a diplomatic response. 'Francesco asked me to come over. I'll give the project any help I can.'

'I think you may've had a wasted journey,' said Sumter. 'Based on the content and linguistic style, I think they're either copies or earlier source texts. Maybe even doctored versions by an unknown scribe – fakes in other words – but I don't think they're by Josephus.'

Moretti, who didn't speak English well, looked at Flora with a puzzled expression on his face. She switched into Italian. 'He thinks they're not Josephus' work.'

He shook his head and rolled his eyes. 'So he's been saying for the last few days. Can you give us a second opinion?'

'I'd be delighted,' said Flora.

'I don't think that'll be necessary,' said Sumter in English, still facing away from them, hunched over the precious texts. Flora had forgotten that Sumter had a few words of Italian.

She turned once more to Moretti, ignoring Sumter's remarks. 'Where do you want me to start?'

'You can give me a hand indexing the –'

'I was talking to Francesco, thanks, Donald.' He's started, she thought: treating me like his graduate assistant already.

Sumter harrumphed, the mask of affability abandoned as quickly as he had donned it. Without speaking, Moretti indicated for her to follow him. 'There's something I'd like you to take a look at,' he said as they headed for the door. 'Something odd.'

'You're wasting your time,' said Sumter, once more without looking up. 'I've told you, it's some form of board game like a larger-scale version of *latrunculi* or *pessoi*. Interesting archaeology, but not what either of us is here for, Flora.'

They returned to Moretti's office. 'Do you think he's serious about the codices not being by Josephus?' asked Flora.

'He seems to be. When he first started he was convinced they were the real thing, but over the last few days he's started to voice doubts.'

'I think I can guess why.'

'So do you think Donald's wrong?' he asked.

'Not necessarily,' said Flora. 'I won't know for sure for days – weeks maybe – but given the cut-off date of August AD 79, even without looking at any of the codex fragments or having the precise archaeological context, I'd say they're earlier, that's all. And that could mean your team's found one of the missing originals. Now the question is, which one?'

'What do you mean?'

'Well, in the preamble to the *Wars of the Jews* – the version he presented to the emperor Vespasian just before his death in 79 AD – Josephus mentions an earlier version, written in Aramaic, but that of course never survived.'

Moretti's face lit up. 'Some of the fragments we've found are in Aramaic so do you think we've got a copy of the early version? That would be wonderful.'

Flora smile back. 'I don't see why not. What a brilliant find.'

'It's incomplete and much of it's damaged but we've done some digital imagery. Do you want to look at the scans?'

'I'd love to,' she replied. 'I'm sure Donald will take his time with the originals: especially now I'm here.'

'Look, Flora, I know he's difficult, but he is thorough and he's good at what he does.'

She laughed and held up her hands in surrender. Yes, I know, and I realise I'm a guest here too, but I just have a feeling he'll be twice as thorough as he needs to be if he thinks it'll hold me up.'

'Perhaps, perhaps not,' said Moretti, flashing a smile at her. 'The conservators have said we can have more of the originals to work with tomorrow and then you can get started on dating them properly.'

'This is worse than looking at your presents under the tree but knowing you've got to wait till Christmas Day,' said Flora, melting slightly under the spell of that smile.

'I know how you feel, but if it helps, there are other finds you can work with right now. Here, take a look at this.' Moretti opened a climate-controlled document safe the size of a small filing cabinet and removed a clear Perspex box about a foot square by a couple of inches deep, containing a flat black slab. 'It's what Donald thinks is a board game.

We've found six of them so far and this is the best preserved. Tell me what you think.'

Flora took it from him and laid it flat on the desk. She swept a loose strand of hair from her eyes and, using a strong oblique light and a magnifying glass, started to examine the pitted metal surface. After a few minutes, she put the glass down and looked at Moretti intently. 'I'm not sure what it is, but it's definitely not a board game,' she said. 'Every square has a letter or character in it.'

'That's what I thought. Now look at this,' he said, handing her a piece of paper. 'It's a digitally enhanced scan of the surface.'

Flora pored over the scan for a few moments. 'Have you found any documents in the same trench, clay or wax tablets, anything that follows the format of the Devil's Codex?' she asked.

Moretti looked puzzled, 'Is that the same as the Devil's Bible?'

'No, you're thinking of the *Codex Gigas* which is much later – thirteenth century I think. The Devil's Codex is a bit of a misnomer, really because it's not one document but lots of fragments, all of which date from the early first century to the beginning of the second.'

'You mean the code thing? I thought it was dismissed as a fake long ago.'

Flora sighed. 'Dismissed by Donald Sumter, yes, but he's a linguist, not a palaeographer and given that no one's managed to decode any of it, it's hard to see his point.'

'So you think it's genuine after all?' said Moretti.

'Maybe, maybe not. There are literally thousands of individual sheets and fragments in circulation, some of which are certainly fakes, but I'm still convinced some of them are genuine. Have you found anything written in what look like random pairs of letters in this dig?'

An expression of suspicion crossed Moretti's angular features. 'Yes. We found two incomplete fragments on papyrus. But how did you know?'

'Because of the copper sheets.'

'I'm still not with you.'

Flora picked up a marker pen and walked over to the whiteboard where she drew a five by five grid and then turning back to Moretti, said. 'Francesco, have you ever heard of Polybius?'

'Vaguely. You mean the Greek historian?'

'That's him. Now look at this.' She filled in the grid with the letters of the modern alphabet:

	1	2	3	4	5
1	A	B	C	D	E
2	F	G	H	I/J	K
3	L	M	N	O	P
4	Q	R	S	T	U
5	V	W	X	Y	Z

Flora continued. 'Polybius invented a way of creating a substitution cipher, so if you stick to a "row-then-column" rule, then "BELLUM" becomes 12 15 31 31 45 35. You don't have to use numbers for the row and column headings, letters or symbols will do just as well. It's not a sophisticated code and was easy to break even then because the same letter is always represented by the same pair of figures.'

Moretti nodded. 'But presumably, if you increased the size of the grid you could have the same letter represented in multiple different ways.'

'Exactly. Which brings us back to the copper sheet,' said Flora. 'It has a grid which is twenty three by twenty three, giving you over five hundred ways of representing the twenty three letters in the Latin alphabet. If you use Greek, then you've got twenty four letters and Coptic has thirty two.'

'But that's fantastic,' he said, eyes wide with excitement. 'If what we've found is in code, then the sheet could be the key.'

'It could, but before we get carried away, even a cipher using a big grid backed up with an additional text key can be cracked. Charles Babbage was doing it in the mid-nineteenth century.'

'So why has nobody deciphered it?' he asked

'Probably because there are multiple layers of encryption or it has a very long text key like the Beale Ciphers use.'

'But you think these copper sheets can help?'

'They could. Especially if trying to be too clever has stopped us seeing the obvious.'

He looked at her with his head cocked to one side and a half smile on his lips. 'Obvious to you maybe. And do you really think you can solve something that no one else has been able to crack?'

'No promises, Francesco, but I've got a couple of ideas. If you can let me have copies of the scans from all the copper sheets and a copy of the encoded text, I'll let you know within the hour.'

Moretti made a gesture of surrender. 'OK, you're on. I'll get you set up with an office and a PC but I'll bet you fifty euros you don't find anything.'

'I haven't got fifty euros,' said Flora with a laugh. 'And besides, I wouldn't want to take your money.'

Chapter Three

The Ionian Sea, September AD 62

For a moment the *Cygnus* hung motionless before pitching into the trough of the next wave. For thirty hours they had been trying to make way against the combined effects of the current and a violent *Euroquilo*, blowing from the north-east and pushing them ever closer to the lee shore of Sicily.

Below decks it was pitch dark. The cooking stove, a fire hazard in seas like these, had been extinguished. The few remaining oil lamps that hadn't been jolted from their mountings and smashed on the deck had long ago burned out. The air was foul with the reek of unwashed bodies, fear, vomit and the stench from the overturned lavatory bucket. Ninety six passengers and crew were all consumed by the same thought and the young Judean was not alone in praying to his god for salvation. To his right he could hear prayers being said in Greek, to his left, others sought the mercy of Lord Neptune in Latin, offering to make extravagant sacrifices should the supplicant come safe home. The ship rolled once more and the noisome slurry received a top-up as seawater cascaded down the companionway, swilling the jumbled collection of flotsam towards where he was sitting. He pulled his knees up to his chest in a futile attempt to avoid another drenching by the revolting cocktail. This time it splashed against the sides of the rough wooden platform on which he sat, perched on a drenched linen palliasse, shivering and soaked. In the darkness, he heard the man to his right being sick again and felt the warmth of the vomit as it hit his leg. He had to get out into the fresh air.

Swaying and cursing, he lurched towards the glimmer of light coming from above. At the bottom of the steep wooden steps he stumbled as the ship pitched forwards and broached hard left. He grasped for the rope that he knew ran either side of the steps but found only thin air and crashed face-first into the ankle-deep slurry. From somewhere above came the sound of splintering wood. He'd heard a similar sound about an hour ago but this was louder: as one who understood nothing of ships, even he knew it wasn't a good sign. Anything, even being wrecked, must be better than this he thought, pulling himself to his feet and bracing himself against the lower rungs.

Pushing open the hatchway, he crawled and half fell onto the heaving deck. Night was over and from ahead, the first grey streaks of dawn lit the eastern sky. Astern lay the jagged teeth of the rocky shoreline. Despite the efforts of the crew, the ship was making no way against the storm – they'd lowered the mainsail long ago to prevent it being shredded by the wind, and with only a shallow keel and just the *supparum*, the small triangular topsail rigged above the yard, the only realistic thing for them to do was to keep the ship's head up into wind and hope the storm would blow itself out before it drove them ashore. He stood, clutching the mast and looked, mesmerised, as the coastline grew closer and more distinct with each passing moment. Timing his rushes, he made his way aft towards the stern-castle and the helmsman's post where the crew were clustered around one of the steering oars. He let go his hold and, profiting from a brief moment when the deck wasn't perpendicular, slithered across to join them. He spotted the helmsman, a man with whom he'd struck up a friendship. He was known as "Gubs" the standard nickname for a ship's *gubernator*. 'Come for a ringside seat then, Josephus?' he yelled, his voice only just audible above the wind screaming through the rigging.

'Is there anything I can do to help?'

'You could try praying.'

'No, I meant to help with the ship.'

'That's what I mean, lad. The *clavus* has broken.'

'Is that bad?'

Gubs ducked as a wall of green water broke over the bow and rushed along the deck at them. 'If it wasn't bad I wouldn't be asking you to pray. The *clavus* controls the steering oars, so it's a toss-up whether we go beam-on and capsize or whether we stay afloat long enough to be driven on to the rocks.'

'And there's nothing I can do?'

'Learn to swim.'

'I know how to swim but in that sea? None of us would last five minutes.'

'Well, you won't have long to wait. Look.' He pointed towards the thin black line of coast. The rain had stopped and as the ship crested another wave, Josephus saw the flickering pinprick of light on the horizon.

'What is it?'

Gubs shielded his eyes against the flying spray. 'It's the *pharos* at Syracuse.'

Josephus moved closer so he could shout into the man's ear. 'Is there any chance we can make harbour there?'

'None,' he yelled back. 'We're already too far south and we'll be on the Siren's Daughters soon.' Josephus looked at him blankly. 'They're a group of rocks and shoals and we're no more than twenty stadia from hitting them.'

'What can we do?'

'I told you. Get ready to swim,' shouted Gubs. 'And watch out for *Lamia*.'

'I don't believe those fairy stories,' Josephus shouted back.

'It's not a fairy story, she's a bloody great fish and I've seen her with her snout out of the water – twenty feet long with horrible, dead black eyes, a big triangular fin and a mouth full of daggers. Jumped clean out of the water with a full-grown seal in her mouth she did. Seen her take dolphins and tuna too off the coast of Malta. If we go down, *Lamia* won't be far away. She never is when there's a wreck.' Gubs peered into the distance once more. 'There, look!'

'Not *Lamia*?' Even Josephus, who held the Jewish disdain for what he saw as barbarian superstitions, was beginning to have doubts. Weather this bad had to be supernatural.

'No,' Gubs shouted in his ear. 'See that line of white?'

'Yes.'

'That's the sea breaking over the Siren's Daughters.'

'Can't we go round them?'

'If we can get steerage I think I can get our course close enough up to the wind to get round to the north. Stand aside and we'll have a try.'

Josephus moved away to shelter behind the cabin leaving Gubs swearing at his green-faced and terrified seamen as they tried to jury-rig a system to give them at least some control over the ship's massive steering oars. He crouched down out of the wind which howled through the rigging as though the entire barbarian pantheon of monsters was mocking their fate. The clouds parted and the grey early-morning monochrome was replaced by low, raking light, showing the sea boiling over the flat rocks which stretched like a wall behind them. He watched, transfixed, unable to take his eyes off the seething cauldron into which the wind was driving their ship. At over one hundred feet long, when viewed at her moorings, the *Cygnus* had seemed vast, impregnable, a force of nature, but now it was being tossed like a cork, a plaything for the angry elements.

A shiver ran the length of the vessel as it grazed against the outliers of the Siren's Daughters and Josephus watched in horrified fascination as weed-encrusted rocks seemed to grasp at the hull as they drifted past, almost touching distance from where he crouched. Any hopes of divine intervention were now long past: the God of the Children of Israel was either angry or too preoccupied to bother with the plight of the handful of Jews on board.

The end, when it came, was not what he'd been expecting: the *Cygnus* checked in the water and with a shudder, came to a halt. Is that it? He wondered. Maybe the stout wooden planking that had looked so solid from the quayside would show that Roman shipwrights were more than a match for anything the seas could do, but another sound, more worrying than the grinding and splintering, jolted him back to reality. Audible, even over the roaring of the seas, came a high-pitched keening, a Babel of screaming, prayers and imprecations: the hull had been breached and the ship was taking on water. Below decks, people were clawing at each other, screaming, gouging and trampling – parents fighting to be ahead of their children, husbands and wives careless of everything save the will to live; those who had already drowned now stepping stones for the living. Josephus peered round the side of the deck-house and watched, horrified, as by ones and by small groups, the survivors tried to run away from their fate by clustering at the bow of the ship which was already beginning to rise as the vessel settled by the stern.

A swell floated the ship off one rock but the next collision turned it broadside onto the sea. With a shudder, its port side was forced against a flat shoal, and now, exposed to a beam sea, it lurched to leeward and the mast gave way, snapping the rigging and pulling its mountings clear out of the deck. A small group of survivors who had just emerged blinking into the daylight from the hatch were caught up in the tangle of rope and timber and swept over the side, their heads bobbing for a moment above the waves before disappearing. Josephus braced himself against the rail and looked down into the water, now barely feet below him, wondering whether it was better to get it over with and choose his moment of dying or to cling to what remained of the ship. Nature took the decision for him as a massive wave smashed through the deck-house, splintering the door and carrying the roof away.

Then everything went green and he tumbled forward, pulled down by invisible hands and so disorientated that he couldn't even tell in which direction the surface lay.

Chapter Four

Manhattan, the East Side

'My sources tell me you're good and you have the overseas connections we require.' The diction was Old South, the slow, precise speech of a man sure of his position and confident of his impact on others. Like his shorter colleague who sat next to him with his hands folded in his lap, he was dressed in a suit and tie and from his neatly-cut grey hair down to the immaculately polished black lace-ups, everything about Andrew Irvine said attention to detail.

The door opened and the two men rose to meet the newcomer, a tall man in his early forties. Raymond shook Irvine's hand, his black skin contrasting with the snowy white hand in his. He looked Irvine straight in the eye waiting for him to look away or to betray the slightest hint of emotion. Raymond had learned from experience: the ones who looked away too soon were the ones you don't trust, the ones who'll screw you over in a heartbeat. Irvine's gaze never flickered and, with a slow-spreading smile, Raymond gestured for him to sit down. He then shook hands with Irvine's colleague – shifty, a mouth that smiled but eyes that didn't: eyes that looked away too soon. Interesting, he mused. Neither of the visitors had given their names. 'Well, gentlemen,' said Raymond, 'you've come to the right place, but let's get some the rest of the introductions out of the way first, shall we? Hey, Luzzo,' he shouted. 'Get your ass in here.'

The short, skinny Italian-American deserted his listening post at the other side of the door, shoved the 9mm pistol back into his waistband. and poked his head into the room. Luzzo's protruding ears and low hairline set above closely-grouped features gave him the air of an inquisitive chimpanzee. 'Yeah, what is it?' The accent was pure Brooklyn.

Raymond noticed an almost imperceptible flicker of disgust cross Irvine's face at Luzzo's appearance: the man was fallible after all. He turned to face Luzzo. 'I'm sure our guests aren't carrying concealed weapons, nor, I hope, are they wearing a wire but hey, in God We Trust, everyone else pays cash. Isn't that right, gentlemen?' he said, turning once more to the two visitors, expecting at least a smile.

'We put our trust in the good Lord, that much is true, sir,' came the frigid reply. It was the first time the smaller man had spoken apart from the pleasantries of greeting and Raymond was impressed by the way he made "sir" sound almost genuine.

They submitted without demur to Luzzo's fast but thorough search. 'Clean,' he said.

'I never doubted it for a moment,' said Raymond.

Irvine fixed him with a cold, blue, Presbyterian stare that left even Raymond feeling uncomfortable. 'We trust in the good Lord – we are men of integrity.'

'Well then you've come to the right place,' said Raymond. 'As for the good Lord, I don't bother him and he don't bother me over-much, and as regards integrity, I think we may be able to help you there because mine is flexible in the face of the right amount of cash.'

The two Southern Gentlemen exchanged glances. 'As I told you on the phone Mr...sorry, I didn't catch your last name –'

'Raymond, just call me Raymond.'

'As I told you, Raymond,' Irvine continued. 'The people I represent cannot pay the sums you're asking and we'd appreciate an opportunity to explain why we think a lower offer is appropriate.'

Raymond glanced at Luzzo who replied with a slow shake of the head. 'It's high risk,' said Luzzo. 'My contacts, the people who source what you're looking for: hey, even talking to those guys I'm sticking my neck out. That price is cut to the bone –'

'And to show our good faith,' cut in Raymond, 'We've even put up some of our own money already. But if you can't honour a fair price then I regret to say we have nothing more to discuss other than to inform you that when you come back to us – and you will, because no one else is capable of meeting your requirements – then you'll find the discount on offer right now will have gone. I can assure you, we're the only game in town.'

'Do you mind if my colleague and I go someplace to talk about this?' asked Irvine.

'You can stay right here,' said Raymond. 'We'll go grab a smoke. Take your time, gentlemen, and if you need to use the phone, please go right ahead. Nine for an outside line.'

Closing the door and leaving them alone, Luzzo and Raymond perched on the desk in reception, each drawing deeply for his nicotine hit. 'What d'you think?' asked Luzzo, blowing a cloud of blue smoke into the cool breeze that streamed from the air-conditioning.

'If they're serious they've got no choice.'

'You reckon they're serious?'

'Sure I do,' said Raymond. 'They're amateurs, but they've obviously got good backers. They're just trying to nickel-dime us, that's all.' After about five minutes, the door swung open and a face peered out. 'Do we have a decision, gentlemen?' asked Raymond.

'Yes, sir, we do,' said Irvine. 'We've spoken to our client and he's willing to proceed at the price you mentioned with twenty-five percent of the money up-front.'

Raymond smiled and shook his head. 'Come now. Let's keep *amour propre* out of this, shall we? Fifty percent up-front are the terms we agreed, take it or leave it.' With a glance to his left, he stood up and Luzzo, taking his cue, did the same. 'I'll bid you a good day, gentlemen, and I wish you a safe and pleasant trip back to Alabama. My colleague will show you out.'

The four shook hands and Raymond was left alone, chuckling to himself at the spectacle of church-going southern white boys trying to hustle him.

***

Pompeii

Later that afternoon Moretti returned to the lab and joined Flora in her temporary office. He looked over her shoulder at the screen of her laptop. 'When do I get my fifty euros?' he asked with a good-natured smile.

'Interesting question,' she replied. 'I'm not sure who's won the bet.'

'What do you mean?'

He could see straight away that Flora was feeling extremely pleased with herself. 'Well, I haven't had any luck with the texts your people found on the dig site,' she said. 'But thanks to the grid on your copper sheets I think I'm getting somewhere with a couple of the Devil's Codex fragments.'

'You're kidding. Let me see.' Moretti was wide-eyed with excitement.

'There you go,' she said, tapping the screen with her pencil and looking up at him, still with a look of triumph on her face.

His face fell. 'But that's still a meaningless jumble of letters.'

'No it's not. Look.' Flora tabbed to a new window showing a scan of what looked like a partially-completed jigsaw. 'This is one of the fragments that Donald dismissed as a fake when it was found at

24

Oxyrhynchus in the early eighties.'

Moretti peered at the screen. 'I can see there are pairs of symbols but I couldn't even tell you what alphabet that is.'

'It's Latin cursive – lower case to you and me. And what's more, I think I've got a translation thanks to grid number three.' She tabbed back to the previous view. 'If you take this pair of letters, RL and go to row R, column L you get the letter A, EM gives you Q and so on until you get AQYR.'

'And what does that stand for?' asked Moretti, looking even more puzzled.

'It doesn't stand for anything but if you try it phonetically, *Alaph, Qoph, Yudh Resh* and then read it right-to-left, you get something that sounds like "ryacka".

'Is that Hebrew?'

'It's Aramaic. It means "fool".'

'Could be a coincidence.'

'It isn't. I've got some complete phrases. Listen.'

When she finished Moretti's eyebrows raised. 'Could be Chinese for all I know, but I'll take your word for it,' he said. 'What does it mean?'

'The name is missing, but from the gender of the direct object, the writer is referring to a male and he says, "...fool....bring him to me" then there's a gap and I think this fragment is the adjective, "alive".'

Moretti looked at her, wide-eyed in admiration. 'But that's amazing, Flora. You're a genius. When I think of all the years –'

'That's because everyone who's tried to decipher it has assumed that because the cipher was written in Latin, then the encrypted text had to be in Latin too. One of the other fragments gives coherent phrases when you take grid one and transliterate the output into Koine Greek – that was the lingua franca of the Mediterranean in the first century. You know something else?'

'N-no,' he stammered.

'I'd put money on there being more grids down there in that trench of yours. How many did you say you've found?'

'Six.'

'Well I reckon there should be seven at least.'

'Why's that?'

'Take another look at your scan of grid two,' she said, handing him the print-out. 'See that image in the top right hand corner?'

He squinted through the magnifying glass. 'You mean the thing that looks like a tadpole?'

'Yes. And now look at grid four. It's the only other one with the top right corner intact. What do you see?'

'The dotted outline of a tadpole.'

'Except it isn't,' said Flora. 'I took the liberty of asking your people to re-run the scans at different magnification and to change the spectrographic filter settings to enhance the relief. Now look at your tadpoles.'

She handed him two more print-outs and Moretti let out a low whistle. 'That's Ursa Major.'

'Not only is it Ursa Major but if you look carefully, there's a faint outline around one of the stars in the tail, see, where it bends. The star's called *Mizar*. And on this one, the bottom left star of the body, *Phecda*, also has a ring round it.'

'But what's it showing us?' asked Moretti, wide-eyed. 'It couldn't be a reference to *The Seven Stars*, could it?'

'I'm trying not to let myself carried away,' said a beaming Flora. 'Depends on whether you believe Suetonius who says the book existed, or Eusebius who says it didn't.'

'But if any of those fragments turn out to be from *The Seven Stars* –'

'Then you've discovered the find of the century. The Church won't like it but you're going to be famous, Francesco.' She jumped up and gave him a hug.

'I'd sooner be rich than famous,' he said, giving her an affectionate peck on the top of her head. 'For now, we can't assume anything about *The Seven Stars*: I think we should look for a more prosaic explanation.'

Flora thought for a moment. 'If you want prosaic then I'd say that whenever someone – let's assume it was Josephus – wanted to tell the recipient how to decipher a message, there'd be something, a mark maybe or perhaps something in the first line of the text, to indicate which grid to use and the stars in Ursa Major correspond to the numbers one to seven. But you know what I'm really looking forward to?'

'No.'

'Donald's face when we show him.'

Moretti looked at her indulgently. 'Please be nice to him, Flora. Remember, he is my guest.'

'Oh, don't you worry, Francesco,' she replied, with a grin. 'I'll be as nice as can be: far better to stick the knife in with a smile on your face. After all, that's what he always does.'

They walked back down the corridor to the office where Sumter was working, their knock receiving a grunt that they took as an invitation to enter. As usual, he didn't bother looking up to see who had had the temerity to disturb him and continued to ignore them, even when Flora went and stood next to him. She politely cleared her throat to announce her presence.

'Yes, Flora. What is, it? I *am* in the middle of something you know,' he said, remaining head-down over his work.

'Just thought you'd like to know that thanks to Francesco and his team, we've had a bit of a breakthrough.'

'Flora is being modest,' added Moretti. 'It's a miracle.'

'Not loaves and fishes?' said Sumter, still with his back to them.

Moretti's English didn't run to sarcasm and he turned to look quizzically at Flora.

'Donald's just made a joke, Francesco. First one since records began in 1965,' she said in Italian.

At last Sumter stood up and turned to face them. 'Listen, Flora, I've got a lot to do. If you've got some information pertaining to the work we're supposed to be getting on with, then please tell me.'

'Oh, it's nothing really, Donald, and if you're busy I can always come back. It's just that thanks to the copper grids, I've deciphered some of the Devil's Codex.' She paused, expecting the news to take the wind out of his over-inflated sails but if he felt any emotion, his face betrayed none.

'I'm impressed. Well done,' he said, making eye contact for the first time. 'I never said the Devil's Codex wasn't old, I merely said that all the fragments we have are either worthless or more recent fakes. What have you got?'

She spread the handwritten text in front of him, trying to hide her anger at his crushing dismissal. 'These are from some of the Oxyrhynchus fragments and using the grids from the dig, they transliterate into Aramaic. Not only that but the grids show the Romans were using this kind of cipher fifteen hundred years before Vigenère came up with it.'

He put his glasses back on and scrutinised her work like a teacher presented with homework that even the dog wouldn't eat. 'Impressive but you've mis-transcribed some of it: that's to be expected, I suppose.'

Flora bristled. 'I think you'll find that I've transcribed it perfectly correctly. If whoever encrypted it made errors, that's hardly my fault.' Moretti caught her eye and his expression seemed to be pleading with her not to start a row.

'It matters little anyway,' said Sumter, 'What you've got is indeed in the Western Aramaic dialect, but deciphering insignificant messages that've been in the public domain for thirty years is hardly what you're here for. I'm more concerned, and I'm sure Francesco is too, about the anomalies in this version of the *Antiquities*. You do realise it's missing the *Testimonium Flavianum* from book eighteen. Now, I'm not saying you haven't been very clever, my dear –'

It was the opening shot in a re-run of the squabble they'd been having since they first met, and being addressed as "my dear" was a provocation too far. 'Listen, Donald,' Flora said, her voice rising in anger. 'Don't you bloody well –' Moretti laid a calming hand on her arm.

'Flora, don't take the bait. He's just being a smart-arse.' He used the Italian word *cacasenno* to make sure Sumter wouldn't understand. 'Let him think he's wonderful if he wants to. Be nice, remember. Now tell me, what's the missing text?'

She turned her back on Sumter to speak to Moretti. 'The *Testimonium Flavianum* is the name for a series of passages in *Antiquities* where Jesus is mentioned by name. It describes him as "the Christ", it also says he was "a doer of wonderful works" and says something along the lines of "after the crucifixion, he appeared to them, alive, after the third day, as the prophets foretold along with tens of thousands of other wonderful things about him."'

'Did Josephus write that or was it added afterwards?' asked Moretti.

'Depends who you ask,' she replied. 'I say it's definitely a later addition, Donald says not –'

'Not even worth discussing,' he said with a snort. 'The *Testimonium Flavianum* is one of many proofs of the New Testament's literal truth. I know that may offend your atheistic sensibilities, but there's no way round it. God's honest truth, like it or not.'

'Any chance of seeing what you've translated so far?' asked Flora, eager to change the subject and to stop the argument before it boiled over into something worse.

'Certainly,' said Sumter indicating a neatly-stacked pile of handwritten papers. 'I'll e-mail it to you when I've transcribed it onto one of those wretched word-processor things.' His tone made it clear that so far he was concerned, the conversation was at an end.

'Oh, before I go,' said Flora, stopping and turning round in the doorway. 'Anything in the version of *Antiquities* from the dig about the number seven?'

'Seven?'

'You know, seven-headed beasts, seven stars, anything like that which wasn't in the existing version.'

Sumter's tone was off-hand and dismissive. 'I think there may've been a vague mention,' he said. 'Why do you ask?'

'Oh, nothing really,' replied Flora, trying to hide the note of triumph in her voice. 'Just thought you'd be interested to see what was in the top right-hand corner of a couple of the copper grids, that's all.' She walked back to Sumter and, ignoring his outstretched hand, placed the print-outs on the table beside him.

Sumter picked them up and although he feigned indifference, Flora noted with satisfaction that he recoiled slightly with surprise at the sight of the star pattern.

Flora and Moretti returned to his office. 'Is this as big as I think?' he asked.

'Probably bigger. Until today everybody accepted that *Antiquities* was published just before the end of the first century. But that's all been chucked out of the window.'

'So do the existing copies date from that time?'

Flora hopped up onto the side of the desk and sat, swinging her legs, looking every inch the schoolgirl on an outing, rather than a twenty seven year-old PhD. 'No. Just like the Bible, what's come down to us has been heavily edited to favour one particular point of view.'

'Not Donald's at a guess.'

'Not Donald's at all,' she said with a smile. 'The earliest fragments of *Antiquities* are from the *Codex Ambrosianus* which was written by sixth century copyists, whereas the earliest full-length copies are as late as the eleventh century. Now, there are a number of academics, me included, who reckon that Josephus' references to Jesus' divinity are all later add-ons – probably originated by Eusebius around 300 AD – given that no other contemporary sources mention Jesus until the fourth century.'

Moretti smiled. 'I can see why Donald doesn't share your opinion,' he said.

'Precisely. So far as he and his friends at William Sunday are concerned, *Antiquities* helps validate the literal truth of the New Testament.'

'And now this new version has turned up – '

'It does just the opposite. Quite.'

'Which is why he's so keen for it to be a copy, a fake or some earlier source document rather than Josephus' original version.'

'It's a pretty contorted way of looking at the facts,' said Flora. 'But

29

that's Donald all over.

Chapter Five

The Ionian Sea, September AD 62

Like a leaf in a mill-race Josephus tumbled end-over-end through the water. To his surprise, he felt no panic, no fear, no pain even: drowning was nothing like he'd expected, a brief pang of regret, but the acceptance that death was inevitable left him strangely at peace. Suddenly, his tranquil, green dreamscape lightened and he bobbed to the surface like a cork, gasping in lungfuls of air, all thoughts of submission to the elements forgotten as he fought to stay on the surface.

The *Cygnus* was now fifty feet away and the waves were driving him further away from her with each second. Despite knowing it was hopeless, some inner force drove him to try and swim back but after the second flailing stroke, his arm crashed painfully into something solid. At first he thought he'd hit a rock but as he tried to grab hold, it moved under his grasp and he saw it was a section of the deckhouse about ten feet square. Ignoring the splintered edges which tore at his skin, he tried to haul himself onto it but it gave under his weight and he slithered back into the water. At the third attempt he managed to get his upper body onto it and by grabbing a cross-beam was able to hold himself in place, too exhausted to do more. On occasions as he was lifted onto the crest of a wave, he saw other survivors struggling nearby, but then his raft would slide down into the next trough and they were lost to sight.

While trying again to haul himself further on to the raft it moved in a way that suggested something was pulling it down from the other side. Rational thought fled in the face of what Gubs had said about *Lamia* and her predilection for shipwrecks. He had to get clear of the water, maybe she couldn't harm him then, and so with a despairing heave, he clawed his way onto the flat planking. As he did so, he came face-to-face with a man he recognised as a passenger from the ship, who was also scrabbling for purchase on the bare boards. 'Here, give me your hand,' shouted Josephus. The man's grasp was weak and no sooner had he taken hold than he let go, so Josephus crawled towards him and, taking hold of the shoulders of his tunic, hauled him onto the wood. Their combined weight pushed it lower in the water, making the task easier and so, now clear of the rocks, the makeshift raft and its human cargo drifted on the swell, driven towards the distant coastline by the wind.

The light began to fade and all Josephus could think of was sleep. He was bitterly cold and the thought of just being able to doze off for a few moments was beyond tempting, but then he remembered the tales Gubs had told him during the first leg of their journey, of his own first shipwreck and the five men clinging to life in a swamped lighter off the coast of Dalmatia, and how the only ones to survive were those who'd fought the temptation to sleep that the cold always brought on, a sleep from which none of the others awoke. He could see Gubs' face now and wondered aloud where he was, talking to him, asking him questions, babbling nonsense, anything not to let his eyes close.

'What did you say?' The voice came from close at hand.

'Gubs?'

'No. I haven't seen him. My name's Alityros. You were rambling.'

'Sorry, I was trying to stay awake. Are you all right?'

'I am thanks to you. We're nearly ashore. Look.' The sight that greeted them was little more encouraging than the Siren's daughters. Long, raking rollers were breaking on a headland, backed by a line of low cliffs. To either side were short stretches of sand and pebble, scoured by the surf and littered with the detritus of the storm.

Paddling and kicking as best they could to steer away from the rocks, the two castaways missed the jagged teeth of the headland by a matter of feet and were swept into the relative calm of the bay to its south. The surf was pounding on the fine shingle and the two men let go of their precious life-raft about three hundred feet from land, letting the waves carry them into the shallows. Alityros tried to stand up but the current pulled his feet from under him and Josephus, half dead with fatigue, dragged him through the breakers, stumbling and falling as he went. At last, the two men lay exhausted and shivering on the beach, unable to move and with the waves still washing over them. By a supreme effort of will Josephus managed to rouse himself and crawled over to his companion. 'Come on, Alityros, we can't stay here. We've got to find help,' he said.

'Just let me sleep first.'

'No,' said Josephus, grabbing him by the back of the tunic and shaking him. 'If you sleep here you won't wake up – you can't give in now. Come on, man, get up.' Like two drunks trying to get each other home but merely making things worse, Josephus and Alityros clung to one another, weaving and stumbling their way up the beach. The shingle gave way to yielding sand as they reached a low ridge of dunes where the effort of each step took on a nightmare quality.

32

On cresting the ridge, there was no sign of life, just the usual low scrub of holm oak, juniper and laurel. Alityros stopped, gasping for breath with his hands on his knees. 'So which way now?' he asked through salt-cracked lips. 'I've got to find water. There must be a river, surely.'

'North,' said Josephus. 'Gubs said we were south of Syracuse, so if we follow the coast we should find it.'

'But it could be miles. I can't walk that far.'

'There's no choice. If we stay here we'll die.'

Night was falling and the wind, which had backed to a northerly direction whistled through the clumps of Marram grass, rendering progress even more difficult, so they moved a little inland to get off the sand but the ground there was rocky and uneven and the coarse vegetation tore at their bare legs. The two men plodded on, bent forward into the wind, each lost in his own little bubble of suffering, their progress hindered by constant detours brought on by the shape of the coastline and the intrusions of creek beds, all tantalisingly dry. Gradually, Josephus, the younger and fitter of the two, began to leave his companion behind, until from behind him in the gloom, he heard Alityros' rasping voice calling for him to wait. He stopped but when the Roman reached him, he just carried on past, seemingly oblivious to Josephus' existence. Now it was his turn to suffer: he'd stopped and the effort required to get going again was almost too much.

Somehow, Josephus managed to take the first step and then the next. In the gathering dusk he could see the dark outline of his travelling companion, about twenty paces ahead. Gaining on him slowly, they both descended into the next hollow, Josephus concentrating more on watching his footing to avoid taking yet another painful tumble into the spiky undergrowth rather than looking too far in front. However, when he looked up, the shuffling form ahead of him was now at least fifty paces distant. He rubbed his eyes and tried to force the pace but his legs just wouldn't respond. 'Wait,' he shouted. 'Wait for me, I can't keep up.' But the wind snatched his words away and the silhouette continued relentlessly on. He called out once more and then saw him stop, turn and retrace his steps. Josephus increased his speed, trying to make up the lost ground before his rejuvenated companion pushed on again. However, on approaching he thought he heard human voices and then the single form split itself into two, once more calling into question years of disbelief and scorn at the notion of barbarian deities. He stumbled closer: no gods, no demons, just two men, deliriously happy to have found one another.

33

'Alityros, is that you?' said Josephus.

'Yes and I've found Gubs,' came a reply from the dark. 'We're going to be all right.' Josephus too embraced the helmsman, delighted that another soul had been spared from the wreck.

'It's good to see you two,' said Gubs. 'I thought we were the only survivors.'

'Who's "we"?' asked Josephus.

'All-powerful Neptune was good enough to save about thirty others. I've left them down on the beach trying to get a fire going while I fetch help. Most of them are in no fit state to walk.'

'So if Neptune is so all-powerful, how come he let us get wrecked in the first place?' snapped Josephus.

Gubs turned on him angrily. 'How would I know? I'm a sailor, not a priest. And besides, fat lot of good you did by praying to your camel-rogering lubber of a god – probably wouldn't know sea water if he fell in it.'

Josephus decided against starting a theological argument and turned to more practical matters. 'So how far are we from Syracuse?'

'Too far,' said Gubs. 'There are villages to the south of the city, so we can try there, but we'll have to be careful.'

In the moonlight, Josephus saw Alityros' eyes widen with alarm. 'Why's that? Are they really cannibals?' he asked.

'No, not cannibals,' said the seaman. 'But wrecking is more profitable than fishing, and survivors aren't treated as welcome guests.'

'W-why's that?'

'Well it's obvious. If you're making off with the contents of a wrecked ship, the last thing you want are witnesses, and secondly, most people will drown rather than see their gold go down to the bottom, so there's a good chance that at least some of those who wash up will be worth robbing. And if they're dead, they're not likely to put up much of a fight or complain, are they?'

'So d'you think they'll try and kill us?' asked Alityros.

'Not if you do as I tell you. If asked, you're members of the crew and I'm your watch commander. Got that?' The two men nodded. 'Good. Now if you can keep up, we should make Arenella in an hour or so.'

The two men followed Gubs, trudging on in silence, thirst rendering conversation a painful necessity rather than something companionable. After what felt more like two hours than one, they climbed to the top of another scrubby ridge and saw firelight about half a mile further on. 'It's not much, but that's Arenella,' said Gubs. 'Remember what I told you, and watch your backs, we may have to fight our way out.'

'Fight?' said Alityros in a quavering voice.

'Yes, fight. I take it you've done your time in the army?'

'No, I got a deferment. I had bad feet. I'm an actor.'

'Great. Now you fucking tell me,' said Gubs. 'Just what we need in a tight corner, a professional bloody pansy. Look, I'll tell you what, if trouble breaks out, offer them your arse and while they're having you, me and the camel jockey here will make a run for it.' That seemed to conclude the debate and the three men continued down the slope towards the village – a group of primitive shacks clustered round a small natural harbour.

They were about fifty yards from the first buildings when the barking started. First one, then another of the village dogs took up the refrain and by the time they'd gone another twenty paces they saw figures, silhouetted by makeshift torches, coming out to meet them, the flickering light glinting from their knives and fishing tridents. 'Stop here,' said Gubs, and moving forward, came to a halt a few paces further on with his right hand held aloft in greeting, addressing the welcoming committee in a rough Latin patois that Josephus barely understood.

'Who the Hades are you and what do you want?' said a burly man, pointing a crude spear at Gubs' chest.

'Social call, that's all,' he replied. 'The *Cygnus* and ninety souls, wrecked on the Siren's Daughters.'

'I asked you who you were.'

'I'm the ship's *gubernator* and these are two of my boys.'

'What were you carrying?'

'Garum and wheat.'

'That all?'

'Yes, and before you go getting your hopes too high, the ship broke up and the only passengers who survived got out in what they stood up in. You might pick up some decent timber, but that'll be about it'

'Ninety souls, you say? We can't look after that many – it's as much as we can do to make a living here.'

'We're not asking you to. There's about thirty survivors on a beach an hour south of here. If you can get water to them in the morning, we'll push on to Syracuse and organise ships to come and take them off. I'll make sure the *Cygnus's* owner knows about what you've done and that you're properly rewarded.'

'How do I know I can trust you?'

'You don't,' said Gubs. 'But you've nothing to lose and plenty to

35

gain by offering three men a drink and somewhere to lay their heads. Now for pity's sake, give us some water. Please.'

The water was stale and tasted of the goat whose skin the bottles were made from but for the three survivors it was nectar. Their hosts, after overcoming their initial misgivings, even offered them food: a watery stew made from fish heads and well past its prime – although to them it was the finest meal they'd ever tasted.

The following morning the sole reminder of the storm was the heavy swell which continued to beat against the rocks of the little fishing harbour as they set off for Syracuse. Good to their word, the men of the village had left at first light with amphorae of water for the other survivors who had passed a miserable night, huddled together for shelter in the dunes.

Josephus and his two colleagues struck inland to pick up the *Via Elorina* which led north east towards the city, and within an hour were picked up by a carter who took them the rest of the way in relative comfort, perched on the back of his load of firewood. Alityros and Gubs seemed to have patched up their differences from the night before and the former entertained them with a series of anecdotes about life as an actor in Rome and with scurrilous tales of the doings of the imperial court.

The sun climbed higher, and rocked by the gentle movement of the cart, Alityros began to snore while the others carried on talking.

'You never did tell me why you were going to Rome,' Gubs asked Josephus.

'Diplomacy.'

'And what's that supposed to mean?'

Josephus shrugged. 'You know, asking favours, doing a few in return.'

'What kind of favours? And who from?'

'Nero.'

Gubs laughed. 'Ask a silly question. Come on, I'm curious.'

'All right,' he said with a sigh. 'I don't see what harm it can do. Without going into too much detail, I'm reasonably well-connected in Judea and three of my countrymen are currently staying as Nero's guests in Rome.'

'Jewish prisoners, you mean? What, like the Christians?'

'No, absolutely not,' snapped Josephus. 'Nothing like them at all, in fact quite the opposite. These are men I know and respect: well-bred, highly-educated members of our priesthood who are friends of Rome.'

'But they're still in chains, right?' said Gubs.

'I wouldn't put is as crudely as that, but let's just say that owing to a slight misunderstanding their liberty is somewhat constrained at the moment.'

'And you're going to ask Nero to let them go, is that it?'

'Something along those lines.'

Alityros woke up and joined the conversation. 'Well I hope it keeps fine for you, Josephus.'

'What do you mean?'

'Are you interested in the theatre? Do you play the lyre, act or sing?'

'No.'

'Well in that case you won't get anywhere with him unless – '

'Unless what?'

'Unless you can get the right side of Poppaea Sabina, you haven't a chance.'

'So they're married now? I'd heard rumours but I didn't know it was official.' said Josephus.

'Earlier this year.'

'So how do I get to meet her?'

'She's a good friend of mine and I'll introduce you,' said Alityros who had woken up. 'Least I can do for someone who saved my life.'

They sat on the back of the bullock cart, legs swinging over the tail in the dust stirred up by the wheels and chatting about nothing in particular until at last they came to the gates of Syracuse.

'So how are we going to get to Rome?' asked Josephus as they walked through the city streets.

'More to the point, when do we eat?' said Alityros.

'I think I can answer both of those. Look,' said Gubs, pointing towards the *pharos* which was just visible above the red-tiled roof-tops.

'What are we supposed to be looking at?'

'The standard of the imperial fleet. I served ten years under Volusius Proculus. I was with him right from when he was a junior officer and now he's commander of the Puteoli squadron. The standard means they're in port.'

'Is that good?' asked Alityros.

'It is if you want to get home before the fleets stop sailing for the year.'

Chapter Six

From somewhere in another world, Flora could hear a persistent bleeping sound: her mobile phone. Pale strands of light showed through the shutters and as she fumbled for the source of the noise, she noticed that the clock by the bedside showed 6:15 AM. She rolled onto her side and answered the call: it was Francesco Moretti. At first, she couldn't make out what he was saying, so loud was the background noise of shouting and what sounded like police sirens but then she realised that she could hear the same wailing, coming from only a few streets away. 'What is it, Francesco, what's the matter?'

'I'm at the lab. There's been a break-in.'

'Oh Christ, is there anything missing?'

Moretti's voice choked with emotion. 'Almost everything from the dig. The codices, the copper plates, the astrolabe. It's all gone.'

She felt for a moment as though someone had punched her in the stomach. 'Oh good God. Is there anything I can do?' she asked. 'I'll come over if you need me there but I don't want to get in the way.'

He asked her to wait while he checked with the police. 'Can you come over now? They want to take a statement and fingerprint you – don't worry, they're doing everyone, it's just routine.'

Flora fell out of bed, pulled on her clothes, tied her hair back and set out for the lab, the chill of the morning air coming as a shock after the warmth of the bed she'd left so hurriedly. The *Carabinieri* had set up a cordon and she had to call Moretti to come and vouch for her before they would let her through.

Inside, an appalling sight greeted her. The lab had been systematically wrecked and the floor was a mess of broken glass, splintered woodwork and awash with spilled chemicals. In the offices, PC screens had been slashed and the few machines which remained had had their hard disks removed; but worst of all, the air-tight, climate-controlled cabinets and safes which held the dig's finds had been smashed open and their contents removed. The lab's server room had been torched and the stench of burnt wiring caught in her throat. Flora felt sick to the stomach and turning to Moretti, asked, 'Have you told Donald about this?'

He looked down at his feet. 'My English is not very good – '

She put a consoling hand on his arm. 'And you'd like me to do it?'

He nodded and Flora dialled. Sumter's response was predictable: he raged and shouted, and "incompetent" was about the most polite thing he said about the Italians in general and the *Soprintendenza Archaeologica* in particular, during the entire tirade.

It took only fifteen minutes for Flora to give the Carabinieri a statement and she rejoined Moretti who was walking in helpless circles in the wreckage of his office. 'Come on, Francesco, let's go and have breakfast,' she said. 'You're not doing any good getting in the way here.'

Around the corner they found a workmen's café. A dozen pairs of eyes turned to look at the strangers and Flora winced as they ran their gaze over her body, mentally undressing her without even bothering to hide what they were doing. She affected not to notice and the two of them took a corner seat. 'So did anything survive?' she asked, taking a sip from her scalding coffee.

Moretti shook his head. 'One or two fragments from the conservation lab, but that's about it.'

'How much had been recorded?'

'Not much. We'd only just started and most of that's gone too.'

'What do you mean?'

'You saw the server room,' he said.

'Yes, but surely you have off-site back up? Please don't tell me – '

Moretti rubbed his thumb and first two fingers together. 'No money, Flora. They saved a few thousand euros and now look at what it's cost them. No offsite back-up and if we can't recover anything from the network, then it's all gone. Your laptop and Sumter's are all we've got, those and a few digital photos on my team's own cameras.'

'And do the Carabinieri have any idea who did it?'

'They think so.'

'Not the ma…'

He held a hand up to silence her. 'I told you, don't use that word. But yes, them.'

Flora was beside herself. 'But if those documents aren't properly conserved, in contact with light and humidity they'll fall apart within months, days some of them.'

'Yes, but you don't understand,' replied Moretti. 'These gangs have been doing it for years, they're professionals. They have people working for them who…I hate to say this, but who have day-jobs as archaeologists and who make more in two or three weeks working for the Camorra, than they can in a year as badly-paid state employees.'

'So you think it was an inside job?' she said, aghast.

'I'm saying it's not impossible, that's all.'

'But who? And why go to all the trouble of destroying the PCs and the servers?'

Moretti shook his head again. 'That's what the Carabinieri want to know. Normally when a gang steals finds they only break what they need to: you know, get in and out as quickly as possible. Well, here, they certainly took their time.'

Flora stared into space, deep in thought. 'It's almost as if they didn't want there to be any trace of these finds ever existing. Surely, that wouldn't increase the black-market value, would it?'

'Just the opposite. If there's no verifiable provenance, then it's far harder to know whether what's on sale is the real thing or not. All I know is that I hate them, Flora. I promise you, if I catch them, I'll kill them myself.'

She reached across the table and patted him affectionately on the hand. 'Come on, let's not talk about killing anyone. How about a walk round the block? The smoke in here is starting to hurt my eyes.'

They wandered back towards the lab, Flora keeping pace with Moretti while he thought aloud about who could have been responsible for the break-in.

'What if it wasn't the Camorra?' asked Flora. Moretti made no reply but just carried on staring into the middle distance. 'Are you listening to me, Francesco?' she asked.

'What? Sorry, I was miles away. It's not been good lately.'

'I'm sorry,' said Flora. 'I didn't mean to be insensitive. This must be awful for you – it's awful for all of us, and it's your dig after all.'

'No, it's not that,' he said, stopping and turning towards her. 'Are you free this evening? To talk I mean.'

She looked at him, perplexed. 'Well, yes. I thought you'd want to be home with Anna though, particularly after what's happened.'

'Anna's away at the moment.'

She thought she detected a slight catch in his voice. 'Sure. Where do you want to meet?'

'There's a place I know just up the road. I'll pick you up at half past seven.'

'Look, Francesco, you've got a busy day in front of you, are you sure you'll have the time? I won't be offended if you'd prefer to leave it.'

'That's kind of you, Flora,' he said. 'But I need the company...' He broke off as his mobile phone rang. She could tell from his expression and the monosyllabic replies that it wasn't good news. 'That was the

Carabinieri,' he said. 'The local police have just called them. Someone's vandalised the dig site too.'

'Oh, Christ, no,' said Flora, the colour draining from her face.

'Come on, we can be there in five minutes,' said Moretti and they broke into a run.

On arriving at the dig the damage was worse than they had feared. Somebody had got the keys to the team's mechanical digger and now, in place of the neat, straight-sided precision of the archaeologists' trench was something more like a bomb crater. Wall plaster bearing traces of paint that hadn't seen daylight for nearly two thousand years lay mixed with brickwork, earth, hardened volcanic ash and fragments of Roman building materials in a series of random heaps. They peered into the hole: whoever had done it had smashed right through the building layers and down to the natural rock below – the trench was robbed out and any hopes of continuing serious archaeology completely gone.

'*Tombaroli*,' said Flora, using the Italian word for grave-robbers.

'I know,' said Moretti, standing with his arms hanging limply by his side and staring in abject disbelief at the remains of what had been potentially one of the finds of the century. 'I know,' he repeated, as if talking to himself. 'But I don't understand is why.'

'Greed, ignorance: those are the usual reasons.'

'No, it's not that. If they were after gold or statuary, something solid, then I could understand why they'd use a digger. But if they were after fragile pieces of written work, and especially working in the dark, all they'd do is smash everything into a pulp.'

'Which is what they've done,' she said, crouching down to sift through the tumbled remains with her bare hands.

The *Sovrintendente* in charge of the crime scene came over to join them and Moretti introduced himself. 'Did anyone see anything? Anyone in the neighbouring flats?' he asked the policeman.

In response he looked at Moretti in a way that seemed to say, *this is southern Italy, you're on a building site owned by the Camorra where the work's being done by companies owned by the Camorra, and you ask if anyone saw anything? Are you quite mad?* Instead, he merely shook his head. 'We've asked around. One or two people said they heard the sound of the digger in the night but just thought someone was putting in overtime.

'Overtime?' said Moretti, incredulous. 'In the middle of the night?'

The policeman shrugged. 'That's what they said.'

'And do you believe them?' asked Moretti, his face colouring with anger.

'What choice do I have, sir?'

'And none of your patrols saw anything?'

'Afraid not.'

'Come on, Flora, we're wasting our time here.' he said. 'I've got to break the news to my team and get them started on seeing if there's anything we can salvage.' They ducked back under the single strand of police tape and into the Via Tenente Ravallese.

'So what happens now?' she asked.

'I'll need to talk to the police and the Carabinieri again, but in the mean time, if you can let me have copies of what you've got left from yesterday – you know, scans of the copper grids, images of finds, anything that'll help us identify what's missing.' Moretti suddenly stopped walking and Flora almost bumped into him as he stood gazing vacantly into space once more.

'Sure,' she replied. 'Do you want me to call Donald and ask him to do the same?' She could tell that his attention was miles away and he hadn't heard a word she'd just said. 'Francesco?'

'Yes.'

'I said, do you want me to call Donald and ask him to bring in what he's got too?'

He looked at her as though trying to work out who she was and what she'd just said. 'Yes. Thank you. That would help.'

She put her head on one side and looked at him intently. 'Francesco, don't you think you ought to go home? You're no use to anyone in this state.'

'No. That wouldn't help.'

'Look, let's forget this evening. It was a nice thought but why don't you call Anna and get her to come home or you go to her?'

'I can't, Flora, she's not coming home.'

'What do you mean?'

'She's left me, Flora. Taken the children and gone back to her parents in Turin.'

'Oh, Francesco, I'm so sorry,' she said, putting a consoling hand on his arm. 'I had no idea. When did this happen?'

'Three months ago. She wants a divorce.' He turned to face her again. The incongruity of having such a conversation between two rows of parked cars in a scruffy Pompeii side-street somehow didn't seem to matter. 'I thought I was coping OK, but this business with the break-in and now this...' his voice trailed away and Flora could see he was close

42

to tears. 'Now you see why I don't want to go back to the flat and all the reminders – at least if I come in to work, I can keep busy. Stops me thinking about it.'

'I understand,' she said, releasing his arm. 'Look, I'm going back to have a shower and make myself semi-presentable and I'll see you at the lab in an hour say. How's that?'

'Perfect,' he said with an attempt at a half-smile.

When Flora returned to the lab she was greeted by the disagreeable spectacle of Donald Sumter sitting at the desk in what had been her temporary office. He looked up from his laptop and nodded vaguely in what she took for a greeting but neither of them spoke. Eventually, she broke the silence. 'Have you been to the dig site yet?'

'No. Why would I do that?'

The question left her temporarily speechless. Finally, she said, 'Oh, it's worth a look, Donald – it's an absolute mess, completely robbed out.'

'So Francesco tells me.'

I've met more talkative furniture, thought Flora, trying not to let her irritation show. 'Did you have much on your laptop?' she asked.

'A fair amount, but not much that would be useful to the police.'

'What about the translations you've done?'

He shook his head. 'Still in hard-copy: I left most of it here overnight and it's all gone.'

She sat on the corner of what had been her desk, something she guessed rightly would annoy him; anything to get a reaction from the wretched man. 'You seem remarkably calm about the loss of what could have been one of the most important archaeological finds in history.'

He looked up at her with large, brown, disdainful eyes. 'I fail to see what my joining in the screaming and shouting would do to help. Anyway, I prefer to leave that sort of behaviour to the Italians.'

Flora gritted her teeth, determined not to take the bait. 'Can you show me what you *do* have left?'

'Certainly,' he said. 'Although as I told you yesterday, I still have no reason to believe what we were looking at was necessarily written by Josephus.'

She glared back at him. 'So not worth stealing then, Donald?'

'Clearly it was,' he said, with a reptilian smile. 'Anything old and rare has a market value. Look at the Devil's Codex for example and think how many bogus copies of *that* there are in circulation. And nearly all of it indecipherable gibberish.'

Sidestepping his gibe at the work she'd done the previous day, she peered at his laptop screen. 'You've been here nearly a month and that's it?' she said. 'Three scanned pages from *The Wars* and some notes?'

'I told you, the rest I left here overnight on my desk. I prefer to work long-hand. Stopping to type is an unnecessary distraction. After all, what I'm doing isn't merely an extension of high-school chemistry – '

'Nor is palaeography,' she replied, at once cursing herself for taking the bait.

A self-satisfied smile crossed Sumter's lips. 'No, of course not,' he said. 'But it is a far more mechanical approach than linguistic and textual analysis, as I'm sure you'd agree.' They'd had the argument many times before and only the arrival of Moretti, accompanied by a Carabinieri lieutenant, prevented it breaking out again. Flora ran an approving eye over the newcomer: a tall, fair-haired man in his late twenties, introduced himself as Antonio Lombardi from the Carabinieri's *Commando per la Tutela del Patrimonio Culturale* or TPC, a specialist unit devoted to solving crimes involving Italy's cultural heritage.

'Am I really going to have to answer the same silly questions all over again?' said Sumter. 'I've already spoken to these people twice already, not to mention the local police; and the interpreter said he was going home –'

'You've no need for concerns on that score, sir,' said Lombardi in English with an accent that seemed to owe more to New England than to Italy. 'I'll try to take up as little of your precious time as possible, but we'd be grateful for any help you can give us.' He turned and spoke to Moretti in Italian who nodded in agreement.

'I'm not sure what you expect me to do, lieutenant,' he said. 'I've told your people what little I know and all my notes have gone. I take it you've no objections to my leaving the country and going home now there's nothing more for me to do here?'

Lombardi showed no outward reaction. 'By all means, sir,' he replied. 'You're under no obligation to do anything you don't want to and you're free to come and go as you please.' Sumter grunted and Lombardi continued, 'If you wouldn't mind leaving us your contact details, just in case we need to follow up, that would be most kind.'

Sumter stood up. 'I've already given them twice this morning,' he said. 'And now if nobody objects, I will bid you all goodbye.'

'Where are you going, Donald?' asked Moretti.

'Back to my hotel and then, to the airport. There's nothing more for me to do here and so I'm going home.' Open-mouthed, Flora and Moretti watched him pack up his laptop and walk out of the door without another

44

word.

Flora felt that she had to say something. 'I'm sorry, lieutenant, he's not always like that. It's just that he's taken the loss of the documents rather badly.'

'I understand,' said Lombardi. And turning to Moretti, said, 'You'll be pleased to know that my people have replaced the local police at the dig.'

'Thanks,' he replied. 'I don't think there's much left to protect, it's completely robbed out.'

'It's a shame you never told us it was there,' said Lombardi. 'We could easily have included it in our standing patrols but we can't protect what we don't know about.'

Moretti recoiled in surprise. 'Nobody told you about the dig? Are you kidding me?'

'No. The first we heard was when we got the 112 call.'

'But that's not possible. I filled in all the paperwork myself – it's something I've done hundreds of times – and I gave it to one of my team to process.'

'Well, we never got it. Who did you give it to?'

'Our chief clerk: guy called Greco. He was as reliable as they come – he'd been with us for years.'

'*Was* reliable?'

'Yes. He's just left us – retired. Let's think...the finds were reported to us a couple of months ago so we'd have filled in the paperwork then, and he went about a week later. I remember because we had a little party for him, you know, drinks, a few nibbles, everyone chipped in for a leaving present, that kind of thing.'

Lombardi nodded. 'Do you have a copy of the notification on file?' he asked.

'Sure, I can get it now if you like.'

'No rush. Do you have an address where I can contact Greco?'

'Certainly.'

Later that evening, looking tired and pale, Moretti arrived at Flora's hotel. He was fifteen minutes late and still wearing his work clothes. 'I'd given you up for lost,' she said as he came into reception. 'What's happened? You look dreadful.'

'I've only just left the Carabinieri.'

'Why, what's happened?'

'You remember I mentioned Greco, our chief clerk?'

'The one who retired?'

45

'That's him. Well, he never came back from walking the dog this afternoon. The dog found its way home still with its lead attached, but there's no sign of Greco and his wife's reported him missing.'

'And Lombardi doesn't think it's a coincidence?'

'Well he might have done if we'd been able to find the paperwork notifying the TPC about the dig. That's gone missing too.'

'Oh Christ,' said Flora. 'You don't think it's an inside job, do you?'

Moretti looked down at his feet. 'I don't want to believe it, but it looks that way…but Greco, after all those years. He never so much as took home a pencil. He was the straightest guy I knew.'

'Maybe someone made him an offer he couldn't refuse.'

'That's not funny, Flora. Not round here, anyway.'

'Sorry, Francesco. Let's go and eat, you can tell me all about it then. Come on, I'm starving.'

As they walked through the streets, the evening ritual of the *passeggiata* was coming to an end but a few remaining groups of locals were strolling in the cool of the evening, standing out in their finery from the more casually-dressed tourists.

Flora stopped to look in a shop window. 'I might be leaving too,' she said.

'Surely not yet.' Moretti sounded almost hurt.

'Well if the Carabinieri have finished with me, there's nothing really I can do and the longer I stay, the more it costs the university. I called Oxford today to talk to Professor Braithwaite. You've met Stephen, haven't you?'

They walked on, imperceptibly closer now. 'Yeah, I think so,' said Moretti. 'Older guy, big bushy eyebrows, speaks excellent Italian.'

'That's him. He's a lovely man, I couldn't wish for a better boss.'

'And what did he say?'

'Not much,' replied Flora. 'I told him about the break in – he seemed as upset about it as we are – and he told me to come home if there was nothing useful for me to do.'

Moretti smiled, the first time she had seen him do so that evening. He turned to look at her. 'Then we'll have to find something for you to do – something to keep you here.' He paused. 'I forgot to say earlier, you look great in that dress, Flora, it really suits you.'

She smiled at the compliment. With her dark hair and skin that turned brown even under an English sun, had it not been for her pale blue eyes, Flora could have passed for Italian. 'That's very kind of you,' she said. 'It's nice to be able to go to work and wear what you like, but I do

46

like to dress up every now and then.'

'I'm sure you're out on the town in Oxford every night,' he said, giving her a playful nudge.

'On my salary? You must be joking.'

Moretti shrugged. 'Find someone else to pay. That's what Italian girls do.'

'My inner feminist doesn't really agree with that, but now you mention it, I think they're on to something. Principles are ok up to a point, but I'm not one for overdoing things.'

'So who's paying the bills at the moment?'

'Me. Just me,' she replied, gazing into the middle-distance.

The conversation was cut short by their arrival at the restaurant. A small neon sign, saying "Al Peschereccio", pointed the way up a set of narrow stairs that looked more like the entrance to a strip-joint than one of Campania's finest seafood restaurants. As they turned the corner at the top of the stairs, a wall of sound hit them – the small dining area was packed with far more people than the fire regulations could ever have permitted, all of whom seemed to be shouting. 'It's full,' said Flora. 'We'll have to go somewhere else.'

Moretti tapped the side of his nose. 'Don't worry, I know the right people: only way you'll ever get a table here.'

A waiter showed them to a table by a window which at least gave them a welcome breeze. 'So if we can't find an excuse for keeping you here, when do you think you'll leave?' asked Moretti.

'Not for a couple of days. I'm going to help out sifting through the spoil tips at the dig and Lombardi wants to talk to me about the missing codices.'

Moretti smiled. 'Yes, I saw you'd taken a bit of a shine to him,' he said.

'Whatever gave you that idea,' she said, her cheeks starting to flush.

'Oh, I notice things, that's all.'

'Well he is rather fanciable – never could resist a man in uniform,' she replied, returning his smile.

'So you've told me. What happened to yours?'

'He's still in the RAF and still an utter bastard.'

'So it's all off then?'

'Has been for a couple of months now. As the old saying goes, there wasn't room in the relationship for three.'

'Another woman? Surely not –'

'No. His ego – kind of crowded everything else out.'

47

'Not good.'

'No, but give it ten years or so, keep me away from sharp objects and pet rabbits and I might get over it. More importantly, what about you and Anna?' The look in his eyes brought her up short. 'Sorry, Francesco, if you'd rather not talk about it I'll shut up.'

He shook his head. 'Nothing to tell really. No other man, no super-sized ego, just a poorly-paid southern archaeologist with a wife from a wealthy northern family who got bored being cooped up in a tiny flat in a backwater like Pompeii with two screaming kids while her husband worked twelve-hour days.'

'But you were a poorly-paid archaeologist when she met you.'

Now it was Moretti's turn to gaze distractedly into the middle-distance. 'Yes I was,' he said. 'So there must've been something else but whatever it was clearly isn't there any more. Not for Anna, anyway.'

Flora reached out a consoling hand. 'You want her back, don't you?'

He nodded. 'Yes. I've told her but she doesn't want anything to do with me. My children... our children are in Turin and it's a long way and a lot of time and money each time I go to see them. She's even turned her parents against me and I have to stay in a hotel.'

'Why don't you take some leave?'

'I was going to and then all this happened. Couldn't have come at a worse time.'

'So what are you going to do?'

'Work, talk to you, work some more, sleep, get drunk. Anything to take my mind off it,' he said. Flora decided it was time to change the subject.

As Moretti had predicted, the food at "Al Peschereccio" was superb, and after the meal he and Flora strolled back towards her hotel in silence, both enjoying the other's company and both willing the evening not to come to an end. 'It's still early. Would you like to go for a drink somewhere, or maybe come back to my place?' he asked.

'I don't think that would be a good idea,' she replied. 'We've both got an early start tomorrow. Why don't you leave me here? It's only a few hundred metres and I'll be quite safe.'

'I'd feel happier if I saw you to your hotel. Look, I'll tell you what, there's a bar on the way back, let's have a last drink. It's still early –'

Flora hesitated. It was warm and she was enjoying his company too much for the evening to end. And he was right: after all, a last one wouldn't hurt, would it?

He ordered the drinks and for the first time that evening she noticed he seemed more like his old self. Without any conscious decision from either of them, one drink turned to two and after the fourth, Flora lost count so by the time they got back to the hotel her head was spinning. 'Thank you for a brilliant evening, Francesco,' she said. 'It's so lovely to see you again.' She put her arms up to kiss him goodnight and he pulled her towards him, kissing her full on the mouth. 'No, Francesco, you mustn't,' she protested but made no resistance when he kissed her again. She felt his hand slide up the back of her thigh as he pressed hard against her. She pulled away again. 'No, not here, you'd better come inside.'

Chapter Seven

An icy wind blew from the Hyrcanian Ocean across the rooftops of the Armenian town of Albanopolis. The garrison troops of the *Legio XV Apollinaris* were confined to barracks, more preoccupied with keeping warm than scouring the frozen hillsides for the scattered remnants of the Parthian army still loyal to King Tiridates. The sleety overcast of the afternoon turned almost imperceptibly to dusk and the few inhabitants who had been brave enough to venture out in such weather wrapped their cloaks around themselves and headed indoors to their firesides.

The sleet turned to hard pellets of snow and began to collect in the gutters of the cobbled streets leading from the citadel towards the port. Josephus, the young Judean who just over two years earlier had witnessed Roman summary justice meted out to Andreas in Patras, pulled up the rough woollen cowl of his cloak in an attempt to protect himself from the stinging white bullets swirling around the narrow defile between the buildings. In the darkness he missed his turning and, cursing, turned to retrace his steps, feet slithering over the icy cobbles. He stopped, looked back into the gloom, and seeing no one behind him, turned into the narrow passageway. They'd chosen well, he thought: the alley was barely wide enough for two men – no need for three hundred Spartans to hold this pass. After about twenty paces the passage opened into a small courtyard and in the corner stood the door he was looking for: had it not been for the light showing through the gap beneath, he would have missed it altogether. Without hesitation, he slammed his hand three times against the solid timbers. The vague murmur of voices from inside ceased at once and he heard the bolts being drawn back. The door swung open. Silhouetted by the firelight from within stood a heavy-set man, at least twenty years older than Josephus and half a head taller. 'I come from the brother of James,' said the younger man.

'Whom do you seek?' came the reply.

'The follower of Christ: Nathanael, son of Talmai.'

'I am Nathanael Bar Talmai. Welcome friend. Please enter.'

He noted with satisfaction that Bar Talmai's Aramaic was spoken with an unmistakable Galilean accent. 'Not now,' he said, staring hard into his eyes. 'There are others; friends who also follow the redeemer's word. I came alone to make sure it was safe. I will fetch them.'

'Very well,' said Bar Talmai. 'But be quick, it will soon be curfew.'

'Don't worry. They are nearby.'

The door closed behind him and Josephus turned once more into the snowy darkness. At the end of the narrow passage, he turned uphill, moving as quickly as he could. In less than twenty minutes he banged on the door once more. As before, Bar Talmai answered the door but this time held it open and stood aside to let him enter. Instead of following his host to join the twenty of so other men crowded round the fire, the young Judean paused on the threshold. Bar Talmai stopped and turned round. He'd heard the sound too – a quiet but distinct ringing sound of metal on metal. 'Tell your friends to come in. There's no need for them to skulk out there in the cold.'

Josephus smiled. 'It'll be my pleasure,' he replied, and returning to the door, beckoned into the darkness, standing aside to let the newcomers enter.

The squad of soldiers from the Albanopolis garrison's *Frumentario* detachment, the Empire's feared and loathed secret service, burst into the room, securing the exits and forcibly restraining the three men who'd been quick enough to try and make an escape. Surprise was total and after a short scuffle during which one of Bar Talmai's companions received a head wound from the butt-end of a *gladius*, a tense calm fell upon the room, the firelight glinting from the blades of the soldiers' short stabbing swords. The commander, a short, scar-faced man who spoke Latin with a strong Mauretanian accent turned to Josephus. 'Which one?' he asked.

He pointed at Bar Talmai. 'Him. The tall one.' Two soldiers moved forward and pulled the Galilean out of the group, kicking his feet out from under him and pinning his arms to the floor. Two others sat on his legs.

'Good lad. You can go now if you like, this isn't for the squeamish.' He turned to face the group of men his troops were holding at sword-point. 'You bastards, on the other hand, are going to have a ring-side seat. One squeak out of any of you and you're next.'

Josephus shuddered at the thought of what was about to happen, and, drawing his cloak about him, disappeared into the dark. By the time he reached the end of the passageway he could hear terrible screaming, worse than anything he'd heard in the arena. A shiver ran through him but not because of the cold: he understood the mechanics of flaying a man alive, but the reality of watching it happen was simply too much.

In time, Bar Talmai would become better known as Saint Bartholomew, but the fact that he died because of his involvement with murder and fraud was wiped from history's slate. Josephus had his revenge but somewhere out there, seven more guilty men still lived and breathed. He would find them all.

Chapter Eight

Pompeii

The next morning Flora's hangover wasn't as bad as she'd feared. The battle with her conscience had been brief and had ended with unconditional and deliciously enjoyable surrender. And now, although part of her felt guilty for sleeping with a married man, another side of her was luxuriating in the sheer naughtiness of what they'd done last night. After all, she thought, in a burst of self-justification, if Anna's left him that's her lookout.

On arrival at the lab she heard Moretti's voice and popped her head round his office door to say hello. He and Lombardi looked up in response and she could tell at once from their faces that the news wasn't good.

'Sorry to interrupt,' she said. 'I didn't realise you were busy, I'll come back.'

'No, please come in, Miss Kemble,' said Lombardi. 'I think we may need your help. You know we were talking about Greco?'

'Francesco's clerk? Have you found him? Is he all right?'

'He's dead.'

'Oh no.' Flora put her hand to her mouth.

Lombardi continued. 'I'm afraid so. Somebody's trying to make a point. We got a call just after midnight and sure enough we found the body. Guess where?'

'Not at the dig? Surely not –'

Lombardi nodded. 'In the bottom of the trench. His throat was slit from ear-to-ear.'

'Do you mind if I sit down?' asked Flora. 'That poor, poor man. Do you have any idea who did it?'

'We thought we did but it turns out we may've been wrong. That's why we're going to need your help.'

Flora looked at the lieutenant, perplexed. 'I'll do what I can, but I'm a palaeographer, not a detective.'

'Don't worry,' said Lombardi. 'You won't be in any danger. I've asked Doctor Moretti to help too. You see, to help us find the "who?", we need start with the "why?" and that's where you come in.'

Flora shook her head. 'I'm afraid you've lost me.'

'It's simple. The TPC deals with thousands of *tombaroli* cases a year and usually, in the case of Roman finds, they're after coin, precious metals, statuary – anything with an established value on the archaeological black market. But this looks different. We're dealing with fragments of work from a known writer and we already have later copies. What made them worth stealing, let alone killing for? And why smash up the dig?'

'Professor Sumter seemed to think it was just people after easily-saleable old documents, but what I can't understand is why they'd want to destroy the provenance too.'

'That's another reason why we think it's more than a simple theft.'

Flora turned to Moretti. 'But Francesco, I thought you said it was the Camorra who did this.'

'That's what the TPC thought,' he replied. 'Lieutenant Lombardi's had some news though.'

'I was coming to that,' said Lombardi. 'You see, Miss Kemble – '

'Flora, please.'

'Of course. You see, Flora, there's been another development this morning.' Lombardi got up and closed the door. 'We've had a visitor. I can't give you names, but let's just say a man the Carabinieri have arrested several times came to see us asking for protection. Third-generation Camorra but small-time: does courier work for them plus the odd break-in, steals cars, scooters, acts as look-out. A foot soldier basically.'

'And he turned himself in because of the robbery?' asked Flora.

'Yes and no,' said Lombardi. 'He was recruited to put a team together for the job, didn't tell his Camorra bosses and now they're extremely unhappy that they didn't get a slice of the action.'

'But I thought the land, the flats and the whole dig site was owned by Camorra companies.'

'It is and that's another reason they went crazy when they found out. Round here, you don't steal from other people's patches. Not if you value your life, that is.'

'Has he said who hired him?' she asked.

'Says they were American: gave him precise instructions, paid in cash and that's all he knows. He's a frightened man and if he knew more, I think he'd have told us. My uniformed colleagues have already threatened to turn him loose if he didn't open up and he promptly wet himself – I don't mean metaphorically either – so I reckon he's telling the truth.'

'And I presume he didn't say why the Americans wanted the finds?'

'Correct, Flora. That's where you come in. We've got very little to go on, but Doctor Moretti has told me you managed to decipher some of the texts: maybe if you can help us read some of the other fragments it might give us a clue.'

Flora shrugged. 'I can try if you like but I can't see what good it'll do. Everything I've seen so far was very mundane stuff.'

A look of consternation spread across Lombardi's features. 'But I thought you'd managed to decipher some of the finds from the dig,' he said.

'A few bits and pieces but that's all – again none of it was earth-shattering. If we hadn't had the copper sheets with the key to the cipher I'd never have been able to do it. From an historical point of view it's brilliant that there are other documents in existence which have been encrypted using the same keys, but it doesn't help you find your thieves.'

'Well it's a start at least.'

'True,' she said. 'But if you're looking for instructions on where to start excavating then I'd suggest trying the thriller section of your local bookshop before coming to me. There's another problem too. The university. My department will want me to come back.'

'And if we funded you?' asked Lombardi.

'Then I don't suppose they'd mind. I'm happy to stay as long as you like – at least until the Autumn term starts anyway. I'll ring and ask. Before I do I take it you haven't ruled out the American Mafia?'

'We haven't ruled out anyone. Our local criminals have friends all over the globe these days but if a small group of our boys have defied family loyalty to get hooked up with "The Mob" then it wouldn't surprise me. But in the meantime, if you could make a start on the remaining documents that would be great.'

'I'll be happy to,' said Flora. She waited until Lombardi had left and then closed the door. 'Is he serious, Francesco? Does he really think I'm going to find anything from a few scraps of first-century code that'll help him solve this?'

Moretti shrugged. 'He's desperate, that's all.'

Flora shook her head. 'I think the poor man's been reading too many thrillers.'

'You could always say no and go home to Oxford.'

She frowned at the prospect. 'I could I suppose. What I want to know is why they didn't ask Sumter. I could've explained the cipher to him and let him get on with it. After all, he's the language specialist.'

'They did. He said no.'

'Figures, I guess,' she said, getting to her feet once more. 'Seeing as I'm going to be cooped up for the rest of the summer decoding Greek and Aramaic shopping lists, do you mind if I go down to the dig first? I just feel the need to get my hands dirty.'

Moretti laughed. 'Who am I to stop you making mud pies?' Sure. I'll give you a lift.'

The atmosphere on the site was very different to that of her first visit. None of the team approached the job with any enthusiasm: they all knew that at best they'd find a few tantalising fragments. Matters weren't improved by the presence of a gang of builders who hung around the trench watching everything that was going on, the foreman repeatedly asking when the archaeologists were going to finish so they could get on with their work.

Doing her best to ignore them, Flora volunteered to help sieving the spoil heaps in the hope of finding anything worthwhile, but after an hour of working in the heat and dust, all she had to show for her efforts were a Roman belt buckle and a few green tesserae. The site supervisor wandered over to look in the finds tray. 'Any luck?' she asked.

Flora wiped the sweat off her forehead with the back of her hand. 'Just these,' she said, indicating the tiny cubes of coloured limestone.

The supervisor picked one of them up and examined it closely. 'This is interesting. Where did they come from?' she asked.

'From the top of the spoil heap. Why?'

'That means they came from the bottom of the trench.'

'True, but what of it?' said Flora. 'It's just the remains of the mosaic floor your people found earlier.'

'But that was blue, white and brown. There weren't any green tesserae in it.'

Suddenly, Flora realised the implication of what she'd said. 'You're right. I think we need to take another look.'

They ran over to the ladder and not bothering to put on hard hats or to ask permission of the diggers, swarmed down into the cool darkness below.

'So where do you think we should start?' said the supervisor.

'Where the trench is deepest I suppose,' replied Flora. She unhooked the wander-light from the trench support and held it up against the side of the cut.

'You see that darker line that slopes down from right to left?' she said, tracing along the faint layer with the point of a trowel. The supervisor nodded. 'Well I think it shows the original surface layer before the eruption. The ash and pumice had the effect of flattening out the humps and bumps, but if I'm right, this house was built into the side of a hill with the ground sloping away to the south-west.'

'And you think there's another floor further down the slope?' asked the supervisor.

In the little pool of light given off by the single electric bulb, Flora's grin lit up like a beacon. 'Well, we won't know unless we try, but I certainly reckon it's worth putting in another trench.'

The two women stayed to help the field archaeologists shift the loose earth and pumice from their new excavation and after only five minutes an excited shout called them back to the face of the trench. 'What have you found?' Flora asked.

'A section of wall that's been cut through by the digger. The earth collapsed back in afterwards which is why we missed it. And guess what's beyond it?'

'A green mosaic floor by any chance?'

'Exactly. The border's green and white but I can't see any pattern yet.'

'That's fantastic,' said Flora. 'I'll get out of your way now. I can't wait to tell Francesco.'

By the time Flora got back to the lab, Moretti was preparing to leave for lunch and she joined him in a small café just round the corner. Bubbling over with excitement, she told him about the mosaic floor.

'You drew a winning ticket today, Francesco,' she said. 'The supervisor was about an hour from shutting the dig down. You're lucky to have her on your team – she's a fine archaeologist – I'd missed the significance of the tesserae and if she hadn't been there, we'd be back to square one.'

'Maybe our luck's finally changed,' said Moretti in a flat monotone. Flora put her head on one side and looked at him intently. This wasn't right: rather than dancing for joy as she'd expected, he seemed to be treating the news more as a source of additional paperwork than anything else.

Unabashed, she continued, hoping some of her surplus enthusiasm might rub off. 'We need to make sure your luck stays changed. There were some very impatient-looking builders hanging around the dig today, and once their bosses hear there are more finds, I wouldn't put it past them to have another go.'

He nodded. 'First thing I do when we get back is to phone Lombardi.

Then I'll fill in the TPC notification and hand it in personally.'

Still buzzing with excitement, Flora found it hard to settle to her work on the document fragments. She began by examining their physical composition: chemical analysis of the inks, of the fragments of binding from the leather covers and of the parchment itself. Once started, she was lost to the world, immersed in the thing she loved best – getting close to the people responsible for producing these wonderful artefacts and understanding what made their two thousand year-old world go round.

At about six o'clock her concentration was broken by a discreet tap on the door, followed by the appearance of Moretti. 'How are you getting on?' he asked.

'Slowly,' she replied, handing him a piece of hand-written paper. 'But I'm making progress. Here, take a look.'

'What is it?'

'It's a translation of one of the fragments. This one to be precise,' said Flora, holding up a dark brown triangle of parchment, sandwiched between two layers of glass. What I've just given you is the translation of the plain text from the front and this one is the decode of what was written on the back.' She laid a second piece of paper on the desk in front of him.

He held them both up and peered at them intently, switching his gaze from one to the other. Then he frowned. 'Unless I'm missing something, these are almost identical.'

'They are identical. The differences in the text comes from the fact that I've only got a fragment of the page to work with.'

'So are you saying Josephus isn't telling us anything we don't know?'

'Depends whose point of view you take,' said Flora. 'For me it's fascinating, but for Lombardi, what he hoped was going to be the key to his mystery looks like nothing more than a coded version of what's on the other side of the paper. The discrepancies come from the fact that they're both written right-left and so where there's damage, different things are missing from the two sides.'

'So it's been a waste of time,' he said. To Flora's ears he sounded almost relieved.

'Not at all. I came across what I call "mirror-image text" in one of the documents I was looking at the other day. This one to be precise,' she said, tapping the screen of her laptop. 'And so I wondered if the same recto-verso, plain text-cipher technique had been used on the fragments from your dig. None of the keys I had from the existing copper grids worked so I fooled around, seeing if I could reverse-engineer the key by simply transposing the two sets of text. And guess what?'

'You're not telling me it worked?' asked Moretti, suddenly animated once more.

'It certainly did and now I've got about a quarter of the missing key already. Assuming all the others use the same one then I should have the whole key by tomorrow.'

'You've done brilliantly, Flora. That's fantastic.'

She held up a hand in caution. 'Steady on, Francesco, let's not get carried away. It may let me work backwards to create a missing grid, but all we've got is the same thing written in two different ways on the same piece of parchment.'

'Hardly the Rosetta Stone, I agree,' he said. 'But it's still an incredible piece of detective work. There's one thing that bothers me though.'

'What's that?'

'Why bother? I mean, if you're going to write "the cat sat on the mat" on one side of the page, why go to all the effort of encrypting it word-for-word on the other?'

Flora shifted her reading glasses onto the top of her head. 'It's been puzzling me too,' she said. 'Maybe it was his way of making sure that his scribes, or anybody else's, come to that, didn't change his text when they copied it out. If they did, all you'd need to do – assuming you had the key of course – would be to decode it.'

'How would that work? And again, what reader would go to all that effort?' asked Moretti, perching on the corner of the desk and looking over her shoulder.

Flora put her hands up in a gesture of despair. 'Well, it's a hopelessly weak theory, I know, but say someone copied it and the plaintext didn't match up with the encrypted text then it would show the copy was inaccurate.'

'And if whoever copied it didn't bother copying the encrypted text because they thought it was gibberish, then what?'

'Then my theory falls apart. Why do you think he did it?'

'I haven't a clue,' said Moretti. 'Everyone likes a good mystery and I'm sure people were no different then. Maybe you're right and Josephus deliberately got the word out that there was secret learning embedded in the cipher-text in the hope it would encourage future scribes to copy it rather than just copying the plain text.'

'I think we'll be getting into UFO territory if we're not careful,' laughed Flora. 'Old Josephus was a past-master at looking after number one, so I can't see him going to all that effort if there wasn't something in it for himself.'

'Of course, the entire theory falls down when we come up against the pages where there's no plain-text,' said Moretti. 'But whatever he was up to, you've done an incredible piece of work.'

'Thanks. But more importantly, what's happened down at the dig?'

Moretti smiled. 'I think you'll like this. They've uncovered what looks like an extension to the scriptorium on a lower level and apart from the area the mechanical digger tore up, the mosaic floor's in fabulous condition.'

'That's great, but what makes them think it's an extension of the scriptorium?'

'I was coming to that in a minute, but you just wait till you see the design on the mosaic.'

Flora was beside herself with excitement 'What is it?'

'Well, we're not 100% sure yet, but it looks like a representation of Ursa Major. Just like the copper grids. The seven stars motif again – it can't be a coincidence.'

'I've got to see this – '

'Hold on, there's more. My diggers have found what look like duplicate copies of some of the copper grids. The *tombaroli* didn't get everything after all.'

'Can we go down there now?' asked Flora, bouncing up and down in her seat with excitement.

'Well, strictly speaking, no. But I'll call Lombardi and ask him if his boys will let us in: the site's better guarded than Fort Knox right now.'

Chapter Nine

Syracuse, AD 62

It was stiflingly hot inside the city walls as Josephus, Gubs and Alityros made their way towards the harbour. That the Puteoli squadron was in port was evident: from an inn on the corner of the narrow lane came the sound of drunken singing and as they drew closer, to loud cheers, two bodies flew through the bead curtain and out into the street followed by the appearance of a man wearing a wine-stained apron whose bulk filled the doorway. 'If you two girls want to cause trouble, you can do it in someone else's place and not here,' he shouted after them while the two men continued brawling in the gutter.

'Nice place,' said Josephus, stepping delicately around the cursing tangle of arms and legs.

'Oh, there are worse,' said Gubs airily. 'Marseille can get quite frisky of an evening, especially when the *Classis Britannia* is in.'

Alityros snorted. 'Tell me about it. We had two slaves from Britain and they were nothing but trouble. All they wanted to do was to drink themselves stupid. Being chained to an oar is all they're fit for. I'd send the lot of them home if I had my way.'

As they approached the port, the crowds grew thicker and the air rang with cries in a dozen different languages. Shouldering their way through the press of bodies, the three men walked the length of the docks, eventually arriving at a fortified building which sat at the base of the *pharos* itself.

'You two stay here,' said Gubs. 'I won't be long.' He spoke to one of the sentries at the gate who welcomed him in with a slap on the shoulder.

'So far so good,' said Josephus and turned once more to Alityros. For a moment he thought there had been an eclipse, but standing in front of them was a man at least twice the size of the chucker-out at *The Flying Fish* whom they'd seen in action a few minutes earlier.

A voice boomed down from above. 'Are you two looking for work?'

Alityros and Josephus looked around to see who he was talking to, but since there was nobody else close by, it had to be to them. In their dirty, salt-stained tunics he had mistaken them for seamen.

'You auditioning then, luvvie?' asked Alityros.

The giant's brow furrowed. 'Are you trying to be funny, little man?'

'You mean you didn't catch my *Peniculus* in *The Menaechmi*? I got wonderful reviews.' The joke went sailing over the man's head – a considerable altitude for humour to attain – and he picked the podgy actor up by the front of his tunic leaving his feet paddling in thin air.

'Put him down, Quadratus, he's with me.' A tall, angular-faced man in military uniform stood in the doorway next to the stockier form of Gubs. The giant obeyed immediately and dropped Alityros who fell to the ground in a heap.

'Gentlemen,' said Gubs. 'Allow me to introduce Sextus Volusius Proculus, *Navarch* of the Puteoli squadron and who has kindly offered to take us to the mainland.'

'Follow me,' said Proculus, leading them past the sentries who snapped to attention. 'And please try not to pick any more quarrels while you're here,' he said over his shoulder. 'Gubs tells me you haven't eaten since last night. Let's get you sorted out with a meal and then we can get those stinking rags off you – you smell worse than my oarsmen.'

Fed, clothed and bathed, the three travellers passed a comfortable night in the officers' quarters of the fleet barracks and early the following morning followed Proculus along the quayside to where the bireme, *Liburna Minerva,* nodded at its moorings. With a staring eye painted on the bow, an overhanging tail of a stern-post and its long ramming prow semi-submerged in the clear water, it looked more like an exotic water fowl rather than a warship. Gubs followed his former skipper up the gangplank onto the outrigger which sat above the two banks of oar slots. He nodded appreciatively at the row of brightly painted shields lining the sides of the upper deck and the two catapults, one mounted forward of the main mast, the other nearer the helmsman's station. 'Our new toys,' said Proculus.

'Are you expecting trouble then?' asked Josephus nervously.

'Not these days,' Proculus replied. 'Pirates won't risk coming near a ship like this. Don't worry, we'll have you home in no time. Now, I need you to stay out of the crew's way until we cast off. Gubs, you can come with me.'

They watched fascinated as the crew tightened the forestay before hoisting the mainsail. Then came a clatter from beneath their feet as the lower bank of rowers manned their sweeps – reacting as one to the shouted commands of the pilot – to steer the long, narrow craft into the open waters of the straits of Messina where a stiff westerly breeze was already giving white tops to the dark blue waves.

Driven on by its sails, the Minerva made good speed and soon the land began to dip beneath the horizon. Josephus leaned on the lee-side shield wall, watching Rhegium and the toe of Italy recede from view while musing on the task ahead. His thoughts were interrupted by the arrival of Proculus. 'Gubs tells me you're on a mission,' he said.

Josephus pondered his response before speaking. 'With no disrespect, sir, I hoped he'd have kept that information to himself.'

The captain gazed out at the horizon, squinting against the brightness. 'Up to you if you don't want to talk about it, but I think I can help,' he said.

'Go on, I'm listening.'

'Play your cards right and you should have a receptive audience.'

'Meaning?'

'Your work on the Empire's behalf in Patras and also in Judea hasn't gone un-noticed. Nero himself is very appreciative and he has a long memory...when it suits him, and that's the problem.'

'But how do I know when it's likely to suit him?'

'Exactly. You won't. None of us do. I wouldn't claim to know him well but we've met on several occasions.'

'And is he really mad?' asked Josephus.

Proculus wagged a finger at the young man. 'You can start by keeping questions like that to yourself: even wooden walls like these have ears. He's highly intelligent but – how do I put this? – he lives in a world of his own where the usual rules of human conduct don't apply.'

'So what do you suggest, sir?'

'If you want to bring those three priests home in one piece then he needs to believe it was his idea to release them all along. And the way you do that is through Poppaea Sabina: he dotes on her and she's the only one who dares stand up to him. Now I'm only going as far as Puteoli, but I can give you a letter of recommendation to her.'

'That's very kind of you,' replied Josephus. 'Alityros has said he'll introduce me. But at the risk of asking an indelicate question, why would you put yourself out like that?'

Proculus smiled. 'You *are* a diplomat, aren't you, young man? What you mean is, "what's in it for me?"'

'Something like that.'

'I told you. You're a friend of Rome, and we need all those we can get in Judea if what I hear is true. And secondly, Gubs speaks very highly of you: he told me how you saved Alityros' life when the *Cygnus* went down.'

'So what have you heard about Judea?'

'Oh, the same old story. The Jews are upset about something again – not as bad as in Caligula's day of course – but since Governor Festus died, the usual suspects have been stirring things up.'

'The Sadducees you mean? Not my favourite people.'

'Not Rome's either, so just make sure you back the right horse,' said Proculus.

'Even if the horse is called Governor Lucceius Albinus and has his snout so deep in the trough that you can't even see his feet?'

'That's politics, Josephus. It's the price you pay for stability. Which would you prefer: Albinus with his snout in the trough or your country given over to direct rule by the Sanhedrin?'

'Neither.' Replied Josephus. 'All I want is a return to the natural order of things: that those who are born to govern be allowed to do so and that they act in accordance with the word of God.'

Proculus snorted disdainfully. 'You're getting way ahead of yourself, young man. I'd stick to being nice to Poppaea. And forget the pipe-dreams. Talk like that will end in tears.'

'Yes, but if you Romans are going to govern a place, then the least you can do is to do it properly. You talk about the usual suspects stirring things up but you've no idea how bad things got in Judea after Festus died and before Albinus finally deigned to show up.'

Proculus switched his gaze from the horizon and now looked at Josephus full in the face. 'You've got a lot to learn,' he said. 'Whatever position you may've been born to in Judea and what your people see as the "natural order" counts for nothing with us and if I were you I'd be very careful before you start giving lectures in governance to members of the Equestrian class.'

'I'm sorry,' replied Josephus. 'I didn't mean it to sound like that, but we just felt abandoned. Rome took away our ability to defend ourselves and then didn't act when the Greeks attacked us again. And then to rub it in, my uncle was murdered by some of Ananus' people.'

'I'm sorry to hear that. Who's Ananus?'

'The High Priest of Judea.'

'Well that just proves my point, doesn't it?'

'What point?'

'That whatever rank you hold in Judea, your entire system counts for nothing with Rome.' Josephus began to bluster but Proculus cut him short. 'I'm not saying it's right or wrong, but those are the facts.' Josephus stared back at him, his expression a mixture of bafflement and truculence. Proculus continued. 'You still don't understand, do you?'

'Understand what?'

'How your country, your people and your religion appear to civilised peoples.'

'Our civilisation is older – '

'Don't argue and don't interrupt. You're a good lad and I'm trying to help you; now listen to me, Josephus, or you'll end up in the same cell as your three priests.'

'Sorry,' he said, looking down.

'It's distasteful to you, I know, but the view from the Palatine is that all Rome's provinces, yes even Judea, are fly-blown shitholes, fit only to send tribute to the empire. Play by our rules and you'll get along fine: kick up trouble and we won't think twice about crushing you. Not nice to hear but that's how Rome sees things. And the way you Jews behave only makes it worse.'

'What do you mean?'

'Well for starters you're antisocial: you're quarrelsome, you'd sooner huddle together with other Jews than mix with us. You won't eat our food: fat, succulent pigs that would make perfect eating die of old age in your country – what a waste. You won't observe our holy days but put your feet up for an entire day once a week. Then there's your cock-eyed superstition that won't accept our gods, whereas we happily accept gods from all over the empire. Have you seen the altar in the stern?'

'No.'

'Well take a look: it's dedicated to Minerva to whom we entrust the well-being of this ship which bears her name, but it's also dedicated to her British counterpart, Sul. You see; we're a reasonable people so we don't like it when subject peoples disrespect us.'

'It's not that we don't respect Rome,' said Josephus. 'We believe there is but one true God and we follow his teachings as given to Moses and our other prophets. He commands us to fight in his name for what is right.'

Proculus rolled his eyes in despair. 'Don't talk to me about fighting. That's precisely the attitude I'm talking about. Do you know what we say about the Jews?' Josephus shook his head. 'Lock a Jew in a room on his own and within five minutes a punch-up will break out.'

Josephus' features showed that the message had sunk in. 'So you're saying my journey's wasted?'

'Not a bit of it. You as an individual are highly thought-of in Rome and if you can swallow your pride, play the game by our rules and make allies rather than enemies, you've every chance of getting what you've come for. On the other hand, if you strut around the place like the lord of the dunghill, you'll get your comeuppance hard and fast.'

Josephus returned his gaze out to sea and pondered Proculus' words. Finally, he nodded and said, 'Thanks for your advice, and I didn't mean to be rude earlier.'

'That's all right,' said Proculus, clapping him on the shoulder. 'I was no different at your age. I had to learn the hard way, that's all. Now let's get you sorted out with that letter.'

The following day the wind remained favourable and the *Minerva* was soon in the calmer waters of the Bay of Naples, with the towering green pyramid of Vesuvius dominating the horizon. As they neared the coast, Josephus leaned on the rail captivated by the view. Perched above the cliffs or sited in remote coves stood what he thought at first were small villages, but as they drew closer he could see that they were in fact individual villas of enormous size and opulence. One particular example which caught his eye sported a series of linked bathing pools, tumbling hundreds of feet in a single cascade from the cliff-top down to a private jetty where a yacht was being made ready for sea, its white sails, edged in purple an ostentatious reminder to all who saw it of the owner's patrician status.

Alityros joined him on the rail. 'Impressive, isn't it?' he said.

'I never imagined houses like that existed,' replied Josephus, still wide-eyed in amazement.

'This isn't even the half of it. It stretches all the way round the bay from Capri to Misenum – you should have seen it before the quake. A lot of the really grand ones got flattened, including the emperor's place which was a bit further round towards Herculaneum. Poppaea's family have a huge villa at Oplontis with a heated swimming pool two hundred feet long – look, you can see the town there, just to the west of Pompeii – it got badly knocked about and they're in the middle of rebuilding.'

'But how on earth do people afford these places?' Josephus asked.

'You really did come down with the last shower of rain, didn't you?' laughed Alityros. 'New money mainly; patronage, corruption, banking – although that's the same as corruption I suppose – skimming tax revenues, nice little governorship of a wealthy province, property speculation: the list is endless and incredibly vulgar.'

'Looks fantastic to me,' said Josephus wistfully.

'Oh, don't get me wrong, it's fantastic all right but it's a world turned upside down.' Seeing Josephus puzzled expression he continued.

'In Rome and pretty much everywhere else in the Empire it's breeding, family and the right connections that count. Here it's different.'

'Different in what way?'

'Here it's money, pure and simple; and sometimes the weight of money in sufficient quantity is enough to overbalance the social order. That's what's happened here. Freedmen, crooks, chancers, speculators and every other hustler with an eye to the main chance have always done well for themselves round the Bay of Naples and now it's the well-born who have to suck up to them.'

'I'll bet they don't like that.'

'That's putting it mildly,' laughed Alityros. 'Behind closed doors the patricians are happy to sneer, but when it comes down to it, they have to hold their noses and pay court to these people. And then when the earthquake happened it got even worse: the rule of law broke down and it was every man for himself – years of practice at fighting for scraps in the gutter turned out to be a far better training than years studying Greek poetry.'

'Or Greek theatre, I suppose?'

'No need to rub it in,' said Alityros. 'I'd be way out of my depth here and anyway, the risks are too high. Even I have my limits.'

'How do you mean?'

'Well, I'll give you an example. You see that place with the swimming pools? – they're all heated too by the way. The owner was a praetor called Antistius, but apparently one night he got drunk at a party and said something that Nero interpreted as plotting against him and so that was curtains for Antistius and his entire family. The emperor had the Senate condemn him to death – legally sanctioned, but murder none the less.'

'So who owns it now?'

'Are you sure you want to know?' Josephus saw that Alityros was no longer smiling.

'Of course, why ever not?'

'The people Nero gave it to of course. I won't mention the name of the family – what you don't know you can't ever reveal – but they have a ten-year-old son, a very pretty boy: now do you understand?'

Josephus shook his head. 'You're going to think me terribly naïve, but no.'

Alityros gave a sigh. 'Very well, if you must, I'll spell it out for you,' he said. 'It's no secret that Nero likes little boys and this lad's family are extremely ambitious. So as soon as he turns twelve they've agreed to pack him off to Rome and in return for their son's arse Nero lets them keep the villa. Nice people, eh?'

Josephus turned to look at him, expected to see a smile that would tell him that the actor had once again strung him a line. Alityros remained stony-faced. 'But that's terrible,' said Josephus. 'There's nothing in the world I'd do something like that for.'

'Really?' Alityros raised his eyebrows. 'It's a matter of degree, that's all. We all prostitute ourselves when it suits us, we only differ in how far we're prepared to go.' Josephus looked at him sceptically and Alityros continued. 'You might not believe me now, but wait till you get to Rome, then you'll see what I mean.'

Josephus heard the words but nothing Alityros said could break the spell that the coastline and its magnificent houses had cast upon him and he continued to gaze in wonder as the panorama slid slowly by. 'You're right,' he said to no one in particular. 'But it just looks incredible and I don't care if it's vulgar, I'd still love to own a house here one day.'

The Minerva docked at the small harbour of Pompeii and they made their way up the slope to the Marina gate and into the crowded streets beyond. Once inside the walls it was stiflingly hot and the air was thick with the smells from innumerable food stalls and with the cries of merchants and hawkers offering everything from Indian spices to slaves: to Josephus it seemed impossibly exotic despite the omnipresent evidence of the destruction wrought by the earthquake which had hit in February. In places, the town walls, neglected during decades of peace, had tumbled down and their ruins transformed into makeshift stalls and sales pitches. Even in the middle of the day, brightly clad prostitutes, some no older than ten, or so it seemed to him, were openly touting for business, seated on their impromptu grandstand of jumbled ashlar blocks.

According to Alityros who acted as his tour guide, many of Pompeii's inhabitants had died in the quake, thousands were still homeless and many had fled, but nothing it seemed could dent the city's energy. 'I've never seen anything like it,' said Josephus, staring wide-eyed at the relentless tides of humanity which surged around them as they followed the via Marina, past the ruined portico of the temple of Apollo and into the south west corner of the forum.

'And if you don't keep your wits about you, you'll never see your money again either,' replied Alityros, batting away a group of street-urchins who were lining up Josephus for a distraction scam while another slightly older child followed a couple of paces behind them, ready to lift his purse. 'Come on, I'll show you around.

'I'd heard the place had been knocked about,' said Josephus, surveying what had once been yet another temple, now reduced to a pile of rubble fronted by a row of Corinthian columns. 'But I didn't know it was this bad.'

'It may look like a building site now but it'll be back to its old self in no time. There's money to be made here,' added Alityros. 'More so than in Rome if you're sharp enough and don't object to rubbing shoulders with new money.'

Josephus looked at him with a puzzled frown. 'But if half the population's dead, homeless or gone, and most of it's in ruins, how on earth does that work?'

'Simple. But don't take my word for it. I'll take you to meet an old friend of mine – he'll give you the story. If he's still alive of course.'

Alityros led the way to a side-street just east of the city's Ercolano gate. 'Excellent,' he said. 'It's still there.' Josephus looked to where his friend was pointing and saw a wooden sign bearing a painted image of an elephant, a serpent and a pygmy: beneath the painting was written, "Sittius Fine Dining – Meals to Revive an Elephant". Under a canvas awning stood a brick-built counter, open to the street, with a row of tall stools for the customers. They each took a seat and Alityros called out, 'Hey, Sittius, what's a fellow got to do to get fed in this place?'

A small, dark-haired man spun round from his cooking pots, ready to deliver a mouthful in return but on seeing his old friend he broke into a broad, toothy grin. 'Alityros, you old queen! What the Hades are you doing here? I thought you were supposed to be in Athens.'

'I was,' he replied. 'In fact, I should've been back in Rome ages ago but our ship got wrecked.' Josephus sat and listened in amused silence as Alityros told the story, now magnified into epic proportions, while Sittius poured them two beakers of wine and flitted back and forwards between his cooking pots. Although autumn was nearly upon them, the day was warm and the smell of cooking, coupled with a second refill of the excellent Falernian that Sittius kept for his favoured customers, left Josephus feeling entirely at ease with the world. However much the pagan city of Pompeii was everything his religion taught him to despise, there was still something that drew him, a guilty pleasure whose temptations he couldn't resist.

Trade was slack and the landlord pulled up a stool to join them. 'I was just telling Josephus here that if you want to make your fortune, this is the place,' said Alityros. 'I don't think he believes me.'

'Well, if you don't mind my saying so, young man,' Sittius said to

Josephus, 'then you're a mug.' He gestured with his head. 'You see that place across the road?'

'What? The laundry?'

Alityros and Sittius dug one another in the ribs and hooted with laughter. 'He is a mug, isn't he?' said the innkeeper moving closer to Josephus and talking in a stage whisper. 'I've got ten girls working for me over there, and when they're not busy at the washing tubs downstairs, they're looking after my customers upstairs. The places they used to work at got flattened in the quake so if they wanted to carry on earning, their choice was to come to me or take their chances out on the walls with the kids. Know how long girls survive on a beat out there?'

'I dread to think,' said Josephus.

'Less than a month. The *Vigiles* have practically given up so there's nothing to stop the punters doing what they want to the poor little devils. That's why two or three a night go missing: there are some sick bastards out there and my girls know it which is why they jumped at a chance to make a few *asses* working in the laundry by day and two *asses* a trick by night.'

Josephus frowned. 'So you're suggesting I make my fortune by opening a brothel, are you?'

Sittius gave a non-committal shrug. 'Entirely up to you how you do it,' he said. 'Personally, I can live with the competition, I was just giving you some ideas. The building where my laundry is survived in one piece but the owner and his family didn't.'

Josephus looked horrified. 'But what about laws of rightful succession?' he asked.

'Never bothered to read them myself: I just crossed the street and took over. It's as easy as that. Find a nice place that suits you, take it as yours, tart it up on the cheap and sell it on or even better, rent it out – there's plenty of people desperate for a roof over their heads and with winter not far off, well, you can't lose.' Josephus sat open-mouthed listening to Sittius' tales of his other money-making schemes and of the ruined villa he'd helped himself to down near the coast.

Well fed, the two companions left the caupona and continued their sightseeing. To Josephus, it seemed that he'd only just begun to explore the city when Alityros drew his attention to a public sundial which showed that their time was almost up. Sure enough, as they came out of the Marina Gate, the casting-off pennant was fluttering at the *Minerva's* masthead. 'What an incredible place,' said Josephus for about the tenth time that day, reproaching himself as he did so. 'I've got to come back and see more of this.'

'Each to his own,' sniffed Alityros. 'As I've told you, it's all right for those with more money than breeding. The emperor loves the place – need I say more.'

Josephus laughed at his friend's bitchy aside and the two of them watched in silence as Pompeii receded into the haze.

Before they disembarked at Puteioli, Proculus was as good as his word and in addition to the letter of recommendation to Poppaea, he also gave them a letter ordering the masters of all ships to provide safe passage, food and accommodation.

A day later the grain ship, *Ceres*, slipped into the newly-built harbour basin, past the fortress on the end of the concrete mole, and onto its berth at Ostia, the busiest port in the Empire. They were a mere twelve miles from the centre of Rome.

'Reckon you'll find a new ship?' asked Alityros.

'I hope so,' replied Gubs. 'If I can't find work here, I'll never find it anywhere. The owner of the *Cygnus* will be interested to find out what happened to his ship too.'

Alityros and Josephus bade their friend a fond farewell on the quayside, leaving him to report to the owner of the *Cygnus* while they arranged transport for the final leg of their voyage along the *Via Ostiensis* to Rome.

Chapter Ten

Moretti put down the phone and smiled at Flora. 'Lombardi says it's ok. He's going to call his people and tell them to let us onto the site. They jumped into his car and within minutes were peering down into the newly-expanded trench.

They paused at the top of the ladder. 'D'you really think we should?' asked Flora.

'Strictly speaking, no,' he replied. 'But if the boss can't bend his own rules, then who else can? Come on.'

The shadows had lengthened and little natural daylight penetrated the bottom of the dig which was now three metres below ground level, its sides shored up by metal supports, braced against each other by screw jacks. They both turned on their torches and stopped at the exposed section of wall which separated the robbers' trench from the scriptorium.

For almost a minute, neither spoke, too awestruck by what lay in front of them. Flora broke the silence. 'But it's beautiful,' she whispered.

'Absolutely perfect,' said Moretti. 'It could've been made yesterday. I've never seen colours like it.'

In the centre of an intricate pattern of concentric green and white braiding, surrounding representations of the Roman zodiac, was a mosaic starscape showing Ursa Major and the Pole Star picked out in dazzling white against a dark blue background. He read the Latin inscription: '*Disce quod ignoras. Docti Iosephi saepe duplex unum pagina tractat opus.*'

'Oh my God,' gasped Flora, translating aloud. '*Learn what you don't know. The work of learned Josephus often stretches over one double-sided page.* He's talking to us, Francesco, he's actually talking to us.' She paused and stood with her head cocked to one side. 'Hold on a minute. I know those lines from somewhere.'

'You're right,' said Moretti. 'Aren't they from Juvenal?'

'No. I've got it,' she said. 'It's from Martial: so that's where he cribbed it from, the old fraud: all he did was take Josephus' words, change the names, stick on a different ending and claim it as one of his own epigrams.'

'Hardly surprising,' said Moretti. 'He and Josephus were in Rome at the same time and shared the same patron. Just think how much of what's attributed to St Paul was copied from Josephus too.'

Flora nodded. 'It confirms what we thought about the ownership of the villa though. This was Josephus' place all right. And what better place to boast about it than on the floor of your own scriptorium?'

'But the Ursa Major motif: if it's not *The Seven Stars*, what's he telling us that we don't already know?'

'If it's not that, then we've got a problem. Maybe it was all such a well-known in-joke that he didn't need to spell it out,' she said. 'Who knows? Seventh heaven, seven-headed beasts – could be anything – seven turns up in just about every mythology and religion there's ever been.'

'And the Pole Star makes eight,' said Moretti.

'Yes, you're right, I think he's telling us to look at both sides of the page – you know, pay attention or make sure you read the small print. But isn't it absolutely gorgeous? And just think, Francesco, if it hadn't been for the *tombaroli*, you might never have found it.'

He edged forward on his hands and knees, getting as close as he could to the mosaic.

'Remember what I thought were tadpoles on the copper plates?' he asked.

'The Ursa Major design. Course I do.'

'And you found that some of the stars were shown with rings around them?' she nodded. 'Well all seven have rings round them so far as I can make out in this light.'

'Could just be decoration.'

'Probably, but look,' he said, swinging his torch to highlight the Pole Star. 'No ring.'

'I still don't see any significance in it,' she replied. 'Polaris is shown larger than the other stars, so maybe whoever did the mosaic decided it didn't need an outline. I don't know.'

Flora spent the following morning at the lab, working on the remaining fragments from the dig and carrying out further experiments. The precise carbon-dating would have to wait, but so far she had identified three writers, each with his own distinct hand but using chemically identical ink: the thought that one of them might be Josephus himself sent a shiver of excitement down her spine.

After lunch, she turned her attention once more to an analysis of the text itself, comparing it to her scans of existing fragments.

The next day Moretti took an early train to Rome to be interviewed on TV about the finds and the robbery. Lombardi's bosses at the TPC used their media coverage to the full and the fact that many of the documents were in some form of unknown cipher ignited the curiosity of professional and amateur conspiracy theorists alike.

Offers of help from fellow professionals came from as far afield as China and the volume of faxes and e-mails soon became overwhelming, leaving Flora not knowing which document to look at next. Try as she might, she couldn't rid herself of what the Germans call an "ear-worm", that irritating little voice that kept repeating, *"The work of learned Josephus often stretches over one double-sided page."*

Tired and hot after his day in the capital, Moretti joined Flora after work for a drink at her hotel. They had the little bar to themselves and switched on the evening news.

'Fame at last,' said Flora. 'You never know, maybe Anna's watching in Turin: she'll be impressed.'

Moretti muted the sound on the TV as the topic moved on to something else.

'A thirty second interview hardly makes me a movie star,' he said, taking another sip of his beer.

'True. But it's not every day you're on CNN, is it?'

'Do you think it'll help get the finds back?'

She shrugged. 'I can't see what harm it can do. The news coverage means the fragments will be harder to shift on the black market and it'll make genuine dealers more likely to call the police if they're offered anything dodgy.'

'Did you come up with anything new today?' he asked.

'Everyone's being very helpful and I've been sent more scanned copies of just about every piece of writing from 300 BC to 300 AD than I know what to do with.'

'What about the fragments from the dig?'

'As for the palaeography, it confirmed what I expected: three different writers, all using the same locally-produced atramentum ink made from charcoal, vinegar and acacia sap.'

'And the ciphers?'

She frowned and rubbed the tiredness from her eyes. 'I've made a bit of progress but it's very slow and I'm well into diminishing returns. Thanks to what came in today I've added a tiny fraction to the grid but there's evidence of at least two more ciphers that I can't get near. Either they're using an additional key text or I'm being stupid.'

'Hardly that,' said Moretti. 'Maybe you should ask Lombardi if he can get outside help.'

'I could, but I can't see national cryptographic agencies giving up their day job to work on our stuff; not when they've got their hands full snooping on the latest bunch of madmen who want to blow us all to kingdom come.'

'What about a website?' he asked. 'There are plenty of people out there who love this kind of thing and we could set it up as a competition or something.'

'I don't think that would work either. Fine if you can get additional resources, but it would be a full time job just sorting out the few plausible answers from the tens of thousands of mad ones from the conspiracy theorists,' Flora replied, cupping her chin in her hands and staring into space. 'Donald Sumter would be my first starting point but he's probably back skulking in his den at William Sunday.'

'If he won't come to us, then maybe one of us should go to him.'

'Fine if you or Lombardi are paying, Francesco,' she said with a smile. 'It's not all bad news, though. You were right about one thing.'

'What's that?'

'The number seven. In one of the dig fragments I found some text that was encrypted using grid two, and it cropped up in a couple of places. One was a clear reference to the *Seven Stars* but the fragment was so tiny I couldn't make out any context and the other one I found was just part of a word.'

'So do you think they're significant?'

'They could be,' she said placing a hand on his leg. 'Just keep your fingers crossed.' She traced her hand along the inside of his thigh and his breathing quickened. They could hear the receptionist shouting at someone in the kitchen and so leaving their half-empty glasses on the bar, slid upstairs to Flora's room.

Stokeville, Bibb County, Alabama

The driver turned off the headlights and killed the engine.

'Jeez, shut the damn window will you, I'm getting bitten to death back here,' said Luzzo.

Raymond did as he asked and as the glass slid home, the din of the tree frogs and the crickets carolling in the humid darkness subsided to a bearable level. Among the branches of the Longleaf pines lining the remote forest track, swarms of fireflies danced their nightly courtship ritual.

'So now what do we do?' asked the third man.

'We wait,' said Raymond, checking his watch. 'Be patient, it's not eleven yet.'

'Think they'll be there?'

'Sure I do. This shit's more important to them than it is to us,' he replied, patting the lid of the coolbox strapped into the front passenger seat next to him.

Gradually, as the three men's eyes became more accustomed to the darkness, the building became visible, first as a blank against the starlight and then, little by little, as the identifiable outline of a *carpenter-gothic* church with a simple wooden spire.

He looked at his watch: shit, only forty five seconds since he'd last checked it.

They sat and waited, with the temperature in the SUV rising. Then, from the direction of the church a light flashed three times. Raymond removed the lid of the coolbox, releasing a cloud of CO_2 vapour from the dry ice inside. He reached in and removing an oblong package wrapped in canvas, opened the door and moved silently towards the church with the other two following at about ten paces' distance, each one with a hand on the butt of his pistol. As he neared the source of the light, both sank down into cover to await his return.

It was pitch dark inside the church porch and he fumbled for the handle, clutching the precious cargo close to his side. He closed the outer door behind him, knocked gently at the double inner doors and waited. A tiny sliver of light shone beneath it and he stood motionless, listening for any sound from the inside, breathing in the familiar childhood aromas of cedar-wood, furniture polish and candle-wax. Then he heard it: a faint creaking sound, footsteps on floorboards, footsteps that were getting closer.

Choosing what looked like the darkest corner, and shrinking down onto his haunches he pulled the 9mm Glock 17 from his waistband and levelled it at the centre of the doorway. Barely daring to breathe, he heard the bolts sliding back and then, as the doors swung inwards, the porch was filled with light, momentarily blinding him. In the sights of his weapon stood a white man, tall and skinny, barely out of his teens. It took him a few moments to notice Raymond crouched in his corner and at the sight of the pistol aimed at his chest he recoiled in horror, raising both hands.

'Please don't shoot. I – I'm not armed, I haven't got anything to give you, I haven't got any money.' By his accent, the young man was a long way from his New England home.

Raymond stood up and maintained his aim as they moved into the nave of the simple church.

'I don't care whether you're armed and I don't care about your wallet,' he said. 'I need to know whether you're alone.'

'Yes. Just like you said in your instructions, I'm alone, I promise. I've got the details of the wire transfer –' He made to lower his hands.

'Whoa, steady now,' Raymond said. 'Just keep it nice and slow and your hands where I can see 'em. That's it.' From his back pocket the young man slowly withdrew a folded piece of paper.

'Good. Now put it down on the floor and back the fuck away.' Raymond unfolded the wire transfer certificate. He read it carefully, checked the account number, the amount and the sender's details and then, seemingly satisfied with what he'd seen, refolded it and slipped it into his pocket, casually tossing the package onto the seat of the nearest pew.

'Now, turn around, feet apart, hands in the air.'

'B-but this wasn't part of the deal,' stammered the young man.

'Well it is now. If you're carrying a cell-phone, get it out now because if I find one on you, you lose both knees and that's just for starters. Understand?'

The young man's face was ashen with terror. 'Please, no. I'm not carrying a phone, I promise. We kept our side of the deal.' It was an intonation Raymond knew well: panic in the voice of a frightened amateur.

He continued searching him, all the while keeping the gun trained on his back and watching for the slightest tensing of the muscles that would signal a coming move. Finding nothing of interest Raymond shoved him hard in the back, sending him headlong onto the wooden boards, worn to a shine by over a hundred years of worshippers' feet.

He looked down at him with ill-disguised scorn. 'You see, play straight with us, we play straight with you. Pay us what you owe and you get the rest. Screw us over and we sell it to someone else or throw it in the trash: all the same to me. Now, you listening?'

He sat up, rubbing his elbow. 'Yes, sir. I'm listening.'

Raymond threw his head back and laughed. 'Shit. Always thought it would take a nine millimetre to get a white boy to call a nigger "sir" down this neck of the woods. Now you listen good. I'm going to walk out that door and you are going to sit tight for one hour as of now. You even think about leaving here early, my buddies will see to it that you're a dead man. Got that?'

'Yes, sir.'

'Good. You won't see them but they're out there, be sure of that.'

Raymond closed the inner doors behind him and waited, listening once more for any sound of movement. None came, so he cautiously opened the outer door and taking a can of spray paint out of his pocket, melted into the shadows at the side of the church. With a final look over his shoulder, he popped the cap off, gave the can a quick shake and sprayed three letters in four-foot-high capitals on the white-painted boards. Replacing the cap, he retraced his steps to the church porch, and, pausing only to make sure the outer door was shut, burst into the church once more. At his arrival, the young white man, his face now streaked with tears, turned and looked up from the pew where he was sitting.

'Told you I'd be back. Here, catch,' said Raymond, tossing the spray can to him.

'What's this?' he asked, turning it over in his hands.

'Yours and my alibi,' said Raymond with a grin. 'Don't lose it or no more handovers. Clear?'

'Uh, yeah, whatever you say,' he replied, looking at Raymond as though he'd gone mad. He was still gawping at him as he left the building for the last time.

Outside in the darkness Raymond crouched down, taking out a pocket torch and sending three brief flashes in the direction of where he'd left his companions – at night all cats are grey and the last thing he wanted was a friendly fire accident. Moments later, three answering flashes came and he stood up, moving swiftly towards them, seeing their dark outlines detach from cover and jogging towards the vehicle.

At once there was a deafening report from somewhere close at hand and simultaneously, a blinding muzzle-flash lit the scene.

Raymond felt rather than heard the shockwave of a supersonic round as it passed him: instinct told him he'd been lucky by a matter of inches. Cursing, he threw himself to the ground and rolled away from the spot where he'd been standing. Then he turned to face the direction of the shot and saw a figure silhouetted against the glow of the fireflies. He lay still and began to groan as though in pain: the figure moved closer. Raymond tried to remember his training – control your breathing and don't tense your muscles or you'll miss. He groaned again and the figure moved closer: just a few more feet to make sure of hitting him, he thought. He was about to squeeze the trigger when a sound of movement came from the tall dry grass close by – probably an animal spooked by human activity on its patch. The figure turned and ran.

Raymond took aim and fired. Immediately there was a scream, but the muzzle flash from his own weapon had spoilt his night vision and he couldn't see whether the target had fallen or run off. No time to go and check, so, keeping close to the ground, he ran towards the SUV, gesturing to the others to follow. From behind them came another bang, this time from the outer door of the church slamming shut. They turned in time to see a figure run off into the darkness. 'C'mon,' said Raymond. 'Let's get out of here before that motherfucker comes back with his buddies.'

'Sorry, boys, but you ain't going anywhere right now.' They raised their hands to shield their eyes from the glare of the flashlight, which they could see was taped to the underside of a double-barrelled shotgun.

Raymond kept his pistol behind his back and peered closely, trying to make out the man's face: white, in his fifties or sixties, judging by the voice and blowing hard, either from fear or exertion. 'You must be the Reverend Morley,' he said, his accent dropping well below the Mason-Dixon line.

'Sure am,' said the voice from behind the shotgun, and Raymond was pleased to see that the weapon was no longer pointing at them. 'And who in the name of all that's holy might you boys be? And more to the point, what in Heaven's name d'you think you're all doing shooting at folk?'

'What the police aren't willing to do, Reverend,' said Raymond.

'And what's that supposed to mean? Hey, how d'you know who I am anyway?'

'We make a point of it, sir, it's what we do.'

The flashlight beam lit them up one by one as the pastor examined their faces, lingering just that little bit longer on Raymond's – this was the South, after all. 'So what is it you boys do? Stealing altar plate? After the collection box maybe? Well if y'are, y'all out of luck –'

'No, sir, just the opposite. If the police aren't willing to protect the House of God from damage, it's up to decent folk to do so, just like you said in last week's Gazette.' Luckily for them, the Reverend Morley's flashlight wasn't on them or the look of incredulity on the faces of Raymond's two companions as they gaped like the bullfrogs in the nearby creek would have given the game away. 'Look,' said Raymond. 'Let me show you.'

Leaving the others at the SUV he took out his Maglite and lit the way over to the church. 'See what I mean?' he asked, turning the beam onto the wall to illuminate the three stark letters: "K.K.K". 'We heard you'd been having problems with people who don't like us coloured folk in your congregations so we decided to come take a look-see. Third time lucky.'

'What do you mean?' asked the pastor.

'Third night we've been out here, sir. We take the Lord's work seriously even though I could do with the sleep,' said Raymond with a theatrical yawn.

Reverend Morley looked at him in admiration. 'Darn it; I come down here most nights and I never saw you once.'

'Then it's a good job we found them before you did, sir, if you don't mind my saying. Little punks shot at us – nearly hit us too. Man on his own might've come off second best if you know what I mean.'

Morley nodded gravely. 'Reckon you may've hit one of them,' he said. 'I'm sure I heard someone yelling.'

'Reckon we did, and all. I was always told the ones that're hurt real bad keep quiet but if a critter's hollerin', then, he's still got plenty of life in him.'

'Well,' said Morley, 'I reckon I've seen it all. I'm sorry if I didn't seem grateful just now, but I've had a whole heap of trouble – damage to the inside, windows smashed, profanities sprayed on the outside that no Christian soul ought to have to read; you name it – and I thought you was them.'

'Don't mention it, sir. We're glad to have been of assistance. And if you'll pardon me for asking, what are you going to do now?'

'Call the police I guess. Why?'

'If you do, can I ask a favour, Reverend?'

'Sure, name it. I owe you boys one.'

'Just don't mention you saw us and don't mention no gunfire.'

Morley scratched his head. 'Sure, if that's what you want, but can I ask why?'

'First, if we're going to catch the dumb-asses behind this – and believe me, there's someone behind it 'cause yours ain't the only church with problems like this – we don't want them to know we're on their trail. And second, if they find some punk with a nine millimetre slug in his ass, then it sure didn't come out of no twelve-gauge and you'll have some explaining to do.'

'So what should I say?'

Raymond thought for a moment. 'Just say you caught a couple of kids damaging the church, you fired in the air and they ran off. You leave the rest to us and the least said, the soonest we can catch these motherf – sorry, these punks.'

Morley shook Raymond firmly by the hand. 'Sorry, son, I didn't catch your name,' he said.

'No, Reverend,' said Raymond with a smile. 'You didn't. But don't you worry, sir, we're never far away.' And with that he turned, loping away into the darkness towards the SUV.

Luzzo's eyes were wide with fear and surprise. 'What the fuck is going on? We thought you was gonna drop him –'

'Just shut the fuck up and drive,' said Raymond, removing the coolbox from the front passenger seat and climbing in.

The SUV jolted along the track and within five minutes they were on the highway leading towards Stokeville.

There was little traffic at this time of night and they drove on in silence watching the blacktop unroll beneath the beams of the headligh. 'So what is all this Uncle Tom vigilante shit, Raymond? What the hell you been smoking?'

'It's called research, asshole. We get invited by a bunch of shitheads we don't even know to a drop at a church twenty miles from East Jesus and you dumb fucks would just say "yeah" and roll along without checking anything? Shit!'

'So what else are we supposed to do?'

'Like I said, research. For a start, where is the damn church? How many ways in and out are there if things goes wrong? Are there any houses, buildings likely to have security cameras, any streetlights and stuff nearby? Who's the pastor? A country mouse or an ex-Navy SEAL? This is shit that matters.'

'And if your research was so goddam shit-hot, how come we got jumped by some good ole boy with a twelve-gauge?'

Raymond glared at the man in the back seat. 'Listen, you ignorant motherfucker, the whole point about planning for trouble is you never know what form the trouble's gonna take. Believe it or not – and God knows why I bother – but I was protecting your investment and also our client's.'

'Yeah? How?'

'Because by doing the simple stuff like reading the Stokeville Gazette online before we came down there I found out that those charming folk from the Klan have been busting up churches with mixed congregations, painting slogans and shit.'

'So what?'

'So I sprayed "KKK" on the church, just in case anyone saw us near the place or in case somebody like our friend the reverend there turned up. Now I know you may have trouble following the incredibly complex

81

logic underlying this shit, but if you're looking for a suspect, it ain't going to be someone who looks like me.'

'I still don't get it.'

The argument continued all the way along State Route 25 to the cheap motel on the other side of Stokeville. Raymond and Luzzo jumped out leaving the third member of the gang at the wheel. 'I'll go back into town and fill up with gas so we can make an early start. Anybody want anything?'

'Yeah, twenty Marlboro,' said Raymond.

As he pulled out of the gas station he paid no attention at first to the headlights behind him but half a mile later the blue flashing lights and the whooping of the siren made his blood run cold. Just keep calm, he told himself as he pulled over to the side of the road, watching the two State Troopers get out of their car, you're sober, you're not carrying, it's going to be cool.

Pompeii

The door to Flora's office burst open and Francesco Moretti rushed in. 'Lombardi's got news. They've recovered one of the pages from a codex that was stolen from the lab – it's from *Antiquities* too.'

'But that's fabulous,' cried Flora, leaping to her feet and giving him a hug. 'Where?'

'Have a guess.'

'The USA?'

'Right first time. Lombardi's coming to see us at ten and he'll tell us more then.'

Flora continued hopping up and down with excitement and after a couple of laps of the office sat down to try and continue working, but she couldn't settle and the hands of her watch seemed to stand still. Eventually ten o'clock came round and Moretti led Flora and Lombardi into his office. 'So what have you got for us?' asked Moretti, he too betraying signs of nervous excitement.

'Well, it's only one page and it's already in poor condition. Our American counterparts at the ACT – '

'What's the ACT?' asked Flora.

'Sorry, it's the FBI's Art Crime Team. They're based in Washington – a very good outfit. They got a tip-off from a collector in Chicago who was offered an early copy of a work by Eusebius at a price that was too good to be true and that led them to one of the gang.'

'So have they got them all?' asked Flora.

'They've made a couple of arrests but I haven't got the full story yet. The handover was supposed to take place in a church near Birmingham – the one in Alabama, not Britain – but when they got there, all they found were the documents and some local pastor who knew nothing about what was going on. Clearly something had spooked the buyers or they'd have collected the package – a single page from the beginning of *Antiquities*, and a few fragments from Eusebius' *Chronicon*, or what was left of them..'

'So who's got it now?' asked Flora. 'I hope it's being properly conserved.'

'Don't worry,' said Lombardi. 'It's under lock and key at George Washington University. The trick is to get the rest of it back. Now, could you excuse me a second.' Flora stood to leave. 'No, not you, Flora. Doctor Moretti, if you wouldn't mind...?'

Alone with the smartly-dressed Carabinieri officer, Flora felt scruffy and ill at ease in her t-shirt and shorts, her hair tied back out of the way with an elastic band she'd found on the desk and with only the odd dab of makeup. Lombardi waited until Moretti had closed the door behind him before speaking again.

'I know this is going to sound like a strange question but how well known are you, Flora?' he asked.

Flora's eyebrows shot up. 'Well if you mean in academic circles, then we all know each other pretty much. Archaeology's a small world and palaeography's even smaller.'

'So how does that work? You read each other's research I suppose. Do you meet at conferences and so on?'

Flora ran her hand over her thick, dark hair and tried to make sense of what she was hearing. 'Well, yes, I speak at conferences in Britain – maybe five or six per year – and so far I've done one in Greece, two in Italy and I've got another one coming up in Germany.'

'What about the States?'

'No, I've never even attended as a delegate.'

'And who goes to these conferences? Just academics or do you get collectors there too?'

Flora shook her head. 'I'm sorry, why are you asking me this? What's it got to do with getting the codices back?'

Lombardi's eyes met hers. 'I can't tell you right now, but believe me, it's highly relevant. Now, tell me – do you ever get collectors at the conferences you attend?'

'No. The conferences aren't open to the general public.'

Lombardi nodded. 'Good. Now my next question is stranger still but please believe me, it's vitally important. Apart from your friends, family and academic colleagues, would anyone recognise you in the street?'

Flora hesitated again. 'Well, no, not strangers if that's what you mean. Why would they?'

'So you don't belong to any social networking sites or anything like that?'

'Yes, I belong to a couple of sites for archaeologists but under a pseudonym: my alias is *Pyroclastic Flo*.' Lombardi looked at her and frowned. 'Sorry,' continued Flora, feeling rather embarrassed. 'It's a joke. You know, a play on words – *Pyroclastic Flo*, she's hot stuff. Destruction of Pompeii? No? Anyway, it works in English.'

'But no pictures of you on the sites?'

'Absolutely not.'

'And you haven't been on TV? Haven't done any documentaries?' he asked. She shook her head. 'Excellent, we're nearly there. Now,' he fixed her with a steady gaze. 'My TPC superiors in Rome would like to talk to you. We may need you there for a few days.'

'But why?'

'They said there are some additional questions they'd like your help with. That's all I know.'

Flora's outdoor complexion went pale. 'But I said I'd stay and help Francesco. His department's paying for me to stay here and I've just told the hotel I'm staying for at least another three weeks. I've got heaps more documents to look at.'

'Don't worry, Flora, the TPC will take care of all the arrangements. Now, please answer: will you come with me to Rome tomorrow?'

'Well if it'll help then yes, of course.'

Lombardi smiled. 'That's excellent. Make sure you bring your passport and please don't tell anyone, and I mean anyone, where you're going or why.'

Fat chance of that, thought Flora. I was hoping you were going to tell me.

Lombardi left and Moretti came back into the office. 'What was all that about?' he asked.

'Oh, you know just a few more questions,' she replied, trying to sound as natural as possible. 'Where I've been, who I've been in contact with over the last few months – the usual I suppose.'

'And what did you tell him?'

The questioning made her feel a little uneasy. Nothing she could put her finger on, but it just didn't sound like the usual Francesco Moretti. 'Oh nothing, really. Just a list of the conferences I've been to: dates, people and so on. Why do you ask?'

'No real reason. Forgive me, I'm just being nosey,' he said, breaking the tension. 'I'll tell you what, how do you fancy meeting up for a bite to eat tonight? Nothing fancy, just pizza or something. I could do with the company.' Her first instinct was to refuse but feelings of guilt over misleading him about the real reason for her conversation with Lombardi got the upper hand.

'OK, but I don't want a late night, I have things to do tomorrow.'

Moretti peered at her with one eye half-closed. 'Oh really? Such as?'

'Personal things. Private, you know.'

'Invited you out has he?'

Flora blushed. 'What do you mean? Who?'

'Your handsome policeman. I saw how he was looking at you – no wonder he wanted to talk to you alone.'

Nothing in Moretti's face gave any clue as to whether he was joking or not and Flora squirmed uneasily in her seat.

'I don't know what you mean,' she said with an indignant pout. 'Anyway I've got work to do. I'll meet you at the hotel at eight.' With that she stood up and left the office, closing the door behind her, wondering how to explain her absence from Pompeii.

This time Moretti was early and it was his turn to wait in the stuffy hotel foyer under the bored gaze of the teenage receptionist. At exactly eight o'clock Flora trotted downstairs to meet him, forcing a smile as she did so: her heart wasn't in this and she was still no nearer to finding a convincing story to tell him.

The restaurant was full of locals, always a good sign, and the pizzas were superb but from the moment they had left the hotel it was obvious to Flora that things weren't right. Moretti seemed morose and try as she might she couldn't think of anything to say that they hadn't already said to one another during the day.

Taking a seat in a corner, they both tried to force the conversation along but the magic had gone and in its place an invisible barrier had descended between them. She asked him about Anna and the family but that only seemed to make matters worse: something was wrong and the more she tried to be jolly, the more contrived it felt. Finally, Moretti broke the ice. 'What did Lombardi really want when he spoke to you this morning?'

'He wanted me to run away with him and have his tiny babies.'

The joke fell flat. 'Don't make fun of me, Flora. What did he want?'

'I told you. Personal questions about where I'd been and who I'd spoken to.'

'I don't believe you.'

Her temper flared and she only just stopped herself from turning her anger on him. 'Look, Francesco, I know you're having a hard time with Anna and we're all hurting about the break-in, but please don't be like this.'

He shook his head and broke eye contact, his gaze turning downwards. 'You don't understand, Flora, you don't understand how I feel about you –'

'I do, you know. You made that pretty clear when we were in bed last night.'

'That's not what I'm talking about, it goes beyond that.'

Oh God, here comes the declaration of undying love, she thought, please beam me up, Scotty.

'Look, Francesco,' she said, reaching across the table and squeezing his hand tightly. 'You fuck like an angel but let's not over-complicate things. Why don't I go away for a few days? Perhaps it would be better if I wasn't around for a bit. You know, let things cool down.'

He looked at her quizzically. 'And where would you go? Somewhere with Lombardi?'

'It's not like that, Francesco, it really isn't. And anyway, what I do and who I spend my time with is nobody's business but mine.'

'He'll use you and you'll get hurt.'

Flora rolled her eyes, 'Look, please spare me the soap-opera clichés. I've made my mind up: I'm going away for a few days and when I come back I'll decide whether to stay here and help or go home.'

'That's not what I'm talking about.' Seeing Flora's puzzled expression he continued. 'It's all very convenient isn't it, this sudden disappearing act of yours? What's it to be: Naples or Rome?'

'What do you mean?'

'Where's Lombardi asked you to go?'

This was more than Flora could bear. 'Look, it isn't like that, I've told you,' her voice took on a shrill tone that she recognised as her mother's. 'He's asked me to help with the investigation that's all. I wasn't supposed to tell anybody but now you know. I've nothing to tell his bosses at the TPC that I haven't already told you so God knows what use I'm going to be to them. Now listen, Francesco, please get it into your head that I'm not interested in Lombardi.' She stood up, pushing her meal away half-finished. 'Thank you for dinner, Francesco, I'm going now. I'll see you in a few days.'

'Sit down, Flora, and listen to me.' He caught her by the wrist. His grip felt uncomfortably hard. 'I've told you how things are played in Campania, haven't I?'

She sat down. 'You mean the people I keep mentioning and shouldn't?'

'Precisely. If they find out you're working with the TPC then they won't take any chances.'

'Meaning what?' she asked.

'They'll kill you.'

'Oh come off it,' she scoffed. 'How are they going to know and why would they want to hurt me? I don't know anything more about the robbery than you do. Come on, tell me. How would they know if I was working with the TPC?'

'They'd know. Believe me, they have ways. You're English, you don't understand how things work here – it's...it's like the air, they're everywhere.' he said.

'Well, you went to Rome,' replied Flora. 'And you were even on the TV. They haven't come after you, have they?'

He looked at her intently. 'That was different – of course they'd expect me to talk to the police, but you're different, you're an outsider, and if you suddenly show up in Rome –'

'Oh, come off it,' she replied, her cheeks flushing with anger. 'You can't be serious –'

' Of course, I'm serious. I want you to tell Lombardi that you've changed your mind.'

She shook her head. 'I can't do that, sorry, Francesco.'

'Don't go,' he said, squeezing her hand. 'Please, please don't go with him, you don't know what you could be getting yourself into.'

She could see he was close to tears. 'Is this about me or is it about Lombardi, Francesco? I don't know what to believe.'

'Trust me, Flora, you mustn't go –'

'I'm sorry, Francesco. I've got to pack. I'll see you in a few days. And thanks for dinner – next time it's on me.'

***

The following morning, Lombardi collected Flora from her hotel and they set off in an unmarked Carabinieri Alfa Romeo for the two-and-a-half hour drive to Rome.

Flora hadn't slept well and was feeling tired and gritty-eyed. This is sheer bloody madness, she thought. They've mistaken me for something I'm not and they're going to be terribly cross when they find out. Lombardi's voice cut into her reverie.

'There was something I didn't tell you yesterday, Flora.'

'Oh really, what's that?'

'There is an outside chance that the people who've got the codices in the US may be dangerous.'

'Well I can't say that surprises me,' she said. 'Makes me glad to know I'll be stuck away safe in some laboratory somewhere. I don't think I'd fancy your job one bit.'

'Look, Flora,' he said, turning to look at her briefly before concentrating on his driving once more. 'I shouldn't tell you this because you're not supposed to find out until later, but there could be an element of danger for you in this.'

Chapter Eleven

Rome, the Capitoline Hill, AD 62

Josephus looked around him in awe. Although familiar with the grandeur of Roman architecture, the sheer scale of the imperial palace left him open-mouthed with wonder. 'Isn't there someone I should report to?'

'Stuff and nonsense,' said Alityros, marching ahead as though he owned the place. 'She's dying to meet you and wants to hear all about how brave you were during the shipwreck.'

'But I wasn't,' protested Josephus.

Alityros sucked his teeth. 'Ah, well, you see, I got a bit carried away. I'm afraid I added one or two bits.'

'You did what?' shouted Josephus, sliding to a halt on the polished marble floor. 'What on earth did you tell her?'

Alityros looked abashed and studied his sandals with great attention. 'That you fought off a couple of sea monsters.'

'Sea monsters?!'

'Not big ones, nothing to worry about. But just so's you know if she mentions it.'

'Thanks a bunch. I'm about to be presented to the wife of the emperor and now she's expecting to meet a raving lunatic.'

'Oh, don't make such a fuss, this place is full of them. On the scale of the crackpots they have here you won't even register. Come on or we'll be late.'

Josephus followed Alityros along the corridor until they came to a grand entrance, guarded by two sentries.

'Wait here.' Josephus did as he was told while Alityros exchanged a few words with the sentries.

'Come on, she won't bite,' he said, leading him through the curtain and into the room beyond.

'Who won't bite?' The voice was melodious and the words came with a hint of laughter. Poppaea Augusta Sabina stood up from her upholstered bench. 'So you must be Josephus? Alityros has told me all about you.'

She was in her early thirties but looked younger, with pale skin and cascades of chestnut-coloured hair surrounding her finely-drawn features. Josephus could see at once why Nero had been tempted to stray from the aristocratic froideur of his wife, Claudia Octavia. He bowed stiffly from the neck. 'It is a great honour and a privilege to meet you, your majesty,' he said.

'Come and sit down,' she said, and picking up a small copper bell, rang it. A slave arrived and Poppaea ordered wine and fruit for her visitors. 'First things first, Josephus. Did you really fight off five sea monsters to save this old queen from his fate?' She looked at the young Judean mischievously.

'Did he say five, ma'am? I don't recall there being that many.'

She put her head on one side and stared at him. 'Well how many were there?'

'Well, to tell you the truth, I think Alityros got a better look at them than me. I didn't actually see any I'm afraid.'

'Oh that is *such* a disappointment,' she said. 'I've always wanted to know what they look like. Alityros, you are a dreadful fibber, you know that?'

'Yes, ma'am,' he replied, looking down at his feet once more.

'Well, I promise that when I *do* find a sea monster, you shall personally fight it in the arena. How's that for a punishment?' The tinkling laugh rang through the lofty chamber.

'I think it fits the crime perfectly,' said Josephus, joining in the merriment.

The slave returned with a tray and for the next few minutes, the three made small talk, Josephus telling her about their journey and Poppaea updating Alityros on all the latest gossip, in between studying the letter of recommendation from Proculus. Having read it, Poppaea rolled it back up and placed it next to the work of Virgil she'd been reading when they came in. 'So I understand you're here to see my husband?' she said.

'Yes, ma'am.'

'Well, before you get to see him, you're going to have to convince me of the justice of your case first. Then, and only then, will I intercede on your behalf.' The switch from good-humoured banter to steely-eyed statesmanship was instant and it caught Josephus off guard.

'Do you understand me?' He nodded and she continued, speaking this time to Alityros. 'And as for you, you can trot along and make your excuses to your lord, my husband. He has a very special punishment arranged for you for arriving so many days late.'

Alityros went pale. 'But, ma'am, the shipwreck, we got here as fast as we could… it was none of my doing – '

'Since when did that matter? My husband has composed a new poem in honour of Jupiter and has set it to music: you are to listen to it in full and I don't need to remind you of how wonderful you are to find it.'

'But ma'am, the one he wrote in honour of Mercury went on for three hours.'

Poppaea remained stony-faced. 'I've heard this one's even longer. That'll teach you to come in here with sailors' yarns about sea monsters. Now leave!'

For all the studied frivolity in the exchange, Josephus had learned much. He'd seen two brief vignettes – firstly, a beautiful, aristocratic and intelligent woman bantering with a parvenu actor, and secondly, a tiny glimpse of the quick-thinking, ruthless schemer – married off to Crispinus, the leader of Claudius' Praetorian Guard, at fourteen – who then made a timely change of allegiance which led her first into the bed of future emperor Otho, and then, when once more she sensed the wind blowing from another quarter, into the arms of the unstable but talented Nero.

'Come sit by me,' said Poppaea, patting the lush upholstery of her couch. 'I'm intrigued.'

'Intrigued by what, ma'am?' He did as she asked but with a mounting sense of unease, feeling for all the world like a fly on the receiving end of charming small-talk from a hungry spider.

'Oh, by lots of things,' she said with a wave of her hand. 'Why you've come all this way; risked your life to plead for your quarrelsome, antisocial countrymen. And by you in particular: Proculus' letter confirms what Alityros told me about you.'

He swallowed. 'Which is?'

'That you are a young man of noble birth, a member of the priestly class.'

Josephus bowed his head. 'That is true. But you mention Proculus, ma'am. He made it very clear that my rank in Judea makes me a lord of the dunghill in Rome's opinion.'

She smiled at the self-deprecation but the terrible cold eyes sent a shiver through his being, and he thought of the cruelty they must have witnessed over the years: the eyes of *Lamia*. 'You learn quickly,' she said. 'An admirable quality and one that will do much to keep you alive, Josephus. Do you know what the other one is?'

'No ma'am.'

'Loyalty.'

'An admirable quality, I agree,' he replied in deferential tones.

She frowned and studied her manicured fingernails. 'Only up to a point, of course. You see, timing is everything. Loyalty is useless if it's given to the wrong person at the wrong time; remember that and you may well stay alive long enough to die in your bed.'

'I'll do my best, ma'am.'

'A wise decision,' she said, leaning over the table and making great show of deliberating in her choice prior to helping herself to a fig. As she leant forward, the top of her white tunic dress gaped open allowing Josephus a clear view of her pale breasts with their small, pinky-brown nipples. She sensed his unease and savoured the moment before sitting back upright and turning her gaze on him once more. 'Now, to business,' she said. 'I understand you've already done some – how shall I put it? – freelance work on the empire's behalf. I'm intrigued. Loyalty or self-interest?'

'Pure self-interest.'

'I like your honesty. Another admirable quality if applied in moderation – something that dear Lucius Annaeus Seneca would do well to remember – I take it you're familiar with his work?' Josephus nodded and she continued. 'Good, because when you speak to my husband he'll tell you more about it, but Seneca is worried about the personality cult developing around one of your countrymen, the one they call The Christ.'

'It worries me too, ma'am. Evil men are deluding the uneducated with this nonsense and endangering the natural order. I have a personal interest in seeing them fail.'

The cold but beautiful smile flashed once more. 'Good: we're in agreement then,' said Poppaea. 'The leaders of the cult refuse to listen so they're obviously going to have to learn the hard way. Whether you, I or my husband would agree on what constitutes the "natural order", as you put it, is an irrelevance.'

'I think we can agree on enough to make it work,' said Josephus.

Her face told him at once that he'd overstepped the mark. 'Do not get ideas above your station. If we work together it will be on our terms. Learn quickly and remain loyal to those you serve and you won't be the loser. Remember that when you talk to the emperor tomorrow.'

'I thought you said you wanted to hear my case regarding the priests.'

She looked at him intently. 'In all honesty I don't care whether my husband releases them or sends them to the arena. My concern is that you don't waste his time or upset him and from what I've seen you're intelligent enough not to do either.' Her smile faded and she looked away. 'The emperor angers quickly and when he does, it's not always easy for those nearest to him. Anger him and you will answer to me. Understand?'

'Yes ma'am.'

'Good. Now you may leave, but be sure, we will speak again.' With that, she smiled once more, leaned towards him and sliding her hand under his tunic, squeezed his balls painfully hard.

In considerable discomfort and with his mind still reeling, Josephus was led away to a walled garden with a fountain at its centre where he sat in the shade, awaiting Alityros' return. The afternoon wore on and lulled by the warmth, Josephus fell asleep. No sooner had he dropped off than he was awakened by someone sitting down next to him. For a moment, he looked around, unsure where he was, but then the sight of a familiar face brought him back to reality.

'Alityros,' he exclaimed. 'I wasn't expecting you for ages. How did you escape so soon?'

'Oh, I have my ways. It's a trick I can't try too often or he'll rumble it, but when I get to a point where I can't stand his doggerel any longer, I ask if I can join in with the singing, so entranced am I by the beauty of his verse and the sweetness of his voice.' Josephus laughed at the hand-waving, bowing and over-acting of his friend.

'And why does that get you off the hook?'

'You've obviously never heard me sing: for miles around, dogs howl, babies cry and milk curdles. He puts up with it for a couple of verses and then tells me to stop, at which point I fall to the ground in floods of tears – I may be a rotten singer, but I can at least act – and beg leave to withdraw in order to get over the emotional effects of being exposed to such beauty, yet at the same time being cruelly forbidden by my nature to be able to participate in it....or some such guff.'

'And he falls for it every time?'

'He has done so far, but I'd better not try it too often.'

Josephus became serious once more and gazed into the dancing waters of the fountain as though searching for inspiration. 'He wants to see me tomorrow,' he said.

'I know,' said Alityros. 'Poppaea told me. What did you think of her, by the way?'

'She scared me rigid.'

'Yes, she does that sometimes.'

'She flashed her tits at me.'

'Yes, she does that too, just to see how you react. Wasted on me of course.'

'And she doesn't scare you?'

'She's no threat to me,' said the actor. 'And that's because I'm no threat to her. I'm from an ordinary plebeian family, a camp old thesp who makes her laugh and indulges her husband when he wants to play at being a poet and musician. You, on the other hand, are different.'

A worried frown crossed Josephus' face. 'You mean she thinks I could be a threat?'

'Not a threat, no. Her main interest is that you don't become one. Don't forget, you're an outsider and worse still, in their eyes you carry all the baggage that comes with being a Jew. Remember what Proculus told you?' Josephus nodded. 'Play straight with them, swallow your pride and in time, they may start to trust you. But for now, they'll be watching you like hawks and if they so much as get a whiff of anything that isn't right, well – ' Alityros made a throat-slitting gesture that left Josephus in no doubt.

'It's the way she switches the charm on and off that frightened me the most,' he said.

'Count yourself lucky. Showing you what she's like when it's switched off was a gentle warning to remember your place.'

'And then as I was about to leave she, she – ' Josephus blushed.

'She what?'

'Grabbed me by the balls. It hurt too.'

Alityros threw his head back and laughed. 'Don't worry, that's just another of her ways of letting you know who's in charge. If they hurt for a bit, it's a reminder that aching knackers are preferable to having them cut off, roasted and then being forced to eat them.'

Josephus crossed his legs at the thought. 'That isn't funny,' he said.

'It wasn't meant to be. She's done it before if the rumours are correct. She's a connoisseur of men's balls: the "carnal delights", as they're called round here are a very big part of her life.'

'She'll cut yours off if she hears you've been spreading stories like that.'

Alityros laughed. 'It's one of the worst-kept secrets on the Palatine. Nero prefers boys – and before you ask, I'm too old and raddled for his tastes – but when he's with her sometimes he has trouble getting it up so Poppaea has to look elsewhere for her amusement.'

Josephus looked at him aghast. 'Such as where? She's the emperor's wife for heaven's sake.'

'Oh, anywhere she pleases. She'll go for another man if the mood takes her but she likes women too. The emperor likes to watch her perform with slave girls in the bath, dirty little sod.'

'I've obviously led a very sheltered life.'

'Well, if you want to make up for it, you've certainly come to the right place.'

***

Next day, at the third hour of the morning Josephus presented himself, as ordered, at the imperial palace. He was led to a marble bench outside Nero's audience chamber where he waited for what seemed like an age, listening to the sounds of someone playing the lyre and a man's voice singing in a high, thin falsetto. Resigned to spending the rest of the day there, he sat with his elbows on his knees and his chin cupped in his hands, not for the first time questioning the wisdom of undertaking such an errand and daydreaming about life at home in Judea. His thoughts were interrupted by the appearance of a thickset young man, of about the same age as him, with a heavy jaw and a spotty, rather podgy face, topped with greasy brown hair. His toga had seen better days and bore the traces of what Josephus assumed was last night's dinner.

'What are you doing here?' asked the new arrival.

'Waiting,' replied Josephus, with a cursory glance up at him.

'Mind if I join you?' Josephus shrugged. The man clearly hadn't been near a bath-house in several days, but Josephus thought it best not to make any comment, and shuffled along the bench to make room. 'So who're you waiting for?'

Josephus was on the point of making a sarcastic reply when he thought better of it. Never know, he thought, this clod might be one of his personal slaves, better play along with him. 'I'm waiting for an audience with his imperial majesty, Nero Germanicus,' he replied.

'Keeping you waiting then, is he?'

Josephus stuck his well-bred nose in the air. 'It's not for me to complain about his majesty's time-keeping,' he said loftily.

'So what's he like, then, this Nero?'

Josephus turned and looked at him in disdain. 'Well how should I know? I've never met him. Don't you work here?'

His malodorous companion pouted. 'Hmm, I wouldn't call it work exactly. I just wanted to know what he's like, what people are saying about him, you know, what's the word on the Aventine? – that kind of thing.'

The question aroused Josephus' suspicions still more and he

95

retreated further into his diplomatic shell. 'Since arriving in the city, without exception, all I've heard is that he is wise, merciful and generous.'

'Nothing about his poetry and singing then?'

'I hear they are of the highest order – god-like was the expression, I believe.'

The young man gave Josephus a hearty shove that sent him sprawling on the marble floor. 'You creep, Josephus,' he laughed, jumping to his feet. 'What a bum-sucking little toady you are. And there was I looking forward to having you executed for sedition. Bugger!'

Josephus looked up and saw that the man was now surrounded by a group of people, including Poppaea and Alityros, all of whom were bent double with laughter. The young man stretched out a hand to help him up. 'Allow me to present myself: Nero Claudius Caesar Augustus Germanicus, but you can call me "sir".' He released his grasp on Josephus who started brushing himself down and straightening a tunic nearly as crumpled as his dignity. 'Wasn't that a wonderful joke, eh, Josephus? Wasn't it brilliant?'

Over the emperor's shoulder he caught Alityros' eye and the actor promptly went into a dumb-show of pantomime hysterics. Josephus didn't need telling twice and put his hands on his knees, rocking back and forth in what he hoped looked like real mirth. 'Fabulous, sir, utterly superb: words fail me.'

Chapter Twelve

The traffic in Rome was nose-to-tail and even using the car's blue flashing lights and two-tone horns, Lombardi had trouble making any headway. To Flora's surprise, instead of continuing towards the ancient heart of the city he turned right off the Via Appia Nouva towards the central railway station.

'Hold on a minute, I thought we were going straight to the TPC,' she said.

'Sorry, didn't I mention it? There's been a slight change of plan,' he replied. 'I was told to take you to the British Embassy first.'

Flora went pale and swallowed hard. 'No, you didn't mention it. Any reason why?'

Lombardi shook his head.

She noticed his shifty expression and felt a pang of irritation. 'And did anyone think to tell me, ask me even?'

'They said not to mention it…'

'Not even to me?'

'Don't tell anyone is what they said.'

'And who are "they" if you please?'

He took one hand off the wheel and gestured airily. 'Oh, my bosses at the TPC. Worried about word getting out to the wrong people in Pompeii I suppose.'

'Or worried I'd have said "no", more likely,' said Flora, folding her arms. She knew this corner of Rome well and coming back to the ugly concrete slab of the Embassy building – looking for all the world like the bastard offspring of a fire station and a 1960s New Town shopping centre – caused a host of bad memories to come flooding back.

They stopped at a red traffic light. 'Anyway, why would you say no?' he asked.

Flora shook her head but made no reply. Why indeed? she thought.

Just four years ago – another lifetime or so it seemed now. At the outset it had seemed to her like a relatively simple, low-risk operation but things had unravelled frighteningly quickly. First came the web of lies, then the deaths, then the blame-shifting and the botched cover-up. She had a good idea of where the disaster had started and why. She knew the names of the guilty and had met some of them too – many of them subsequently ennobled, knighted, honoured and generally kicked upstairs away from any proof of their involvement. It was in this very building that a younger and more naïve Flora Kemble had been briefed for her part in the drama that was about to unfold.

The tap on the shoulder had come during her final year at Oxford. As a brilliant linguist she made a natural target for the talent spotters and during a discreet lunch at a restaurant just outside the city, was invited to consider applying to join the "Foreign and Commonwealth Co-ordinating Staff", one of the euphemisms for the Secret Intelligence Service, better known as MI6 to the media and "The Firm" to its employees.

As expected, Flora graduated with a first and passed the FCO entry exam with ease. Then, after coming top of her SIS training course at Fort Monckton came the hammer blow: a posting to Rome, a D-category Station.

The SIS rates its highest risk Stations such as Pyongyang and Kabul as "A". The lowest, safest, and to Flora's way of thinking, dullest, were the "D" postings – Commonwealth and EU countries where the threat to British interests was considered lowest. If she expected three years cultivating friendly journalists and fishing for gossip about Italian government corruption, then the reality of why she had been chosen for the job came as a complete shock.

'Flora… Flora,' Lombardi's voice jolted her back to the here and now. 'We're there, they want to see your passport.'

Mechanically, and with a sense of detachment, tinged with disbelief that she was back at the very building where she had worked for eighteen months, she scrabbled in her handbag. The security guard barely glanced at it before handing it back and waving them into the embassy compound.

'Do you like it?' he asked.

Flora was still only half with him. 'Like what?'

'The building. It's very different.'

'Very ugly if you ask me.' she answered in a monotone.

Lombardi caught the change in her mood and looked at her intently. 'Something the matter? Not nervous are you? I'm sure it's just routine.'

She thought for a moment. 'I'm sure you're right. I was just wishing I was back in Oxford, that's all. I miss my cat.'

They followed the signs to the left hand side of the building into a car park shaded by trees and as they drew to a halt, a pink-faced young man, barely out of his teens or so it seemed to Flora, appeared from a side door to greet them.

'I'll wait for you here,' said Lombardi. 'I'm sure they won't keep you long.'

'Glad to know one of us is so well briefed,' she replied, climbing out of the car. The young man introduced himself and led the way up the steps.

'First time here?' he asked as they made their way to the *piano nobile*.

'No I've been to Rome before.'

'But not to the embassy?'

It could have been small-talk or he could be sounding her out, she wasn't sure. 'I don't think anyone could forget a building this ugly,' she said with a laugh, hoping the answer was ambiguous enough.

Not pressing the point any further, he guided her along a marble-floored corridor. A cleaning lady was half-heartedly steering a mop along the skirting and looked up at their arrival – Flora recognised her but the woman made no sign that she remembered Flora. At last they arrived at a light oak door marked "Meeting Room 1D and he showed her in. It was sparsely furnished but elegant and the pink-faced young man invited her to take a seat. 'Mr Smith will be with you shortly,' he said, closing the door behind him.

Flora got up and crossed to the window, gazing down on the shaded inner courtyard – a view she knew well. Was it really only four years ago? Maybe she was reading too much into this: the young man was probably just trying to be friendly and after all, her past had nothing to do with this.

A discreet tap at the door broke her reverie and she turned to see a tall, silver-haired man in his early sixties. The suit was of a local cut and spoke of good taste and expensive tailoring. His shoes were definitely Jermyn Street: old habits die hard, she thought.

He smiled and crossed the room, hand extended. 'You must be Miss Kemble. I'm Giles Smith from the consular department. Very good of you to come.'

Neutral sounding name, vague job title, I don't like this one bit, thought Flora but her expression remained neutral and friendly. 'I thought I was going to the *Tutela del Patrimonio Culturale* offices. It seems there's been a change of plan.'

'Ah, yes,' said Smith. 'We just thought it wise to ask you to pop in and see us first.'

Flora chuckled at this. 'I didn't actually get much choice in the matter.'

'Again, we thought it best to limit the number of people who knew.

News travels fast in southern Italy.'

'So Lieutenant Lombardi tells me.'

Smith shifted his gaze from her and hesitated for a moment as though weighing up what to say next. 'We know you worked for the Rome Station for two years.'

Flora immediately tensed and folded her hands in her lap. Her training kicked in: after the eyes, the biggest give-away are the hands. Don't shift your gaze, don't move your hands.

The corners of Smith's mouth turned almost imperceptibly upwards into what could almost have been a smile. 'Please relax, Miss Kemble, you're not under interrogation, we just need to get one or two facts straight.' And while Flora was wondering who "we" might be, he reached down into his leather briefcase and drew out a file with a blue cardboard cover. 'This is an extract from your personnel file,' he said, placing it on the low table in front of them. 'Heavily redacted but it's only fair to tell you that we're aware of your work for The Firm.'

Flora maintained eye contact, waiting for him to look away. 'And does that change anything? I hope that file of yours tells you I resigned four years ago and that I'm now a dusty old academic.'

This time, the smile looked more genuine. 'Hardly old, Miss Kemble and Professor Braithwaite speaks very highly of you.'

Now it was Flora's turn to smile. 'Stephen Braithwaite,' she said with a shake of the head. 'I should have known.' The Professor, who was Flora's faculty Dean at Oxford had talent spotted her for the SIS and had been present at the restaurant when she had agreed to try for the FCO exam.

'He's very upset about the robbery.'

'I think we all are,' said Flora.

'And after you phoned him, he called me. He thought you might be able to help.'

At this, her eyebrows went up. 'I retired four years ago. This is police work.'

Smith nodded. 'It is indeed but there are complexities.'

'Such as?'

Smith drummed his fingers on the table. 'There's an international twist. The Cousins have evidence that the ultimate destination for the Josephus finds may be the USA. The FBI's Art Crime Team are on the case but this is the first time they've handled a case involving documents of this age.'

'I'm sorry,' said Flora. 'You've lost me. I've told the TPC

100

everything I know and my old job's got nothing to do with this.'

Smith looked at the file once more. 'It doesn't say why you resigned.'

'That's because I didn't give a reason.'

'I'm assuming there was one.'

'Of course.'

'And I take it by that you mean you're not telling me,' said Smith, closing the file once more.

'No I'm not. I don't want to be found in the woods with my wrists slashed.'

'Point taken,' said Smith. 'As I said, the FBI and the TPC think there's an American connection. The ACT – apologies for all the acronyms, but that's the FBI's Art Crime Team. Well they want to set up a sting but they don't have the specialist knowledge to carry it off.'

'And let me guess. You think I do?'

'We know you do, Miss Kemble.'

'I resigned, don't forget,' said Flora.

Smith regarded her intently. 'We haven't forgotten. It's just that we, well Stephen Braithwaite and I, thought you'd be well placed to advise them. That is, assuming you're willing to, of course,' he added.

Flora shook her head. 'No, this isn't right. It's not the sort of case The Firm would bother itself with and there are plenty of palaeographers in the States who could help. There's more to this than you're telling me.'

'Let's say we owe one or two favours.'

'And I'm the favour. Should I be flattered? Do I have to jump out of a cake?'

Smith laughed at this and the tension eased a little. 'I don't know about flattered and certainly no cakes, but we wanted to sound you out first and also to put your mind at rest that all the diplomatic niceties have been squared. The TPC and the FBI representative you'll meet have been told that you have helped in enquiries of this sort before, but purely as a subject matter expert. They know nothing about your work for HMG so you will need to play the innocent abroad.'

Flora sighed, turned away and gazed out of the window. 'Every instinct tells me to say no,' she said.

Smith's disappointment was palpable. 'I was afraid you might say that.'

She thought for a moment. 'If it was "for Queen and Country" you know I'd tell you to get stuffed.' The silence hung heavy between them.

At last Flora continued. 'But this is different. The Josephus finds are something I care about.'

He brightened at once. 'Really? You mean you'll help.'

'Yes, I want those codices back. I couldn't care less about The Firm, nor about the Special Relationship for that matter, but this goes beyond all that.' He made to speak but she cut him off. 'Now listen, I don't trust The Firm, nor its political masters any further than I can throw them. I'll help you, but there are strings – things I want put in writing.'

'Very well. Name them.'

They spoke for another five minutes, with Flora doing most of the talking and Smith taking notes. When they had finished he reached into his briefcase once more and took out a sealed envelope. 'Take this with you to the TPC,' he said, handing it over. 'You'll be told when to open it.'

***

Five minutes later, Flora was back in the car park. Lombardi put down his newspaper and reached to open the door for her. 'Everything ok? he asked.

'Probably not but that's my look-out.'

He made a puzzled frown. 'Meaning?'

'Meaning, let's get moving before I change my mind.'

They set off into the organised chaos that is Rome's traffic system and turned into a maze of narrow side-streets, mid-way between the Pantheon and the Trevi Fountain, until at last the Alfa's tyres rumbled to a halt on the cobbles of the Piazza di Sant'Ignazio.

Opposite the basilica of the eponymous saint stood a three-storey baroque building, painted in Tuscan yellow and white, with light Prussian blue iron-work and shutters. Two wings jutted slightly forward from the central façade giving it a concave appearance, and over the front door, which bore the oval badge of the Carabinieri, flew the Italian and the European Union flags. Around the front of the building stood robust earthenware urns, each containing an evergreen shrub, forming a protective square. Inside this palisade were two black Mercedes with diplomatic plates and Flora was about to ask how they'd got in there when Lombardi reached down to the central console and picked up a small remote control which he pressed. As if by magic, two of the urns lifted up on hydraulically-operated steel platforms and pivoted gracefully outwards to allow the car to pass through.

'I just love doing that,' said Lombardi, with a small boy's grin.

'So I can see,' replied Flora, shaking her head indulgently.

102

With the sun almost directly overhead there was little shade in the square and the buildings seemed to focus the heat down onto their heads so she was grateful to get into the cool, dark interior of the headquarters of the *Comando Carabinieri Tutela Patrimonio Culturale.*

'Not bad for a police station, eh?' he asked, leading her up the marble staircase to the second floor.

'I think it's gorgeous.'

'And don't worry, the natives are friendly, you'll see.' He tapped at a delicately carved door and went in, with Flora following behind. The meeting room was wood panelled to half height and around the walls marched oil paintings of bewhiskered military men in parade uniforms of a bygone age. As they entered two men rose from their seats at the highly-polished table which dominated the room. Lombardi presented Flora to each in turn. First was the commanding officer of the TPC, Colonel Andretti, a tiny man with a pointed nose and a small moustache, which gave him the air of an inquisitive mole. The second introduced himself as Michael Hayek from the US Embassy's Legal Attaché's office.

They sat and Colonel Andretti gave a short speech, thanking her for her efforts to date and willingness to help.

'I still don't know what you're expecting me to do,' said Flora, shifting uncomfortably in her seat and hoping the act was working. 'I don't know the first thing about detective work.'

'Miss Kemble is being modest as usual,' said Lombardi. 'She is one of the most highly thought-of palaeographers in the world and the work she's done on helping date and read the codex fragments has been of enormous value to our search for a motive.'

'It has?' said Flora, who was growing ever more puzzled with each passing moment. That was clever of me, and I didn't even notice, she thought.

The colonel then nodded towards Hayek, who leaned forward and caught Flora's eye. To her he looked every bit the streetwise, hard-bitten downtown lawyer but surprised her by speaking grammatically-perfect Italian with a slight Piedmontese accent.

'Miss Kemble, first let me add my thanks for offering to help us. Let me explain why I'm here. My department, like all our overseas "Legat" teams is part of the Office of International Operations and I report straight into the Director of the FBI. Because we believe the break-in at the lab as well as the attack on the dig were financed by US-based criminals, together with the fact that fragments from the missing codices have turned up in our country, that makes it a problem for us as well as for our Italian colleagues. We know you've provided expertise in cases like this before and we're grateful you've agreed to help.'

'I'll do my best.'

Hayek continued. 'I can't yet reveal why, but we believe all the artefacts stolen from Pompeii are in the USA. We also believe there was a falling-out between those who did the job and those who financed it, and that the collection has been at least partially broken up and is being offered for sale.'

'So where do I fit in?' she asked.

'The market for ancient documents is extremely lucrative and is also a club with a very small and select membership. It's awash with forgeries and with later copies being passed off as being much earlier as I'm sure you're aware.'

Flora nodded, she was back on home turf now and feeling less like a small child facing interrogation by grown-ups. 'Much of what I do involves validating documents and placing them in the right country and in the right period: some of it's scientific and some is more based on language, style, calligraphy and so on,' she said.

'So you'd know the real thing if it was put in front of you?' he asked.

'I won't say I've never got it wrong, but in most cases, yes.'

Hayek nodded. 'Good. Since the recovery of the title page to Josephus' *Antiquities* in Alabama, Federal agents have made a number of arrests, one of which we believe to be particularly significant. Miss Kemble, have you ever heard of the FBI's Art Crime Team?'

She nodded. 'Heard of them but that's all.'

'The ACT's a small unit – thirteen agents – who specialise in the recovery of stolen art works, catching forgers and so on. Now until recently, the guy who headed up the team knew the art world backwards, but the problem is he's retired.'

'Right,' said Flora, eyeing him suspiciously.

'His speciality was working with other national agencies, posing as an art collector to lure criminals into situations where they could be arrested and successfully prosecuted.'

'A sting, in other words,' she said.

'Correct.'

Flora rolled her eyes. 'And now he's retired, you want me to try and convince a bunch of professional criminals that I'm a high-rolling art-collector with millions to blow on a couple of codices by Josephus.' She paused. 'You must be out of your tiny minds. They'd spot me for what I am a mile away. The answer's no.'

'Miss Kemble,' said Hayek. 'It's not as insane as it sounds. Please would you hear me out first?'

She folded her arms and looked at him warily. Hayek continued. 'We've no intention of throwing you into something for which you've had no training. We have an agent who's been understudying this role for over a year and although he trained as an archaeologist before joining the FBI, neither ancient documents nor ancient languages are his speciality so he's going to need help. We'd like you to come to the US to help us find the people who did this. Do you want to hear more?'

Flora unfolded her arms and the tension slowly lifted from her features. 'Of course. Please carry on and I'm sorry if I was abrupt just now, this is all a bit much to take in.'

Hayek spoke gently but firmly. 'OK, now this is where it gets serious. If we continue from here, everything I tell you is in the strictest confidence and if you divulge it to anyone, you'll be committing a felony, a criminal offence, irrespective of what country you happen to be in at the time. Still want me to go on?'

'Please do,' she replied, curiosity getting the better of her.

'Very well. Federal Special Agent Benjamin Cohen has been seconded from the FBI's New York Field Office to the ACT for this case. Given the provenance of the stolen artefacts, his role in the hunt for the criminals will be to assume the role of a wealthy Israeli collector, keen to see these works back in the native land of their author. As for you, Miss Kemble, we'd like you to join him as his assistant.'

'But these people, the criminals, would only have to Google me and they'd find out who I was.'

'I believe you were given an envelope to bring here, Miss Kemble. Would you open it please.' Flora did as he asked. 'In the envelope is a passport, a driving licence, credit cards, library membership and other cards, bank statements and utility bills all in the name of a British National living in Italy and working at the University of Bologna for the department of archaeology. I believe you studied there for a year.' He consulted his notes. 'Greek and Latin epigraphy – am I correct?'

There was something about him that didn't chime right with Flora. Just a little too self-assured, and certainly far too condescending. 'You are, and what big ears you do have, Grandma,' she replied.

'Take a look,' Hayek said.

She examined the passport: it bore exactly the same photograph and date of issue as her own, only the passport number, name and date of birth were different.

Suddenly, she stopped reading. 'Lavinia Hilda Crump!' she spluttered. 'Are you pulling my leg? Nobody's going to believe any parent would inflict a name like *that* on a child.'

'I agree it does seem a little old-fashioned,' he said. 'But the late Miss Crump really existed. Sadly, the airliner carrying the infant Lavinia and her parents hit the side of a mountain in Ecuador twenty six years ago. There were no survivors.'

'Oh, God. I'm sorry I made fun of her, I'd no idea,' said Flora, clapping her hand to her mouth.

'Please don't worry; you weren't to know. Now if you take a look at the front pages of the passport, you'll see there are a number of Israeli entry and exit stamps, all of which correspond to your trips to visit a Mr Benjamin Grossman – which is agent Cohen's alias – for whom you provide consultancy services and advice on the purchase of ancient texts.' Noticing her quizzical expression he continued. 'Just for your information, we've given Agent Cohen's alter-ego the same first name, firstly because it's one less thing to remember and secondly, if he ever bumps into someone he knows while under-cover – and believe me it happens – and they say "Hi, Ben, how ya doing?" in front of one of his targets, then it's going to take a lot less explaining than if he was passing himself off as Fred, say.'

'OK, so now what?' asked Flora.

'The "now what" is that we'd like you to memorise this,' said Smith, holding up another envelope. 'It's Lavinia Crump's CV from cradle to now. Please don't copy it or take it off the premises. We'll test you on it and you don't go anywhere till you're word-perfect.'

'But what if someone Googles Lavinia Crump?' asked Flora.

'That's all taken care of. We've created social networking profiles for her, online links to various academic papers and other references which have all been given the right search engine optimisation so they'll come up exactly where you'd expect and not just all over the first page.'

Flora paused again. 'Look,' she said. 'I'm one of the privileged few who've actually seen the codices, so I'm as keen to get them back as anyone. And I hope the people who stole them get locked up and the key thrown away, but it's not as simple as that.'

'Meaning what?'

'Meaning that you seem to have forgotten that it's all very well changing my plans to help you out, but I do have a day job – academics don't roost like bats until term starts – and outside that job I actually have a life: you know, friends, plans I've made, bills to pay, my house to look after.'

'You've nothing to worry about,' said Hayek. 'We've already spoken with Giles Smith about that. We can look after your house, make sure the garden's done, bills are paid and any emergencies – burst pipes and so on – are dealt with. I take it you run a car?'

'Only an old one.'

'Well, we can have it serviced, make sure the battery's charged for when you come home. We won't leave you in the lurch.'

Flora paused, choosing her words with care. 'Of course I want to help but I need assurances – just like my Embassy has agreed to give me. I need to know I can trust you people if things go wrong.'

'I'm listening,' said Hayek.

'Firstly, I want to know exactly who I'll be working for and that they'll guarantee me something approaching diplomatic status – I don't want to end up rotting in jail somewhere when one of your stings goes wrong and I'm trampled in the rush to be first out of the door.'

'I think we can manage that without any problems. Anything else, Miss Kemble?'

'Yes. I'm not carrying a gun or any other kind of weapon, and furthermore, you undertake never knowingly to put me into a situation where I might need one.' Hayek signalled his agreement and she continued. 'And finally, I want to be able to continue the work I've started for Francesco Moretti.' She sat back and fixed her gaze on Hayek, hoping he wouldn't notice she was pretending to be far more confident than she felt. She looked once more at the three men sitting around the table and caught Lombardi's eye. In return he gave her an approving nod.

'So are we all agreed then?' asked Colonel Andretti, receiving nods and general murmurs of approval in reply. 'Splendid,' he said, rubbing his hands in anticipation. 'In that case, I suggest we continue this conversation over lunch.'

Chapter Thirteen

Rome, the Capitoline Hill, AD 62

Nero led Josephus away from the little group of dutifully laughing people and into his private apartments, all the while, treating the Judean to a non-stop description of his most recent poetic works and their rapturous reception by all who'd been lucky enough to hear them. 'Poppaea tells me you're not keen on music or theatre.'

'I just prefer rhetoric and prose, that's all.'

'Fair enough,' said Nero over his shoulder. 'You've no need to flatter me, you know, just in case you thought you did.'

'It wasn't my intention, sir.'

'Good. I have plenty of people to do that for me and who think I don't notice.' He stopped at a doorway and motioned at Josephus to enter. The room was surprisingly plain – decorated plaster above half-height on the walls its only concession to opulence, with pudgy-cheeked *putti* playing hide-and-seek with a lascivious-looking *Bacchus* in between tresses of delicately-painted vines.

'Please sit down,' said Nero, all traces of the slapstick buffoon now gone. Either side of a low table stood two couches facing one another. Josephus sat and the emperor continued. 'I understand you want your priests back. Is that right?'

'Yes sir. They're old friends.'

'Do you know why they're in custody?

Josephus answered cautiously. 'They were arrested on Governor Festus' orders, sir.'

'And do you know what the charges were?' Josephus' perplexity was growing by the minute and his features showed it. 'Don't worry, these aren't trick questions,' said Nero. 'There was a report; I did read it but Jupiter only knows what's happened to it, and given that Festus is dead, he's not going to be able to tell us either.'

'I don't wish to be impolite, sir, but had you thought of having someone go and ask them?'

'No, it's not impolite, it's a very sensible question to which the answer is yes.'

'And if you don't mind my asking, what did they say?'

Nero made a dismissive gesture. 'All three gave the same story:

Festus had them arrested for preaching sedition. According to their version of events, they were merely preaching to the Jews to maintain the Jewish law.'

'That's what I heard too, sir,' said Josephus.

'Oh, well, that at least confirms what I've thought all along.'

'What's that?' asked Josephus, waiting with trepidation for the outburst which he was expecting at any moment.

'That under Roman law they've committed no offence and we've no grounds for holding them.'

'But that's wonderful news,' said Josephus, unable to believe his ears. 'Would it be all right for me to see them, you know, make sure they're all right?'

Nero smiled. Unlike Poppaea, the smile looked genuine – to fake a smile that well takes genuine madness, thought Josephus, still waiting for the unstable emperor to turn on him. 'Of course you can see them, Josephus, but all in good time. We have more important matters to discuss first, don't we?'

'We do?' he asked nervously.

'Yes, we most certainly do. Do you really think I had you come all this way just to talk about three Jewish mumbo-jumbo merchants? Please credit me with some intelligence. No, Rome has a problem and I understand you have a dog in the same fight.'

'The Lady Poppaea told you then?' said Josephus.

'She confirmed what I already knew. We have a common enemy: the followers of the so-called anointed one: the *Chrestos*. You've given my local commanders valuable help, but we all know there are others.'

'That's correct, sir.'

'And you're serious about hunting them down from what I've seen so far,' said Nero.

'I am, sir.'

'Good. So am I. Let me explain. It was Seneca who first realised this cult posed a serious threat. Phony Jewish messiah cults are two-a-denarius all the way from Syria to Egypt, and usually their followers lose interest when a better one comes along, but what Seneca spotted was the organising genius behind this one and that's what makes it different.'

'He's right,' said Josephus. 'The people behind it are evil and manipulative, but highly intelligent.'

Nero snorted with amusement. 'I wouldn't start feeling too smug; you obviously haven't heard what Seneca says about the Jews.'

Josephus did his best to hide his wounded pride. 'And what's that, sir?'

'Well I don't know what you've done to upset him but if I remember correctly, his precise words were *"sceleratissima gens"* – a most wicked people.'

'I hardly think a sweeping generalisation like that is fair, sir –'

'Life isn't fair,' said Nero, scowling at him. 'Get used to it. Seneca's a great one for spotting other people's shortcomings and ignoring his own. He rightly mocks Jews for not eating pork when he himself subsists on a diet of radishes.'

'That does seem a little inconsistent, doesn't it?' said Josephus, choosing his words more carefully this time.

'Inconsistent or not, he talks a lot of sense and what's more he lumps you Jews and the followers of this wretched cult in together – to him you're as bad as each other.' Josephus thought about interrupting but the expression on the emperor's face made him think better of it. 'As for the cult itself, he says it's the perfect combination: apparent fulfilment of earlier prophecy plus a personality cult based around a real individual who demonstrably existed and onto whom a whole slew of supposedly miraculous conjuring tricks has been grafted.'

'A perfect description,' said Josephus.

'Quite. And where they've been clever is in controlling the message so tightly. Normally with these things the rumour mill runs out of control and within five minutes all the idiots who've persuaded themselves that the messiah has finally come are at each other's throats over whose version of the truth is best.'

'If they can make it work, it's the ultimate political triumph, isn't it sir?'

Nero half smiled. 'What do you mean?'

'Turning superstition into perception: and from there you're only one step away from reality.'

'Very astute, Josephus, but where does your personal animus against these people stem from?'

'My father, sir. They had him killed.'

'Saw through them did he? What was his name.'

'Yeshua Bar Yosef, sir. It wasn't that he saw through them. In fact he started the movement that's been twisted into this dreadful cult –' Josephus paused; a mixture of sadness and hatred washed over him as he recalled the words of his adoptive father when he'd finally broken the truth to him all those years ago.

'Go on. I'm intrigued.'

110

'He was an aristocrat,' said Josephus. 'A member of the priestly caste and by all accounts a decent, pious and just man. I suppose because he'd never wanted for anything he was able to preach against the love of money – for him it truly was the *radix malorum* – and to encourage the creation of a society based on those things which unite us, rather than carrying on slaughtering one another in the name of a merciful God.'

Nero wrinkled his nose. 'I don't see anything to object to in that. What happened to him?'

'That's the whole point, sir. As an intelligent, charismatic man he attracted a different calibre of person than the usual rabble and that was his undoing. It all started with a small number of ambitious, unscrupulous men – there were eleven of them at the start – led by a man called Simon Kefas, better known as Peter: they even got my father's brother involved. They realised that by turning my father's message, and the movement which was developing around it, into something it wasn't they could ride his coat-tails to fame, power and the wealth that comes from leading the credulous.'

'Seneca says credulity will be man's undoing.'

'I think he's right. These men were all wealthy, the sort who can play at being hair-shirt ascetics when it suits them and then return to their villas when they get bored. As you can imagine, the appearance of rejecting worldly wealth harnessed to my father's charisma and piety made for a powerful force and the mob lapped it up. They took his basic message that it's the vain striving after wealth that causes discord and turned it into something that looked to his less-educated followers like an attack on the rich and hence on the status quo ante.'

'Hmm,' said Nero, stroking his unshaven chin. 'I can't imagine that went down very well with the procurator at the time – remind me who that was.'

'Pilate. At first, there were no problems because there was never any violence, in fact my father always preached against it. He saw there was plenty to gain by co-operating with Rome and far more to lose by living down to your stereotypes of us.'

Nero fixed him with a penetrating stare. 'And is that the view you hold, Josephus?'

'It is, sir, as I hope the Lady Poppaea has told you.'

'She has indeed. She also told me you seem to think rather too highly of yourself. That, on the other hand is not a quality I admire in those who are offered the privilege of working for me: you'll do well to remember that.'

Josephus lowered his head as if in submission. 'I'll bear that in mind, sir, but I can assure you that on this occasion perception is not reality.'

At this, Nero's features darkened and he stared at him in a way that caused Josephus to wish he'd kept quiet. 'That's a very diplomatic way of suggesting that the emperor and his wife are talking out of their collective hindquarters.'

'It's not for me to tell you how to interpret what I say, sir.'

The anger seemed to melt as quickly as it had arisen. 'You're good, Josephus, I'll grant you that,' said Nero with a chuckle that Josephus didn't like the sound of. Caution: at all times caution – no more clever answers; don't give the cobra an excuse to strike. 'So back to your father. What happened then?'

'Well, gradually they reduced him to nothing more than a figurehead and then falsely attributed all manner of words and deeds to him until eventually, the Sanhedrin took against him, which of course was the idea all along. The prophecy had to be fulfilled.'

'What prophecy?'

'That the messiah, Jesus the *Chrestos*, would rise from the dead.'

'Only gods can do that,' said Nero.

'But that was it, you see. Their idea was to present him as the God of Israel's incarnation on earth. Other messiahs have claimed to be that but for obvious reasons, none of them have ever pulled off the rising from the dead stunt.'

'And to rise from the dead, someone had to kill him: his twelve good friends and true presumably?'

'No, sir. It was more subtle than that. With the right bribes in the right places and their heavies controlling access to the streets leading to the procurator's palace, they engineered it such that a mob, ably encouraged by the Sanhedrin, persuaded Pilate to have him crucified.'

'And presumably his chums cut him down overnight and claimed their Jesus had risen from the dead with nothing worse than a few puncture wounds and smashed ankle bones for his pains?' said Nero, shaking his head. 'Cynical, cruel and very effective.'

To Josephus, the words sounded uncomfortably like approval. 'No, sir. They let him die, took him to the family tomb and after three days opened it up, dumped his body on a midden and claimed he'd risen from the dead.'

Nero slapped his thighs – he seemed to be enjoying the story far too much for Josephus' taste. 'Fascinating. So how did they get away with it without him being there as proof?'

'Easily. By then, people were so used to this group acting as my father's spokesmen that his followers swallowed the story of the risen Jesus hook, line and sinker. And as soon as the awkward questions started, they made up a few more miracle stories about him to distract the mob's attention and finished it off with him last seen floating up to heaven on a column of golden light to sit at God's right hand.'

'It's staggering what people will believe, isn't it?' said Nero, half in admiration. 'But what about his family, why didn't they intervene? Why didn't they expose these men for what they were?'

Josephus took a deep breath. He'd told the story very few times and on each occasion, the pain grew more acute.

'It happened in the first year of Gaius Caesar's imperium, just before I was born. My poor mother was pregnant but that didn't stop them coming after her. Luckily, being a well-connected family – my mother has royal blood through her descent from the Hasmonean line –'

'Can't say I've heard of them,' said Nero, picking at his fingernails.

Josephus flinched at the insult but continued, 'Matthias, one of my father's cousins, took her in and protected her: six months later I was born but she died in childbirth. It's unusual in our culture, but he adopted me which is why I bear his name. Everything I know about my father's life and his murder come from Matthias. I owe him my life.'

Nero frowned. 'Are you telling me the rest of this aristocratic family of yours just sat on their hands and let it happen? I can't see a noble Roman family being so cowardly.'

'From what Matthias told me, it wasn't anything to do with cowardice – they simply never had a chance. My father's brother, James, could have helped but they'd already thought of that – they lured him out of Jerusalem on a fool's errand to Alexandria. From my father being under no threat to going on trial for his life all happened in the space of two days and none of the family knew what was happening until it was too late. Afterwards, James and some of the others tried to stem all the nonsense about him rising from the dead, being Jesus the *Chrestos*, God's incarnation and so on, but by then, there was such a tide of mob hysteria that they nearly got lynched just for trying to speak the truth.'

'So after your good work in Achaea, you've got eleven left to track down.'

'Not exactly, sir. One of them, Judas, was so appalled at what they'd done and all the lies that he threatened to make the whole affair public.'

'And what happened to him?'

A look of disgust spread across Josephus' face. 'The others drugged him and then hanged him to make it look like suicide. They even left a note and concocted a story about how he'd accepted thirty pieces of silver to betray my father.'

'An interesting way of disposing of someone,' said Nero. 'I'll bear that in mind for future use. And has fate been kind enough to remove any of the others?'

'Yes, Yaakov Bar-Zebdi was put to death on the orders of the first Herod Agrippa. My father's brother, James, the one I told you about, well he was never part of the plot and he'd been helping me until earlier this year.'

'What happened to him?' asked Nero.

'It's as I told the Lady Poppaea yesterday; after Festus died and before Albinus arrived in Judea, the Sanhedrin had him convicted on trumped-up charges and stoned

'So then there were eight. With my help you should have them all in no time flat.'

'It's a bit more complicated than that, sir,' said Josephus. 'Of the original twelve, four are now dead, but another man joined the inner circle, a Cilician called Paul – '

'Damn. I wish you'd got here a week ago,' said Nero, slapping himself on the knee. 'If it's the same one I'm thinking of, I've just let him and another cult preacher out of the *Lautumiae* prison. How ironic, that's where your three friends are right now: if I'd known Paul and Peter were leaders of this wretched movement I'd have had them crucified.'

Josephus' eyes lit up. 'Do you think they're still in Rome?'

'No idea,' said Nero. 'That's going to be up to you to find out. It can be your first task and you'll be doing it somewhere where I can keep a close eye on you. What could be better?'

'If I might finish, sir –'

'Of course, please go on,' said Nero, with mock humility.

'In addition to my father's brother there's another of the twelve who turned against them and helps me when he can – Ioannis, known as John, he's the brother of the one who was killed by Herod Agrippa – but they're on his trail. They've come close to catching him on several occasions. They hope once he's silenced, there'll be no one left to tell the truth about what happened. He's holed up on Patmos at the moment, living like a dog in a leaking hovel. By now they probably know about what happened to Andreas in Achaea, but whether they've connected the death to me is anyone's guess. If I'm to win this, the longer they don't know who I am and what I want the better.'

'It's the winners who write the history, Josephus. That's another thing Seneca never stops telling me.'

'And that's precisely what I aim to do. With the remaining eight out of the way I can put the record straight and clear my father's name from the taint of this wretched cult.'

Nero looked at him gravely. 'Seneca thinks we may already be too late. He says it's too big to stop'

'With all due deference, sir, I beg to differ. With the leaders out of the way, the rest of the illiterate rabble will fall to fighting one another and it'll die out in months. It's like you said, control of the message and consistency in delivering it are everything: nothing else counts.'

Nero stood up and stretched. For a moment, he didn't speak and started pacing around the small chamber, occasionally stopping to help himself to a date from the Samian-ware bowl on the table and then spitting the pits onto the marble floor. 'So what do you need to get the job done?'

Josephus' answers were well rehearsed: it was the question he'd been willing the emperor to ask.

'Information, access to the imperial signal stations chain and people to help me – people I can trust. I'll also need letters of authority from either your highness directly or from the senate, authorising me to requisition vessels, horses or accommodation, to draw cash from the imperial treasury and so on.'

Nero raised an imperial eyebrow. 'Don't want much, do you? You left out the war elephants, siege towers and the regiments of cavalry.' Josephus could see the emperor's attention span was close to its limits. 'I'll tell you what. I'll sign the letters and you can have your three priests as your private army. That should do for now.'

'You are most gracious, sir,' said Josephus. 'And if I might be so bold as to ask –'

Nero gave a half-snort, half-laugh. 'I suppose you want to know what Rome will do in return for ridding it of these vermin?'

'Something along those lines, yes, sir.'

'I'll make sure that Lucceius Albinus has his nose forcibly removed from the trough, as you so indelicately put it.' Josephus jaw dropped at hearing the words of his ship-board conversation with Proculus repeated back to him. Nero smiled at his discomfiture. 'Oh, don't you worry, everything you say gets back to me one way or another. Let's say that if you keep your side of the bargain, your personal star will rise greatly in Rome's eyes and your people won't be the losers from it either – even if they are a quarrelsome, anti-social bunch of camel-jockeys.'

'Thank you, sir,' said Josephus, with a sigh of relief.

'My pleasure,' said Nero. Josephus watched him carefully for outward signs of sarcasm but there didn't seem to be any.

'Now let's go and take a look at those priests of yours. Then you can listen to some of my poetry.'

Chapter Fourteen

At nine o'clock the following morning, Flora returned to the TPC headquarters. She was greeted by one of Colonel Andretti's men who took her to the same room on the second floor. Already present were the American, Hayek and the British diplomat, Giles Smith. At her arrival he sprung to his feet and greeted her warmly.

'Delighted to see you again, Miss Kemble,' he said.

'You didn't expect me to do a bunk did you, Mr Smith?'

'I must confess the possibility had crossed my mind,' he replied. 'But, I'm very glad you didn't. You'll also be pleased to know that we've got the written undertakings you asked for,' he said, pushing a buff envelope across the table to her. 'One signed by HMG, the other by the US Department of State. Take your time over them and if you've got any questions don't be afraid to shout. Mr Hayek and I are here to help.'

'Thanks.' Flora took the documents to a side table and studied them carefully, making sure she understood the implication of every last sentence. At last, satisfied that her interests were being looked after, she pushed her reading glasses up on top of her head and returned to join the four men.

'There you are, gentlemen,' she said, passing over the copies which she'd signed. 'I still think I must be out of my tiny mind, but I guess I'll have to trust you.'

Smith lowered his gaze. 'It was very nice meeting you again, Miss Kemble, but now I have to return to the Embassy.' The smile did not quite reach his eyes but Flora tried to return the gesture despite her misgivings about his sincerity. 'You'll fly to Washington DC, but don't worry,' he added. 'We'll be in touch before you go and , you won't need to come looking for us, we'll find you. And now I'll leave you in the capable hands of my counterparts.' He stood, shook her firmly by the hand and took his leave.

The rest of her morning was spent in a vacant office learning her new identity, immersing herself in the history of this stranger who'd gatecrashed her little world and whose life mirrored hers in so many ways. Lavinia Crump was two months and a few days older, she'd attended the same schools as Flora, had uncannily similar exam results, a string of boyfriends and lovers who differed only by name and it was only when it came to their postgraduate studies that the stories diverged, and she read on, amazed at the detail and care with which Lavinia Crump's life had been assembled, even down to a dog-eared identity photograph of her younger self showing her membership of the Bologna University choral society.

After lunch Hayek returned to test her on the details of her alias. 'Let's have a run-through on Miss Crump.'

'Fine with me,' said Flora. 'But I do have one more question. What happens if someone who isn't on the side of the angels tries to check me out? Goes digging around at Lavinia's old school, or at Oxford's alumni department, say?'

'It's incredibly unlikely but you just have to face the fact that no cover story can ever be completely watertight. That said, I'm willing to bet that this one will keep you dry long enough for us to catch the bad guys.'

The bad guys, who until now had seemed an amorphous entity like some obscure sub-atomic particle that she knew existed but never impinged on her life, now became solid: real people, real criminals with the power to harm and probably years of practice at doing so. For a moment Flora's resolve wavered and she was on the point of telling Hayek she'd changed her mind, but then she thought of Francesco Moretti and his team of archaeologists who'd had the find of a lifetime snatched from under their noses, not to mention all the other academics who, unknowingly, now depended on her – well, on the FBI really if she was honest – to get it back.

Her reverie was interrupted by Hayek who began firing questions at her. Lavinia's parents: both dead; father to cancer, mother to drink. Brothers and sisters: older brother, now living in New Zealand – a handy combination of distance and time zones could be trusted to keep that one safe. University – Magdalen College Oxford; that was easy enough to remember because it was where Flora herself had done her first degree. Their parallel paths then led to Bologna, but whereas Flora returned to England after a year's study, her ghostly twin had stayed and was now on the academic staff. The questions grew harder but however he tried, Hayek was unable to catch her out until he got onto her relationship with Benjamin Grossman, as agent Cohen would be known. For a reason she couldn't understand her mind began to wander and all manner of unpleasant memories crowded in. She began to make mistakes.

'What's up, Flora, you were doing so well?' It was the first time he'd used her first name and she realised he was doing his best to put her at ease.

118

'Sorry, Mr Hayek –'

'Mike, please.'

'Sorry, Mike. It's not that I don't know this stuff it just, well...' she hesitated, trying to find the words that would convince him. 'And I know you're going to think this is silly and fluffy of me, but talking about Grossman and the trips I'm supposed to have made with him makes it all seem so very real all of a sudden, and to be honest, I'm frightened.'

He smiled at her and she saw a little of the compassion that was so well hidden behind Hayek's tough exterior. 'Do you know what would worry me the most?'

'No.'

'If you weren't frightened. Anyone who wasn't scared at the prospect of what you're facing would be dangerously overconfident or hadn't understood what they'd gotten themselves into. You're good, you'll be fine.' He watched her reaction as the words sunk in – then he continued. 'Let's go again, when did you last visit Israel?'

'May this year – fifth to the eighth.'

'Correct but the wrong answer.'

Flora pulled a puzzled frown. 'I'm not with you.'

People don't remember travel dates for more than a week or so after the event. No, the right answer to that one is something like, "I think it was early May, I'll have to check". Now do you see?' She nodded enthusiastically and her competitive streak took over, making her determined not to let him catch her out again. 'OK, so why did you go to Israel?'

'To see Mr Grossman and to discuss our forthcoming trip to Switzerland.'

'And where did you stay?'

'The Crown Plaza in Haifa. I've stayed there before – Mr Grossman lives in the Ahuza district which is just round the corner.'

'What was your room number at the hotel?'

Flora was about to show off her perfect recall of the script when she checked herself. 'I can't remember. What I do remember is that it was near the lift shaft and the noise kept me awake. I think I'll stay somewhere different next time – maybe try the Shulamit.'

'Excellent. And what did you and Mr Grossman discuss?'

'A purchase he was planning to make in Geneva for his collection.'

'What was he buying?'

'I'm afraid I'll have to refer you to the post-sale report from the auctioneers – I never discuss my clients' personal affairs.'

Hayek nodded again. 'Good,' he said with a smile. 'You're a natural at this – and please don't take this the wrong way – nobody but an Englishwoman from a certain background can load such a simple sentence with so much goddam, ice-cold "mind your own goddam business and kindly go screw yourself while you're about it". It's a great gift.'

'Thanks. You do realise it's mostly an act to draw attention away from the fact that my knees are knocking together?' she said, feeling secretly pleased at the way Lavinia's character was taking shape.

'Are you professionally trained in acting?' he asked. 'That would explain a lot.'

If only you knew, she thought, but instead replied, 'I was in the school play.'

'I hope they gave you the lead,' said Hayek.

'Third shepherd to the right of the manger.'

'Oh well,' he laughed. 'Guess all great acting careers have to start somewhere. Now, let's go back to your friend Grossman and from now on, no more blanking me for asking impertinent questions: tell me how you got involved with him.'

The quick-fire questions continued for another thirty minutes and Flora was word-perfect, recounting in detail how Lavinia and two colleagues from Bologna had been working in Israel on early Hebrew papyrus scrolls when their discoveries made the national press. On reading the article, Grossman, one of the richest men in Israel and one whom many considered a crook, used his extensive network of contacts to track them down and then insisted that they examine a series of ancient documents that he considered to be even more important than the Dead Sea scrolls. Of course they jumped at the opportunity, but to his chagrin, the redoubtable Miss Crump took very little time to reveal them as fakes – incredibly well executed, but fakes none the less – and in the process, making it very clear to a crestfallen Grossman that he should always take expert advice before spending his money.

At first he had stormed and raged, told the team – and Lavinia in particular – that they didn't know what they were talking about, rammed the documents' certificate of authority under their noses – another fake she detected instantly – but however much he blustered, she refused to be intimidated. Grossman wasn't used to people who stood up to him, let alone women – to him an inferior species – and was fascinated by this ferociously bright young Englishwoman to such an extent that he asked her to come and work for him, offering her several multiples of her academic's lowly salary. He expected her to jump at the offer, but instead, she calmly informed him that she had no intention of giving up her post at the University of Bologna, but when and if she could fit him in, then there might be time to do a little consultancy work.

As the relationship developed, she helped him avoid buying any more fakes and more importantly, guided him towards priceless artefacts being offered at a fraction of their true value by sellers unaware of what they had. For all her academic rigour, oddly enough she never once showed the slightest concern regarding the provenance of these treasures, even the ones that had obviously been stolen from other collections or from dig sites before they had even been recorded. Grossman was delighted by her discretion and the number of consulting opportunities multiplied.

'I'm not sure I like Lavinia very much,' said Flora.

'Nor do I,' said Hayek. 'She isn't meant to be liked. Think you can carry her off?'

'I'll give it my best shot. Being such a full-time bitch isn't going to be easy.'

'The less likeable she is, the more realistic she'll seem. And the colder you play her, the easier you'll find it to keep people at arm's length. That way they're less likely to want to know about your background and that'll keep you safe.'

Flora nodded. 'Good point,' she said.

'And tomorrow, you get to meet Grossman.'

'I do?'

'Special Agent Cohen will be catching this evening's United flight from Dulles which gets in tomorrow morning. Lavinia will be at the airport to meet him. He'll give you a full briefing on the people we're targeting.'

***

In southern Italy two men sat in the corner of a bar smoking and sipping coffee while they waited. Later than expected, the call came from Rome and the younger, taller of the two answered his mobile, replying in a series of monosyllables. Finally he said, 'No, don't try anything. Stay close and see what she does. Send the others home.

Chapter Fifteen

Rome AD 62.

Nero led Josephus towards the imperial palace's north-eastern wing. As they passed, everyone either sprang to attention or leapt out of the way to let them past. Josephus noticed how their eyes avoided the gaze of the emperor – anything rather than attract his attention – but were riveted instead on his own face. Who was this young foreigner? How had he gained Nero's favour and more importantly, which faction within the imperial household did he support?

Suddenly, Nero stopped and Josephus nearly cannoned into him. 'I've changed my mind,' the emperor said. 'There's something I want you to see first.' And with that, he turned to the right, up a staircase leading to a semi-circular balcony looking over the valley between the Palatine and the Oppian, the southern spur of the Esquiline Hill. Nero led him to the centre of the colonnaded sweep of white marble where he stopped and leant over the parapet, gazing at the red-tiled housetops below. 'What do you think?' he asked, sweeping his hand from horizon to horizon.

'Nice view,' said Josephus, hoping he'd given the right answer.

'Too many houses though. That's the problem.'

'Er, I'm not sure I follow you, sir.'

'I want to extend the palace. You see the buildings on the hill there?' he said, pointing eastwards to the Caelian Hill. Josephus said yes and Nero continued. 'Well, I want to build out from here, across to the Caelian and on to the Oppian. All of it, one big palace in its own grounds: an artificial lake, vineyards, pastures – there'll have to be shepherds of course – a theatre set in a woodland glade and a statue of me playing the lyre. It's going to be my very own *rus in urbe* – just think what an improvement that'll be over all those horrid apartment blocks, and all of it designed to my own specification.'

Josephus noticed the look of bliss on the emperor's face and chose his words with care. 'I don't think the people who're living there now will be too impressed when they find out.'

Nero made a dismissive gesture as though swatting away an insect. 'Oh, I'm sure they'll get over it – anyway, it's too late, I've already started building at the Esquiline end and my people have acquired lots of properties in between. As for the plebs, I'll have the senate fund building of new houses for them somewhere, I'm sure we can fit them in: we usually do.' He rubbed his stubbly chin, deep in thought and then brought his hand down on the marble balustrade with a slap. 'That's it. Why didn't I think of it before? Once I tell them they're getting new houses then, all I have to do for a couple of years is to double the *Annona* –'

'The what?'

'The *Annona* – you know, the grain dole?'

'Er, yes, of course,' said Josephus who until then had no idea that the citizens of Rome were regularly bought off by such handouts.

'Then, listen, listen, it gets better.' Nero's excitement was almost manic. 'Once the palace is finished, we'll have the games, gladiatorial combats and I'll race my own chariot. And what's more, you can be sure I'll win – I take it you've heard that I'm the finest and boldest charioteer that's ever lived?'

Josephus was learning fast – the man was completely unhinged and the only thing to do was to go along with him. 'I had and I'm overcome with admiration. Little wonder the citizens hold you in such awe.'

Nero took his eyes off the cityscape below and as he did so his mood seemed to alter, turning to look at Josephus with cold, dead eyes. 'Awe is understandable, but it's not what I seek: let me explain. Fear and respect are close cousins. First, I made people fear me, then they came to respect me, but now I wish them also to love me. In fact I insist on it. Come to my next concert and you'll see what I mean.'

'It would be a great honour,' said Josephus, secretly dreading the thought. According to Alityros, anyone falling asleep or showing any symptoms of flagging enthusiasm during one of the emperor's interminable performances risked summary execution. Men had been known to feign death and women to pretend to go into labour just to escape from them.

'Now, let me think when my next performance is –'

'Sir, please forgive me for interrupting,' said Josephus, his voice quavering. 'But we were on our way to see my three countrymen.'

'Yes of course. I quite forgot. Each time I come up here I can see in my mind's eye the greatest palace the world has ever known and everything else – except my music of course – just seems so petty and irrelevant. But you're right, come, I'll take you to them myself – I could do with some fresh air and the populace could do with seeing their beloved emperor.'

As they continued downwards through the palace complex painted plaster and roughcast took over from the marbled walls of the higher floors and at last, on a subterranean level they came to a broad landing with a guard-post. About a dozen soldiers of the Praetorian Guard, a permanent detachment from their barracks on the *Campus Martius*, were sitting on simple wooden benches surrounding the walls of the room, the entire area suffused with the characteristic smell of the oil lamps – combined with the tang of sweat and second-hand garlic – whose dirty yellow light glinted dully on the men's oval shields.

At Nero's appearance, the *Evocatus* in charge of the detachment called the squad to attention. Each soldier was armed with a *gladius* at his waist and outside, in a rack against the wall were the soldiers' *pila*, the army's standard issue infantry javelins. The guard commander saluted and with a nod of his head, Nero beckoned him and his men to follow.

A flight of stone steps, barely wide enough to allow the passage of two men abreast, led down to a brick-lined tunnel about ten feet high and the same wide. It was lit by pitch-soaked torches and at the far end daylight filtered through the bars of an iron gate. A soldier unlocked it and the emperor and Josephus stood aside. The troops of the guard filed past and formed three ranks in the sunshine outside.

With six of the Praetorians in front of them and six behind, they marched through the courtyard and into the south side of the forum, past the Temple of Saturn and the Basilica Julia, then left towards the Capitoline.

No trumpet-blowing, shouting or announcement of the emperor's passage was required and the crowds melted before the marching feet of the guard, the eyes of the curious straining to get a look at the emperor, who waved cheerfully to the mob as they passed.

People craned their necks to try and identify the young man who walked beside Nero – nobody had troubled to tell Josephus to keep a respectful three paces behind.

Passing in front of the *rostra*, the raised platform used by orators and for official pronouncements, they climbed the steps at the north west corner of the forum, passing beside the low, two-storey *Carcer* prison and up towards the *Carceris Lautumiae*, the jail where the three priests, Josephus' friends, were being held.

The officer commanding the prison was missing and one of the jailors scuttled out through a back door to look for him. Nobody could find the right keys. Nero watched the pandemonium with detached amusement.

'Now you see why I like to pay surprise visits, Josephus,' he said. 'It doesn't give anyone time to paint over the cracks or hide things in cupboards. I'll have somebody's balls for this and I don't mean that metaphorically.'

Eventually the keys were found and a jailor led them into the dark heart of the prison. The stairs widened out into a broad ante-chamber with a vaulted ceiling, and Josephus was surprised to see natural light coming from high, barred windows set into the eastern wall: lack of space in the forum had obliged the builders of the *Lautumiae* to enlarge the galleries of the former quarries on the south-eastern slope of the Capitoline Hill in order to squeeze it in between the other buildings. They were climbing the inside of a man-made cliff-face.

As the next door opened, the stench and the noise hit them. On either side of the vaulted passageway, the floor of which was raised on wooden duckboards, were iron grilles against which pressed the faces of the prisoners, some in rags, others naked: all covered in sores and paddling ankle-deep in their own filth. They beat against the unyielding metal, pleading in every language of the empire. Josephus pulled his cloak around his nose against the stink and tried to hurry on, but Nero, seemingly oblivious, continued his measured pace, nodding and smiling in satisfaction at the plight of those who had offended against Rome and its laws.

He laid a fleshy hand on Josephus' shoulder. 'You'll be pleased to know we have a good number of *Chrestos* cult members in here,' he said. 'And I'm sure you'll be equally pleased to hear that they burn well too, and light up the night sky in a *most* amusing manner.' Josephus shuddered.

At last they came to a smaller chamber with only one other door and where the air was clearer. The lock clicked open and Nero signalled a halt. 'We're now in the more select part of the prison,' he said leading Josephus to a low, barred window with a view over the forum. 'Nothing but the best for our esteemed Jewish guests. Now, if you take a look down you'll see we're right above the main prison and that opening in the top leads to the cell where Vercingetorix was held before Gaius Julius had him executed – the roll-call of famous names who've spent their last hours in there is quite impressive and nearly as long as that of the not so famous in the cells you've just passed: never forget that.'

The young Judean was suddenly aware of a chill in the poorly-lit chamber as the emperor beckoned him back to the open doorway. To his surprise, the three priests were accommodated in a spacious suite of rooms, lit by natural daylight from windows in the eastern wall. They looked up as the guard pushed the door open: hidden in the shadows, neither Nero nor Josephus were visible to them. 'Go on, what are you waiting for?' asked the emperor, giving him a nudge in the back. 'Tell them they can go home. Hurry up before I change my mind.'

Josephus cleared his throat and took a step forward into the light. 'Philo, Giora, Jozar, it's me, Josephus. I've come to take you home.' At first they just stared at him in disbelief, then as one, leapt to their feet and ran to hug him, all shouting at once in Aramaic.

'Please say this isn't a joke,' said Giora, the youngest of the three. Despite his time in jail, his burly embrace left Josephus worrying for his ribs. Laughing and crying at the same time, he kissed Josephus on both cheeks, his wiry beard temporarily blocking his friend's view, but the laughter died in his mouth when he saw who was standing in the doorway. 'It's a trick, Josephus. Look who's behind you...it's him, the emperor. He's going to lock you up too.'

'Don't worry,' said Josephus. 'And be careful, he may understand what we're saying for all I know. There's no trick. He's agreed to release you and I've come to take you home.'

Next to greet him was Jozar, also bearded but at fifty-five, the oldest of the group. Josephus was appalled at how much older he looked – he tottered into Josephus embrace on legs that seemed barely able to support him.

Last came the scholarly Philo. Clean-shaven in the Greek style, he approached warily as though unable to believe the good news. He and Josephus were life-long friends who shared a passion for knowledge and the history of their people. Clasped him tight to Josephus breast, emotion finally got the better of him and he burst into tears, babbling his relief and gratitude,

Retracing their steps with the three men still chattering excitedly to Josephus, the Praetorian Guard formed up around them to march back across the forum, the former prisoners shielding their eyes against the unaccustomed brightness and Nero waving to the crowd.

Once inside the palace Nero turned Josephus and the three priests over to one of his administrative clerks. 'Marcus Vedius here will look after your needs,' he said. 'This evening I am giving a recital of my Ode to Venus and you are most cordially invited to attend: until then I bid you a good day.' With that, he turned on his heel and left.

Later that day, bathed, fed and wearing fresh clothes, the three former captives were still all talking at once and Josephus had to shout to make himself heard. 'Gentlemen, please, there are things I need to explain to you.' They fell silent and he continued. 'This may not be what you want to hear, but you're not free yet. Nero has released you for a reason and if you want to see your families again, you've got to keep your side of the bargain. Let me explain –'

'What bargain?' said Giora, leaping to his feet, towering over Josephus with his bearded chin thrust forward. 'We haven't agreed to anything. You heard what Nero said – there were no charges against us and our account of events was entirely satisfactory.'

'Sit down, Giora,' said Josephus. 'And hear me out. The deal involves the two men who were in prison with you until recently: the two *Chrestos* cult preachers, Paul the Cilician and Peter the Galilean.'

'What? Those idiots?' snapped Giora. 'In all my born days I've never heard of such a pair. If age begets wisdom, those two are going to have to live longer than Methuselah before they have the common-sense of a five-year-old.'

'Nero didn't realise who they were. When he released them he thought they were just a couple of ranters.'

'A pair of charlatans,' said Giora. 'One of our jailors was a follower and kept trying to convert us – I've never heard such a lot of half-baked nonsense in all my born days.'

'Nero's been listening to Seneca and Seneca thinks they're dangerous. What do you think?'

'I think they're soft in the head, the pair of them.' Giora turned to the other two. 'Well, what do you reckon? Harmless madmen or dangerous?'

Jozar, the eldest of the three, thought for a moment. 'I believe Seneca may be right. It's easy enough for us to see through their nonsense but don't forget the mob aren't capable of rational thought. If the cult catches hold it could spread like wildfire, nonsense or not.'

'Nero wants us to find them,' said Josephus. 'He thinks they may still be in Rome.'

'And when we do?' asked Philo. 'What then?'

'He didn't say. I presume he'd prefer them delivered alive, knowing his taste for sadism, but on the other hand I don't think he'd shed any tears over two corpses. Do you reckon you could find them though?'

'And then Nero lets us go home?'

'That's what he said anyway,' Josephus replied.

'And I suppose the fact they were involved in your father's killing has no bearing on the fact?' asked Philo, looking at him suspiciously.

'What are you suggesting?'

'Nothing, just making a logical deduction. With Seneca dripping poison in one ear about the Christians, it would certainly make Nero a more receptive audience to anything you had to say in the other. Am I right?'

'No, you're wrong. Until now I've been working pretty much on my own with the help of one or two local Roman contacts who have similar views on these people to mine. Word of what I was doing got back to Nero but this is the first time he's actually offered to help.'

'And we're the price for that help.'

'Wrong again, Philo. He was the one who suggested it, not me. And if you must know, I stuck my stupid neck out and said I'd only do it if he let you three go. If you like, I can go back and tell him I've changed my mind.' He got to his feet and walked over to the window. With his back turned to the three men he stared out over the city, his adoptive father's words ringing in his ears: *"Never expect gratitude, Josephus, and you'll never be disappointed."*

Philo remained seated with his head in his hands. 'I'm sorry, Josephus. I misjudged you.'

'I understand,' Josephus said. 'In your place, I'd probably feel the same. Now, all of you, it's your decision and I won't pretend there aren't risks involved.'

The three whispered together while Josephus retreated out of earshot to the far corner of the room. 'Tell him we'll do it,' said Jozar.

'Good. So where do we start? I need to show Nero we've got a plan.'

'If we're to find them, I think Jozar has the best chance of any of us,' said Giora.

'Oh thanks,' said the older man. 'Why me? I've got a wife and family don't forget.'

'I'll tell you why,' he replied, clapping Jozar on his bony shoulder. You're the only one who knows what they look like.'

'Well, that's a start at least,' said Josephus.

'Hardly,' replied Jozar. 'It was only a few weeks ago. I saw two other men in chains being taken past the door to our cell. I asked our jailor – the idiot who kept trying to convert us – who they were.'

'And he said they were Paul and Peter?'

'Exactly.'

Josephus thought for a moment. 'Would you recognise them if you

128

saw them again?'

'Definitely,' said Jozar.

'Did they see you?'

'Yes. I think they were as surprised to see me as I was to see them.'

'In that case, we'll need to make sure they don't get a decent look at you,' said Josephus. 'But we'll be four against two and once we find them Nero can do the rest.'

'I still don't like the sound of it,' Jozar said.

'You'll be fine. I've got a plan. Bring your chairs and gather round, we're probably only going to get one chance at this so we need to get it right. Now, tell me, assuming both of them are still in Rome, where are they likely to be?'

Jozar shrugged. 'With the rest of the cult, I suppose.'

'And where's that?'

'Could be anywhere. Most of them are of the members are of the more biddable, less intelligent classes – freedmen, slaves, beggars and the like – and what passes for their leadership is, I'm ashamed to say, made up of Jews who've gone over to them.'

'Any names?' asked Josephus.

'Afraid not' said Jozar.

'So where do we start looking?'

Jozar gave a shrug. 'The poorer areas I suppose. Maybe start at the rough end of the Aventine. Then you could try asking around the *Porta Capena* or near the *Porta Octavia*.'

'And those gates, where are they?'

'The *Porta Capena*'s where the Appian Way comes into the city, near the Caelian Hill – about five minutes walk, certainly no more. And the *Porta Octavia* is west of here, near the Tiber.'

'Good,' said Josephus. 'We'll start there. From what Alityros has told me, if we go poking our noses into the tenements of the Aventine, it'll be us who end up with our throats cut, not them.'

'Thanks for the warning,' said Jozar. 'Really fills me with confidence, that does.'

Josephus ignored him. 'Good, that's settled then. Tomorrow morning, we'll split into two pairs: Giora and I will take the Octavia; Jozar, you and Philo take the Capena. We're all new in town and we're looking for Paul the Cilician because we've heard such wonderful things about his preaching. It's not subtle but it's the best I can think of for now unless anyone's got a better idea.'

'Sounds all right to me,' said Giora while the other two shook their

129

heads. 'But what I could do with now is another pitcher of wine.'

'Take my advice and don't,' said Josephus. 'If you drink too much and fall asleep during Nero's performance this evening he'll have you killed on the spot. He does it to Roman citizens so he wouldn't think twice about doing it to any of us.'

'From what I've heard, after an hour of his wailing, death would be a merciful release,' said Giora.

Chapter Sixteen

'Nervous?' Hayek asked Flora as they waited in the arrivals area of terminal five at Rome's Fiumicino Airport. It was her first outing as Lavinia Crump and although there was no risk involved, she still felt a frisson of excitement.

'A little I suppose. Is it that obvious?'

'It is to me,' he replied.

'And I thought I was doing a good job of hiding it,' she said with a look of disappointment on her face.

'You are, but you're acting just a little over-excited and that's what gives you away.' Seeing her expression he continued. 'But if I didn't know you and hadn't been working with you, then I'd never know.'

'That's a relief,' she said, allowing herself a brief smile. Lavinia Crump was hard, cynical and calculating she kept telling herself, so no outward displays of emotion. Try to remember your training

The status for the United Airlines flight changed to "Arrivato" on the screen above them. 'OK, I'm going outside for a smoke and then you'll find me over there.' He pointed towards an area round the exit from customs where a group of drivers were clustered, each holding a sign with the name of the people they were waiting for. 'Just remember the brief and you'll be fine.'

'But what if I don't recognise him?' asked Flora.

He put his hand on her shoulder. It was the first time he'd touched her but it felt reassuring rather than over-familiar. 'You've picked him out of every picture we've shown you and don't worry, he knows what Lavinia looks like too. You're both pros, so just relax.' As he walked away, Flora allowed herself a little flush of pride. She knew he was only saying it to boost her confidence, but being called a pro by someone like Hayek felt good – it was just like old times with The Firm. For now the grown-up game of charades was still fun and the bad memories were banished from her mind.

As the first passengers started to file through, Flora scrutinised each male face in detail, looking for Cohen in the crowd. The first man she identified as a possible candidate glared back at her with a look that said "who are you staring at?" Relax, she told herself, or you'll look like a stalker: you're Lavinia meeting her client – just relax.

When he did arrive, there was no doubt: mid-thirties, well-cut blue wool suit, tall, athletic build and close-cropped dark hair that didn't really suit him she thought. He spotted her too, gave an almost imperceptible nod and approached, his well-defined features lighting up into a broad grin. 'Lavinia,' he shouted, hurrying towards her with one arm outstretched, the other towing his carry-on bag.

Flora's stage fright vanished and her old training kicked in as she assumed the mantle of the frosty Miss Crump. She gave what she hoped was a suitably icy smile and replied, 'Good morning, Mr Grossman. I trust you had a pleasant flight.'

'Yeah, not too bad thanks,' he replied: New York overlaid with an Israeli accent. 'Hey, it's great to see you again, come here.' He tried to give her a kiss on each cheek but she kept him firmly at arm's length.

'Please, Mr Grossman, I've told you before, let's be businesslike,' she said, making sure other bystanders heard and holding out a hand to shake his. 'Now if you'll kindly follow me, your car is here.' She led him towards the scrum of drivers where they found Hayek, standing under a "no smoking sign" with a cigarette in his mouth, wearing a battered peaked cap and holding up a sign saying "Sig Grozemann". Flora permitted Lavinia her second smile of the morning.

As Hayek drove down the exit ramp. Cohen loosened his tie and sat back in the seat with a contented sigh. 'Damn, you've no idea how much I hate wearing those things,' he said to Flora. 'Sorry, didn't really introduce myself back there. Ben Cohen, FBI Art Crime Team.'

'And I'm Flora Kemble,' she said, returning his smile.

Cohen nodded approvingly. 'Mike said you were good – he wasn't kidding. Lavinia's a ball-breaker, isn't she? Please, no offence,' he added hastily.

Flora laughed. 'None taken, Mr Cohen.'

'Ben, please,' he said.

'Of course, Ben. Just give me time to get out of character.' She felt at ease in his company and her fears of being teamed up with an over-aggressive, TV stereotype bad cop disappeared as they chatted in the back of the car.

Hayek headed through the traffic towards the US Embassy – a collection of four-storey buildings painted in a shade of pink that reminded Flora of artificial food colouring on an over-sweet cake – before pulling up in front of the first set of sliding metal gates which protected the entrance to the compound. At the car's approach, the orange lights on top of the centre post began to flash and the gates slid noiselessly aside, allowing the car to approach the picket post, closing behind it as they advanced. Four CCTV cameras tracked their progress as the US Marine Security Guard corporal, invisible behind a pane of reinforced smoked glass, cleared them through the final series of protection. The second set of gates opened and two retractable metal barriers folded down flush with the roadway.

Once inside the compound Hayek led the way, swiping his identity card against the readers to open the doors as they went. Soon, Flora, was completely lost. Taking the elevator to the third floor, he showed them through a heavy sliding door into a small entrance hall. They stopped. Hayek picked up a tray and pointed to a sign on the wall. It read: "No recording devices, electronic apparatus, cameras, cell-phones, pagers or similar allowed beyond this point." Leaving their mobile phones in the tray, they continued into a lecture theatre, with tiered rows of tip-up seats and at the front, a low stage with a lectern bearing the seal of the United States. Flora noticed the room had no windows and that their voices sounded strangely muffled. Hayek spotted the puzzled expression on her face. 'Don't worry, it's the sound-proofing and anti-vibration dampers – they stop the structure of the building transmitting anything we say to the outside walls. Thirty years ago, both we and the Soviets could pick up speech from the vibrations of window glass, but the technology has moved on a bit from there, so best to be careful.'

He showed Flora to a seat in the front row. What have I got myself into? she wondered for about the thousandth time in the last few days. Hayek's voice called her back to reality 'Special Agent Cohen's going to give us an update,' he said, leaving him to plug his laptop into the audio-visual system which after the customary false starts and head-scratching, finally responded to a reboot and sprang into life, displaying the FBI Art Crime Team's logo on the screen.

'First of all,' said Cohen, 'I'd like to add my thanks, Flora, for agreeing to help us. The people we're up against are pros and we're only going to get one chance to make them think we're fellow collectors. They're going to be skittish as hell and if they see or hear anything that doesn't ring right, we'll never see them again. That's where you come in.' To Flora, his pale grey eyes seemed to exude an infectious confidence.

'I do?' she said, playing the innocent.

'Sure you do. You've obviously got grade-A pain in the ass Lavinia Crump nailed down and it's her presence that's going to convince these guys that I'm the real deal, because if they start quizzing me on the stuff I'm supposed to be collecting then maybe I'd be able to snow them for five minutes, certainly no more, so we're relying on you to make us look like the real deal and to stop Grossman making a schmuck of himself in public. Plus, from what Mike tells me and from what I've seen already, I can tell you're a natural.'

I only wish I felt as sure about that as you two do, thought Flora, looking up at him with what she hoped was an expression of steely determination.

Cohen continued. Next on the screen was a mug-shot of the SUV driver who'd been arrested in Alabama. 'We've got a name for this character but he's not co-operating. Luckily for us, he was carrying a credit card which led in a roundabout way to this guy here.' He flicked to the next screen which showed a intense looking man, aged forty three and called Giovanni Luzzo according to the information board in front of his chest. 'We have another name: a black guy who's called Raymond but who doesn't seem to match any known offender profile.'

'Any form on Luzzo?' asked Hayek.

'Sure. The usual lowlife CV. String of felonies long as your arm: handling stolen goods, robbery with violence, possession with intent to supply – we're pretty sure he's got links to the mob – and it's not the first time his name has come up in connection with stolen archaeological finds.'

'Anything involving works of art or first-century documents?'

Cohen checked down the printed sheet on the lectern in front of him. 'Arrested in possession of stolen goods – whole bunch of twenty-sixth dynasty Egyptian stuff that went missing from the Royal Ontario Museum a couple of years back – but released for lack of evidence. Said he'd found it under a hedge and was about to hand it in. As if.'

'What was he carrying?'

'Oh, funerary items from a pharaoh called...hell, how do you pronounce this guy? P-sam something –'

'Psamtik probably,' said Flora, happy to be back on home turf. 'There were two pharaohs of that name in the twenty sixth dynasty and according to Herodotus the first one did the first ever recorded experiments in linguistics,'

Cohen shot a worried glance at Hayek as if to say "what the hell have we got here?" Flora spotted the unspoken exchange, and, nervous that she'd said too much, sunk down in her seat and stared up at the screen, hoping she wasn't about to make a fool of herself and that her former training would see her through.

'So if the driver is taking the fifth how've you managed to link these guys to events in Pompeii?' asked Hayek.

Cohen moved on to the next photograph. 'Just coming to that,' he said, as a picture of a Ford SUV filled the screen. 'The vehicle was rented from Hertz using a cloned credit card which was found on the driver. We managed to trace it back to this guy here.' The screen now showed a much younger man with long unwashed hair and a straggly goatee beard. 'Now the good thing about him is that as soon as we threatened him with a grand jury he started singing his dear little heart out.'

'What are you holding him on?' asked Hayek.

'Plenty. He was their IT guy and a specialist in internet fraud as well as being a one-man credit card and driver's licence factory. He's already given us three other names but they've gone to ground. The good news is he's also given us an insight to what's going on with the haul from Pompeii.'

'Which is?'

'That it's all in the US of A as we speak,' said Cohen. 'Every last scrap of it.'

Hayek frowned. 'That's one big haystack to find a needle in. Any idea where?'

'Not yet, but what we do know is that there was a screw-up. The guys in Italy had specific instructions about what to steal but they exceeded their remit. Now here's where we got lucky. The Italian team were paid off but when it came to the US end of the chain, there was a bust-up with the client. Luzzo's people wanted paying for everything but the client only wanted to pay for the stuff he asked for and there was a row. That's all we know because the geek wasn't party to the full details.'

'Can you be sure of that?' asked Hayek, looking up from his notes.

'Pretty sure. He's had no dealings with the law before and now he's got the FBI all over him. We've also told him what'll happen to his pretty young ass if he goes to prison – he's in Arthur Kill Correctional Facility on Staten Island right now.'

'What's it like?'

'The usual,' said Cohen with a casual shrug. 'Medium security joint which in English means rough as hell. Right now we got ourselves one scared young white man – our biggest problem has been trying to get him to shut up.'

Hayek winced. 'You gonna leave him there?'

'Nah. They're moving him to someplace upstate within the

135

Incarcerated Witness Scheme until we need him to testify. He says Raymond and Luzzo have been trying to sell the stuff the client didn't want in order to cover their losses.'

'But we still don't know who the end client is?'

'We've got a name, sure to be an alias, and a hotmail address that was set up from behind a proxy server anyway, so we're none the wiser.'

'How'd you get the driver?' Hayek asked.

Cohen laughed and shook his head. 'The handover was supposed to go down in a church of all places but like I said, there was a screw-up. We got good footage of the driver from a security camera at a gas station where he used the same cloned credit card to pay on two days running. The same evening the county police got a call from a pastor reporting vandalism at his church – told them he's been keeping an eye on the place at nights to deter kids and Klan crazies from tagging the place. State Troopers pulled the SUV over for a random check, didn't like what the driver had to say and because of the call they held on to him.'

'And when they got to the church they found the page from the *Antiquities*?'

'Correct,' said Cohen. 'Along with a can that had been used to spray "KKK" on the church wall. We've got good prints and DNA from it too.'

Hayek frowned. 'I still don't see how this hooks up.'

'I'm not sure I do yet and if the collector from Chicago hadn't told us that someone was out there trying to sell document fragments, we'd never have connected Luzzo with the case.

Trouble is, the only hard evidence we've got is the cloned credit card: we can't hold him on that, and we still can't prove he was involved with what was found at the church, let alone the body –'

'Hold on a minute,' said Hayek. 'You never mentioned a body.'

'I was coming to that. The following morning a farmer in his pickup saw what he thought was a pile of clothes on the roadside, about a couple of miles from the church, stopped to take a look and it turned out to be a dead body.'

'Anyone we should be interested in?' asked Hayek.

'Not sure. Police surgeon puts the time of death at around midnight – about the same time the driver was arrested so he's in the clear. But here's where it gets weird; the deceased was a local college kid from William Sunday University who'd collected a nine millimetre round, probably from a Glock.'

'Not your typical profile, I'll admit. Any ideas?'

'None. Autopsy showed he'd been shot in the leg from behind. The round severed his femoral artery and he bled to death. Folks at the college are as puzzled as we are – straight-A student, devout, no known enemies, didn't drink, didn't smoke. Like you said, he doesn't fit the profile for a murder victim.'

'Couple of miles away you say? Could be a coincidence.'

Cohen shrugged. 'Could be but gut says something went wrong with the handover and the kid was involved. Local cops think maybe he walked into it by accident.'

Hayek's eyebrows rose into a sceptical arch. 'Walked into it by accident? At a rural church in the middle of the night? I know William Sunday's a Bible college, but hey, there are limits. Even God deserves a night off.'

'Trouble is, we're screwed,' said Cohen. 'We can't tie Luzzo or this Raymond guy to the shooting, nor to the handover. The vehicle was a rental so the interior's going to be contaminated with the DNA of every John Doe who's sat in it. There's powder residue too, but nothing that can be linked to the college kid's shooting. We can throw a credit card misdemeanour at the driver, but that's it and for now he's not saying anything.'

Hayek chewed the end of his pen as he mulled over what he'd just heard. 'So how do you propose to flush the buyer out if he's got everything he wants?'

'That's the good news. He hasn't – least we don't think so. According to the kid, Luzzo's boys are holding on to a bunch of the finds as a bargaining chip. I reckon negotiations are probably still going on.'

'Interesting,' said Hayek. 'So all we need to do is find Mr Luzzo and see who he's talking to these days.'

'Yeah, that's what we thought. The IT punk wasn't sure but he seems to think they kept at least one Josephus codex section and all the copper sheets.'

Flora looked up from her notes again. 'Ben, can I ask a question?'

'Sure, Flora, go right ahead.'

'Did this kid, the IT geek or whatever his name is, seem to have any idea of what the copper sheets were for?'

He shrugged. 'Dunno to be honest. We never asked him.'

'Well far be it from me to tell you how to do your job,' she replied. 'And please tell me to shut up if you've already thought of this, but I think the grids could be your best way of smoking the buyer out of hiding.'

Another rapid glance flashed between the two men before Cohen answered. 'You're going to have to help us here, Flora. We know they're in the form of Polybius squares – an early form of Vigenère cipher – and that you've proved they can be used to decipher some of *The Devil's Codex*, but that's all.'

'That's really all there is to know,' she replied. 'The big problem for whoever's buying, is that without the copper sheets, they can't decipher the texts. If they can't decipher them they can't validate them and the market's knee-deep in forgeries. Now some of the fragments from the dig have plain text on one side of the page and the exact equivalent, word-for-word, in encrypted format on the other. However, at least forty percent of what Moretti's people found is encrypted and there's no equivalent plain text. So no copper sheets, no way of telling whether the codices are the ones the buyer wants.'

'Ah, I see where you're coming from,' said Hayek.

'Now please stop me if I'm teaching granny to suck eggs,' said Flora. 'But from what little I know about the antiquities trade, I reckon that if Mr Grossman lets it be known that he's in the market for the grids to help translate parts of his own collection, I don't think the customer could take the risk of sitting tight and potentially losing his chance of reading them for ever.'

'That's assuming he knows of their existence and what they're for,' Cohen said.

'That's easily done,' said Hayek, snapping his notebook shut. 'We put out another press release about the theft, concentrating on the grids – how important they are, what they're for and so on. Then we get the word out on the street that Grossman and his wallet are in town. Our buyer – as Flora has pointed out – has to react.'

Cohen nodded. 'Sounds good to me,'

'Good. I'll call DC and tell the Director. Now, run us through the rest of what you've got.'

Chapter Seventeen

Rome AD 62.

Jozar looked back over his shoulder but Philo was nowhere to be seen. Trying to stem the rising tide of panic, he turned into a side-street he thought he recognised but realised at once it was another wrong turning. A shouted warning from above gave him just time to dodge to one side as the contents of a chamber pot splattered into the street from a third-floor window.

In the canyons between the timber-framed brick tenements of the Aventine the sun didn't reach street-level but it was nonetheless unbearably hot and a mixture of blood and sweat ran into Jozar's eyes as he stumbled down the hill, searching in desperation for a road that would take him out of these slums and back towards the Palatine – safety beckoned only a few hundred yards away but he couldn't see it, nor did he know in which direction it lay.

***

Their mission to the Capena Gate area had yielded results straight away. At a tavern just outside the city walls, they found a willing helper who gave not only a name, but directions to an address on the Aventine belonging to one of Paul's lieutenants where the Christians were said to meet. Their informant claimed to have attended one of the cult's meetings, but when Jozar and Philo tried to press him for more details he made off, claiming a previous engagement.

At first, the directions were easy to follow and they arrived at the temple of Minerva. It had seen better days but was in better condition than many of the buildings around it which seemed in imminent danger of toppling into the streets. As they moved higher, searching for the temple of Ceres, the apartment blocks hemmed them in ever more closely and the air became thicker with the smell of open sewers, rotting garbage and with the stink from the tanneries. 'I think we should turn right here,' said Jozar.

Philo looked around. 'Are you sure? I think we've come round in a circle, I'm positive I've seen this corner before. Let's ask.' He stopped a man who was carrying an amphora over one shoulder. 'Excuse me, we're looking for the temple of Ceres: are we in the right area?'

The man grunted something in return that Philo only half caught – the man's accent was so far from classical Latin that all he understood were a couple of lefts and a right, accompanied by a jerk of the man's head in the direction of a street leading up the hill. 'Did you catch any of that?' he asked Jozar.

'Two rights and then second left is all I got.'

'Damn. I got two lefts and first right. Come on, let's try up here and if we can't find it we'll ask again.'

It soon became apparent that they were heading away from the main thoroughfare. The crowds were thinner, the shops and food stalls on the ground floors of the tenements looked even more poverty-stricken, and as the two friends went on they realised they were starting to attract attention. This time Jozar tried his luck. 'Excuse me, sir, we're looking for the temple of Ceres.' Without a tooth in his head, the old man's reply was incomprehensible. 'I'm sorry, we're new in town and I didn't quite catch that,' he said.

'Who's new in town?' a voice demanded. They swung round and saw a strongly-built young man, hands on hips and glaring at them from his one remaining eye: what looked like a healed sword cut ran vertically from his forehead down to his disfigured jaw, his injuries twisting his words into sibilant menace.

'We are,' said Jozar. 'We're looking for the temple of Ceres.'

'There's one in the forum. And anyway, what are two Jewboys doing looking for a temple?' He stopped and screwed up his eye, staring at each of them in turn. 'You're up here looking for a bit of trade aren't you?'

'No we're not merchants –'

'Don't worry,' he said with a mocking laugh. 'You've come to the right place. Second on the left, knock on the green door and ask for Callista; tell her Marcus sent you and she'll find you a couple of nice young Egyptian girls – fresh in off the boat, and very well trained if you get my drift.' He tapped the side of his disfigured nose and leered at them.

'No actually,' said Philo. 'That's not what we're here for at all –'

'Oh, so it's boys you're after is it? After a spot of Greek, eh? Well, each to his own I s'pose.' He shrugged. 'Now, in that case you need to – '

'No really,' said Philo. 'We're trying to find the Temple of Ceres because it's near the house of Thaddeus the Syrian.'

The mask of affability disappeared in an instant and the young man took a step towards them, placing his hand on the hilt of the knife he wore at his belt. 'And what do you want with him?'

'Just to talk to him.'

'Balls,' he said and spat on the filthy cobbles. The knife glinted as he whipped it up under Jozar's chin, the point only inches from his windpipe. 'Tell me why you want to talk to Thaddeus.'

Jozar took a pace backwards, his eyes wide with terror as he blurted out, 'W-we were told he could put us in touch with Paul the Cilician.' Philo wanted to kick Jozar in the shins to shut him up but he was out of range. To make matters worse, from the doors leading to the filthy stairwells, other figures were moving towards them, attracted by the altercation.

'And what if you've been told wrong?' The single eye flicked from one to the other.

Despite Philo trying to shut him up, Jozar's mouth had come disconnected from his brain. 'Well then perhaps someone else could kindly tell us where to find him...' He took another pace backwards away from the knife and trod on someone's foot. A voice from behind cursed him and powerful hands shoved him in the back, almost pushing him onto the point of the blade.

'You still haven't told me what you want with this Paul: you see, for all I know he might be very picky about who he talks to – people round here are like that.'

'That's quite all right,' said Philo, grabbing Jozar by the arm and trying to steer him away. 'We'd heard so much about his preaching that we wanted to come and listen – no need to bother him, so if there's somebody who could tell us where and when the next meeting is, we'll be on our way.'

The crowd had grown and, emboldened by the numbers, the one-eyed man stood blocking their way, body-checking Philo as he tried to lead his friend to safety. 'Tell you where the meeting is? So you can send the *Cohortes Urbanae* along to it? You must think I was born yesterday.'

His remark drew hoots of derision from the mob pressing around them: the sound was anything but friendly and a call of, 'Cut their bloody throats for them,' was greeted by a general murmur of approval. Pushing the knife under Jozar's chin once more, he held up his hand for silence.

'Be quiet, all of you, and listen. I've a fair idea who these jokers are, or at least who sent them. Now if we kill them, it'll send the wrong message. If that lot over there,' he jerked his thumb in what Philo assumed was the direction of the Palatine, 'find these two clowns with their throats cut, all manner of shit will fall on us and we don't want that, do we? Anybody would think we knew where this Paul the Cilician was,' he jeered and the mob joined in the hilarity. Then he turned to Philo and Jozar once more. 'Right, you two, you can fuck off out of it and tell whoever sent you that we don't know where this Paul of yours is. Never heard of him. Got it?'

He shoved them away and the crowd parted, forming a narrow corridor of jeering humanity. They were almost clear of the square when Philo felt hands scrabbling at his belt, and looking down, saw a bandy-legged street urchin – the boy can have been no older than seven – trying to steal his purse. Instead of hurrying on he made the fatal mistake of cuffing the child away, sending it howling into the nearest stairwell. In an instant, shouts and yells followed them down the street and, too late, the friends started to run. Jozar looked back and saw a face he recognised: the man they'd spoken to earlier in the tavern near the *Porta Capena* was now leading the rush towards them.

The next thing Philo felt was a blow in the stomach. At first he thought he'd been punched and although winded, carried on for a few more steps before sinking to his knees, blood pouring from his mouth. The assailant's knife had found its mark. Jozar stopped to try and help but someone lunged at him with a blade. He parried it but his right hand and wrist were slashed to the bone. Another downward thrust tore a gash in his scalp and as the mob closed on his fallen companion, he fled in panic. All he could think of was to get off the hill; downwards lay safety, uphill was the mob. For a moment the sounds of pursuit appeared to have gone so he stopped, bent almost double, gasping for breath and with his uninjured hand against the rough brickwork of a shop front. Then he heard it again, like the baying of a pack of hunting dogs and getting ever louder.

Two years in the *Carceris Lautumiae* had taken their toll on Jozar's physique. Despite his leg muscles screaming at him to stop, he stumbled on, looking back at regular intervals in the forlorn hope of seeing Philo coming down the hill towards him. The voices sounded louder again, like a nightmare where the nameless terror gets ever closer but running becomes impossible. His tunic was soaked with blood and at his approach, people turned away – life was precarious enough in Rome's *Regio XIII* without sticking your neck out for strangers.

Jozar was now hopelessly lost but at least it felt like his steps were carrying him in the right direction. However, his instincts had played him false and somehow, instead of coming back down into the *Regio I*, the area around the *Porta Capena*, he had gone in the opposite direction and was now heading westwards towards the Tiber. Even though he could see the river below him glinting in the sun above the waterside roof-tops, no safety lay there because the more determined of his pursuers were still not far behind. Weakened by his injuries and with blood running into his eyes from the head wound, in desperation he turned into a narrow side-street in the hope of throwing them off his scent. As he did so, his feet skidded on a pile of rotting offal, pitching him hard to the ground, his head striking the rim of the gutter. The impact left him stunned and splattered with filth.

'Are you all right? Can you stand?' The voice seemed to float disembodied in the air as though coming from far away. A hand shook him by the shoulder and he opened one eye to see a woman kneeling beside him. 'Hey, you there,' she shouted at a couple of youths who'd stopped to look at the prostrate figure, their eyes fixed on the purse at his belt. 'Come and give me a hand, you useless pair of lumps. Don't leave the poor man lying there, help him up for goodness sake.'

With a sigh, they shambled over and under her direction manhandled Jozar through the gap in the butcher's shop counter and into a room at the back. Propping him up in a chair, the woman dismissed the two idlers, scolding them as they left. Next she fetched a bucket of water from the cistern in the courtyard and, using a floor-cloth, began to bathe his wounds. In the distance, Jozar heard the sound of raised voices as the last of his pursuers made their way past.

'I need to get back to the Palatine,' he said through gritted teeth. 'I have an urgent message for the emperor.' At this, the woman dropped the blood-soaked rag in horror.

'The emperor? Are you in some kind of trouble?' she asked. 'This is a respectable household and I'm not having any trouble here, d'you hear?'

'Please, it's just – '

'Right, you stay put. I don't know who you are or what you're up to but I'm going to fetch the *Vigiles*.' Stopping only to sling the bucket of water out into the street, the woman swept out, locking the connecting door to the shop behind her. Alone in the cool darkness, Jozar slid off the chair and crawled over to the low wooden cot that stood against the far wall. Pulling a tattered woollen blanket over himself, he curled up in the foetal position, trying to smother the pain in his head and wrist with sleep.

Dusk was falling by the time the woman returned. A patrol from the *Cohors XI Urbana* had turned out from their barracks near the port and in the darkened back-room they found Jozar delirious and rambling in Aramaic. It wasn't until they pulled him to his feet and walked him out of the shop into the fresh air that he regained the ability to talk to them in something approaching comprehensible Latin.

'Where do you live? Where are you staying?' asked the commander, shaking him to try and get a response.

'On the Palatine...'

'Yes, but where?'

'The palace.'

'Come on, don't mess me about, I haven't got all day.'

'We're guests of the emperor,' said Jozar.

The guard commander looked at his senior non-commissioned officer. 'He's clearly not Roman. What do you think, take him to the palace or leave him for the *Vigiles*?'

'If I were you, sir, I wouldn't risk it. If he's telling the truth and he dies before you get him back, you'll be in it up to your neck. If he's lying, the Praetorian boys will kick his arse out into the street so either way, we don't end up with the problem.'

Pushing his plumed metal helmet back on his head, the commander wiped his brow with the back of his arm. Although dusk was falling there wasn't a breath of wind to provide any relief from the day's stored heat radiating from the brickwork of the closely-packed buildings.

'All right,' he said. 'Let's get him down there.' With a curse, he gave the order and a semi-conscious Jozar was half carried, half dragged the few hundred yards to the palace.

Nero joined Josephus and Giora at Jozar's bedside. The doctor, a Greek, like most who followed his calling, was not the emperor's personal physician, but a surgeon specialising in treating wounded gladiators to get them fit for a return to the arena. He managed to stem the bleeding from Jozar's damaged hand and made him drink copious amounts of clean water. Next, he turned his attentions to the gaping head wound, dressing it with cobwebs to staunch the bleeding and honey to prevent infection. Slowly, and without rushing his patient, the doctor coaxed the story from Jozar.

'You mean you asked for Paul the Cilician by name?' asked Josephus, aghast.

Jozar nodded, wincing now, in spite of the drink of milk laced with opium that he'd been given to ease the pain. 'I don't know why. I'm sorry, Josephus, I'm so sorry, this is all my fault – poor, poor Philo. We should never have gone to the Aventine.'

'Shhh, don't blame yourself,' said Giora, patting him on the shoulder. 'I'm sure you did what you thought was best.'

'We were betrayed, Giora.' Jozar's words were barely audible. 'It was the barman from the tavern by the *Porta Capena*.'

Josephus shot Giora a worried look and Jozar continued, each word a painful effort. 'I can't remember the name of the place, but there's a carved stone boar above the door. We told him we'd heard there were Christian preachers in town and we were interested to hear what they had to say. He mentioned Paul by name and –' The opium was taking effect and they could see his pupils growing ever wider.

'Come on man, get a grip, we haven't got all evening,' snapped Nero. 'Give me names and addresses and I'll have the buildings pulled down and the inhabitants executed.'

'But that's the point,' replied Jozar. 'The barman told us to find the Temple of Ceres and ask for Thaddeus the Syrian. We were lost and got into an argument with some thug with only one eye. And when the mob set on us, there he was.'

'There who was?' asked Nero. 'The man with one eye?'

'No, not him, the barman. He must've run on ahead of us.' Jozar's speech was slurring, almost incoherent and despite the heat he was shivering. 'I'm cold, can someone please get me a blanket?'

'You're bloody useless, the lot of you,' stormed Nero. 'Jupiter only knows how many pig-ignorant low-life have managed to find this cult and listen to its leaders preach their mumbo-jumbo, yet four of Judea's finest minds can't even manage it in broad daylight without two of them getting lynched. Explain to me why I shouldn't put you in the arena? And as for –'

'Sir, could I have a word please?' The doctor interrupted Nero in mid-sentence.

The emperor raised a hand as if to strike him but then slowly lowered it. 'Yes. What is it?' he asked, his eyes burning with cold fury.

'Not here, sir.' He gestured with his head towards the door. 'It won't take a moment.' With a sigh, Nero followed him outside. Once out of earshot, the doctor continued. 'He's going to die, sir. There's nothing more I can do: it's probably just a matter of a day or so. Maybe less.'

Nero thought for a moment and glared at the diminutive Greek, his fists resting on his hips. 'So you're suggesting you take their place in the arena while I send for a sawbones who can tell an arse from an elbow in

145

a well-lit room?'

'With respect, sir –'

The emperor took a pace forward and lifted him up by the front of his tunic. 'If you value your life, man, don't you dare "with respect" me. Every time somebody says that it's an excuse for outright disrespect and I won't have it.'

'If you wouldn't mind putting me down, sir, I can explain.' replied the doctor, not in the slightest cowed by the tirade. Nero let him go and the doctor continued. 'Based on my medical knowledge and after years of experience in treating injuries like these, I can see that the head wound is infected and it's too far advanced for me to do anything about it: his blood is poisoned and he's going to die.'

'Poisoned? So you're saying the hag who found him on the Aventine poisoned him?'

'No, sir. You heard the guard commander's report. The woman said she found him lying in the gutter in a terrible state and tried to clean him up.'

'What's that got to do with it?' shouted Nero.

'Dirt from the weapon, polluted water used to clean him, filth from the gutter – any of those could've got infection into the wound. Whatever it was, it's the effects of the dirt that've poisoned him, not anything the woman did.'

'So he's going to die and you can't do anything about it?'

'I'm afraid not, sir. He already has a fever, he's lapsing in and out of consciousness and he's delirious. I've seen the symptoms before and –'

'Guards!' Nero barged him out of the way and kicked the door open, breaking the catch and slamming it against the inside wall, bringing down a chunk of painted plaster. 'Guards!' He shouted again, his voice rising to a scream, and almost at once, the sound of iron-shod feet clattering down the hallway signalled the arrival of two Praetorians. 'That man there,' he said, pointing at Jozar. 'Take him outside and kill him.' The doctor made to protest but Nero turned on him once more. 'What's your problem? You told me he was going to die, Mister know-it-all. I'm merely confirming your diagnosis for you.' Giora started to take a step forward but Josephus held him back.

Nero stormed out, slamming the already damaged door behind him, followed closely by the two soldiers who dragged Jozar away, half-crying, rambling incoherently in Aramaic: it was the last time they ever saw him.

Chapter Eighteen

Bedford-Stuyvesant, Brooklyn, NY

Giovanni Luzzo checked the address scrawled on the piece of paper. No mistake, this had to be it. Christ, what a dump. He searched for a bell but it had long ago been torn from the rotting frame leaving two lengths of wire sticking out. The glass in the door beside the boarded-up shop-front had been replaced by plywood and at a prod from his foot it swung open, revealing a wooden staircase which, from the paint marks, he saw had once been carpeted. At the top he flicked at the light switch but the bulb had gone the way of the stair carpet and so he groped around in the dark until he found the door. He was about to knock when it swung open and a familiar black face peered at him over the security chain.

'You're late,' said Raymond.

'Late? Yeah, as in "the late Giovanni Luzzo": I'm lucky to be alive coming to a 'hood like this,' he replied as the door closed behind him. 'Them boys dealing on the corner was looking at me like I was their lunch.'

'For shame on your scrawny Italian ass, my friend,' replied Raymond as Luzzo followed him through a grubby hallway, piled high on one side with cardboard boxes. 'Those boys ain't dealing, they're my people, my very own eyes and ears.'

'Yeah, yeah, ok. I'm sorry. No offence meant.'

Raymond laughed, a deep baritone rumble that shook the flimsy sheet-rock walls with their peeling wallpaper. 'And none taken. I want it to look like they're dealing: keeps attention away from us right here and keeps law-abiding taxpaying folk inside their cars with the doors locked. Come on; let me show you the new office suite.' He opened another door which led into what may once have passed for a bedroom: the carpet and the walls had turned a matching shade of yellowy grey over the years and the whole scene, with its few sticks of cheap furniture – including an unmade bed in the corner – was lit by two bare bulbs hanging from a nicotine-stained ceiling. 'What d'you think?'

Luzzo shook his head. 'What do I think?' he said. 'I think that even the fucking roaches must've moved out. What the hell are you doing in a shithole like this?'

Raymond looked at him over the top of his half-moon reading

glasses. 'I take it you'd have preferred something downtown Manhattan?'

'Wouldn't we all. But Bed-Stuy, for chrissakes?'

'Nowhere safer,' said Raymond. 'Take a look out the window. Go on, it won't bite you.' Luzzo moved the damp-stained curtain aside and peered out. 'Now tell me what you see opposite.'

'An abandoned car, houses. What d'you expect me to see?'

'True, but what kinda houses?'

'Shit, Raymond, I ain't got time for no dumb-ass games. I dunno, vacant lots; rat-infested dumps like this one.'

'Ah, but they're not like this one are they? All those windows are bricked up. Anyone trying to get close enough to take a look at us is going to have their work cut out.'

'Yeah, terrific. It's gonna give me a real warm fuzzy when I collect a bullet on the way outa here knowing the police couldn't see in the freakin' window. Anyway, what do they want?'

'A meet at Woodchester,' replied Raymond.

He snatched the printed sheet out of Raymond's hands. 'They want to meet where?'

'I told you: Woodchester.'

'And where the fuck's that?'

'Alabama – just read the goddam letter will you,' said Raymond with a sigh. He'd had a last name once but that was years back – maybe Raymond *was* his last name, even he wasn't so sure these days – but to everyone else he was just Raymond.

'Alabama? Is he seriously suggesting we go all the way back down there just so's his people can screw up again?'

Raymond maintained his usual implacable calm in the face of Luzzo's ranting. 'Well, I don't see we've got any choice.'

'I don't trust them,' said Luzzo, throwing his cigarette end on the floor and treading on it with a vehemence that suggested he wanted to grind it clean through the cheap carpet and into the boards below. 'These assholes damn near got us killed last time, they've already cost us money and good people. Those Alabama motherfuckers need to understand the price just went up.'

'Why don't we go to Woodchester and tell them in person?' said Raymond, looking up from his laptop.

'And anyway, how do they expect us to get there? Fly to Birmingham and rent a car like last time? Feds'd be all over us before we could say "shit". Why can't they come here?'

'How would I know?' said Raymond. 'All we got's that damn letter
–'

Luzzo screwed up the piece of paper and threw it into the corner before beginning yet another bad-tempered circuit of the room. 'And who the fuck writes letters in this day and age anyway? What are they playing at?'

Raymond got to his feet and calmly retrieved it, smoothing out the page on the table, taking care to avoid the worst of the coffee stains that formed a pattern of rings on its cracked Formica surface. 'You don't get any smarter, do you, Luzzo?'

'What's that supposed to mean?'

'You've got previous so we have to assume you've already got the Feds all over your sorry ass. Do you really think they're not listening to your cell-phone, following your car around the place with some fancy piece of technology stuck on with a magnet – that's if they can find enough bodywork that isn't made of filler? Why d'you think I've got those boys on the corners?'

'And so letters are safer than phones or e-mail? And if the Feds find the address, then what?'

Raymond looked at him, more in pity than anger, waving the envelope under his nose. 'Your name ain't Gloria Washington, nor's any of ours,' he said. 'If her mail gets sent to the store downstairs, that's nothing to do with us.'

'Yeah, but they could be reading them.'

'And if they do, they read a jumble of characters. Again, nothing to do with us.'

'How d'you know they can't decode this shit?'

'Because they haven't got the keys. This Josephus guy had access to grid-style ciphers that weren't re-discovered for nearly fifteen hundred years, he's the one who gave me the idea.'

'You're confusing me with all this code and cipher shit, Raymond,' said Luzzo, lighting yet another cigarette. 'So could the Feds read it or not?'

'Eventually, but it would take them one hell of a time because the text key that tells you how to use the grids is long and unique.'

'So's my dick, but where does that get us?'

Raymond looked at Luzzo and shook his head. 'When you come out with crap like that, I start to wonder if the human race isn't regressing. It's the King James Bible, asshole.'

'What is?'

'The source of the cipher key. Look, come here, knucklehead, and I'll show you.' Raymond spread the crumpled sheet out and weighted it down at the top with a well-thumbed copy of the Bible that he took out of his briefcase. Written underneath the groups of seemingly random groups of characters in his neat, almost feminine, hand was the decoded version, inviting them to meet the men whose money had paid for the robbery in Pompeii. 'Now, take a look at the first line.'

'It's a bunch of letters and numbers.'

'Excellent. Your mother and I are so glad to know all those years at Harvard weren't wasted.'

'OK, Raymond, cut the smartass crap. Letters and numbers. What of it?'

'Third number, third group is what?'

Luzzo sighed. 'Seven, teacher. Can I be excused please?'

Raymond ignored him and continued. 'Which is an odd number, right?'

'If you say so.'

'And the word "odd" starts with the letter "O" so we go to "O" for Old Testament. Now if we count another three groups along from there, third character we get the number three, so we go to the third book of the Old Testament.' Raymond picked it up and thumbed through to the relevant page. 'And that happens to be Leviticus.'

'Reckon I'll wait till they make the movie.'

'OK, well the rest of it's very simple. This group of characters tells you that the key comes from chapter nineteen, starting at verse six – that information's known as the indicator block – and you use the text from the Good Book, Leviticus nineteen, verse six to tell you which squares on the grid to use to generate your cipher-text. You with me?'

'I think so,' lied Luzzo.

'Of course if you know what you're doing you can brute-force decode a book cipher and each try has about a 1 in 2^{40} chance of success, but I've lengthened the odds by flattening out the frequency distribution of the letters rather than using what's called a *tabula recta* – so my grid's got lotsa Es, Ts, As and so on, but not many Js, Qs and Zs. Simple as ABC,' he said, rubbing his hands.

'Maybe to you,' said Luzzo. 'Makes me glad I never finished high-school if that's the kinda shit you had to sit through.'

Raymond laughed. 'No, this was stuff I got interested in when I was at college: I was a math and stats major.'

'Shit, I bet you had to fight the chicks off with a stick. So how much closer to Nowheresville Alabama does this get us?'

'It means we go there with a stronger hand than they do. We've got the grids and they haven't. I haven't done any Latin or Greek since I was eighteen but I've managed to decipher a couple of lines and where the plain- and cipher-text are written recto-verso – '

'Rectum what?'

'Recto-verso. Same text on different sides of the page: one side in clear, the other side in code.'

Luzzo scratched his head. 'And this rectum-version or whatever gives us a stronger hand?'

'Sure does. Shows them what we've got is for real. Like your Italian buddies said, all that stuff in the papers about all the grids having been recovered is just police bullshit and I've told the Good ole Boys as much. They pay us for the rest, every last goddam scrap of it, or we go looking for someone who will.'

'So what do you want me to do about Alabama?' asked Luzzo.

Raymond pondered for a moment. 'You go down by train. We'll get you a new credit card and you can rent a car once you're down there. I'll fly down and you can pick me up. And in case you're worried about the Feds, or the local State Troopers pulling you over, you'll be tailed by my people to make sure there's no one tailing you. If there is, you turn around and come straight back here.'

'What about the finds and stuff?'

'You leave all that to me. They're being looked after by people who do this kind of shit for a living. However, as far as our buyers know, they're sitting in someone's leaky shed in the back yard being eaten by ants – that'll give them even more incentive to come to the right decision.'

'So you're going to agree to the meet?'

'Already done so. The letter's in the mail,' said Raymond, patting the laptop. 'I've written a little piece of code that turns plain-text into cipher-text and automatically generates the indicator block.'

'What if someone steals the laptop? We'd be screwed then.'

'No we wouldn't. Even if they get past the BIOS password, the code's obfuscated –'

'It's what? Speak English will you.'

'Obfuscated,' repeated Raymond. 'It stops anyone looking at the code and working out what it does or reverse-engineering it. I've got other little goodies in there that make it impossible to get at, so don't you worry about a thing.'

151

'Have they talked money?' asked Luzzo who walked back to the window and began surveying the street scene below.

Raymond shook his head. 'Nope, they just said they wanted to negotiate face-to-face. And this time they've guaranteed no screw-ups.'

'Can we trust them?'

'Nope. Can't trust nobody in this business. But while we've got something they want then I can't see them doing anything stupid.'

'Well that's something at least.'

'You'd better get your ass down there,' said Raymond, handing him a scrap of paper. 'Go find a payphone and call this number. Tell them it's from me and you need train tickets and a driver's licence. Don't carry a weapon on the trip down – we'll get one to you.' Luzzo stood up and turned to leave but Raymond called him back. 'One more thing, make sure you've got a good cover story in case you get stopped. You need to have a watertight reason for going down there. Got that?'

'Yes, teacher,' Luzzo replied from the doorway without even turning round.

'Fool,' muttered Raymond under his breath.

Chapter Nineteen

Colchis, Pontus Cappadocius, AD 63

'We've found it. I think I can see a light up ahead.' Giora had to shout to make himself heard above the wind which was howling down the pass from the north and piling the snow into drifts beside the track.

Josephus kicked at his pony's flanks to try and drive the exhausted animal forward. Finally he drew level with his companion. Squinting against the swirling flakes he looked where Giora was pointing. Through the gloom he could just make out a dark shape on the crest of the rise and a guttering yellow light. 'I just hope the natives are more friendly than the last place,' he said, pulling his cloak tighter around himself.

'We're safe, Alityros,' he said, half turning in the saddle. 'Did you hear me? I said we're safe. Alityros? Alityros? Damn, where is he?'

'I thought he was back with you,' replied Giora, pulling his cloak down from his mouth in order to reply.

'And I thought he'd gone on ahead. When did you last see him?'

'Must be half an hour or more, he just gradually slipped behind, I thought you'd scoop him up.'

'I didn't pass him,' Josephus yelled into the wind. 'He must've wandered off the track.'

'Hardly, it's seven hundred feet up on both sides of the valley. Look, it's my fault, I'll go back, you go on ahead and tell them to make ready for three travellers.'

'And if Paul's people are already there waiting for us and I turn up on my own?'

'No,' Giora shouted back into the gale. 'They can't have got ahead of us. This is the only road, we'd have seen them for sure.'

'Just like we saw Alityros, you mean? Come on, we'll both go back.' Josephus turned his horse's head to retrace their steps, Giora's further words of protest were carried away on the wind and he turned to follow, noticing with unease that their two animals' hoof-prints were already buried by fresh snow. Their tough little Sarmatian-bred ponies were ideally suited for the conditions but the extreme cold, lack of fodder and a day's march had pushed even them to the limits of their endurance.

After ten minutes there was still no sign of their missing friend and Giora steered his horse alongside Josephus' mount. 'If we go much further, none of us is going to make it to that *caupona*, Josephus.'

'Don't think I hadn't thought of that, but we can't leave him to die out here. Another five minutes: all right?'

Giora muttered something inaudible into his cloak and they set off once more, hunched against the cold, the only sounds now the moaning of the wind and the clatter of the horses' hooves muffled by the carpet of snow which was by now fetlock-deep.

Josephus had drawn slightly ahead of Giora and so didn't hear his shouted calls that they should turn round. For a moment, the snowfall cleared and ahead of them, standing forlornly in the middle of the road was Alityros' pony, its head and back already covered with a layer of snow. It was then that they saw him, a heap of what looked like abandoned clothing left by the roadside and it was only because he had one leg in the air, still attached to the horse's saddle that they recognised it as a man. Jumping down, they ran over to Alityros and after detaching his foot from the stirrup, brushed the snow off him, hauling him into the sitting position.

'Just let me sleep,' he protested. 'Five minutes, that's all I need. Please let me sleep. I was warm there but now I'm cold.'

Giora put his arms under those of Alityros and grasping him round the chest, hauled him to his feet. 'Come on. Go to sleep in the snow and you'll never wake up. What happened to you anyway?'

The actor could barely speak for shivering and his words were slurred. He stared at Giora like a drunk, as though trying to bring him into focus. 'I don't know. I was so cold and then I wasn't any more. I was comfortable. Please let me sleep.'

'Must have gone to sleep in the saddle and fallen off,' said Josephus. 'You're a lucky man, Alityros, if it hadn't been for your foot catching in one of those stirrup things, the horse would've carried on and we'd never have found you. Come on, there's a *caupona* at the head of the pass and we'll get you thawed out there. Just a few more minutes.' With much puffing and heaving they manoeuvred him back into the saddle and riding in close proximity, to make sure he didn't fall off again, managed to get him to the primitive wayside *caupona*.

Little more than an overgrown hut, it was a large, single-storey building, built from the dark local stone and topped with a steeply-pitched roof designed to shed the snow. From the chimney a thin line of smoke streamed away horizontally in the freezing wind.

They left the horses with the stable lad and opened the door into the welcoming fug of the inn, supporting Alityros between them. The hubbub of conversation fell silent and at least thirty pairs of eyes turned their way.

A burly figure pushed his way towards them, barging customers and furniture aside. 'Are you blind? Didn't you see the sign?' he bellowed in execrable Greek, hands on hips. 'No room at the inn – we're full. Go on, get out.'

The innkeeper stood head and shoulders over the three travellers and Giora was readying himself for a fight when out of the corner of his eye he saw Josephus reach inside his cloak. 'Throw us out in this weather and it's murder,' he said calmly.

The innkeeper wiped his hands on the front of his grubby linen apron. 'I don't care what it is,' he said. 'We're full, now get out before I throw you out.'

'Recognise this?' said Josephus, pulling out a cylindrical leather case and holding it under the man's nose.

'Yes I do and we're still full, imperial seal or no.'

Josephus gestured for the man to follow and led him out of earshot to a corner. He waved the leather case at him. 'I take it you yourself can read seeing how you brought the topic up?'

'If you're trying to be funny you and your poncey friends can go and do your comedy act outside –'

'In here are letters of passage signed by Nero himself giving me, amongst other things, the right to requisition anything I need – such as an entire caupona should the need arise – so if anyone's going to end up outside, you're first on the list.'

The innkeeper, unmoved, continued to glare at the Judean with undisguised contempt. 'You're a long way from Rome in case you hadn't noticed. Nero may not even be emperor any more for all I know.'

'Talking treason isn't going to help your case. You put us out of here and the emperor will know about it. There's a ship of the *Classis Pontica* arriving to pick us up from Phasis and if we're not there to meet it, the soldiers on board are going to come straight down this road asking questions.'

He took a step towards Josephus who stood his ground, leaving them almost toe to toe. 'Balls,' he growled in Josephus' face. 'The *Classis Pontica* is holed up whoring and drinking in Trapezus for the winter. You must think I'm stupid, little man.'

'As a matter of fact I do,' replied Josephus. 'So stupid that you seem to relish the thought of dying in the arena. Any of that lot,' he said, jerking his thumb towards the *caupona's* patrons, 'would betray you for

155

three *asses*. Now, do you want to take your chances with the army or do we get a bed for the night, hot food for ourselves and fodder for our horses?'

The argument had drawn a little knot of curious spectators from whom came a stream of barracking and profanities. Their presence had clearly unsettled the innkeeper and Josephus noticed that the man's fists were clenching and unclenching; for a moment he feared the idiot would sooner face the wrath of a distant emperor than lose face in his own *caupona*. Eventually he took a pace back and his arms fell limp by his side. 'Very well – looks like I've got no choice, does it? There's no beds spare but you can get your heads down wherever you can find space. The boy will take care of your animals and if you find yourself somewhere to sit I'll bring you some food – payment in advance, mind.'

Once it became clear that a fight was out of the question, the group of onlookers lost interest and melted away towards the fire, treating the innkeeper to a few choice comments about the probable state and size of his manhood as they went. He waited until they were out of earshot and then demanded a price which Josephus knew was three times the going rate. Deciding it was better to let him salvage something in return for the public humiliation he'd just suffered, he counted the silver coins into the muscular hand without demur. Stuffing the money into a leather purse at his waist, the innkeeper made to return to his cooking stove in the far corner of the stone hut when Josephus called him back.

'I've got a favour to ask.'

'A favour? You've got a bloody cheek,' said the innkeeper, his words dying on his lips at the sight of the gold *aureus* Josephus held up between his thumb and forefinger.

He gazed at the coin spellbound while Josephus continued. 'Do as I ask and when we leave in the morning you'll have three more of these.'

'I'm listening,' he said, almost twitching with greed.

'There are a group of men, hostile to his majesty the emperor, who wish us ill. They've already tried to stop us reaching Phasis and they may do so again. If anyone else comes here tonight, do not let them in under any circumstances and if they turn up after we've gone, then you haven't seen us. Understand?'

'Certainly, sir. It'll be my pleasure,' he said, snatching the coin from his outstretched hand and winking at him in a way that made Josephus feel distinctly uncomfortable.

'Good. Bolt the doors now, secure the stables and make sure no light is visible from outside. Oh, and tell your boy to put a sack or something over our saddles and not to say anything about them to anyone.'

'The saddles?'

'You heard me. Any more questions and you don't get paid. Now move.'

Their conversation was interrupted by a gust of icy wind sweeping into the room. It blew the thick woollen curtain over the door almost horizontal and treated the guests sitting nearby to a dusting of snow. The door slammed shut to the accompaniment of shouted protests from those caught in the freezing draught.

'Where are they? Chuck 'em out,' shouted the innkeeper, pushing his way across the crowded *caupona* and looking around for the new arrivals. 'I said no one else was to come in.'

'They didn't.'

The innkeeper swung round to see who'd spoken. 'Don't talk crap or I'll throw you out too,' he snarled at the young Parthian sitting by the door. 'You saw the door open. Stop playing silly buggers and tell me who it was.' He scanned the faces of his clients, trying to work out whether any of them looked like newcomers.

'They left,' said the Parthian. 'Three of them.'

'Left? What, in this weather? Stop pulling my leg.'

'Suit yourself,' he replied with a shrug and gesturing to an empty bench. 'But I can promise you they were sitting right there.'

'Bastards left without paying. Well I hope saving twenty *asses* is worth freezing to death for,' said the innkeeper with a snort of disgust and stamped off in search of the food he'd promised Josephus.

Josephus joined the others at a table near the fire and heard Alityros complaining that his toes, fingertips and nose were hurting and itching abominably. 'It's a good sign,' said Josephus. 'Remember what they told us? If they hurt and itch you're going to be all right, if they don't it means they'll turn black and fall off.'

'I told you I wasn't cut out for this. I've got bad feet,' wailed Alityros for possibly the thousandth time since they'd set off on their mission to track down Nathanael Bar Talmai.

'Serves you right for fibbing to Poppaea about sea-monsters,' said Josephus. 'In fairness, she did offer you the option of fighting in the arena instead of coming with us.'

Alityros looked across the table at his companions with the expression of a whipped puppy. 'At least in the arena I'd have had a speedy end rather than freezing to death in the back of beyond.'

'Oh don't be such a drama queen,' said Josephus. 'The only reason

Giora and I knew we'd lost you was because we couldn't hear your whining any more. Two more days, three at the most, and we'll be in Phasis.'

Josephus knew there was nothing to gain by bringing up the unspoken worry that beset them all. Bad weather and a near fatal encounter with members of the *Chrestos* cult, loyal to Paul, had delayed them by three weeks. None of them knew whether the ship would still be there; and cornered for the winter in a place like Phasis where the writ of imperial law ran fitfully at best, it would be a matter of time before Paul's people caught up with them again.

Giora, who'd stayed out of the conversation, leaned forward over the table and beckoning them closer. 'I hate to put a dampener on things,' he whispered. 'But I think we've got a problem on that score.'

'What d'you mean?' asked Josephus.

'It may be a coincidence, but I think three of Paul's people may have been in here.'

Josephus' face went white with horror. 'How do you know?'

'Just now when you were talking to fatso there and the door opened.'

'What of it? I saw it all for myself. Whoever it was, he didn't let them in.'

Giora shook his head. 'Letting people in wasn't the problem, it's the three who left that bother me.'

'In this weather? You'd have to be mad –'

'Or fanatical,' replied Giora. 'If they're who I think they are and assuming they survive the weather and get to the next *caupona* then, well…. we're done for.'

Chapter Twenty

Flora folded her arms and glared across the table at Hayek and Cohen. 'I made it quite clear I wasn't having anything to do with weapons and you promised not to put me in a situation where I might need one.'

'We promised to do our best,' said Hayek. 'We can't guarantee what other people might do. Surely you understand that.'

'Yes, Mike, I do; and please don't patronise me.'

'C'mon, be reasonable, Flora, let's say that if despite our best efforts, Special Agent Cohen here runs into trouble and he dies because you can't use a pistol, then how are you going to feel?'

'Sorry, Mike. If you think you can emotionally blackmail me by concocting scenarios where I fail to save the world because I won't use a gun, then you're wasting your time.'

'OK, have it your way.' He turned to Cohen who was sitting next to him across the table from Flora.

Cohen shrugged. 'Tell her, Mike,' he said.

'Tell her what?' asked Flora.

Hayek sucked his pen and paused before speaking. 'Flora, I don't want you to take this the wrong way and I need you to know we did it with the best of intentions –'

'Did what, Mike? Don't talk in riddles.

'Well…we thought we were acting for the best by not telling you a couple of things that, I dunno, might've spooked you.'

'So when you said there'd be no risk you lied to me.' She stood up to leave. 'Very well. In that case, gentlemen, if you'll excuse me, I'm going back to Pompeii, I've got work to do.'

'Sit down, Flora, you can't go anywhere right now.'

Flora bit her bottom lip. 'Oh can't I?' she snapped. However, as she stood up she remembered she'd surrendered her passport, credit cards and driving licence and, more embarrassingly, didn't even know how to get out of the building.

'If you try to go back to Pompeii you won't make it beyond Naples. Assuming you even get that far…'

The chill in Hayek's voice stopped Flora in her tracks and she spun round to face him. 'Are you threatening me, Mr Bloody Hayek?'

159

'No, Flora, of course not. Please come and sit down and let me explain. You're potentially in a lot of danger. Hear me out and then if you still want to go home, we'll make sure you get back to Oxford safe and sound and that you have all the necessary protection – I've already spoken to Giles Smith at the British Embassy and London have confirmed it.'

Flora walked back to her seat and sat down. All the bad memories came flooding back. 'Protection? Whatever for?'

'We think there may've been a leak. Word's got out that you're in Rome giving specialist advice to the TPC.'

'But how can they possibly know?' she asked, the anger rising in her voice.

Hayek's eyes never left hers for a moment. 'Perhaps you should tell us, Flora,' he said, the menace in his voice all too apparent. 'Who knew you were coming to Rome?'

She thought for a moment. 'My mum and dad. I called them on my mobile after I'd spoken to Captain Lombardi.'

'Where were you when you made the call?'

'Outside the lab in the car park.'

'Could anyone have overheard you?' asked Hayek.

'I don't know…I don't think so, and besides I was speaking English.'

'That's no guarantee. Did you tell anyone else?' Flora thought for a moment. 'Come on, who else did you tell? Don't lie to us, Flora, we'll find out in the end.'

Livid with herself for being so stupid, she answered. 'Only Francesco Moretti. We went out to a pizza place and he was in a funny mood: God knows why but I think he's jealous of Lombardi and he kept pestering me about why I was going away for a few days. He seemed desperate for me not to go – kept telling me how dangerous it was.'

'And *are* you seeing Lombardi?'

'Oh for Christ's sake, don't *you* start. No I'm not and if I was it'd be nobody's business but my own.' She thumped her elbows down hard on the table.

'Look at me, Flora,' said Hayek. She glared defiantly back at him. 'Lombardi asked you not to tell anybody, didn't he?' She made no reply. 'Didn't he, Flora?' he repeated.

She broke eye contact. 'Yes, all right: *mea culpa*. I know I wasn't supposed to, but he just seemed so depressed and I didn't want to make it worse by lying to him, that's all.' She paused for a moment as the realisation sank in. 'Surely you don't think he told anybody? Not Francesco.'

'We don't know, Flora. They could be listening to your cell-phone, someone could've overheard you talking to Moretti. Whoever it was, we'll have to find out, but for now we've got to do a bit of re-planning.'

'I screwed up, didn't I?' she said, furious with herself for such a beginner's lapse. 'I'm really sorry.'

'It's a bit late for sorry,' said Hayek. 'You of all people should know that when someone asks you to keep quiet about something, they mean just that. The entire Campania region is riddled with Camorra influence, from the regional government right down to the waiters in the restaurant you ate at: it touches everything –'

Another wave of guilt for adding to Moretti's weight of unhappiness swept over Flora. 'That's pretty much what Francesco told me,' she said, inwardly kicking herself.

'Well he was right. In that part of Italy you just have to think of everyone and everything as linked to the Camorra. You trust nobody.'

'So what do you suggest?'

'You call Moretti, you tell him you've had enough and you're going back to England. You call your folks and tell them the same thing. You spend a few days back in Oxford and then we'll get you on a flight – as Lavinia Crump of course – to DC. We'll leave it up to Giles Smith and his people to make it look like you're still in the country. It's not perfect, but it might just work.'

Flora raised her eyebrows. 'And if it doesn't?'

'Then you might end up wishing you'd had some weapons training.'

The memories came flooding back once more. Oh, Christ, Mr bloody Hayek, if only you knew, she thought.

Hayek shrugged. 'Anyway, it's your choice but I think it's a bad one. Now, to business,' he said, tapping a buff-coloured folder on his desk. 'This has come from DC. 'It's a report from the ACT on a series of thefts from museums. You can read it if you like.'

'Is it your friend Luzzo?'

'We think he may be part of it. Whoever it is, the problem just got a whole bunch bigger. All the different national agencies: the specialists like the ACT and TPC and the generalists like Scotland Yard, do their best to share information but it doesn't always work out how we'd like: data formats are different, there are language problems and it takes more time and people than we've got to pull it all together. It's needle in a haystack stuff, but occasionally we get it right.'

161

'And today's the day?' asked Flora, her face brightening at the thought of recovering the codices.

'Yup. How much do you know about the market for stolen art works?'

'Not a huge amount. Anyway, you're the experts, why are you asking me?'

'Because the report tells us that documents, manuscript fragments, even entire works have been disappearing from museum archives over the last five years, maybe longer, and nobody knows why or who's been taking them.'

'And none of the museums ever missed this stuff? That ought to surprise me but the way some of these places operate it doesn't.'

'So you're saying that the museums just leave these texts to gather dust?'

'Until recently, yes. But the technology is so good these days that we can read and date texts that were unusable a few years ago. It's great for researchers but the backlog of stuff needing cataloguing and recording is huge.

'Well, I guess that's kinda appropriate because if it wasn't for a researcher they probably wouldn't even have known anything was missing.'

'What happened?'

'A German doctoral student at Göttingen was researching one of the early church fathers – guy called Origen: I take it you've heard of him?' Flora nodded and Hayek continued. 'The Städtisches Museum had a collection of writings attributed to Origen – scrolls, pages, fragments and so on – from a nineteenth century dig in Turkey and although it was listed in the archives as probably being late fifth century, the individual elements of the collection had never been properly catalogued.'

'That's absolutely standard,' said Flora. 'Typically only about five percent of any document collection is catalogued.'

'Anyway, the museum assumed the collection had been mislaid and started looking for it. In the process, they found that a bunch of other stuff was missing too and reported it to the police. Then, by a stroke of luck the German report found its way to the ACT and they put it in the hopper with the others.'

'I think I can see where this is going,' said Flora.

'Exactly. It was good, honest-but-dull police work that did it. Then when they looked at the report on the finds from the Royal Ontario Museum that our buddy Luzzo claims he found, it turns out that the museum did an audit of its archives as a precaution and realised that several collections of early writings had gone. That one was in the hopper too but they'd missed it. Same deal in Copenhagen earlier this year, the British Museum, then Berlin, Cairo, Milan – the list just goes on: the more they looked through the data, the more they found and the more it looked consistent. No sign of a break-in in any of the cases and the thieves only seem to have taken uncatalogued collections of ancient writings: every one has to be an inside job and the ACT guys are sure they're linked – question is how?'

Flora put her glasses on and thumbed through the report. 'Can I ask a silly question?'

Hayek nodded. 'Sure,' he said.

'If all these robberies were done by museum staff without anybody noticing, what's that got to do with what happened at Pompeii? Using a mechanical digger and smashing up a conservation lab doesn't seem to fit the pattern of stealing things on the quiet.'

'Normally, I'd agree, but it's the very specific nature of what's been stolen that suggests a link. Trouble is though, proving it's going to take time. We're dealing with different jurisdictions, and in a lot of cases we don't even know when the finds went missing or exactly what was in the collections.'

'And you still don't know why.'

Hayek stood up and moved to the window, looking out across the embassy grounds. 'Money. It's always money,' he said. 'Follow the money and you'll find out who and why.'

Flora looked puzzled. 'But if there's little or no commercial value, what's the point?' she asked.

'The market value may not be much, but that doesn't stop money being involved somewhere. That's where Mr Grossman and Miss Crump come in. As soon as you start offering big bucks for anything you'll start seeing people coming out of the woodwork. Our media release about the copper sheets hasn't produced anything yet so maybe good old fashioned cash will help.'

Flora tapped at the report with her finger. 'Well, I can see one place where you could try.'

'Really?' asked Hayek, coming to look over her shoulder. 'Where?'

'William Sunday University. It says here they had a work stolen – a well-known one too. The Dean of the college is also head of the faculty of ancient history and biblical studies: a character by the name of Donald Sumter. He and I can't stand one another but I think we're professional enough to put our differences aside over something like this…well, I am anyway.'

'Wasn't he the guy who was on-site with you at Pompeii?' asked Hayek.

'Yes, that's him. Once there was nothing more for him to do there, he did what he always does – was rude to everyone and cleared off home.'

'Sounds a charmer,' Hayek said.

Flora pulled a face. 'Don't get me started.' She read on for a minute or so and then sat up with a jolt. 'This is really interesting, Mike. I never even knew it had gone missing. Donald Sumter never mentioned it.'

'What's gone missing?' he asked.

'The work stolen from William Sunday University: a book from the *Apocryphon of John*. It's one of a number of works mentioned by Eusebius, but which didn't make the cut when they were picking the team for the New Testament – anything Eusebius or his predecessors like Irenaeus considered heretical or unfitting, like the Gnostic texts for example, didn't get in. Copies of some of these documents still exist, others were thought to have been lost but turned up at places like Nag Hammadi – the Gospel of Thomas is a case in point – and others are just plain old missing.'

'Like the *Apocryphon of John*?'

'Yes and no. Three slightly different versions of the *Apocryphon* were found at Nag Hammadi. The entire work is mentioned by Irenaeus and in later copies of Eusebius and although Irenaeus describes the whole thing as "secret and illegitimate" and really goes to town on the evils of the last book, he gives no details about its content. That's what's so fascinating.'

'It is?' asked Hayek.

'Yes. It's reputed to be an early version of the Book of Revelation, so as you can imagine, there was a big hoo-hah during the 1950s when what looked like a third-century copy turned up in Greece. It was eventually written off as a fifteenth-century fake and interest in it waned.'

'Then presumably someone got interested again?'

'Exactly. New technology to the rescue. A team at the University of Athens managed to read more of it and it turned out to be second-century, so it's really early, which was fantastic. Unfortunately, the research team ran out of funding and so Sumter stepped in with an offer to carry on where they'd left off.'

'Do you think he'd be willing to help us?' asked Hayek.

Flora nodded. 'I think he might. Whatever you say about him, he's passionate about ancient writings, languages and the history of the early Church – not for the best of reasons if you ask me – but passionate none the less.'

'So what's wrong with his motives?'

Flora sighed. 'Where do I start?' she said, pausing for a moment. 'OK, and bear with me because this is the cut-down version. As I'm sure you know, William Sunday is a Bible college and gets a lot of its funding from the wackier fringes of the Evangelical Movement – TV preachers, that kind of thing. A good chunk of that cash goes to Sumter and his team to pay for their efforts to find historical evidence supporting the idea of the Bible as literal truth. That's why he was so keen to dash to Pompeii when he heard that works attributed to Josephus had been found.'

'Because Josephus backs up what it says in the Gospels?'

'Well yes and no,' said Flora. 'He doesn't mention Jesus, the disciples, virgin births, miracles, resurrections, none of it; which when you think about the detail he goes into on other fairly minor subjects is pretty telling if you ask me.'

'So why's Sumter so keen on him?'

'Because in one of Josephus works, the *Antiquities of the Jews*, there's a paragraph that appears out of the blue saying what a fantastic miracle-worker Jesus was, how everyone followed him and how he rose from the dead after three days.'

'And that's it?'

'That's it, no other mention. A bit like someone writing a detailed history of the twentieth century and devoting one paragraph to the Second World War – you just wouldn't write it like that. And nor did Josephus in my opinion.'

'So you think the Jesus paragraph was grafted on later?'

'Most certainly. As do most serious historians without a selective blind spot; but not Donald Sumter. He'd been in Pompeii for three weeks before I arrived and I think he was already looking for an excuse to leave when the break-in happened. He hadn't found what he was looking for and was therefore happy to ignore what Moretti's people had dug up: he could either dismiss the texts as fakes or as precursor works, possibly not written by Josephus.'

'We'll bear him in mind,' said Hayek. 'If our agents strike out trying to find Raymond and Luzzo then it might be worth a trip to William

Sunday.'

'Donald would have a fit if you turned up with me in tow.'

'We can leave you out of it. The fewer people who know you're helping us the better, even if they *are* on the side of the angels.'

Flora laughed. 'Donald? On the side of the crackpots more like. By the way, any chance I could take the report back to read at the hotel?'

Hayek looked serious once more. 'There's been a change of plan. Just in case anyone's looking for you in Rome, we thought it safer if you stayed at the British Embassy; Giles Smith's sending a car for you and tomorrow morning you're leaving for London under your own name – he'll give you your own passport back and you'll get Lavinia's again before you leave for the US. And in case you were wondering, while you're air side and on the flight, Giles tells me you'll be watched by *The Friends* as he calls them, so you've no worries on that score.'

'But what about my things? I've got clothes at the hotel at Pompeii and the one here.'

'Already taken care of: they'll be waiting at the embassy for you.' Hayek looked at his watch. 'I'll take you downstairs to wait for the car, but before I do I just wanted to thank you for agreeing to help and to wish you luck. You're good, better than a lot of our people, but for Pete's sake, don't let it go to your head. Remember that and you'll be fine.'

The subtle rebuke was not lost on Flora. 'I will, don't worry, Mike,' she replied. 'I wasn't really trying to be difficult.'

He cracked a smile. 'I never doubted it for a moment. Now, just a bit of housekeeping. Phone Moretti this evening and tell him you're still at the same hotel but the whole business in Pompeii has upset you so much that you've decided you want to go back to England. Don't tell him you've spoken to anyone other than the TPC and only if he pushes you, tell him they've been asking you a bunch of questions and getting you to look at mugshots. Got all that?'

'Every last word, Mike.'

'Good, now, let's get you downstairs. And don't think you've seen the last of me,' he added, shaking her warmly by the hand. 'I'm sure our paths will cross again. And as for Agent Cohen, he's got work to do in Israel and Switzerland but we'll arrange things so you'll meet up with him for your flight to the States. Good luck, Flora, and this time, please keep things to yourself.'

'Don't worry,' she said. 'I won't let you down.'

166

Chapter Twenty-one

Colchis, Pontus Cappadocius, AD 63

Josephus looked at Giora aghast. 'But you said you put them in these stalls last night.'

'I did,' he replied. A movement by the door caught his eye. It was the stable lad. 'Hey, you, stop skulking around and come here.' With a look of sulky indifference the youth wandered over. 'Well?' asked Giora. 'Where are they?'

'Where are what?'

'Our horses, idiot. We left three ponies in your charge and now they've gone.'

The stable lad blinked several times and looked around as though searching for inspiration or in case the animals had somehow hidden themselves behind a pile of hay. 'Someone must've taken them by mistake.'

'What?' roared Giora, picking up the lad by the throat and pinning him against the wall. 'You little shit, if you don't tell me who took them I'll break your –'

'You just leave him be.' The sound of a weapon being unsheathed brought Giora up short and they turned to see the innkeeper framed in the doorway, a sword in his hand. 'I brought him into the warm after I'd settled everyone down. If he'd spent the night out here, he could've died of cold, you know that as well as I do. If someone stole your horses, well, I'm sorry it happened but it's nothing to do with him, or with me come to that.' Giora let the boy go and he scuttled away into an empty stall.

'So what are we supposed to do?' said Josephus. 'We've got twenty miles to cover today and we can't do it on foot.'

The innkeeper shrugged his indifference. 'You could stay till it thaws I suppose but that could be months and I'll need paying in advance – give you a nice discount of course.'

I'll bet you bloody will, thought Josephus. 'Do you have any animals we could borrow, just to get us to the next *caupona*?' he said.

'Borrow?' said the innkeeper, incredulous. 'If it's charity you're after you've come to the wrong place. As a sacrifice, I can sell you my three best horses –tack will be extra of course – but they won't come cheap.'

Giora and Josephus exchanged glances and at a nod from the latter, the innkeeper kicked open a half rotten door that led to where three elderly mounts were chewing listlessly at a ration of hay. 'There we go,' he said, wandering over to pat the bony rump of the nearest animal, causing a cloud of dust and horsehair to rise into the frosty air. 'Mercury, Pegasus and Rapidus. You won't find three finer mounts this side of Trapezus: four *aureii* each, but seeing as how you're such good customers, I'll call it ten for cash. Two more for the saddles and they're a steal at twelve, what do you say?'

Josephus who was no judge of horseflesh looked first at the hollow ribs and the knock knees of the wretched animals and then turned to Giora. 'What do you think?'

'What do I think?' asked Giora. 'I'll tell you what I think. This crook probably sold our horses to the highest bidder and now he wants to rob us again. Now you listen,' he said, taking a step towards the innkeeper. 'You've seen the letters and now you're going to give us these broken-down heaps of dog-meat and be grateful we don't take you with us under arrest.'

Instead of reacting angrily the innkeeper began to rock with laughter, shaking his head in disbelief. 'You forget where you are, boy. Carry on like that and I'll leave your bones in the valley bottom for the crows to pick over come the thaw.' He turned a scornful gaze on Josephus. 'And if you mention your precious bloody letters again, I'll take them off you and burn them. Now, twelve *aureii*: take it or leave it.'

Half an hour down the pass it was clear that the horses were in worse condition than they had feared. Mercury, a sorely misnamed animal, was struggling under Giora's weight and each time they waited for him to catch up it proved almost impossible to persuade the other two nags to move on again. The snow had stopped and now they trudged on in thick cloud, cocooned in an unreal world where white merged with white in a disorientating dreamscape with no clear indication of up and down.

Alityros, in the lead for once, would have collided with the other horse in the mist had it not been for Pegasus coming to a sudden halt. Giora reined in Mercury and jumped down from the saddle.

The riderless animal was several hands smaller than their rangy nags but was in far better condition and lifted its head at his approach. He patted the horse's shoulder and took hold of its bridle. 'That's not possible,' he said.

'What isn't?' asked Josephus, who dismounted and led Rapidus over to join him.

'This is one of ours, it's even got the same Parthian saddle, look.'

Josephus examined the animal closely. 'You're right. But why abandon it here?' he asked.

'I think I know why,' said Alityros, pointing ahead.

From the snow by the roadside protruded a human arm. Josephus brushed the snow away to reveal the body of a man lying face upwards, his clothes black with frozen blood from multiple sword cuts and puncture wounds. The bone of the right shoulder joint gleamed white against the now solidified tissue of the livid gash that had laid it bare.

'I think we should go back,' said Alityros. 'I don't like this.'

'No,' said Giora. 'We have to go on. And anyway, the body's been here several hours, whoever did this is long-gone.'

'Giora's right,' said Josephus. 'We have to go on. For all we know, the bastards who stole the horses may've had a falling out.'

Alityros looked down at his companion with disbelief. Long months of being jollied along, prodded, cajoled and gently deceived by the others had left him wary of shows of optimism like this. 'And leave a valuable horse and its tack standing in the middle of the snow? Come off it, Josephus, he was ambushed, probably robbed if you ask me. There was obviously a fight and whoever did this will be back for the horse, you mark my words.'

Faced with the option of returning to the *caupona* on his own, Alityros grudgingly agreed to continue, trailing in the wake of Giora who now rode the Parthian pony, with Mercury's reins tied to its saddle. They had barely gone twenty paces when Giora held up his hand for them to stop. From out of the mist loomed two dark shapes: the other ponies, standing miserably shoulder-to-shoulder for warmth. A trail of reddish-black bloodstains in the snow led them to two corpses, their limbs frozen into bizarre contortions.

The travellers stared at one another in horror. Josephus broke the silence. 'Listen, you two, if either of you wants to go back I'll understand. You won't get a ship till Spring and you won't have the protection of the imperial seal, but don't feel you have to come with me.'

'I think we should go back,' said Alityros, turning his gaze away from the gory spectacle at the roadside.

'Up to you,' replied Giora. 'But if you do, you're on your own, I'm going on with Josephus.

'Anyway,' said Josephus, jumping down into the snow and wading over to examine the nearest corpse, sinking almost up to his knees at every step, 'we're well over half-way to the next *caupona* and from there it's only a day at the most to Phasis.' He turned the body onto its side and started to examine it.

'Found anything?' called Giora.

'Yes,' he replied. 'It wasn't robbery. This one's got twenty *aureii* in his purse.'

'Keep it,' said Alityros.

'I fully intend to. But I think I know why these three were killed. Whoever did this thought they were us.'

'Paul?' asked Giora, his voice betraying the nervousness they all felt.

'Who else?' said Josephus. 'His people are probably at the next caupona with their feet up in front of the fire congratulating themselves on a job well done.'

'So that means we'll be all right then,' said Alityros. 'If they think we're dead then we're safe.'

'I wouldn't put money on it,' said Josephus. 'Here, take this,' he said to Giora, handing him one of the swords he'd taken from next to the bodies. 'I think you might need it.'

They set off once more, their horses plodded along inside what felt like a motionless white sphere. 'Stop. I can smell burning,' said Alityros.

'So can I,' said Josephus. 'Must be woodsmoke from the caupona. We're nearly there.'

Alityros reined his pony to a halt. 'No. It's not woodsmoke, it doesn't smell right.'

'Nonsense,' said Giora, clapping him on the shoulder as he rode past. 'Come on or you'll freeze if you don't keep moving. It'll be dark soon.'

'I still don't like it,' said Alityros as Giora and Josephus disappeared into the gloom a few yards further on. Not wanting to be left alone he kicked on and after only a few seconds almost collided with the others who had come to a halt. In front of them stood the outlines of a low range of buildings; one of which had been reduced to a fire-blackened shell. 'Told you so,' he said.

From the chimney of the undamaged part of the caupona, a thin stream of smoke drifted lazily into the milky whiteness but no lights showed from its closely-shuttered windows. In silence Josephus led them on, looping round the roofless structure, its walls blackened with soot and its interior a charred heap of timbers and roof-tiles.

Josephus dismounted and made his way towards the stable which, like the still standing portion of the Caupona, had also escaped any damage. He pushed the door open and peered into the warm gloomy interior. At last, satisfied that there was no one around he stuck his head round the door and motioned to Giora to join him leaving Alityros holding the ponies. 'Six horses,' he said in a whisper. 'Not great odds but we'll have the advantage of surprise and they may be drunk –'

Josephus eased the door shut behind him and as he did so a sharp metallic ring made them both spin round: in time to find a sword at their throats. 'Drop your weapons and neither of you move,' said a voice. Then Alityros appeared, also at sword point.

The leader, a cube of a man with a jet-black beard covering most of his face, stood back and appraised his captives. 'Kill them,' he said with no more emotion than someone ordering a drink at a *caupona* bar. His companions raised their weapons.

'Stop! What in the name of Hades d'you think you're doing?' A burly figure stood silhouetted in the doorway to the interior of the building, his hands on his hips in a pose of indignation. Taking no chances, Josephus and the others threw themselves flat on the floor.

'We found three more, sir,' said the cube. 'More of Paul's mob by the look of it.'

The newcomer strode into the stable, and ignoring the captives, took a cursory glance at the horses. 'You've no idea who they are have you, idiot? And if they are Paul's we need to find out how many more there are out there.'

The man's voice seemed vaguely familiar and Josephus propped himself up amongst the straw and dung which coated the earth floor of the stable. 'Gubs? What on earth are you doing here?'

'Josephus,' he shouted. 'The gods be thanked you're alive.' And pulling his friend to his feet, warmly embraced him, ignoring the residue clinging to Josephus' clothing. 'We thought those bastards had killed you.'

'Which bastards?' asked Josephus, still shaky after his close call at the hands of the cube.

'The ones Paul sent. But how on earth did you get away? They said they'd killed you all about an hour back up the pass. Not that they volunteered the information straight away, you understand.'

'I don't think I understand anything,' said Josephus. 'I need to thaw out and I could murder something hot to eat.'

Leaving the six horses in the care of the stable lad, who looked to Josephus worryingly like the one from the previous *caupona*, they trooped into the warm fug of the inn. Unlike the main room of their previous night's stay, this time, save for the detachment from Gubs' crew, the place was deserted. The innkeeper brought three steaming bowls of soup.

'So what on earth are you doing here?' asked Josephus when they had finished eating.

'Looking for you of course,' replied Gubs. 'When the weather started closing in I decided to make a run for it back down the coast to Trapezus even if it meant leaving you behind till Spring.'

'I wouldn't have blamed you if you had,' said Josephus. 'We all expected you to have sailed weeks ago.'

'We were taking on stores,' continued Gubs. 'And one of my lads got chatting to a bunch of what he thought were army deserters in a tavern. Anyway, after a fair old skinfull, they started trying to get him to convert to their religion.'

'Christians,' said Josephus.

'Exactly. Anyway, being a good lad, he reported them to me and it just seemed like too much of a coincidence so I did a bit of digging to see if I could find out what they were up to. Don't know if it that was coincidence too or something I said, but the next night when we went back to the tavern, they'd paid their bill and cleared off.'

'So you decided to follow them?' asked Alityros. 'That was brave.'

'Not really, but the fact that they were here and you lot were so far overdue, we decided to try and find you. The idea was for a quick look: two days out, and if there was no word, we'd assume the worst and come back.'

'And at a guess, you weren't the only one looking for three travellers,' said Josephus.

'Exactly. At around midday, the five men we'd seen at the tavern came in to the bunk house out the back and without going into too much detail, let's just say that the conversation between them and my lads got a bit heated if you'll excuse the pun.'

'Where are they?'

'Dead. The lads got three of them straight away, but don't worry, we got plenty of information out of the others before we finished them off.' Gubs slid a wooden-framed message tablet onto the table. 'Here, take a look at this. I think you'll recognise it.'

Josephus undid the cord and unfolded it to reveal the wax writing surface beneath. What he saw made his blood run cold. 'I sent you this from Albanopolis, Gubs.' Traced in the cold, hard wax was the description of their successful operation against Nathanael Bar Talmai,

172

their intended route back to the shores of the Black Sea and an estimated date for their arrival.

'I know you did,' said Gubs. 'But it never reached me. They must have ambushed the *Cursus Publicus* and once they'd got the message block that's how they found you.'

'Hold on a minute,' said Giora. 'What about the three men we found on the road? Who killed them?'

'Paul's mob,' said Gubs. 'One of them was blind drunk and came into the bunk house shouting his mouth off about what they'd been up to, so we thought you were done for. One of my lads recognised him from the bar in Phasis and naturally assumed that if you three were dead then he'd been traipsing through the snow for nothing – he's Carthaginian you see and they're not very keen on snow. That's when the fight kicked off. Pity about the bunk house but at least three of the Christians got a decent funeral pyre.'

'I can see why you thought we were dead,' said Josephus. 'Whoever stole our horses this morning ended up doing us a big favour.' He paused for thought. 'If we're going after Paul himself next we need to make sure we've got a more secure form of communication. All this has given me an idea.'

'What have you got in mind?' asked Gubs.

'It's Greek.'

Gubs snorted. 'Whatever it is, I don't like the sound of it,' he replied, casting a sideways look at Alityros.

'No, it's nothing to do with that.' Have you ever heard of Polybius?' Gubs shook his head and Josephus continued. 'He was a Greek mathematician who came up with a way of turning messages into code. The problem is, his method isn't difficult to break even without the key. Mine will be impossible to read unless you have both keys.'

'You've lost me again,' said Gubs.

Josephus smiled. 'I think you'll like it. It could even be useful for the fleets. I'll explain it to you when we get to Phasis.'

Under normal circumstances, even in the relatively sheltered coastal waters of the Black Sea, no sane captain of a *liburna* would ever leave port during the winter months, but Gubs, now master of the *Celer* and with supplies dwindling, decided to take a chance and head west from Phasis towards the fleet base at Trapezus. Starting at first light, relying mainly on the oars during the bitterly cold but clear days and running for shelter at the first hint of bad weather, they made the journey in five days.

Josephus, Giora and Alityros leaned over the rail as the ship, driven on by the rhythmic beat of its sweeps rounded the eastern end of the mole into harbour.

'Hardly Ostia, is it?' said Alityros as the *Celer* coasted through the ranks of warships, their masts waving gently as the *liburna*'s wake stirred them at their moorings.

'Cheer up,' said Josephus. 'Only three more months and we can sail for home.'

Alityros stared down into the black, scummy waters of the harbour. 'My career's ruined, you know,' he said. 'By the time we get back, no one will even remember who I am.'

'So long as the emperor does, you'll be all right,' Josephus replied.

'Assuming he's still emperor,' said Alityros, watching distractedly as a dead dog drifted slowly astern.

'You'll have to hope so,' added Giora, slapping him on the back, otherwise you'll have to spend the rest of your days traipsing around the arse ends of the empire with Josephus here.'

'Perish the thought,' he replied with a shudder.

Later that evening, Josephus gathered Gubs and his two friends around one of the long wooden forms in the fleet mess which was to be their home for the remaining months of winter. Darkness had fallen early under the leaden skies and he set a ring of oil lamps and candles around the squares of papyrus which he spread out on the table.

'You asked to see this, Gubs,' he said. 'And I've even created a special version for military use, but we'll come on to that later. By my reckoning, there are seven leaders of the Chrestos cult still alive: Simon Kefas, who's known in the cult as Peter; Paul who changed his name from Saul; Philippos; Matityahu or Matthew if you prefer; Didymus, known as Thomas; Yehudas who sometimes goes by the name of Thaddeus and finally, his sidekick, Simon Kananaios. I call them the "Seven Stars", and each one of them is going to fall.'

'So how does this message system of yours work?' asked Gubs.

'For each of the targets there's a separate grid that allows you to encrypt and decrypt messages. Each man is assigned to one of the stars in the constellation of Ursa Major, that way we don't have to use names and even if one of the grids falls into the wrong hands, no one will be any the wiser.' Josephus looked around at each one in turn to make sure the message had sunk in, his face lit from below, which in the echoing darkness of the mess hall gave him an appearance of demonic fanaticism.

'The cipher for Paul is different, for obvious reasons,' he continued.

'And that's the one I think you'll like, Gubs. But let's start with the first one: Peter, represented by *Phecda*: that's the star at the bottom left corner of the body of Ursa Major.' He spread out a papyrus sheet on top of which was a simple drawing of the constellation with the relevant star surrounded by a circle. Underneath lay a grid, with the twenty three letters of the Latin alphabet written left to right along the top, and from top to bottom down the side to form a matrix with 529 squares: in each square was a letter.

'Right, gather round and pay attention,' said Josephus. 'This is how to use the grids and the key.'

At first his friends were baffled by the logic but gradually they grasped that each letter in the encrypted text was represented by two letters and to decode the message, all the reader had to do was find the letter represented by the row and column pairs. 'So,' said Josephus, 'If you want to send a message about Peter that starts with the letter "E", pick any old "E" from the body of the grid – here's one, at the intersection of row H and column N – and write down the letters corresponding to the row and column: HN.'

'And so when I receive the message,' said Gubs. 'All I have to do to read it is go to row H, column N and see what letter's at the intersection.'

'You've got it in one,' said Josephus. 'Or, on the same grid the person writing the message could've used "S" and "O".'

Gubs ran his finger along row "S" until he got to column "O". 'Which gives us another letter E.' He looked up and grinned. 'This is fantastic, Josephus, and it's dead easy too. Even the dimmest of my crew could use this.'

Josephus moved quickly through the grids for the next five stars before arriving at the grid for Paul. 'Now, for the last one,' continued Josephus, laying a new grid over the previous one, 'you're going to have to concentrate. Paul is represented by the star *Merak*; bottom right of the Bear's body.' He tapped the circled star with his finger to emphasise his point. 'As you'll see, the grid is different. Instead of the letters in the squares being all jumbled up, here they're in order. Take a look.'

	A	B	C	D	E	F	G	H	I	K	L	M	N	O	P	Q	R	S	T	V	W	X	Z
A	A	B	C	D	E	F	G	H	I	K	L	M	N	O	P	Q	R	S	T	V	W	X	Z
B	B	C	D	E	F	G	H	I	K	L	M	N	O	P	Q	R	S	T	V	W	X	Z	A
C	C	D	E	F	G	H	I	K	L	M	N	O	P	Q	R	S	T	V	W	X	Z	A	B
D	D	E	F	G	H	I	K	L	M	N	O	P	Q	R	S	T	V	W	X	Z	A	B	C
E	E	F	G	H	I	K	L	M	N	O	P	Q	R	S	T	V	W	X	Z	A	B	C	D
F	F	G	H	I	K	L	M	N	O	P	Q	R	S	T	V	W	X	Z	A	B	C	D	E
G	G	H	I	K	L	M	N	O	P	Q	R	S	T	V	W	X	Z	A	B	C	D	E	F
H	H	I	K	L	M	N	O	P	Q	R	S	T	V	W	X	Z	A	B	C	D	E	F	G
I	I	K	L	M	N	O	P	Q	R	S	T	V	W	X	Z	A	B	C	D	E	F	G	H
K	K	L	M	N	O	P	Q	R	S	T	V	W	X	Z	A	B	C	D	E	F	G	H	I
L	L	M	N	O	P	Q	R	S	T	V	W	X	Z	A	B	C	D	E	F	G	H	I	K
M	M	N	O	P	Q	R	S	T	V	W	X	Z	A	B	C	D	E	F	G	H	I	K	L
N	N	O	P	Q	R	S	T	V	W	X	Z	A	B	C	D	E	F	G	H	I	K	L	M
O	O	P	Q	R	S	T	V	W	X	Z	A	B	C	D	E	F	G	H	I	K	L	M	N
P	P	Q	R	S	T	V	W	X	Z	A	B	C	D	E	F	G	H	I	K	L	M	N	O
Q	Q	R	S	T	V	W	X	Z	A	B	C	D	E	F	G	H	I	K	L	M	N	O	P
R	R	S	T	V	W	X	Z	A	B	C	D	E	F	G	H	I	K	L	M	N	O	P	Q
S	S	T	V	W	X	Z	A	B	C	D	E	F	G	H	I	K	L	M	N	O	P	Q	R
T	T	V	W	X	Z	A	B	C	D	E	F	G	H	I	K	L	M	N	O	P	Q	R	S
V	V	W	X	Z	A	B	C	D	E	F	G	H	I	K	L	M	N	O	P	Q	R	S	T
W	W	X	Z	A	B	C	D	E	F	G	H	I	K	L	M	N	O	P	Q	R	S	T	V
X	X	Z	A	B	C	D	E	F	G	H	I	K	L	M	N	O	P	Q	R	S	T	V	W
Z	Z	A	B	C	D	E	F	G	H	I	K	L	M	N	O	P	Q	R	S	T	V	W	X

'Provided you don't use "AE" every time you want to use the letter "E" you could probably get away with using this grid as it stands. However, what I've done is to make sure that any message sent using this method can never be read by anyone without the key. Here's how it works. I take it you're all familiar with *Caesar's Gallic Wars*?'

'Painfully so,' said Alityros, rolling his eyes. Our magister was a brute and used to beat me black and blue.'

'I thought you liked that sort of thing,' quipped Gubs.

Alityros pouted, 'Well there are limits, you know…'

Josephus showed them another piece of papyrus on the top half of which were written the first few lines of Book 1:

"*Gallia est omnis divisa in partes tres, qvarvm vnam incolvnt Belgae, aliam Aqvitani, tertiam qvi ipsorvm lingva Celtae, nostra Galli appellantvr. Hi omnes lingva, institvtis, legibvs inter se differvnt."*

He uncovered the bottom half. 'Now, take out the spaces between the letters and you get this.'

"galliaestomnisdivisainpartestresqvarvmvnamincolvntbelgaealiamaqvita nitertiamqviipsorvmlingvaceltaenostragalliappellantvrhiomneslingvainst itvtislegibvsintersediffervnt"

'That's the key that locks the message from prying eyes.'

Giora scratched his head. 'I'm sorry, Josephus, you've just lost me,' he said.

'Don't worry, it's dead easy. I'll explain. Suppose we want to send a message, itself taken from Gallic Wars.' Underneath, Josephus had written:

"Horvm omnivm fortissimi svnt Belgae": "the bravest of all these are the Belgae."

With a flourish, Josephus produced yet another piece of Papyrus. 'Let's just look at the first two words with the spaces taken out.' By the light of the guttering oil lamps they read "horvmomnivm". 'Now write the key underneath it and you get this. Plain text on top, key underneath: got it?' They all nodded.

h	o	r	v	m	o	m	n	l	v	m
g	a	l	l	i	a	e	s	t	o	m

'Now here's the clever bit. We encode the first letter of our message, "H" using the row given by the key, in this case "G": so where row G and column H intersect we get O from the grid and our encoded message looks like this.'

Message	h	o	r	v	m	o	m	n	i	v	m
Key	g	a	l	l	i	a	e	s	t	o	m
Code	o	o	d	h	v	o	q	f	d	k	x

'So when you receive "oodhvoqfdkx", to read it you just reverse the process using the key and the grid. Then all you have to do then is work out where the gaps between the words go. Provided you've got a copy of the Gallic Wars to hand, you can always decode any message.'

'Hold on a minute,' said Gubs. 'What if the message is longer than the key?'

Josephus smiled. 'Easy, you just repeat the key from the beginning. If the key was something short like, oh, I don't know, "CANIS", say, then you just keep repeating it so it would look like this.' He dipped the worn metal nib into the ink pot and wrote on a corner of the papyrus.

Message	h	o	r	v	m	o	m	n	i	v	m
Key		c	a	n	i	s	c	a	n	i	s	c

'The important thing to remember, is that the longer the key, the safer the code. I'm confident that what I've come up with will never be broken.'

Chapter Twenty-two

William Sunday University, Bibb County, Alabama

That the Reverend John Mortlock was not happy was plain to see. Illuminated like a Raphael saint by the light slanting through the stained glass windows of the refectory, he stood up and thumped the table, gesturing towards Irvine who sat at its head acting as chairman of the thirty-strong group. From their heavy frames set at regular intervals along the wood-panelled walls, the censorious faces of William Sunday's founders and benefactors gazed down on the debate.

'You told us your student body was made up of pious and disciplined young men, not thieves and racists. This isn't the publicity you promised,' shouted Mortlock, pausing to wipe a trail of spittle from his chin. 'The whole evangelical movement is all over the press and TV with us looking like fools. That's the last thing we needed.'

Irvine remained impassive and sat fiddling with one of his gold cuff-links, not even looking up in the face of the tirade.

'Sit down, John, and please don't raise your voice,' he said. 'I grant you that through no fault of our own, the evangelical movement in general and this great university in particular have been damaged by the actions of two well-intentioned but foolish young men who committed a serious crime. You can be assured that we are co-operating fully with the authorities.' Irvine looked up as though seeking higher inspiration and his voice moved down half a register for maximum impact. 'Sadly, one of them, a highly intelligent and diligent student, paid the ultimate price for his folly and we can only hope and pray that the good Lord will have mercy upon his soul.'

Mortlock leapt to his feet again, provoking a chorus of tutting from the other members. 'Andrew, we weren't born yesterday. Do you really expect us to believe that a fragment from a hoard stolen in Italy just happened to turn up on William Sunday University's doorstep by chance? Go tell it to the Marines.'

Irvine turned his attention away from the sleeve of his shirt and fixed Mortlock with an icy blue gaze. 'I'll say it again for those of you who haven't been paying attention for the last hour. Professor Sumter was present in Pompeii at the invitation of the Italian authorities, working on a priceless body of previously unknown first-century document fragments when the robbery happened. Somehow, and I'm hoping we'll find out how very soon, these young men were able to obtain some of the pages from the thieves. I can only assume money changed hands – maybe bad things were done with good intentions, who knows?' He raised his hand once more in response to a volley of questions. 'There'll be plenty of time for questions later, so please let me finish. Now, I've shown you copies of the digital photographs the Professor managed to take before the theft; sadly, he was only able to record a fraction of what's now been lost, but its significance is beyond description.'

The representative of the Kentucky United Evangelist Congress raised his hand to speak. 'But, Doctor Irvine, the Reverend Mortlock has a good point. The good name of this college, and by association the entire evangelical movement, has been dragged through the mud by the media.' More nodding of grey heads. 'Like it or not, these two students of yours have gotten us connected with the theft in Italy and the media have already found us guilty by association. What do you propose to do?'

'Why, to turn it to our advantage of course.' Irvine's words set off another buzz of conversation. His smile brimmed with self-satisfaction. 'We show Christian penitence for having missed the completely unsuitable nature of the two young men responsible and we use our new-found position in the media spotlight to escalate the battle against those who seek to undermine the truth of the Gospels. We're going to take the fight to them and we're going to win.'

A snort of derision came from the far end of the table. 'So how's that gonna work? Are you telling us two of your students went off the rails, got everyone here involved with receiving stolen goods and now you're going to try and spin your way out of it?' asked an octogenarian pastor, his voice barely audible above the general hubbub.

The same smile; this time edged with steel. 'There's no need for spin as you put it, sir. It was only as he began the arduous work of deciphering and translating the texts, that Professor Sumter realised the importance of what he'd found. For reasons I'm sure you'll all understand, not least of which are the robberies from Pompeii and also from this very university, the Professor decided to keep the knowledge of the finds confined to a small group of people, including the two students who were helping him translate and catalogue them. It appears that the zeal of youth over-rode common sense and somehow they made contact with the criminals in a misguided quest to retrieve the rest of the finds.'

The piping voice cut across the muttering that broke out when Irvine stopped talking. 'That's all well and good, boy, but you still ain't answered my question.'

Irvine had to shout to make himself heard. 'Gentlemen, if you please. You asked me how this works, sir, and I'll explain everything, but right now – and I make no excuses for repeating this – you must understand that we are under attack, gentlemen. This is war, make no mistake. The forces of Satan have rallied against us before and this time their weapons are bogus science and silver-tongued tricksters well versed in misusing the media – the Christian church has beaten worse foes than this before and in answer to your question, we make it work by turning their own arms against them.'

The old pastor shook his grey locks. 'Well, that sure sounds good, son, but how will I know the elephant when I see it?'

Irvine smiled, waiting just long enough for the tension to build before replying. 'Evidence. I'm from Missouri, so show me. Understand?'

'Nope, not a darn word,' drawled the veteran, turning up his hearing aid and causing it to emit a high-pitched squeal. 'We're simple folk in my part of Georgia, son: the flag, this great country of ours and the King James Bible; outside o' that, we're inclined to struggle.'

Irvine levered his angular frame out of the chair and began to pace the oak boards of the refectory. He turned once more to confront the expectant faces looking up at him. 'In this modern, secular world, the need for evidence – tangible, laboratory-tested, repeatable proof – has elbowed faith aside but now we get to play them at their own game.' He paused, his taut features lit as though by an inner radiance. 'What I am about to tell you is nothing short of earth-shattering.' He stopped once more: perfect silence, the assembled clergymen scarcely daring to breathe. 'Thanks to the documents that Professor Sumter was able to photograph, we can now validate the existence of a cannon of early Christian writing that proves beyond any doubt that the New Testament represents a true, eye-witness account of our Saviour's life and works. Clear, irrefutable proof that our faith is based in solid, verifiable reality and not, as some would have the gullible believe, on the few scraps that science hasn't gotten around to working out yet.'

Irvine's voice was drowned out by an excited buzz of chatter. 'And what's so wrong with faith?' called out a cadaverous individual whose plucked-chicken neck would have fitted five times over into his ecclesiastical collar.

'Nothing,' replied Irvine, turning to face the questioner. 'It's what's sustained us for the last two thousand years. But we've all heard it, haven't we? "Faith in something that's not there" – that's what our detractors say of us. But we know they're wrong – hey, the President said so himself on TV not ten days ago – only now we have the means to prove it and at the same time show them we have something they don't; the one thing they always demand: tangible evidence.'

'What if Sumter's wrong?' asked the representative of the Florida Baptist Union in tones that left his opinion of the great man in no doubt.

'Professor Sumter, if you please, Henry,' said Irvine, bringing up a new series of images on the projector screen. 'He isn't wrong. These are photographs he took of the documents at Pompeii before they were stolen.' Heads nodded around the table in approval. 'Probably like me, you don't know Aramaic or ancient Greek well enough to understand them, but when his work is complete and the findings published, we'll have unshakeable evidence that Titus Flavius Josephus was in possession of writings that prove the Saviour's divinity beyond any shadow of a doubt.' He paused for effect, nodding gravely as he paced in front of the raised dais. 'The prophecies are coming true, gentlemen, and I don't think it's an exaggeration to say that we may be nearing the End of Days.' A chorus of "amen to that" rippled around the assembly.

'Let's see 'em argue with that,' shouted Mortlock, banging a bony fist on the table in delight. 'When do we let 'em have it?'

'All in good time,' replied Irvine with a half-smile. 'We've waited two thousand years for this after all. Even if the authorities don't recover the remaining documents, Professor Sumter is confident that we'll soon have sufficient material to go ahead with a full disclosure of the facts.'

'What about *The Seven Stars*?' shouted Florida, struggling to make himself heard above the din of whooping and back-slapping.

Irvine returned him a knowing look, confident now that the group was under his spell. He called for quiet and waited, hands clasped behind his back, for complete silence. 'For those of you who didn't catch that, our brother in Christ from the State of Florida has raised the question of *The Seven Stars*. You'll be pleased to know that Professor Sumter has news for us there too. It appears that a work of that name was indeed written by Titus Flavius Josephus, who, as you know, was no friend of our Saviour nor of his apostles.' He stopped pacing and wagged an admonitory finger in the air as though trying to scold the Judean from down the years. 'A Jew,' he spat, leaving his listeners in no doubt of what that meant. 'A man, remember, who by his own admission was a turncoat, a liar, a traitor to his own people and who did his utmost to suppress the truth of the Messiah's life and resurrection.'

By the end of his tirade, his audience's reaction to Josephus' name was like the greeting accorded to a pantomime villain. Waiting once more for them to quieten down, he continued. 'Professor Sumter believes that Josephus may have begun work on *The Seven Stars* in response to writings subsequently found in the remains of his villa at Pompeii, the very writings that prove the truth of the New Testament. So ashamed was he of what he was doing, Josephus decided to write most of it in a code of his own devising – many later versions exist and these mis-transcribed copies are what we all know as "The Devil's Codex" – but thanks to the work done at this very university, we are now able to read some of it and we'll shortly be showing the unbelievers that it was nothing more than self-justifying cant from a bitter man who felt he'd been denied his true status in life.'

'So what are we supposed to do?' asked sceptical Florida. 'Keep this stuff quiet or go tell our parishioners?'

'Every journey starts with a single step,' replied Irvine, basking in Sumter's reflected limelight. 'And that single step will start with each one of you. The Professor would prefer you to wait for now – there's nothing to be gained by rushing. But once he gives the signal, word of mouth borne on the wings of prayer will have the media beating a path to your doors.' He nodded to the small group of TV evangelists sitting just to his right; sleek, contented creatures with capped, whitened teeth and expensive hair implants. 'And you, gentlemen, will be key to our success.' Four well-practised smiles shone back at him in response. 'What's more,' he added. 'I'm sure that success will be amply rewarded in this world as well as the next.'

'Amen to that,' they chorused in return.

Irvine looked around the room with satisfaction: nothing succeeds like telling people what they want to hear.

From his vantage point behind a half-open fire door Donald Sumter had heard every word. Just a few loose ends to tie up and then they could begin.

***

Pompeii

'So where is she?'

Moretti looked across the table at his dinner companions – two short, heavily-built men of indeterminate age, their faces wrecked by a diet of cigarettes and alcohol. One was almost entirely bald and his pate shone under the stark light of the bare neon tubes overhead. The other, as if in deliberate contrast, sported a full head of jet black hair, combed straight back from a heavily-lined forehead in an Elvis quiff. The last of the diners had gone home and the owner of the restaurant began piling chairs onto tables but making sure to keep well away from the trio.

'She told me she was going to stay another couple of nights in Rome and then come back here,' said Moretti.

'One of you is lying,' said Elvis. 'How about you tell us who it is?'

Moretti looked at them pleadingly. 'I'm telling you the truth, that's all I know.'

Elvis shook his head and smiled in the same way a crocodile might smile at its next meal. 'Then how do you explain that she checked out of the hotel but hasn't been seen at the airport? We've got people watching Fiumicino and Ciampino and they'd have seen her for sure. You sure she didn't tell you where she was going and why?'

'Yes, Rome. No, London... I mean, that was after she'd come back here... she didn't say why.... Look I've told you all I know.' Flustered, he put his head in his hands and tried to think.

'Francesco, be calm,' said the bald one, reaching out a bear-like paw and resting it just a little too heavily on his shoulder. 'We want to help you. You want to be with Anna, so we know you'll help us. We're not asking you to break any laws.'

A bit late for that, thought Moretti, racking his brains for an excuse to change the subject. 'Someone from the police collected her things from the Hotel Sorrento so we know she's not coming back here,' Elvis said.

'So why are the TPC taking so long to question her and why Rome rather than here or Naples? Come on, Francesco, what story does she have that takes three days to tell? What does she know that you don't?'

'How the hell am I supposed to know? I'm not a mind-reader!' shouted Moretti.

'Shh, not so loud,' said Elvis with a smile that was half-way to an unpleasant leer. 'You'll upset the other clients.' Moretti assumed this was the nearest the man ever got to a joke and glanced over at the owner who abruptly looked away, busying himself with his broom, studiously rearranging the dust in between the cigarette burns on the cheap laminate flooring.

'OK,' said Elvis. 'Let's try again. When Lombardi was questioning you two, what did he ask, what was his angle?'

Moretti shook his head, trying to show a casual indifference he was a long way from feeling. 'He gave the impression they knew who robbed the dig and smashed up the lab, but he said they didn't know why.'

'And what did you say?'

'I said the robbery looked like a classic *tombaroli* job, but I couldn't understand why anyone would destroy the lab and our entire IT system.'

'And Kemble?' asked Elvis. 'What did she tell them that was so important that they took her to Rome and left you behind?'

Moretti thumped his elbows down onto the grimy plastic tablecloth and buried his forehead in his hands once more. 'Look, I've told you a dozen times, she's a palaeographer; an historian, a linguist, an expert on ancient languages and on the chemical and biological process of dating and validating documents. She's one of the best in the world. That's why I asked her to come and help: this find could've been globally important.'

'But that still doesn't explain why they've been keeping her for all this time in Rome.'

Moretti looked up, fixing Elvis straight in the eye. 'Then why don't you leave me the fuck alone and go and ask her yourself.' He immediately cursed himself for saying it.

'What an excellent suggestion,' said the bald one, shooting a quick glance at Elvis. 'Do you know where she works?'

Moretti half choked and took a deep breath, trying to maintain his crumbling facade of bored irritation. 'Sure. Oxford University. Why?' The look on the bald man's face told him his worst fears were about to be realised. Please, God, no, not that. 'And where does she live? Do you have an address?'

'No, I've no idea where she lives,' he lied, fighting back a wave of nausea at the thought of what could happen to him and possibly to Anna if these two caught him out in such a simple untruth.

'Then I suggest you find out for us,' said Elvis, all vestiges of humour gone from his voice. 'Remember, your loyalty is to Anna and not to Flora Kemble. We just want to have a quiet word with her that's all.'

Just like the "quiet word" you had with Greco before you slit his throat, thought Moretti.

The following day, the subject of their conversation, travelling on her own passport, checked in at Fiumicino for the 1145 BA flight to London. A queue of frustrated travellers streamed back from the only two security checkpoints which were manned. Just before her turn came she noticed two men standing on the departures side of the security barrier. The years fell away and her training kicked in: something in the way they looked at her wasn't right. Flora was used to men giving her the once-over, but this was different – nothing she could describe, just different. Heart pounding, she swallowed hard and tried to remember Mike Hayek's words about the presence of *The Friends:* nothing about these two looked at all friendly. She let her gaze rest on them just a fraction too long. One nodded to the other and the two men disappeared though a service door. This didn't look right.

Mind racing, she considered an about-turn and a dash for the taxi rank but as she craned her neck, looking for the easiest route to safety without drawing attention to herself, she spotted the second pair. No doubt about it, no need for training where these two were concerned: they didn't even look away when her eye caught theirs. She'd seen armed police on arrival in the booking hall so there should be others air-side: find one and stand next to him until the flight's called, that'll work, she thought.

Once through the detector arch the security guard gave her the all clear and she rushed over to the moving belt, fumbling with nerves, to gather up her belongings.

Flora glanced to her left, but to her horror there was no sign of them. Where the hell were they? With trembling hands she pulled at the zip of the laptop bag which refused to budge and so leaving it half open, bundled her things under one arm, planning her dash into what she hoped was the safety of the crowds in departures when she felt a hand grasp her arm. Spinning round in horror, she was about to scream for help when she did a double-take. Rather than the two men who'd been watching her, she saw what she could only think of later as an unmade bed. The man was over six feet tall and with such a huge pot belly that he seemed to be in imminent danger of falling over forwards. His hair stuck out from beneath an ancient straw hat in frizzy white clumps and his clothes, right down to the odd socks poking between the straps of his sandals, looked like the result of a bungled night-time raid on a charity shop. 'Flora!' he boomed, hugging her so tightly to his chest that she couldn't breathe. Then, 'Just pretend you know me from Oxford, I'm a friend of Giles Smith's,' he whispered. 'How simply splendid,' he said aloud. 'What a lovely surprise.'

'Who are –?' she started to say but he cut her off.

'I do so hope you're flying to London, we've got so much catching up to do. I simply can't remember the last time I saw you – absolutely ages,' he shouted, kissing her on both cheeks before linking his arm through hers and leading her in a wide sweep round the two men. 'Sorry for the abrupt arrival but you may've been about to have unwanted company,' he said under his voice as they hurried along through the slow-moving herd of passengers grazing in front of the airport shops.

'Thanks. You mean those two by the security post?'

'Yes, and there were two more in the queue behind you. We thought for one horrible moment you were going to make a run for it.'

'Is that the royal "we"?' she asked in a weak attempt at humour. Her new friend made no answer and steered her out of sight along a service corridor towards a door marked with a red and white *Ingresso Vietato* sign. He opened the door with a swipe card, only releasing her arm once they were inside.

'No, I'm not alone, it's just that we weren't expecting any of them to turn up behind you like that. Nearly caught us on the hop: it was the pair by security who were our biggest concern.'

Flora stopped and turned to look at her rescuer. 'If it's not an indelicate question, why are you disguised as a scarecrow? And seeing as you've probably just saved my life, might I at least know who I should be thanking?'

He treated her to a smile and a shake of the head. 'One question too many, Miss Kemble. I could give you a name but firstly it wouldn't be mine and secondly it wouldn't mean anything to you. As for the scarecrow routine as you put it, the idea was to make me look like an archaeologist: from what I've seen of the ones on TV I think I've got the look down to a T, though I say it myself.'

Flora looked at him, unable to hide a look of amusement as the adrenalin drained slowly from her system. 'I'm a palaeographer actually, not really a proper field archaeologist.'

'Yes, I know that, but none of us knew what one of those looked like so we settled for archaeologist. I thought the socks and sandals were a good touch, don't you?'

Flora smiled at him. 'It's very realistic, believe me.'

'The AISI boys thought it was hilarious,' he said, leading her further along the windowless corridor.

'Who are the "AISI boys"?' asked Flora.

'*L'Agenzia Informazioni e Sicurezza Interna* – that's the Italian domestic intelligence agency: they've got people here too. Anyway, the last thing I wanted was to look like what I am: far better to make them think you had a chance encounter with an old chum.'

'And if you won't tell me who you are, I presume it's no good asking what you are?' Flora asked.

187

'Like I said, I'm a friend of Giles Smith's and he's very concerned that you get home safely.'

***

In a bar in Naples, Elvis answered his mobile phone. 'The London flight? Good. How many? Three?' he raised his eyebrows in surprise. 'She must have had interesting news for them then. We'll speak with her.' He rang off and nodded in satisfaction to the heavily-built bald man sitting opposite.

Chapter Twenty-three

Rome AD 64

'Shhh, don't make so much noise,' Josephus hissed at Giora.

'Well I can't see a bloody thing.' In the darkness beneath the wooden seating of the *Circus Maximus*, the disembodied voice was the only sign that his companion was still there. They crept forward, feeling their way over and around the web of beams that supported the tiered grandstand above their heads.

Josephus looked upwards: between the curving rows of seats, the stars of the constellation of Draco, winding its tail around the Great Bear, looked close enough to touch.

Although night had fallen long ago, the heat of the day radiated back at them from every solid object. A breeze from the south east had sprung up but its stifling breath only made things worse.

Edging round a brick pillar they neared their goal. In front of them, a sliver of light shone through a gap in the wooden boards forming the back wall of a row of shops, warehouses and workshops clustered under the high point of the grandstands. Barely daring to breathe, Josephus crouched down and peered through the crack into the cooper's workshop. 'What can you see?' asked Giora. Josephus motioned to him to be quiet. The interior was lit by a series of flickering oil lamps and he counted: twenty of them, all men and seated in a semi-circle facing the speaker. Standing on a barrel, and with his back to Josephus, an elderly man was speaking in heavily-accented Latin. He could only catch the odd word but the topic of his address left no doubt.

Josephus stood up and motioned for Giora to follow. 'It's him all right,' he whispered. They stole along a narrow alley separating the cooper's workshop from the neighbouring building, home to a lamp oil seller according to the sign. At the corner they stopped and waited, peering into the darkness and straining to catch the merest sound – anything that would suggest the presence of look-outs. Finally, Josephus, satisfied that the coast was clear, tapped his companion on the shoulder and they made their way through the shadows to the front of the building. 'Now,' he whispered and Giora cupped his hands to his mouth, giving the owl hooting signal for the Praetorian Guard detachment to move. Then they saw them: thirty men, each armed – like Josephus and Giora –

with the army's standard-issue short stabbing sword; ideal for close-quarter action.

Without breaking stride, a team of four guardsmen carrying a short ram used by the *Vigiles* for breaking into burning buildings, smashed down the entrance, and with a yell, the rest of the squad poured through the breach. To Josephus, this was familiar territory: as with Andreas in Patras and Nathanael Bar Talmai in Albanopolis, he'd done the detective work and now it was up to the professionals to do the physical side of the job. However, the Christians had other ideas. Well drilled, two of them pulled swords from under their cloaks and hustled the speaker, now clearly identifiable as Peter, towards the rear door of the workshop. Those still standing after the Praetorian's first assault also drew weapons and stood in a single rank, defying the soldiers to take them on. For a moment, the officer commanding the detachment hesitated but then, leading the charge, hurled himself at the Christians. Screams filled the air. Lamps, the cooper's tools and half-finished barrels were scattered left and right as the battle raged.

Suddenly, Giora grabbed Josephus' arm. 'Look,' he shouted. 'They're getting away.' All the Roman soldiers were fully occupied fighting for their lives, so with no time to explain, Josephus and Giora ran back down the alley and into the darkness beneath the grandstand. Light now streamed from the open door and ahead of them, lit by the flames of a fire from a fallen oil lamp, were three figures: two taller men were half carrying, half dragging the third, their progress hindered by the maze of struts and girders below the seats. Swords drawn, the two Judeans advanced and were nearly on them when one of the Christians turned and saw their pursuers silhouetted against the light.

They charged on, Josephus calling out into the darkness behind him as though summoning the Praetorians to his aid. Expecting the two Christians to run and abandon the elderly preacher to his fate, they received an unpleasant surprise when instead they turned on them, swords drawn.

Josephus had no combat experience and while struggling to remove the *gladius* from its sheath, he got the hilt tangled under his belt. He heard rather than saw the downward rush of his opponent's sword, and with a thud, the blade bit deep.. Josephus fell sprawling on his back. For a moment he wondered if he'd died and why, if he was still alive, he felt no pain. He looked up to see the blade embedded in one of the diagonal bracing struts and the Christian sawing up and down on the hilt to get it free. To his left, Giora and the other Christian were fighting over the same sword. Seizing his chance, Josephus rolled over, got up onto one knee, finally managing to disentangle his sword which he grasped with both hands. The Christian bore down on him, his sword blade glinting in the reflection of the fire which now engulfed the workshop. In panic, Josephus drove his weapon upwards. He thought he'd missed and was about to die when the sword-tip seemed to meet a slight resistance. It was only as the figure looming over him pitched forward onto its face, snatching the weapon's hilt from his hands, that he realised he'd run the man through.

Just a few feet away, Giora was losing and Josephus tugged at the sword to try and release it from the dead Christian's body. At last, with a nauseating sucking sound, the blade came free. Twice Josephus made to strike but held back for fear of hitting the wrong target. At last he saw his opportunity and swung the blade horizontally at the man's neck. This time, he felt the blade slice through flesh and stop as it hit something more solid. The two figures span away from each other, Giora falling backwards and the Christian lurching away into the darkness.

To Josephus' horror, Giora lay motionless. His eyes were half open and staring straight ahead. Illuminated by the light of the fire raging twenty yards behind them, Josephus could see that his face, neck and the front of his tunic were drenched in blood. He threw his arms around his friend's neck and sobbed. 'Oh, Giora, please forgive me. Oh, God, what have I done.' He pressed his face hard against Giora's, matting his own hair with blood. Suddenly he felt movement and drew back. Giora's eyelids flickered.

'I don't know what you've done, but my head hurts. Here, help me up, would you.'

'Giora! You're alive,' shouted Josephus in delight, putting his hands either side of Giora's face. 'I thought I'd killed you. Look at all this blood.'

Groggily, he sat up and felt himself over for damage. Then he blinked and squinted, trying to bring Josephus' tear-stained but beaming face into focus. 'You know,' he said after running a hand over his head. 'I don't think it's mine. Whatever you did, I think you got him.'

'Can you walk?' Josephus asked.

'I think so.' He pulled Giora to his feet and they stumbled on past the dead Christian and away from the flames which had now spread to the woodwork of the grandstand above them. They had only gone a few paces when Josephus noticed movement off to their right; crouching behind a wooden pillar and trying to lose himself in the shadows was a hunched figure.

'Stay here,' he told Giora and, unsheathing the *gladius*, moved towards the man whose name had haunted him for so many years.

Peter cowered, trying to back further into cover. 'Please don't harm me,' he said in Latin as Josephus stood over him, levelling the sword at his throat. 'I am but a humble servant of the Lord and I bring a message of love to all mankind –'

The reply which came in Aramaic cut him off short. 'A bit late for that, Simon Kefas, you two-faced old bastard. It's a pity you didn't think about "love for all mankind" when it came to my father.'

Peter's mouth dropped open at the sound of his Aramaic name. 'Y-your father? I haven't harmed anyone's father. I'm a man of peace...you're making a mistake...you must have me mixed up with someone else, my name's Peter.'

In his peripheral vision Josephus could see that Giora had joined him. He nodded in the old man's direction. 'Funny how memory fades with old age, isn't it, Giora?' Turning his attention to Peter once more, he said, 'Then let me give you a clue. Does the name Yeshua Bar Yosef mean anything to you? The one you people now call "The Christ"? The man you loved so much that you had him killed. Remember now?'

Peter stared at him in disbelief. 'Why do you take the Messiah's name in vain? Who are you?'

'I'll tell you who I am,' said Josephus, dragging him to his feet and pinning him against an upright, the tip of the sword now inches away from Peter's throat. 'I'm his son.'

'But that's not possible.'

'Oh yes it is,' said Josephus, his voice becoming a snarl. 'There are two ways it can have happened: either my mother was already pregnant when you people had him murdered by the Romans or alternatively he came back to life, as you would have the gullible believe, so perhaps he fathered me then. Which do you think, Peter? And do please be quick because I'm in a hurry to cut your guts out.'

Giora placed a hand on Josephus' shoulder. 'No, not that. Not here. Nero wants this one alive.'

Josephus lowered the sword. 'You're right. I'm sure he's got something far slower and painful in mind after all the trouble his fairy stories have caused.'

Peter shook himself free and glared at Josephus. 'The Lord is merciful and forgives all. Remember your teachings, young man. If you're who you say you are, you should know better than to threaten your elders on the basis of a distorted version of events that happened nearly thirty years ago.'

'You were a liar then and I see nothing's changed,' he said, grabbing him by the scrawny throat. 'Nero wants you alive and if I have anything to do with it, your death will be even more harrowing than the one you had inflicted on my father. But at least there's one consolation.'

'What's that?' Peter asked.

'That when you're dead and the dogs have eaten their fill of your mangy carcass, people will have more sense than to believe in any superstition based on your worthless life.'

The southerly wind drove the flames ever closer and, pushing their captive ahead of them, they rejoined the detachment of Praetorians outside the stadium. Of the original twenty who had been listening to Peter, only six had survived and three of the soldiers were dead. Four others were having their wounds tended by an army surgeon. 'I see you got him then,' said the commander. 'What happened to the other two?'

'Back under that lot,' said Josephus, indicating the blazing grandstand.

'I don't fancy the *Vigiles'* chances of putting that out in a hurry,' said the commander.

'And I don't fancy your chances when the emperor finds out how it started,' replied Giora.

'Unless of course we tell the truth. Just like you always do, eh, Peter?' Josephus said. 'We tell him the Christians started it on purpose. After all, it's just the kind of thing they'd do.'

Driven on by the wind, the fire raced through the buildings on the eastern end of the Palatine hill. Soon, the entire city was in pandemonium and the air rang with the screams and shouts of desperate Romans, some throwing furniture and valuables from upstairs windows while others frantically piled their belongings onto handcarts, all desperate to get away. In the confusion, Peter tried to escape so Giora tied his hands behind his back, keeping a tight grip on the free end of the rope and treating him to a cuff around the head. 'You were lucky, Bar Yeshua,' Peter said to Josephus, his face contorted with rage. 'Phasis is far from Rome and our friends there few in number. Take my word for it, once the Lord's elect hear of this, your days will be numbered.'

Josephus grabbed the rope and hauled it up behind Peter's back, causing him to bend almost double. 'All our days are numbered, you old fool. Have you forgotten everything you learned?' he said. 'You're an apostate, a liar and a murderer. My father was a good man: an aristocrat and a scholar, a man whose boots you weren't fit to lick. Now move!' he shouted, giving Peter a vicious kick up the backside.

It took them over an hour to cover the few hundred yards from the *Circus Maximus* to Nero's private apartments, their progress hindered by the blaze that had now spread to the buildings at the eastern end of the palace complex itself. Giora handed Peter over to the custody of the Praetorian Guard commander while Josephus set off to report in person.

'So the first of the seven stars has fallen,' said the emperor, his face lit by the inferno which raged almost directly beneath the balcony on which he leant. 'You must be feeling very pleased with yourself, Josephus.'

'My only hope is that you are satisfied with our work, sir, and that you'll continue to give it your support.'

'Oh of course I will,' said Nero, still with his back to Josephus, unable to tear his eyes away from the spectacle of the fire. 'I haven't had so much fun in years. And you say the Christians started it deliberately?'

'Yes, sir. Peter himself gave the command.'

At last, Nero turned round to look at him, leaning against the marble balustrade, everything around them suffused with the glow of the flames. 'Seneca was right about these people. They tell me only six of his followers survived. Is that true?' Josephus nodded. 'Seems such a pity; I always think mass executions are so much more fun. What do you think best fits the crime, the arena or crucifixion?'

'It's not for me to say, sir,' replied Josephus, anxious not to overplay his hand. 'But given that Peter was responsible for having my father scourged and then crucified, well, it seems only fitting –'

'That he should suffer the same fate.' Nero clapped his hands. 'I think that accords perfectly with Roman justice at it's most merciful – a splendid idea – would you like to watch? You can even hammer the nails in if you like.'

'I'll pass if I may, sir. I'm a little squeamish.'

Nero shook his head. 'You Jews never cease to amaze me. The man was responsible for your father's death, you've been hunting him for years and now you don't want to take part in his punishment? Still, each to his own I suppose, but you'll be missing a treat. Now tell me, who's next on the list?'

'Paul.'

'Ah yes. Paul.' said Nero. 'Proculus tells me that if it hadn't been for the crew of a Black Sea Fleet *liburna*, you wouldn't have made it home because of Paul.' Without waiting for Josephus' reply, the emperor

194

turned on his heel and wandered distractedly in through the doors as though searching for something he'd forgotten but couldn't quite remember what it was. Moments later he returned, carrying a lyre. 'Are you familiar with *The Sack of Ilium*, Josephus?' he asked.

'I've studied the works of Homer, if that's what you mean, sir,' he replied, with a puzzled look on his face.

'No, the ballad, the one by Arctinus of Miletus. He was one of Homer's pupils.'

'Can't say I've ever heard it, sir.' Josephus cursed himself the moment the words left his mouth: he knew what was coming next. Sure enough, with a beatific smile the emperor raised the lyre and began to strum, singing in a high falsetto of King Priam gazing down on his burning city and of the rage of Athena at the rape of Cassandra by Ajax of Locris. At least he's most of the way through the Trojan War, thought Josephus, if he'd started with the judgement of Paris, I could be here all night. For a moment his spirits rose as help, in the form of two palace officials, rushed onto the balcony with news of further outbreaks of fire in the eastern wing of the building, but the sulphurous look on Nero's face at their interruption sent them scurrying away again.

Seizing his chance, with a quick, 'Excuse me, sir, there's something I must do,' Josephus ran after them.

Before Nero had chance to call him back Josephus was out of earshot. The corridors of the palace had begun to fill with a haze of smoke and the smell of destruction was everywhere as he hurried down the steps to the Praetorian guardroom. There he found Giora who was toasting their success with the squad who'd raided the meeting. Peter was locked in a cell, scowling and cursing at anyone who came near. The detachment commander invited Josephus to join the party and so he went to find something to drink from.

On entering the stone-flagged pantry adjoining the kitchens he was surprised to see a balding, heavy-jowled man – he looked about sixty to Josephus – sitting on a stool with a half-empty Samian drinking vessel in one hand and his other cupping a strong, upward-tilted chin. What surprised him even more were the two broad crimson stripes – a colour the Romans called purple – that ran vertically from the shoulders to the bottom hem of the man's tunic: the mark of a senator. 'Can I be of assistance, sir?' asked Josephus. 'Are you lost?'

'Lost? I wish I was,' said the senator, looking up at him with sorrowful brown eyes. 'I've been waiting down here for the last ten days.'

'What are you waiting for? Perhaps I can help.'

He made a noise that was something between a snort and a laugh. 'I think I'm past helping, young man. I'm waiting on the emperor's pleasure: sooner or later I find out what he's going to do with me.'

Josephus looked at him nonplussed. 'But aren't you? –'

'A senator? Yes I am. Titus Flavius Vespasianus, better known as Vespasian.'

Josephus in turn introduced himself. 'I thought you were governor of North Africa,' he said.

'I am,' he replied, 'Or rather I was until a few weeks ago. My tenure's over and I was due to join the emperor's personal staff until this happened.'

Curious, Josephus pulled up a stool and sat next to him. 'If it's not an impertinent question, sir, until what happened?'

Vespasian gave another ironic laugh. 'Until I became so highly esteemed in Nero's eyes that he invited me to one of his recitals.' Their eyes met: fellow sufferers, there was no need for either of them to risk saying what they thought. 'I'm not as young as I used to be, I hadn't fully recovered from the voyage and, if I'm honest, I'd fortified myself for the ordeal – sorry, for the concert, with rather too much wine.'

'And you fell asleep?'

'Worse,' said Vespasian, 'I'm told I snored so loudly that I drowned out his singing. Anyway, Nero was furious and sent me down here to wait on his pleasure while he went down to Antium to give a private recital at his villa.'

'If it's any use, he got back yesterday,' said Josephus.

'Do you know him?'

Josephus chose his answer carefully. 'I wouldn't flatter myself that far, sir,' he replied. 'But I have the privilege of working directly for the emperor and he seems satisfied with what I do.'

'I don't suppose you could put a word in for me do you?' asked Vespasian.

Josephus tried to hide his surprise; a senator asking a favour of a foreign hireling. He hesitated. 'Er, I'll do what I can, sir, it's just –'

Vespasian looked him straight in the eye. 'It's just that you want to know what's in it for you, isn't that right, Josephus?' He made no reply and the senator continued. 'You can't have too many friends in this city. Who you know is more important than what you know.'

'The lady Poppaea said the same to me the other day, sir.'

Vespasian nodded. 'Then she was right. Even emperors come and go. You help me out of this jam, young man, and you won't be the loser for it. I have a long memory.'

'I'll do my best, sir,' replied Josephus, getting to his feet. Despite the drunken barracking and cat-calls he declined the offer to join the celebration, and with a final glance into the cells at his father's nemesis, retraced his steps along the maze of corridors towards the imperial apartments.

Chapter Twenty-four

Pompeii, the present day

The three men sat on the hard stone tiers of the Pompeii arena. Ahead of them to the north, just visible above a row of umbrella pines, the summit of Vesuvius loomed out of the haze. 'Her number just keeps bouncing to voicemail,' said Moretti. 'I've left messages, sent her e-mails, tried to call the university. Nothing.'

Elvis and the bald one looked at each other. 'OK, that's good, just don't overdo it,' the former said. 'Tell me, Francesco, how well do you know her colleagues at Oxford?'

He shrugged. 'Not well. I met a few of them when I was over for a conference last year, but that's all.'

'How about this one?' Moretti frowned as he studied the first photograph.

'Never seen him before.'

'This one?'

'No.'

'How about the third one?'

Moretti peered at the image: tall, overweight, middle-aged, florid English complexion, frizzy hair that looked as though it had been cut by the council, and dressed like a flood victim.

'Definitely not,' he replied, handing it back with a shake of his head. 'I think I'd have remembered someone like that. 'Where was this taken?'

'Fiumicino. Two days ago.'

'Who is he?' asked Moretti.

'That's the problem,' said the bald one. 'We don't know. She checked in as normal and was just picking her things up after going through security when this character greeted her like a long-lost uncle, said something about being on the same flight and then never left her side.'

'So she bumps into a friend at the airport. It happens. What of it?'

'What he means,' cut in Elvis, 'is that before our people could get close to her, she and this haystack disappeared out of sight. We're not even sure she boarded the flight. If she did, she certainly didn't go through the gate with the rest of the passengers. We've got lots of friends at Fiumicino – reliable people – and not only does Flora Kemble disappear into thin air but there's no trace of a passenger fitting the description of her long-lost colleague boarding a flight that day either. Once is coincidence, twice stinks. We need your help, Francesco. Find out what she's doing, what she knows, who she's working with.'

Moretti had prepared what he was about to say. He'd lain awake in his stuffy flat the entire night endlessly rehearsing and refining it. He took a deep breath. 'No, gentlemen, enough is enough. I've already told you everything I know and all of it's true. You've offered to help me financially in order to get back with Anna and the kids. Don't think I'm ungrateful...but I've been thinking –'

'Clearly not thinking straight, Francesco –' said Elvis.

'Just let me finish. I've decided I don't need your help any more and it's clear that I can't help *you*, so if you'll excuse me, gentlemen, I've got work to do.' He stood up to leave but the bald one caught him by the arm. In the other hand he held a semi-automatic pistol.

'Just sit down and stop being so bloody silly. You were born in Naples, right?'

Moretti looked at him with contempt. 'Sure. What's that got to do with it?'

'Everything. Now sit down.' Moretti sat. 'You of all people should know how things work round here. You're forgetting that we're the ones who decide when it's over, not you. Co-operate with us and what we discussed as a loan could well become, let's say... a gift. Screw us around and people near to you could get hurt.'

Moretti's face went the same colour as the pale stonework of the arena, his hands bunched in rage. 'You leave Anna out of this. If you've got a problem, you sort it out with me –'

'Be careful what you wish for,' Elvis said with one of his crocodile smiles. He nodded to the bald one who slipped the gun back into his pocket. 'You're right you know,' he said with a shrug. 'Maybe you can't help us, or maybe you don't want to. Either way, all I'd ask is that before you go you take a look at some more photos.' He handed Moretti an envelope. He recoiled as though it were toxic. 'Go on, open it, it won't bite you,' Elvis said.

Moretti slid open the flap to reveal a deck of photographs all showing the same subject: Anna. Anna cycling alongside the river Po with their youngest child in a carrier on the back of the bike, Anna walking with the children in the Giardini Reali, Anna out shopping under the porticos of the Via Roma, Anna outside her parents' house.

'You bastards,' he said, turning on them, his face a mask of pure,

199

undiluted hatred. 'Touch my family and I swear to you that I'll –'

Elvis looked at him like something he'd just stepped in. 'That you'll do what, Francesco?' his voice dripping with contempt. 'Please remember who you're talking to and don't make silly threats. Just do as we ask; nobody gets hurt and I promise we'll help you get your little family back together again. It'll be just like old times, you'll see. Now, first things first: we want you to find Miss Kemble for us.'

Without a word Moretti handed the envelope back to Elvis and lowered his head almost to between his knees, his thick black fringe flopping down over his face and hiding his tears.

***

Flora took a taxi for the short journey from Oxford station to her house near the Iffley road. It was all very odd: her front garden, far from being overgrown, had been tended and when she turned the key in the lock, instead of having to push the door against a mountain of junk mail, it swung open unhindered to show the envelopes neatly stacked on the hall table next to a vase of freshly-cut flowers. Curiouser and curiouser, said Alice, Flora thought, leaving her bags in the hall and making her way into the sitting room, her initial delight at the state of the house mingled with unease as to who could have let themselves in. Here, unseen hands had tidied, vacuumed and dusted, leaving nothing but the smell of furniture polish. She clapped her hand to her forehead and sighed with relief. You idiot, it must've been mum and dad, she thought, bless their cotton socks. She opened the French windows to her small courtyard back garden: instead of the usual sea of healthy weeds and dead bedding plants, there wasn't a weed in sight and someone had been watering.

After bundling her washing into the machine and checking her voicemails, she locked up once more and made her way down the path. I hope the car starts, she thought. As she drew closer, she realised that there was something odd. Then she realised: instead of being coated in a year's worth of traffic film, the bodywork was shining like new. She pressed the plipper on the key fob, expecting a dead battery to deny her access after so long away, but again she was wrong. With a satisfying clunk the doors unlocked and inside, she saw that for probably the first time in the car's existence, the interior had been valeted and all her receipts, shopping lists and assorted junk tidied up into two plastic bags. A handwritten note was wedged into the steering wheel: it read, "Hope this fits the bill. Best Regards, Giles S." All very thoughtful but it left her with a strange sensation: a mixture of gratitude but also of disquiet that strangers, even well-intentioned ones, had once more let themselves into her life with such ease.

The car started first time and on setting off towards her parents' house, she noted with satisfaction that it had lost its lifetime urge to pull to the left. She turned off the main road to Chipping Norton, diving into the cool darkness between the high, tree-lined hedgerows that transformed the narrow Oxfordshire lanes into dappled green tunnels. As she bowled along with the windows down and the wind tousling her thick, dark hair, the unease she'd felt earlier slowly faded from her mind.

The following morning she left Shipton-under-Wychwood and with the cat on the back seat, yowling his displeasure at being shut in his box, headed back for Oxford.

The brief reacquaintance with normality felt wonderful but every time she thought of what lay ahead it put her stomach into knots. The episode at the airport haunted her by day and even her dreams by night, giving her the sensation of jumping – being pushed was more like it – into waters that were way out of her depth. She resolved to go and talk to the Dean but then hesitated: presumably, her vow of silence included him too.

Flora had only been at her desk for half an hour when the phone rang. It was the Dean's secretary. Could she pop over for a cup of tea and a chat? Guess the decision's just been made for me, she thought. She locked her PC screen and set off round the quad, the afternoon sunshine filtering through the leaves of the horse-chestnut in the middle of the lawn. She stopped and ran her hand along the weathered stone of one of the pillars supporting the cloisters: it was warm to the touch. This was home, an island of security and permanence far from the world of *tombaroli* and organised crime. By the time she reached the Dean's office, Flora had almost convinced herself that Mike Hayek, Agent Cohen and "*The Friends*" would surely have forgotten all about her by now.

Flora hesitated at the doorway of the outer office, almost afraid to break the silence that pervaded the college out of term-time. The Dean's secretary beckoned to her, 'Just go right on in, dear, Stephen's expecting you.'

Flora knocked, walked in and Professor Stephen Braithwaite looked up from under the bushiest eyebrows in Oxford. His face lit up with affection as he stood, hand outstretched, to greet her. 'Flora, how absolutely wonderful to see you again. Margaret,' he called to his secretary. 'Could you be a dear and bring us some tea, please? Now then,' he said, closing the door and showing Flora to an armchair.

The office showed no trace of a woman's touch. Inside, there wasn't what Flora would have called a smell – that would have been pejorative – it was more an atmosphere, a distilled essence of Oxford bachelor academic, made up of gently mouldering paper and leather binding, blended with hints of pipe smoke, floor polish, linseed oil and elderly dog.

Braithwaite took a seat beside her. 'I understand you've been living in interesting times. I heard about what happened in Pompeii – dreadful business, absolutely frightful. But it's what you've been up to in Rome that I want to hear all about. Do tell.'

Flora hesitated and broke eye contact. 'I'm sorry, Stephen, but it's on a need to know basis.'

'Good answer,' he replied, leaning forward to knock out the bowl of his pipe into the grate. 'You're quite right and in the normal course of events you'd be perfectly entitled to tell me to take a running jump. Now I know you'd never be so rude, but in this instance I do need to know if I'm to help our dear friends the woodentops keep you safe and sound while you're in Oxford.'

'The woodentops?' she asked, perplexed.

'Better known as the Thames Valley Constabulary,' replied the Dean with an avuncular twinkle. 'Inspector Morse, a police officer of towering intellectual capacities, remains, sadly, a fictional character.'

In an instant, Flora's illusion of security vanished. 'Why would the police need to protect me here? Surely I'm safe in Oxford.'

'Sorry, Flora. You're probably as safe as houses but it's best to make sure. The kind of people who can organise a raid like the one you saw at Pompeii, then spirit themselves into and out of air side at Fiumicino, aren't going to be too worried about having a go at you over here if the mood takes them.'

'I hadn't thought about it like that,' said Flora.

'Forgotten your training already?' he asked with a smile.

Flora laughed. 'Rusty, that's all.'

'Luckily for all of us, Giles Smith has everything covered. I presume he told you we were at Cambridge together?'

'He did.'

He looked up at the ceiling and chuckled. 'A great climber in his day was Giles Smith.'

'You mean mountains and things?' Flora was used to the byways and back-roads by which the Dean arrived at the point he was trying to make, but this time he'd lost her.

'No, colleges mainly. Usually after rugger or cricket and always after a skinfull. Have you ever heard of Whipplesnaith?'

'Er, no,' replied Flora. 'Is he a colleague of Giles Smith's?'

'Good heavens, no,' chuckled Braithwaite. 'Long dead by now: Whipplesnaith was a pseudonym used by a fellow called Symington who wrote a definitive guide to climbing Cambridge colleges in the nineteen-thirties. The tradition pre-dates Whipplesnaith of course; there was another chap called Winthrop-Young who wrote *The Roof-climber's Guide to Trinity* in nineteen hundred. He and his friends used the colleges as practice for their trips to the Alps during the long vac, East Anglia being a bit short on mountains of course.'

Flora shook her head in disbelief. 'Giles Smith climbed colleges while drunk?'

'You bet he did,' chuckled the Dean. 'Left a chamber pot on top of the "Wedding Cake" – that's the New Court building at St John's College. Then he stole a policeman's helmet after a May bumps dinner and put it on one of the pinnacles of King's College Chapel – nearly got sent down for that, silly beggar.'

'And he seemed such a stuffed shirt when I first met him.'

'Oh don't let that fool you, he may've calmed down a bit over the years but he's still sharp as a tack: speaks very highly of you by the way, and let me tell you, he doesn't do that about many people. It was thanks to him that you didn't run into trouble at the airport.' Flora winced and Braithwaite continued. 'And now he wants to make sure nothing happens while you're here. I hope you realise you've got yourself mixed up with some pretty unpleasant characters, don't you?'

'Mike Hayek said as much.'

'Did he say any more?'

'He said they were something to do with the people who smashed up the lab at Pompeii,' replied Flora. 'And presumably the same people who were at the airport...' she stopped in mid-sentence as though struck dumb. 'Hold on a minute, Stephen. Assuming Giles Smith or someone he works with sent that man to rescue me at the airport –'

'You only met one of them. Let's say there were quite a few *Friends* around that day.'

'Which means they knew I was in danger and they obviously could've got me straight to the aircraft without going through the terminal if they'd wanted to....' Her voice trailed off once more.

'Keep going, Flora. Glad to know you haven't forgotten your

training after all,' the Dean said, still smiling.

The colour drained from her face. 'But that's the whole point... they didn't want to. They were using me as bait...'

'Fieldcraft, Flora. You know how it is.' he said. The smile had gone. 'Rather than arrest those men, the Italians wanted to find out who they're working for. And in fairness, the chances of your coming to any harm were minimal otherwise I'd have advised them not to go ahead.'

'Oh, well, that's a huge relief,' said Flora, her voice dripping with sarcasm as she got up to leave.

'Please sit down, Flora. I haven't finished.'

Red in the face, she continued towards the door, burning with fury at these men – it would be bloody men, she fumed – who'd got her into this.

'Flora, there are things you need to know.'

At this she stopped and turned to face him. There was something indefinably decent in the lined, kindly face looking up at her from the depths of the ancient armchair that held her back. 'Stephen, I'm sorry if I was abrupt just now but I don't like being used. I resigned from The Firm four years ago, remember?'

'Come and sit down, Flora. There are one or two things I need to explain.'

'Such as?'

'Without your help, you do realise this entire operation is likely to fail?' he asked.

Flora frowned. 'I'm still not sure what the operation is. I know I'm supposed to act as some big-shot collector's blue-stocking sidekick. The ACT want to set up a sting in the US and they need my help.'

'Something like that,' replied Braithwaite. 'It's not just this case, it's about breaking the link between the organised crime gangs in Italy – the *tombaroli* who do the grunt work daren't even stick so much as a trowel in the ground without their say-so – and the money men at the other end. If you help solve this case, you won't just be helping a few policemen and the odd spook improve their annual statistics, there's the whole cultural element too. That's what's really important.'

'I'll remember to have that chiselled on my gravestone.'

Braithwaite smiled. 'I'm sure it won't come to that,' He looked at her intently. 'I flatter myself that I know you, Flora. With a mind like yours you could've earned a fortune in the legal profession or in the City, but instead you chose to be a badly-paid academic. We do it for love. It doesn't pay the bills –'

Flora snorted. 'Tell me about it,' she said.

The Dean continued. 'Not only does it not pay the bills, but sometimes the objects of our affection – just like the real flesh and blood ones – don't always repay us in quite the way we'd like but we stick with them none the less. Just like Giles and his American friend, Mr Hayek, told you, you can walk away from this any time you like. I just don't see you doing so, that's all. Not you.'

Flora's first instinct was to rail and scream at him. Cheap, emotional blackmail, and she wasn't going to fall for it. But then a small, calm voice told her that however much she hated to admit it, everything Stephen Braithwaite had said was true. She cared about her work and even though the job – not to mention her students – got her down at times, her passion for the ancient world and the excitement that bringing it to light gave her, wouldn't let her stand by while some thieving low-life made off with priceless eye-witness accounts of the first-century. Mentally, she cursed them all – good guys and bad guys together. She bit her lip. 'Don't worry, Stephen. I told Mike Hayek I'd see it through and I will.'

'Good, splendid, I hoped you'd see it like that,' he said. 'What none of us can work out is the motive. Seems most odd to go to such a lot of effort to pinch a few codices that you'd expect only crusty old academics – present company excepted,' he added quickly, 'to be interested in. Now, an intact Phidias bust or Nefertiti's tomb, those I could understand someone killing for – I'd be tempted myself – but this defeats me. Anything in the texts caught your eye?'

'Not yet.'

The Dean raised both enormous snowy eyebrows at once. 'Waiting for divine inspiration are you?'

She laughed. 'I'll leave that kind of thing to Donald Sumter. No it's the encrypted stuff that's looking most promising. Thanks to the copper grids, I've made a bit of headway with deciphering some of it – that's what I've been working on since I got back.'

'What do you think it is?'

'It's too early to stick my neck out,' she said. 'But I think it may be from *The Seven Stars*.'

The eyebrows went up again. 'So you think the work exists as a distinct text?'

'It's looking that way. Trouble is, so few of the finds had been properly recorded and catalogued by the time the robbery happened, that we've lost our best chance of proving it.'

'So let's get this straight. Your friend Moretti found originals of *The Wars*, *The Antiquities* – minus the *Testimonium Flavianum* of course – some personal correspondence and possibly an encrypted copy of something that might be *The Seven Stars*. And that's it?' asked Braithwaite, standing up and gazing out of the window into the quad where one of the gardeners was mowing arrow-straight stripes in the immaculate turf.

'No, they also found some of the keys to the ciphers.'

'Still doesn't seem worth killing for, does it? We're all missing something, Flora, and I'm blessed if I know what it is.'

Chapter Twenty-five

Rome AD 64

The *Campus Vaticanus*, the scrubby plain around the *Circus Gai et Neronis* – Caligula and Nero's Circus – and the fields stretching down to the Tiber, were covered by a new city: a Rome comprised of makeshift shelters; tents made from blankets; wooden huts, anything that would give shelter from the sun to the tens of thousands of homeless refugees encamped there. Hungry children wandered around while stray dogs competed for scraps. Elsewhere, trails of smoke from cooking fires wound upwards, merging imperceptibly into the smoggy, high-summer overcast, and already the effects of a lack of sanitation had begun to compete with the stench of burning and decay in Roman nostrils.

The inferno had raged for five days and a quarter of the city, including most of the imperial palace itself, stood in smoking ruins.

'I think that could've gone better, don't you, Josephus?' Nero pulled off the leather gloves he wore for chariot-racing and sat with his elbows resting on his knees. He watched as the silent, sunburned hordes streamed out of the arena which bore his name, kicking up clouds of dust as they went. The *spina,* the central divide of the *Circus Gai et Neronis* was decorated with a grisly forest of crosses and charred wooden stakes: on the former, the emperor had arranged a mass crucifixion of Christians, including Peter and many of his followers; the latter bore the greasy, burnt traces of those who had been transformed into human torches for the crowd's amusement.

The cries and shrieks of those condemned to a lingering death on the crosses had subsided to a harrowing chorus of groaning and pleading that jarred on the listener's nerves like fingernails on a slate: as he looked across the imperial box at his host, he noticed that even the notoriously callous Nero seemed disturbed by the sound.

'The whole human torch thing doesn't really work in daylight, does it?' Nero's tone became petulant as though complaining about rain on his birthday.

'I think people have had enough of suffering, sir,' he replied. 'It was probably a bit soon after the fire.'

'They liked my display of chariot-driving though, didn't they?' he

207

said hopefully, like a small child seeking a parent's approbation . 'I could hear them cheering me.' Josephus made no reply and looked away. Nero's idea of using human torches to illuminate his triumphal passage around the Circus had raised little more than dutiful applause from those who felt they might be being watched. Bolder souls, perhaps with less to lose, had greeted him with catcalls and accusations of having started the fire himself. The uprising of public hatred against the Christians that the three-day festival of executions and games was supposed to create had failed to materialise. 'We've got five hundred more to execute, Josephus, what do you think I should do?'

Josephus wasn't sure how to reply. Nero's reputation for asking people what they thought and then turning on them when they gave the wrong answer was well deserved. 'Is Paul among the captives?'

'No. I asked the Praetorians to check. Just the typical credulous riff-raff: the usual suspects. They must be made to pay for their treason.'

'Then why not set them to work tearing down the damaged buildings or digging temporary latrines for the people living rough out there?' he jerked his thumb over his shoulder towards the squatter camp that spread across the *Campus Vaticanus* from horizon to horizon.

'Good idea, I can always crucify them afterwards...' Nero stopped mid-sentence and a puzzled frown came across his face. 'Hold on a minute, forget the Christians, you mentioned people living rough. What are they doing for food and water do you think?'

Josephus did a double-take. 'Looking at the state of them I think they're not far off starving to death and if there isn't an outbreak of disease, I'll be amazed. You do realise people are drinking from the *Aqua Alsietina* rather than going all the way down to the cisterns by the Aemilian Bridge?'

'But the *Alsietina's* water's not fit for human consumption, it's only supposed to be used for irrigation. Everybody knows that.'

'That's my point, sir. They're not just going to sit up here and die quietly. You're days away at most from food riots and the city – what's left of it – will soon be full of people carrying diseases.' For the first time, Josephus saw Nero not as the all-powerful tyrant but as a frightened young man out of his depth.

He clutched at Josephus' arm as though afraid he might leave. 'What do you think I should do?'

'It's not for me to say, sir, but I'd close the *Alsietina* and put guards on it to stop any illegal tappings, organise carts to carry water to distribution points all along this side of the Tiber, order your engineers to build new siphons from the *Aqua Appia* and the *Aqua Anio* to get a permanent water supply established and start a daily bread distribution this afternoon. If you don't, there's every chance the mob will turn against you.'

'Brilliant,' said Nero, nodding vigorously. 'I couldn't have put it better myself. The people will love me for this. How can I ever thank you?'

The question was supposed to be rhetorical but Josephus took a deep breath and spoke. 'Actually, there are a couple of things, sir.'

'Very well, name them,' he replied, eyeing him suspiciously.

'I'd like more manpower to help me look for Paul.'

They both knew that in the newly-devastated city, manpower was in short supply but Nero meekly nodded his head. 'I think I can manage that,' he replied. 'What else?'

'Favours for friends.'

'Such as?' Nero said, narrowing his eyes.

'Let Alityros go back to doing what he does best. He's an actor, not a soldier and he's more of a hindrance than a help to me most of the time.'

'Very well. I'll mention it to Poppaea, it was her idea in the first place to make him work for you.'

'I know,' said Josephus. 'Then there's Giora.'

'What of him?'

'He wants to go home. You freed him two years ago. He's been a loyal servant to the empire but he misses his family.'

Nero thought for a moment. 'I thought he was pivotal to your operation.'

Josephus hesitated. He was treading on thin ice. 'He was but he's tired and homesick – it's not for me to say, but I think he's done more than enough to earn his freedom. If we're to crush this wretched cult then all I need is one loyal intelligent man to replace him, preferably one with good connections in the empire.'

The look of suspicion returned to Nero's face. 'If I didn't know better, I'd say you had someone in mind.'

'I have, sir. Titus Flavius Vespasianus.'

'Vespasian?' shouted Nero, going puce in the face and almost choking. 'A senator, a condemned criminal and you want him to work for you?'

'Not *for* me, sir, I wouldn't be so presumptuous. I'd like him to help me, if he's willing to.'

209

'You realise where he is?'

'In the condemned cell of the Mamertine Jail at a guess.'

'Correct,' said the emperor. 'Your timing's impeccable. His execution was to be the star turn in the arena tomorrow.' Nero waved him away, turning his back. 'Have him, do as you will, just don't let him near any of my recitals.' Josephus bowed his head in compliance. 'That it?' Nero asked.

'That's all, sir. And I'm most grateful.'

With not another word to Josephus, Nero stood up and called for his attendants to fetch his carriage. Nobody paid the young Judean any attention as they prepared for the imperial departure and after a few minutes he was alone, his sole company the soldiers guarding the *spina*, the last few spectators unable to tear themselves away from the ghastly sights stretched along its length, and the groaning victims themselves.

Josephus lifted the catch on the side gate of the imperial box and walked down the gangway between the tiers of sun-bleached wooden benches to the low fence separating the crowd from the blood-stained sand of the arena. Vaulting over, he made his way towards the *spina*, looking for Peter. The guards paid him no heed as he walked towards the obelisk which marked its centre point. Just after the obelisk, he found him – not as history records, crucified head-down, but in the normal position, assuming such things can be described as normal. Peter's head had slumped forwards onto his chest and a scrawny crow, which had settled on top of the vertical post, flew off at Josephus' approach. 'Now do you understand?' Josephus called up to him, but there was no reply: death had come quickly. 'I hope it hurt, you sanctimonious old bastard,' he said, turning his back on the inert form and heading across the sand towards the eastern exit. The first of the seven stars had fallen from the sky.

Unnoticed by Josephus, two pairs of eyes followed his progress. The men sat in the last row of the north grandstand under the shade of the Circus's canvas awnings and watched him intently. They spoke in Aramaic. 'You sure that's him?' asked the first.

'No doubt about it, I'd recognise him anywhere. Get it right and he won't suspect a thing before it's too late.'

'Don't worry, you can rely on me, Paul.'

Chapter Twenty-six

Oxford

For an entire blissful week Flora was able to convince herself that she'd got her old life back. Her work days passed in a pleasurable blur – lost in translation as she called it – surrounded by copies of first-century texts, some in Latin, others in Aramaic, Coptic or Greek, many encrypted by unknown scribes into a confusing jumble of letters. Her social life regained some of its normality too; there was even a voicemail from her ex-boyfriend, telling her he'd been posted to train as a flying instructor at a base she'd never heard of somewhere amidst the potato fields of Lincolnshire, and would she call him. To her immense satisfaction, she was able to delete the message without the slightest pang of regret: perhaps time does heal after all, she mused.

As for the call from Francesco Moretti, she wasn't sure what to think. He sounded nervous, guarded even, and afterwards she hadn't a clue why he'd called: the Carabinieri had no more news about the break-in, no new finds had turned up at the dig and given that he didn't seem to want to bring up the subject of Anna, she thought it best not to do so either.

On Saturday she went to the theatre with friends and out for a curry afterwards. It was almost midnight as she turned into the street that led to her cottage and she paid no attention to the silver-grey Ford that had been sitting behind her all the way from the city centre but now continued south towards the ring-road.

The following morning she'd just settled down with a mug of tea and the Sunday papers, with the delicious prospect of doing precisely nothing stretching ahead of her, when the phone rang. It could have been one of a dozen people, but Flora's sixth sense told her it wasn't going to be good news: it wasn't. Mike Hayek was friendly but to the point. In the guise of Benjamin Grossman, Special Agent Cohen had been making a nuisance of himself in the sale rooms of Tel Aviv and Istanbul. He was now in Geneva where Lavinia Crump's services were urgently required to cast an expert eye over a number of antiquities on sale at Sotheby's. 'Come on, cheer up, Flora,' he said, in response to her unenthusiastic replies. 'You'll be staying at the Hotel Beau Rivage.'

'Is that good?'

He laughed. 'At fifteen hundred Swiss Francs a night it better had be.'

'Well I'm glad you're paying, not me. When do I leave?'

'Tomorrow first thing. Sorry for the short notice but we nearly dropped the ball on this one. The pre-sale exhibition started Saturday and the auction itself is on Tuesday.' Flora's mind went blank: there were a dozen or more questions she knew she ought to ask but luckily, Hayek anticipated her. 'Don't worry about the Dean, he's been briefed. A car will pick you up at four thirty tomorrow –'

'Hold on,' said Flora. 'I thought you said it was a morning flight....oh, God, you don't mean four thirty as in AM, surely?'

There was a brief silence at the other end of the line. 'Yup, sorry about that, you're on the 0645 from Heathrow, but hey, we've booked you in business class. Flora,.... are you still there?'

'Yes, I'm still here,' she said. 'I'm just calculating how much I hate you. It's hardly going to be worth going to bed.'

'I know, and I really do apologise. Now, in the car will be a briefing pack, all your travel docs in Lavinia's name of course, a US cell-phone and a sales catalogue from the auction house. A driver will meet you at Geneva airport to take you to the hotel and Mr Grossman will meet you there. You got all that? Flora, are you listening.... Flora?'

'Four thirty in the morning? Couldn't you just shoot me, it would be kinder? And what am I supposed to tell my parents and my friends?'

'Tell your friends whatever you like so long as it's not the truth. Your folks – well, I guess you could always tell them that the Italian police have asked you to go to Zurich to identify what could be documents from the theft at Pompeii.'

'Zurich? I thought you said Geneva.'

'I did. Safer that way, just trust me. And anyway, you're only going to be there a couple of nights because you leave Geneva at midday on Wednesday for DC. You're booked into the Marriott.' Hayek continued his list of instructions and Flora scribbled on the pad by the phone as he spoke: "Zurich", LHR terminal five, Washington DC, Marriott, 0430, take cat to Mum's.... Finally, he rang off and cursing to herself at their intrusion into her own little paradise she padded upstairs to start packing, leaving the papers unread and her tea going cold.

***

There is a pitch of tiredness that can only be attained in the small hours of the morning when the body's cycle is at its lowest ebb and every neuron and cell is screaming for sleep. In a state verging on hallucination, at four thirty on Monday morning Flora opened the door to the uniformed driver who greeted her with a cheerfulness that made her want to hit him. The roads were empty and they made good time, Flora keeping herself awake by reading her briefing. 'Remember to leave those in the car when you get out, Miss,' he said, glancing at her in his mirror. 'And Mr Smith asked specifically that you leave your own passport in the white envelope.'

Heathrow airport, grey and dirty, loomed out of the early-morning mist and the black Mercedes dropped her at Terminal Five – indistinguishable from any other out-of-town shopping centre save for the presence of airliners and its far surlier staff. Lavinia Crump was off on her travels.

The flight was on time and a gritty-eyed Flora was met by a taciturn driver who grunted at her in accented French, treating her to a blast of last night's garlic. As the Mercedes bumped over the level crossing into rue de Chantepoulet she spotted the famous Lake Geneva waterspout, *le jet d'eau*, arcing above the buildings. Flora looked at her watch: five past ten – five past nine in Oxford and most of the academic staff wouldn't be in for another twenty five minutes.

Hayek had been right about the Hotel Beau Rivage. After checking in she'd only just set foot in the tiled atrium with its pink marble Corinthian columns and a circular fountain at its centre when her bags were whisked away and taken to her lakeside room on the second floor.

In the middle of the bed lay a monogrammed envelope with her name printed across it and inside she found a message to contact Mr B. Grossman in room 306. Picking up the bedside phone she dialled. 'Yes, what is it?' The voice was barely recognisable, more of a snarl, and overlaid with a thick Israeli accent.

Flora cleared her throat. 'Good morning, Mr Grossman, it's Lavinia here. I got a message to call you.'

'Right. Meet me in reception in five minutes. Don't be late.' The line went dead. Charmed, I'm sure, thought Flora.

He looked up from his newspaper as she walked into the atrium. 'You're late,' he said. 'Come with me, we're going for a walk.'

'Yes, Mr Grossman, sorry, Mr Grossman,' she said, but he was already on his feet striding towards the door with Flora trailing behind him like a dutiful middle-eastern wife. Without another word they crossed the busy Quai du Mont Blanc and turned left towards les Bains

213

des Paquis. At last she caught up with him. 'Good trip?' Cohen asked once they were clear of other pedestrians.

'No, bloody awful since you asked,' she replied. 'I've been up since half three this morning.'

'Yeah, sorry, there was a screw-up. Happens all the time, you kinda get to expecting it after a while. You read the brief?'

'Yes, this afternoon we're going to –'

'Forget it,' he said, interrupting her. 'That's changed too. We've got outside help.'

'Anyone I know?'

'Doubt it. It's Sotheby's – I take it you saw their set-up in the hotel?' Flora nodded and he continued. 'A couple of the documents in the sale catalogue are fakes and two others have a provenance that a blind man could see is questionable.' He stopped talking as they waited to clear a gaggle of Japanese tourists. 'OK, make like you're on holiday,' he said, pointing at the miniature lighthouse on the tip of the Bains de Paquis promontory. As he did so, Flora felt him press something against her hand. It was an envelope which she immediately slipped into her bag.

'What was that?' she asked.

'A list of the dud sale items. I'm sure you'd have found them blindfold, but what the hell, eh?'

'So what am I supposed to do?' she asked.

'I'd like you to take a casual look round and identify the fakes and the stolen items. I'll make a big public fuss about it and Sotheby's will pull them from the auction and put out a press release after the sale, by which time you and I will be on our way to DC.'

The subterfuge went as planned. In front of the astonished members of the Sotheby's team who weren't party to it, Lavinia Crump was prissy and offended at what she dismissed as little short of outright fraud, Benjamin Grossman stormed, shouted and swore in a mixture of English and Hebrew, working himself into a pitch of fury just short of spontaneous combustion.

Later that afternoon they went for a drink at a lakeside café. 'It's not often I get to do that kinda stuff,' said Cohen.

'I could see you enjoyed it,' said Flora with a smile. 'By the way, what does "benzona" mean?'

Cohen blushed. 'Literally it's "son of a whore" but if you use it like you would "sonofabitch" you won't go far wrong.'

Flora smiled. 'Thanks, I'll remember that. So what do we do tomorrow, now we're not going to the sale?'

'I'm afraid we're going to have to check out. They've got us on the DC flight tomorrow so we save the US taxpayer the cost of another night in the Hotel Swank.'

Cohen ordered another two beers. At last Flora began to unwind and, for the first time that day stopped wishing herself back in Oxford. Had she known, she'd picked a very good night to be out of town.

* * *

The silver Ford slowed to a halt and then turned between the wooden gate-posts, bumping over the track that ran through the centre of the allotments. Its headlights went off and two black-clad figures climbed out, one of them holding a small canvas holdall. Moving soundlessly between the vegetable patches and the wigwams of runner bean supports they reached the foot of the wall and crouched down in its shadow. At this time of night during the week, most of the inhabitants were asleep and only the flickering light from a television three doors down from Flora's cottage betrayed any signs of human activity.

At a pre-agreed sign they stood up. Even a close observer would have struggled to make out any more than two shadows sliding over the wall and into the seclusion of the courtyard garden below. Once more they waited and after five minutes motionless in the lee of the garden shed they moved towards the house itself. In the dark only a cat could have seen precisely what tool was removed from the holdall, but in seconds its effects were evident as the door to the living room swung open with a barely audible squeak of protest from the lower hinge. Treading carefully, they climbed the stairs and pushed open the door to the main bedroom. Just enough light filtered through the window to show the bed was empty. Years of experience clicked into action as they systematically checked all the drawers and cupboards, rearranging the contents to leave no trace of their passing.

A whispered order: 'Check the other one,' and they tiptoed across the landing to the second bedroom which Flora used as her office. One of the figures closed the curtains while the other shut the door and snapped on a pencil torch. The desk was clear of paper and in the drawers, nothing on her neatly-filed credit card or bank statements indicated the purchase of a ticket to anywhere. On the other hand, there was no sign of her passport.

'So where the hell is she?'

The living room and the kitchen were treated to the same painstaking

215

examination but even the pinboard next to the fridge gave no clue, so after a murmured conversation they decided to abandon the search; after all, they'd done most of what they'd been paid for; but luckily for Flora, not all of it. As they left the kitchen, the one holding the torch swept its pale, narrow beam around the hall. 'Hold on a second,' he said, advancing towards a Victorian bureau just inside the solid front door.

'What is it?'

'Probably nothing....hold on a minute, I think this is... bingo, we've got it,' he said in a whisper, focusing the beam on the notepad Flora kept by the telephone.

'Got what?'

'Just listen.' He read: 'Zurich, BA, LHR – that's Heathrow I think – yes, that makes sense... Marriott... 0430... Washington DC. I think we've found her.'

'What the fuck's she doing at the Marriott in Zurich for Christ's sake?'

'Shagging some rich bloke, how should I know? Come on, let's go: we've spent too much time faffing about in here as it is.'

Exactly seven minutes after the silver-grey Ford left its hiding place on the allotment behind Flora's house it passed a black Audi coming the other way. The Audi drew up outside the cottage and two men let themselves in through Flora's front door with a key. Closing all the curtains they began turning lights on and one of them walked over towards a nondescript black box, about two inches square and seemingly wired into the lighting flex that ran along the top of the picture rail in the living room. Then he removed what looked like an old-fashioned mobile phone from his pocket and pressing a button on its side, held it up towards the box. The readout told him all he needed to know so he replaced it in his pocket and pulled out his real phone.

On the third floor of a serviced apartment block, just off Kensington Church Street, Giles Smith cursed as he rolled over in bed, fumbling in the darkness for his mobile phone. 'Smith here. What is it?'

'We've got a problem, Giles. You were right.'

'What's happened? Is she all right.' He was suddenly wide awake.

'She's had visitors. According to the IR detector in the sitting room, someone let themselves into the house through the back door at 02:08 and left the same way nine minutes later: two distinct heat sources. We can't have missed them by more than ten minutes. Pros I'd say because there's no sign of forced entry.'

'Any damage inside? Anything taken?' Smith asked.

'No. That's what worries me. I reckon they were looking for her.'

'Shit. That's all we need.'

'I can get a forensics team here if you think it'll help.'

Smith thought for a moment. 'No. Firstly, given the likely suspects I don't think they'll have left anything for us to find and secondly, if we have the Thames Valley forensic brass band marching in and out of the place all day, chances are our friends will get to hear about it. Leave it for now and call me later at the office.'

Chapter Twenty-seven

Rome AD 65

'Bloody thing gets bigger every time I see it. No good will come of this, you mark my words.' Vespasian folded his arms and turned away from the construction site of the new palace in disgust. For the past nine months both he and Josephus had been monitoring the progress of what the senator referred to as "Nero's folly" with a mixture of alarm and disbelief. Paul seemed to have vanished into thin air along with the five other survivors of the "Seven Stars".

'You know what the mob are saying, don't you?' Josephus asked, trotting to catch up with him as he paced up the slope.

'Of course I do,' he snapped. Even Lady Poppaea was talking about it the other day. They're saying the fire was started on his orders just so he could enlarge the palace. The emperor of course says the Christians started it.'

'They did. I was there when it happened, remember?'

Vespasian stopped, sat down on a pile of bricks and stared down towards the forum. 'Doesn't matter what he says: nobody's listening any more,' he said with a rueful shake of the head. 'Worse still, Nero's stopped listening to what people are telling him. Even Seneca can't get through to him.'

Josephus sat down beside him. 'Do you think anyone will make a move against the emperor?' he asked.

Vespasian's reply was as matter-of-fact as it was horrifying. 'They have already. It's started.'

'What? B-but we've got to tell him,' said Josephus, panic-stricken. 'Without Nero's support I won't be able to find Paul and the others.'

Vespasian snorted and looked down his well-bred nose in disgust. 'Nice to see you've got Rome's wider interests at heart, young man. No, we wait. If we tell the emperor now he'll go after the tiddlers, the bait fish. Wait a bit and we'll help him find whoever's holding the rod.'

'So what do we do?'

'We don't do anything until I've spoken to Volusius Proculus –'

'You mean the admiral?' asked Josephus.

Vespasian raised his eyebrows. 'Do you know him?' Josephus nodded and the senator continued. 'He's due to arrive in Rome tomorrow. You can come along and say hello if you like.' He stood up and made to leave. Suddenly he turned round. 'Oh, I nearly forgot, there's one more thing.'

'What's that?'

'You're now an accessory to the crime. Putting aside what I just said about bait and fishermen, if anyone finds out you knew and didn't report it, I wouldn't rate your chances. The worst Nero can do to me as a Roman citizen is cut my head off but I'm sure he'd come up with something far more inventive and prolonged for you.' Josephus' face fell and he stared back at Vespasian open-mouthed. 'Still want to run with the big dogs, Josephus?'

'Er...yes, I think so, sir.'

'Good lad. Come to my house at the fifth hour tomorrow and don't be late.'

The next day when the Nubian slave showed Josephus through to the garden at the centre of the villa, Proculus and Vespasian were deep in conversation. Despite their difference in rank, Proculus rose as the young Judean entered, greeting him like an old friend. 'Glad to see you're still in one piece,' he said, embracing him warmly. 'Your old friend Gubs wishes to be remembered to you.'

Josephus smiled. 'I owe Gubs my life,' he said.

'Gubs was too modest to put it that way,' said the admiral. 'But he's back working for me now; the *Classis Pontica* is a bit of a backwater if you'll pardon the pun so he asked if I'd have him back.' Josephus sat down on the bench next to them and Proculus' face became grave. 'Vespasian tells me you understand the personal risks you're about to take. Now you've slept on it, do you still want to be involved?'

'Yes, sir.'

'Even at the risk of being crucified by the very man you're trying to help?' Josephus nodded and did his best to look grimly determined. 'Right. Here's what we know so far: Gaius Calpurnius Piso thinks Nero is mad.'

'As do a lot of people,' added Vespasian.

Proculus continued. 'Piso also thinks he's leading the empire to ruin – again, a widely held sentiment in certain circles – and he thinks he'd make a better emperor than Nero. He's cobbled together enough support to have a reasonable chance of success and we have most, but not all, of the conspirators' names. Once we've got the complete list, we can shut the conspiracy down and thereby gain the emperor's undying gratitude and loyalty.'

'You mean you'll own him?' asked Josephus.

'I wouldn't put it as cynically as that,' replied Proculus. 'Let's just say there's a possibility he'll be somewhat dependent on those who remained loyal if he plans on staying alive.'

'Nice,' Josephus said with a smile.

'The players we know about are Piso himself, Faenius Rufus from the Praetorian Guard, Subrius Flavus who's a member of the Praetorian Court and a centurion called Sulpicius Asper.' He then reeled off a list of senators and Equestrians, most of whom Josephus had heard of. 'Now you're probably wondering how I got involved,' said Proculus. 'My wife is friendly with a woman called Epicharis – her husband is a senator and they've got a summer villa near Puteoli, that's how we got to know them. Anyway, while the senator is in Rome, Epicharis tempers her boredom with drink.'

'Luckily for Nero, *in vino, veritas*,' said Vespasian.

'Very true,' continued Proculus. 'Now, we were entertaining friends a few weeks ago, Epicharis got drunk, cornered me on the terrace and started on about Nero. I was going to explain, very politely of course, that I didn't like my guests talking treason when she told me about a conspiracy to kill him involving the Praetorians. Naturally, I assumed it was just the drink talking but the more she said, the more names she mentioned, the more credible it became. I confided in her that I was no friend of Nero's either and we agreed to meet the following day. Basically, she repeated the same story word-for-word with a few more names thrown in and I said I'd gauge support among senior officers in the fleet and get back to her.'

Josephus, who'd been listening in stunned silence, asked. 'So what do you intend to do?'

It was Vespasian who spoke. 'I told you. We wait. We've got the names of other conspirators but no proof against them. My people are working on getting it and they reckon they'll be ready the day after tomorrow. By which time –'

'The lady Epicharis will be under arrest in Puteoli,' said Proculus.

'But where do I come into this?' asked Josephus.

'You help us buy time so we're not forced to act until the net is fully closed. Keep close to the court: Nero himself, ideally, but if not, then go and talk to Poppaea or to Alityros; see if you can find any hint the emperor knows about the plot. If he does, then tell us and we'll bring our plans forward.'

'Who else knows about this?'

'The ones you need to know about are Nerva, who's Praetor elect, and Tigellinus, the Prefect of the Praetorians,' said Vespasian. 'They won't move without my say-so.'

Josephus left Vespasian's house on the southern slopes of the Pincian Hill and set off towards the Palatine. He had just passed through the Saepta Gate when he heard someone call his name. Turning to look, he failed to see three figures approach from behind and at once a hand was clamped over his mouth, his arms were pinned by his side and he felt himself being bundled through a shop doorway. Someone put a bag over his head and he felt the point of a knife blade pressing into his neck. A voice said, 'Keep quiet or you're dead.' In the circumstances it seemed wise to comply.

What followed next was even worse. Rough hemp rope bit into his wrists and ankles as it was pulled tight and knotted, rendering him completely immobile. Then, unseen hands grabbed him and threw him like a side of beef into the back of a cart. He cried out in pain but once again the sharp jab of a knife into his leg accompanied by a volley of curses made him hold his tongue. Next, the few glimmers of light he could see through the weave of the bag disappeared as heavy objects were loaded on top of him and all around. With a jolt, the mule cart got underway and clattered off over the cobbles.

For what seemed like an eternity, the cart lurched along, each bump sending bolts of pain through his arms which were pinned behind his back. Josephus began to groan. A disembodied voice swore and someone kicked him. Finally the cart stopped, he heard bolts being drawn back, and with a final lurch, it moved forward a few more paces on a smooth surface and stopped. Then the bolts slotted home again. He could hear the cart being unloaded and once more saw flickers of light and movement through the weave. Someone untied his ankles and for a few moments as the circulation returned to his feet, the pain was unbearable. The same pair of hands dragged him into a sitting position and pulled the sack off his head. He seemed to be in some kind of store-room or workshop at the back of a shop.

There were five of them and none of the faces were friendly or familiar. 'Come on, move, we haven't got all day,' one of them said and pushed him off the cart-tail. As he landed, his feet went out from under him and he crashed to one side, his hands still pinned behind his back. Two of them hauled him to his feet, frog-marching him up the steps to the upper storey and into a small room, containing two chairs, a bench and a bed with a straw palliasse. The only light came from the open

221

shutters of a small dormer window set in the sloping roof.

However much Josephus shifted his position on the bench, the pain in his arms just got worse and his head and neck hurt abominably from falling off the cart. He gritted his teeth.

He'd only been sitting for a few minutes when he heard footfalls on the wooden stairs. As they pushed aside the tattered sacking curtain and came into the room all his bravado evaporated in an instant. It was Paul.

Chapter Twenty-eight

Arthur Kill Correctional Facility, Staten Island, NY

At five foot eight and one hundred and forty pounds, the prisoner looked down into one of the inner circles of hell. Although the walkway was ten feet above the heads of the inmates in the mess hall below and the two armed guards who held the chains attached to his handcuffs were both over six three and two hundred pounds, he was almost knocked off balance by the wave of hatred aimed at him. "Faggot", "queer" and "punk" – the latter, prison slang for male prostitute – were some of the milder insults hurled his way as the guards led him over the seething cacophony of noise, from the Special Housing Unit towards the waiting truck.

Paperwork screw-ups are not uncommon when it comes to prisoners – after all they're not valuable goods – and the one which had led to the young man being put into a holding cell with ten other detainees for five hours while they processed him, nearly cost him an eye. After another delay while they sorted out his paperwork and following surgery to re-attach the retina, he was finally leaving the SHU for the "Incarcerated Witness Program" and the anonymity of a special unit in an upstate jail.

Virginia, USA

An unmarked Lincoln Town Car collected Flora and Agent Cohen from Dulles airport and set off to do battle with the DC downtown traffic. Cohen checked his voicemails as they hit their first jam. Flora dozed in the back seat by his side. 'You see, they can't leave me in peace for five minutes, let alone ten hours,' he said, bringing her back from the edge of sleep.

'What's happened?' she asked, her head snapping forward with a jolt.

'Dunno. My supervisor says he wants to talk to me urgently. Usually means some trivial shit about my time-sheets.'

He dialled and Flora could tell in an instant from Cohen's voice that whatever it was, it wasn't trivial. Snapping the phone shut, he turned to her, looking as though he'd aged ten years. 'We've got a problem. Fucking idiots have lost our witness.'

Flora blinked in surprise. 'What, as in escaped?'

'No. Lost, as in dead. Murdered.'

'Who?'

'The one I told you about – the IT guy who worked for Luzzo. They'd got him in protective custody, moved him to some minimum security joint up near the Canadian border and then instead of keeping him safe in the "hole", some dork put him in an open dorm with twenty other inmates. Third night there and he was found strangled this morning. And, guess what? By one of those miracles which only happen in prisons, no one, not even the guy on the top bunk a couple of feet above him heard or saw anything. Shit, that's the last thing we needed.'

'How badly does it hurt the investigation?' she asked.

'Pretty bad. All we're left with is the driver of the SUV and names for two people we can't find: Luzzo and Raymond. Luzzo knows the score and he'll be jumpier than a motherf... let's just say he's gonna be pretty jumpy. If we want to get anywhere near without spooking him, we're going to have to get lucky. And as for Raymond, we don't even know what he looks like.'

'So when do we start?' asked Flora.

'I've got to go straight to the office because of this crap. You can take the evening off, go stroll round DC if you like. I'll pick you up from your hotel at nine tomorrow morning.'

The car dropped her at the Marriott. Fighting off the urge to sleep, Flora unpacked, started her laptop and set to work making a few last-minute changes to the presentation she was giving to Cohen's colleagues on the FBI Art Crime the following day. Once more, her head started nodding and a vigorous walk along the National Mall only delayed the inevitable: even working on her current obsession, the decryption and translation of the Devil's Codex fragment couldn't keep her awake so she turned on the TV to keep her company while she got ready for bed. She picked up the remote and started zapping through the channels. All the news feeds seemed to have synchronised their ads to stop people channel-hopping and she was well down among American TV's extensive intellectual shallow-end when a familiar face stared back at her from a panel of talking heads: Donald Sumter. Brilliant, she thought, this is too good to be true. All thoughts of sleep banished from her mind she sat on the bed, drew her knees up to her chin and settled down to watch. A press of the "information" button told her she was watching the "God's Truth Revival Channel". She'd seen pale imitations of such programmes on UK TV, but this was the real deal and Sumter was in fine form: the anchor, a face-lifted and hair-weaved man who looked like

Liberace's ugly sister, lobbed gentle questions to the panellists who took it in turns to hit them out of the ground.

Sumter was damning to hell-fire the lost souls who obstinately refused to accept the veracity of the New Testament, with an especially warm corner reserved for those responsible for stealing priceless relics from the archives of William Sunday University. Then he started talking about the Pompeii finds and his photographs of from the "Q Source" document. Obediently, the anchor interrupted, and almost on bended knee, implored Sumter to enlighten them about "Q". Flora nearly choked with surprise and indignation. You sly old bastard, she thought, you played that one pretty close to your chest.

He cleared his throat and with a look that was supposed to betoken sincerity but reminded Flora of a child-molester, Sumter began to hold forth: "Q", from the German *Quelle*, meaning "source", was the common document on which the gospels of Matthew and Luke were based. 'What's more,' he said, trying to add gravitas by speaking in a register so low it was barely audible, 'the translations my staff and I have completed, prove beyond doubt that the existing Gospels are but an abridged version of the Lord's life. For the first time we have corroborated, eye-witness accounts of the miraculous deeds of our Saviour's childhood, right through to the start of his ministry where the extant gospels rejoin his journey to the Holy Cross and subsequent resurrection.'

Sumter paused for effect and the anchor gurned at the camera in what Flora assumed was an attempt at a rapturous smile – not too rapturous of course or the caked TV make-up would have cracked – before lobbing another under-arm question to him. 'But, Professor Sumter, this is such wonderful news and we're deeply honoured that you chose our humble programme to make the announcement, but why isn't this all over the headlines and the news channels?'

'Oh it will be, don't you worry,' said Sumter. 'And don't forget, this isn't news, it's been God's Truth for the last two thousand years. All that's changed is that we now have tangible proof of something we knew was there all along – a bit like when J J Thomson discovered the electron....'

He rambled on in similar vein for another ten minutes, prompted, lauded and cajoled by the anchor and the other panellists, and when they announced it was time for a prayer break, Flora decided she'd seen enough. Part of her boiled with anger at Sumter for comparing scientific fact with unauthenticated documents, but on the other hand, she couldn't help admiring his nerve. She looked at her watch: half past nine and her eyelids were on the way down again. So, she did the east-to-west jetlag classic: asleep early and wide awake at four in the morning.

Only a lover of nineteen-sixties brutalist concrete, or maybe at a push, its mother, would describe the J Edgar Hoover building as attractive. On the inside it is even worse which came as quite a shock to Flora who'd been expecting FBI Headquarters to be far more modern and high-tech. Cohen led the way from the elevator through a maze of corridors to a conference room where his FBI supervisor from New York, no fan of the ACT, and an assortment of other agents were gathered.

After the usual fight to get laptop to speak to projector, Cohen went first, giving an overview of art crime in Italy and the sources of the money – drugs mostly – that funded the *tombaroli's* activities. What shocked Flora most were the details of how highly-trained but poorly-paid archaeologists and art historians were earning a fortune helping manufacture provenance to hide the stolen artefacts' true origins.

Flora stepped up to the lectern and introduced herself. Starting with the historical context, she outlined the clash between the world view of the Jews and that of Imperial Rome. Next, came a brief but concise scamper through the history of the first century: the more noteworthy emperors from Augustus to Trajan, the internal conflicts within Israel, culminating in the Jewish revolt and the destruction of the Temple in AD 70. Then she moved on to the life and works of one of the few chroniclers of that turbulent century; Titus Flavius Josephus, born Joseph son of Matthias and whose writings were the subject of the current joint Carabinieri-FBI enquiry.

Next, she showed them scanned images from the stolen collection and explained how she'd managed to decipher the encrypted texts, working from the copper polyalphabetic substitution grids.

A hand went up in the audience. 'Do you have formal cryptographic training, ma'am?' asked a voice from the back.

'No, not really,' lied Flora. 'It's like doing crosswords, if you stick at it long enough and use a bit of common sense, it's not that hard. Mind you, finding out about frequency analysis of letter usage was a big help: I've got Charles Babbage and the internet to thank for that one.' A ripple of laughter ran round the room. Even Cohen's supervisor permitted himself a smile.

'And so what's it say? What's it telling us?' he asked.

'Well, I'm not sure yet because I've only just started and also there's a lot of text that I can't get anywhere near deciphering. I suspect Josephus – presuming he was the author – may've used a substitution grid we don't have. Some of it seems to be to do with finding people – we've got the names Philippos, Matityahu and Yehudas: one Greek and two Hebrew names meaning Philip, Matthew and Jude respectively, but given that Josephus himself was Judean and Greek names were used by non-Greeks as well, all we've got is the modern equivalent of references to Phil, Matt and Jude in a population the size of the DC Metro area.'

Another question came from Cohen's supervisor. 'And does he say anything about these guys that makes this stuff worth stealing?'

Flora thought for a moment. 'No and that's what's been puzzling me from the start. Josephus clearly didn't like these three individuals – that's all we know. The most valuable find at the dig was a beautiful first century mosaic, but the tombaroli ignored it and took the texts and the copper grids instead.'

Another hand went up. 'Were there any other writings?'

'Yes, there were early versions of his works that have come down to us as later copies made after his death. Together, these writings make up Josephus' slanted and self-justifying history of the Jewish people and the revolt against Rome. Needless to say, he was the hero throughout, but he was a rotten copy editor because in trying so hard to justify being two-faced and disloyal whenever it suited him, he contradicts himself all over the place.'

At this the supervisor shook his head and Flora noticed a look of alarm spread across Cohen's face.

'It's an interesting story, Miss Kemble, and I thank you for sharing it with us,' said the supervisor, staying just the polite side of sarcasm. 'But if I understand you correctly, nothing you've found to date has any possible relevance to the case: who stole this stuff, why it's in this country and who's got it right now?'

Flora took a deep breath. 'I'm sorry, but I can't agree with you.' He made to speak but she continued. 'And nor does your own Art Crime Team.'

'I think you've got me wrong there, Miss Kemble,' he said. 'I'm not ACT, I'm a supervisor from the Agency's New York division and I happen to have lost one of my people, Special Agent Cohen to be precise, on secondment to a wild goose chase that's stopping him doing his duty back home.'

'So you haven't read the ACT report on the theft of documents from museum and university archives?'

'Can't say I have,' replied the supervisor.

Flora remained unmoved. 'Then I take it *das Städtisches Museum von Göttingen* won't mean much to you?'

'Never been much of a one for foreign food – how's it cooked?' A dutiful ripple of laughter from the non-ACT agents in the audience ran round the room.

Flora had dealt with bigger egos than this and she turned the full force of her sarcasm on him. 'OK, for those of you who are struggling with this let me recap,' she said, smiling at the supervisor. He glared at her with a look that could've stripped paint. She smiled once more and continued. 'The ACT report shows beyond any doubt that over the past five or more years there have been a number – how many, nobody seems to know – of thefts involving uncatalogued papyrus and parchment fragments dating from the first century BC to the fourth century AD –'

'Tell me who and why and I might be interested,' interrupted the supervisor, trying to regain the upper hand.

'Very well, I will,' said Flora. 'I haven't enough proof yet, but I think it goes something like this. Firstly, the thefts are connected. Secondly, people steal art works because they can sell them on. In other words, the buyers create the demand – a bit like drugs I suppose. So who are the buyers?' Nobody risked a reply so she carried on. 'The end buyers are usually collectors – an illustrated manuscript or a first folio by Shakespeare are things of beauty, things you can gaze on in wonder and adore.... but this stuff? Most of it's incredibly dull – a laundry list is still a laundry list even if it's two thousand years old and apart from telling us what people were wearing back then, its interest is limited – so limited that nobody's ever got around to cataloguing, yet alone reading it. Even the museums they were stolen from thought these finds so uninteresting that they didn't even bother putting them on display. So I'll ask the question again: who's paying for this stuff to be stolen and why?'

'Someone looking for information about something?' ventured an agent sitting in the front row.

'Like buried treasure, you mean?' asked Flora. This raised a laugh and the tension eased a little. 'And why not? You're the experts, you tell me, but I don't think that's far off the truth. Somebody, somewhere in your country thinks these writings are capable of telling them something. What that something is, I don't know yet, but they want to have it to themselves.'

'Nice theory,' said the supervisor, putting his hands behind his head and stretching his feet out in front of him. 'Perfect for keeping yourself in a job. While you take the next ten years on Christ knows what daily rate decoding King Tut's Christmas card list, we all sit around on our dumb asses watching in admiration. Is that the plan?'

Instead of reacting how he'd hoped, Flora just laughed: at him or with him, he wasn't sure. 'If only I'd thought of that first,' she smiled. 'In case you're wondering, I'm not getting paid for this. I have a day job, teaching and researching at the University of Oxford: term starts in a few weeks, I have a huge pile of documents to work through if I'm to help you and,' she smiled at the supervisor once more, 'I have better things to do than waste my time in an intellectual fencing match with an unarmed opponent.' The barb found its mark. 'I'm going to hand back to Special Agent Cohen, and unless there are any other questions, I'll leave you with what I think is the most plausible theory. Your buyer is someone who sees a message in these works, particularly the encrypted ones, at a guess: a message that may not be there or one we haven't found yet. If I find it, I'll tell you and you'll have your motive.' Flicking the projector to the blank at the end of the presentation, Flora walked off the stage and resumed her seat next to Cohen. She noticed he'd gone red in the face and for a moment thought he was crying. Then she realised he was doing his utmost to suppress a fit of the giggles at his supervisor's public humiliation.

The mood of good humour was short lived. As Flora and Cohen left the room, they noticed the supervisor deep in conversation with the head of the Art Crime Team. 'So what's that all about?' she asked as they walked back to the elevator.

Cohen gave a resigned shrug. 'At a guess, it's my boss bitching like hell to get me back. With the exception of the head of the ACT, we're only seconded for as long as they need us, or more usually, until they get fed up with our supervisors' whining.'

'And yours wants you back?'

A double ring announced the arrival of the elevator. 'It's not so much about wanting me back,' said Cohen, pressing the down button. 'He fought like hell not to let me go in the first place. His clear-up stats for this year suck and stats are all this organisation rates you on.' As they stepped out into the lobby, Cohen's cell-phone began to ring. 'That'll be him now. You dropped me in some deep shit back there, you know that?' He answered. 'Yes, she's with me right now.' He looked at Flora and she saw his face go pale. 'Shit! When? Fuck. Yeah, OK, I'll tell her. We're on our way down.' He rang off. 'Change of plan, Flora, we've got a problem.'

'Look, I'm sorry if I was a bit brusque with him but –'

'No, it's nothing to do with my supervisor. He's pissed off at you but it's not that; I'll tell you about it when we get to the basement.'

'The basement?' Flora asked, trotting along behind to keep up with his long strides. 'What's down there?'

'The garage and a paddy wagon with no windows for putting bad guys in. You're going for a little ride as they say on TV.'

Chapter Twenty-nine

Rome AD 65

Josephus screamed again: begging, gasping, the last vestiges of resistance destroyed. The rope around his wrists was now looped over one of the roof beams, pulling his arms, which were still fastened together behind his back, upwards into a position of indescribable agony. The first time the two men hauled on the rope, his toes remained just in contact the floor but the pain in his shoulders was unbearable. Then, they pulled him clean off the ground, leaving him hanging for five minutes while he screamed.

Ignoring the tears, the cries and the pleading, Paul nodded and the rope was slackened just enough for Josephus to take some of the weight off his shoulder joints and to get his breath.

'I'll ask you again,' said Paul in a matter-of-fact voice and this time don't lie to me or we'll break your arms. 'You're going to die anyway, so it's up to you whether it's quick or whether we take our time over it.'

'Please,' sobbed Josephus. 'I've told you everything. Vespasian's helping me, Giora's gone home and the emperor provides manpower and money. That's all. Now for God's sake let me down, I can't stand it –'

'But that's the whole point,' Paul replied, savouring his victim's agony. 'If you could stand it, you'd carry on lying to us. Now, for the last time before I have your feet burnt off, who betrayed Peter?'

'I've already told you I don't know his name,' sobbed Josephus. 'Somebody at the theatre told Alityros there was a meeting so we checked it out to make sure it wasn't a trap. We got to the workshop, found them all there and gave the sign to the Praetorians. Please, you must believe me.'

'You really are a bore and a stupid one at that,' said Paul stroking his beard. He signalled to one of his men. 'Go and tell the blacksmith and his boy to clear off for an hour, we're going to need the furnace. Give him this,' he said, tossing him a gold coin.

Josephus began wailing again, twisting in a vain attempt to ease the pain shooting through his whole body. Then, at the sound of returning footsteps on wooden boards he screamed in terror, but instead of strong arms bearing him away to the smithy, the end wall exploded in a shower of splinters as a squad of Roman soldiers burst through the jagged hole

231

into the room. 'Which one's Paul?' shouted the commander and Josephus felt the rope go slack as two soldiers piled into his torturers, cutting them down with their swords.

'Him, the old one with the beard,' he gasped. One of the soldiers untied him and he collapsed onto the floor, his arms flopping uselessly by his sides.

'Come on,' said the guard commander, Nero's having a meeting with Proculus and Vespasian and he'd like you to join them.' He helped Josephus up, and supporting him around the shoulders, led him back down the stairs.

By the time they reached the palace Josephus had regained some use of his arms although still couldn't raise his hands above waist height.

Seated around a circular fountain were the emperor, Proculus and Vespasian: Nero, he noted with concern, wasn't smiling. Behind Nero's chair stood two men, one displaying senatorial rank, the other in the uniform of a Praetorian centurion.

'So glad you could join us, Josephus,' the emperor said, his voice laden with menace. 'Perhaps you can explain to me why you kept the news of this foul conspiracy to yourself.'

Josephus looked nervously at his two high-ranking friends but neither of them would meet his gaze. 'I was advised,' he said, 'that evidence against the plotters was incomplete and that there would be no risk of harm to you, sir, if their arrest were delayed while the final proof was obtained.'

'And did that seem reasonable to you? Did it sound like the truth?'

He wasn't sure how to answer. 'It sounded plausible, sir. Admiral Proculus told me about a woman in Puteoli – Epicharis, I think…'

'Go on,' said Nero.

'Well that's it. She told Admiral Proculus about the conspiracy, he pretended to go along with it to get further information and by now she should be under arrest.'

The emperor made no reply and turned to the senator who stood behind him. 'Well, Nerva, what do you think?'

Nerva snorted in disdain. 'He's learned his lines well. All Jews are liars and this one's no different. All three of them were in it up to their eyes and now they're trying to wriggle.'

Nero turned the other way. 'Tigellinus. What about you?'

'I think they could be telling the truth. One second if you'll permit, sir?' Nero nodded and the centurion left the room to return about three minutes later. 'I've just spoken to my detachment commander. Just as

Vespasian said, sir, the Christian Paul and some of his followers have been taken. This man,' he pointed at Josephus, 'was present. I believe that if Epicharis really is under arrest as Proculus has said, then they're telling the truth.' Nerva glared at him and muttered something under his breath.

'Very well,' said Nero, turning once more to his three unhappy guests. 'You gentlemen are under house arrest. If you are found outside the precincts of the palace I will take it as an admission of your guilt.' He stood and spoke to Tigellinus and Nerva. 'You two, get me a full list of names. Arrest those you can find. Those in the provinces, you are to inform them it is my will that they commit suicide. You may leave, all of you.'

Josephus, Vespasian and Proculus were led away. 'So what went wrong?' asked Josephus as they sat together at the meal table, for the moment all differences in rank forgotten.

'Nerva,' said Vespasian. 'Like I told you, I'd briefed him on what we'd found, I even told him when we planned to make the arrests and he simply moved a day early to make himself look like the empire's saviour while we, by implication, looked like members of the plot. Our lives depend on Tigellinus now.' He looked towards Josephus. 'There's something else.'

'What?'

'Nerva will get all the credit for catching Paul.'

Josephus shivered. 'He was about to kill me, you do realise that?'

'Yes. Sorry about that,' Vespasian said, looking down at the floor. 'My fault I'm afraid.' The emperor has known for a long time that Paul has been trying to track you down. Paul knows who you are and what you're trying to do so Nero gave me an order: use you as bait.'

'And so you set me up?' asked Josephus, his face a picture of stunned disbelief.

'Given a choice between risking your life and disobeying a direct command from my emperor, I'm sorry, but you came a poor second. We tipped Paul's followers off that you'd be leaving my house to walk back to the palace and we had you followed to see where they'd take you. The idea was to grab Paul and then send in the Praetorians before he had time to do you any harm.'

'With all the respect I owe your rank, sir,' spat Josephus. 'You were several hours late. Those bastards nearly pulled my arms out of their sockets....' Josephus broke down and wept.

Proculus put a comforting hand on his shoulder. 'There was nothing

233

either of us could do. We've both spent most of today arguing for our lives in front of the emperor. Paul's dead and so are the others who abducted you: there's nothing more to worry about.'

'Did they manage to get any useful information out of him?' asked Josephus, still fighting back the tears. 'We all wanted him dead but there's a whole network of his followers still out there.'

'I doubt it,' said Vespasian. 'If what Nerva said is true they dragged the survivors outside and decapitated them on the spot.'

Time hung heavily as their house arrest dragged on. First to be released was Proculus. Epicharis had indeed been arrested in Puteoli the day before Nerva exposed the conspiracy, thus validating the admiral's version of events. Vespasian's release came a few days later, Nero, in a rare fit of lucidity having realised that attempted coups rarely come as single spies and securing his future would require all the loyal supporters he could muster.

Josephus was released at the same time but Piso's abortive conspiracy had changed his relationship with the emperor for ever. At Nerva's suggestion, Vespasian was sent on a diplomatic mission to Greece and Josephus filled his time planning the next move against his father's killers. Didymus, it was said, had achieved little success in peddling the Christian cult to the Armenians and so had drifted further east, eventually finding more success on the south-east coast of India, almost at the limits of the known world.

So Josephus turned his attention closer to home. Word had come from Giora that Yehudas and Simon Kananaios were preaching at towns along the Syrian coast and both made frequent trips to the Phoenician city of *Colonia Berytus*, modern Beirut. However, without a date for Vespasian's return and access to the emperor limited, the risks of tackling them on his own were too great.

While studying one of Pliny's maps of Phoenician Syria, he heard a knock at the door. 'Alityros, what a lovely surprise,' he said, getting to his feet to greet his guest. 'Please come in...' his face fell. Alityros stood in the open door, red-eyed and clutching a parchment scroll to his chest.

'I'm sorry, I can't,' he said, shaking his head. 'I've got to get straight back to the emperor.'

Josephus rose from his seat. 'You look like you've seen a ghost. What on earth's the matter?'

Alityros' face crumpled. 'It's the lady Poppaea. She's dead.' He burst into tears. Josephus stood rooted to the spot, unable to think of anything to say. 'She went into labour last night. The baby got stuck and the doctors couldn't do anything. They're both dead. Nero's beside himself.'

'Oh God, no. Please send him my condolences,' said Josephus. 'Sit down, Alityros. Let me fetch you a cup of wine.'

'No, Josephus, there's more.' He handed him the scroll which bore the imperial seal.

Josephus took it. 'What's this?'

'Read it. The emperor wants me to return with your answer.'

The message was short and simple. 'Do you know what it says?' Josephus asked, turning round to face him.

'I haven't read it but I know the rough gist and I'm sorry, Josephus, I really am. I tried to talk to him but it's no good: I think he's gone mad, really and truly mad this time.'

With trembling hands, Josephus gave back the letter. 'He says I talked him into persecuting the Christians and now their god has punished him by taking Poppaea and their baby son. I've got two days to leave Rome or face trial for treason.'

Alityros bit his lip as a fat tear rolled down his cheek. 'I know. You mustn't stay: you'll be convicted and crucified if you accept a trial.'

Josephus took a deep breath. 'I'm not stupid. Tell the emperor... I don't know... tell him I'll go, tell him I'll miss his musical recitals and the stupid chariot-driving. I don't care – just tell him what he wants to hear: after all, that's what everybody else does, don't they?' Alityros sniffed and nodded in reply.

'Thanks, Alityros, I appreciate it.' The actor made no reply and turned to go. Josephus called him back. 'And thanks for everything. We couldn't have done it without you.' They embraced a last time and Alityros left, his face streaming with tears.

Chapter Thirty

Washington DC

Flora followed Cohen across the basement car park of the FBI building. Near the ramp up to street level stood a custody wagon with two uniformed guards in the cab. He opened the rear door, helped Flora into the neon-lit confines of what was effectively a cell on wheels, and sat down beside her on the bench. The door slammed shut. 'You still haven't told me what this is all about,' she said.

'Your house in Oxford was broken into.'

She clapped her hand to her mouth and tried not to burst into tears. 'Bloody bastards. Is there much damage? What have they taken? I can't believe it,' she spat.

'Just hold on a minute,' said Cohen, putting a consoling arm round her shoulder. 'There was no damage and so far as they know, nothing of value was taken.'

Trying to hide how dejected and homesick she felt, she looked at him imploringly. 'I don't understand. Who are "they" and how do they know what's valuable to me?'

'While you were in Rome, some of Giles Smith's "Friends" as he calls them, let themselves into your house and your car. Correct?' She nodded and he continued. 'During their visit they fitted movement sensors, so small even you wouldn't notice, and the detectors picked up a couple of intruders. They were only in the house a few minutes, time enough to look in all the rooms and turn on your computer. The Friends had a good look round afterwards and judging from the imprints on your notepad by the phone it's possible whoever broke in may've got a copy of the travel itinerary you'd written on it.'

'So they weren't burglars? But that means –'

'Precisely. The people who hit the dig site and the lab. Probably not the same ones, but working for the same employer.'

'And now they know I'm here. I want to go home, Ben,' she said, staring straight ahead.

'You can if you like,' he replied, giving her shoulder a squeeze. 'But you're a lot safer here, you do realise that, don't you?'

'I suppose,' she said. 'Where are you taking me?'

'To the safest place on the eastern seaboard. Does the name

236

"Quantico" mean anything to you?'

Her face fell. 'Whatever for? Are you really going to lock me up for leaving notes by the telephone?'

'Flora, nobody's locking you up. As I'm sure you know, Quantico is a US Marine base which also houses the FBI Academy, the CIA Academy plus a whole bunch of folks who officially don't exist but are very much on our side. Safe enough for you?'

'Sorry,' she said. 'I was upset about the house that's all. I'm not thinking straight.'

'That's OK,' he replied, removing his arm from around her shoulder. 'Your house will be fine. And in case you're worried about your things, one of our agents will collect them from the hotel.'

She thought for a moment. 'But hold on, I was booked in as Lavinia Crump. They'd never have found me.'

'Some of them may know what you look like. All they'd have to do was sit in the lobby of the Marriott and wait. We couldn't take the risk. Still, it's only for one night and then we're off again.'

'Where to?' Flora asked.

'New York. Christies have a sale of pre-Christian and Common Era art and Mr Grossman, with your help, is going to make a nuisance of himself again. My little tantrum in Geneva got picked up – hardly front page stuff but anyone active in the market will have seen it. '

'But what if somebody spots me in New York?'

'They won't. They probably won't even come looking – this is just a precaution.'

'I'm not sure whether I should feel happier now,' she said.

'Listen, when we get to New York, unless I say otherwise, stay in the background and duck if anyone points a camera at you: good practice for guns.' Flora scowled and made no reply.

The FBI accommodation at Quantico was basic and functional – liveable but not the Marriott, she thought as she unpacked for the second time in two days. Later she decided to go for a walk but on strolling out through the reception area, her eye was caught by the headline of the Washington Post. "Evangelicals claim fresh evidence on New Testament". Underneath was a photograph of a beaming Donald Sumter holding aloft a piece of paper. According to the caption, it was a copy of an early first-century parchment fragment. The article went on to cover Sumter's claims that it was but one of many, recently translated by the team at William Sunday University and which "proved beyond doubt", as Sumter put it, that the New Testament, was founded in documented fact.

The article repeated the same line she'd seen him give on the TV show, but as she read on her mouth fell open in disbelief at his claims of having single-handedly saved much of the document hoard found at Pompeii for posterity. He alone had possessed the foresight to photograph many of the fragments subsequently stolen during the raid. Flora snorted with disgust: you kept that one to yourself, didn't you, Donald? she fumed. Typical bloody Sumter, just the kind of thing he'd do. On the inside pages was a feature on the Professor, describing him as the Republican Party's favourite evangelist. Challenged – relatively gently – by the interviewer over his failure to condemn the recent spate of threats and attacks aimed at pro-choice groups, stem-cell research labs and doctors who carried out abortions, his response took the form of a counter-attack against Roe v Wade and the "baby-killers in our midst", as he called them, with just enough criticism of the recent murder of two doctors in Michigan to keep himself onside.

Midtown Manhattan

The New York salerooms of Christie's are in the Rockefeller Center and Flora sat in the back row watching in fascination. The first lots under the hammer were figurines and pottery from Asia Minor. Cohen, in his guise as Benjamin Grossman, made sure everyone knew he was there by bidding enthusiastically and helping the price along but then, with an uncanny knack, dropping out just three rounds short of the sale price. Later, he made successful bids for papyrus and parchment fragments preserved in air-tight glass blocks and for a series of Akkadian clay tablets inscribed with cuneiform script.

Just after twelve thirty they took a break and Cohen led the way, turning into East 50th Street, weaving his way through the lunchtime crowds with Flora struggling to keep up. He checked, halted by a bump with another hurrying New Yorker. Both men apologised and moved on. Flora caught a glimpse of the other man – small, wiry, with close-set features and dark, slicked-down hair – just another face in the crowd, and she wove her way through a gaggle of tourists, finally reaching Cohen's side. 'In here,' he said, showing her through a nondescript doorway and up a flight of steps. 'Best food in Midtown.'

They ordered and settled down to discuss the lots that had gone under the hammer during the morning session and also the phenomenon that was Donald Sumter. According to Cohen, the Professor had also made the New York Times. 'Seen anyone of interest in the sale room,

238

Ben?' asked Flora, eager to change the subject.

'Not so far, and I don't really expect to. And hey,' he said, adopting his Israeli accent once more, 'don't be getting so familiar: it's Mr Grossman, Lavinia, and don't you forget it.'

'Whoops,' she said. 'Sorry about that.'

He smiled and reverted to his normal way of speaking. 'In here it's not a problem, but I don't want you letting it slip when we get back to the sale. And coming back to your original question, I'd be very surprised if I recognised anyone here; I'm hoping people will start to recognise me –' He paused, distracted by his cell phone announcing the receipt of a new text message and put his hand inside his jacket pocket to silence it. 'What the fuck - ?'

Flora looked up, 'What's happened? Bad news?'

'I dunno,' Cohen replied, pulling a folded piece of notepaper from the same pocket. He read the handwritten message and handed it across the table to Flora. 'Looks like things have started moving already. This just turned up in my pocket.' She read: "I see you're a buyer. I'm selling. Call me." Underneath was a telephone number. 'It'll be a prepaid cell-phone,' he said. 'Dollar to a dime when I call it'll bounce to voicemail. Let's give it a go.' Cohen dialled the number. 'Yeah, hi, this is Grossman. I'm interested. Call me at this number.' He rang off and turned once more to Flora. 'Did you get a look at the guy I bumped into just before we got here?'

'Sorry, no.'

He held up the piece of paper between forefinger and thumb. 'Well, whoever he was, he's a damn good pickpocket to pass me this without my noticing.

'So now what happens?' she asked.

'I call in the number to my colleagues in DC, just in case it's known, then I wait for a call-back, we'll set up a meet and take it from there.'

From opposite him came a sharp intake of breath. 'Does that "we" include me?'

'Yup, I'll need you to validate anything they bring along. But don't worry,' he said. 'We'll have company.'

Bedford-Stuyvesant, Brooklyn

Raymond picked up his cell phone and dialled Irvine's number. As expected, the call diverted to voicemail. 'Hi, this is Raymond, we met a while back and I think you should get in touch with me. I know you prefer to write but this is urgent: I have another customer, an Israeli gentleman by the name of Grossman – I assume you know the name. My offer of first refusal still stands but if you're not interested, please let me know and I'll take my business elsewhere. A very good day to you, sir.'

'Think it'll work?' asked Luzzo. 'What if Grossman's not interested? What if he goes to the police?'

'Don't panic. He won't go anywhere. After all, Grossman left you a voicemail, didn't he?' said Raymond, lighting a cigarette. 'So long as he offers enough to cover our losses, we can wave goodbye to Irvine and the Alabama Rednecks and get on with our lives. I've had enough of their bullshit.'

'You want I should talk to anyone back home about this?'

'No. They'll only get excited and start shooting at people. That's not how I operate. Just set up the meet.'

'Where? D'you wanna use the offices again?'

Raymond thought for a moment. 'Yeah, why not? Just in case friend Grossman isn't legit. It'll be safer.'

Midtown Manhattan

During the afternoon session Benjamin Grossman put in bids for four more lots, buying a set of Assyrian cylinder seals carved from lapis lazuli. Flora stuck to her briefing and kept to the back of the room, making sure she wasn't photographed. Grossman, although networking and handshaking as though his life depended on it also managed to keep his face out of shot.

They'd barely arrived back at their hotel when the call came. The screen on Cohen's cell phone showed "number withheld" and he made a great show of tracking down something to write on, then more time was lost while he searched for a pen that would work, all in the hope that his colleagues in the technical division were triangulating the caller's location. 'Look, if you're going to waste my time, you can forget it,' said Raymond after yet another pen was dismissed as useless.

'No, it's OK,' replied the heavily-accented voice. 'I got a pencil now. Let's meet at my hotel…you don't want that? OK, where *do* you want to meet?' Cohen jotted down the address on the East Side: it was walking distance from the hotel. 'No, I'm busy tomorrow. How about Friday?' They bickered over the date and finally Cohen yielded. 'Yeah, OK, have it your way, ten AM tomorrow if we have to. What are you selling?'

'First century stuff. Latin, Aramaic and Greek manuscripts plus a few Coptic pieces. Rock-solid provenance: been in the same Syrian family for years.'

'Family provenance ain't worth ass-paper. I want my assistant to verify it,' replied Cohen.

'Your assistant you say? Hold on,' Raymond muted the call and spoke to Luzzo. 'I thought you said he was on his own?'

Luzzo shrugged. 'He is so far as I know.'

'Says he wants to bring his "assistant" to verify the goods. I don't like the sound of it.'

'A cop?' asked Luzzo, a worried frown on his face.

'Could be. Wait a second.' Raymond unmuted and continued. 'Mr Grossman, I had assumed any meetings would be one-to-one: a third party adds an... an increased level of risk. As a fellow private collector, I'm sure you realise that...how shall I put this, "misunderstandings" can occur and false accusations of all sorts can lead to tiresome conversations with the authorities. Conversations I'm sure neither of us has time for –'

'Now just you wait,' interrupted Cohen. 'First, I don't even know your name and second I don't like people suggesting my assistant is a cop or that I'm setting you up. *Benzona*, screw you, I'll take my business someplace else –'

'No, don't hang up, Mr Grossman, please. It was rude of me not to introduce myself: my name is Raymond and I can assure you I had no intention of insulting either you or your assistant. If you could just let me know his name so I can tell reception to expect you both –'

'Her name: he's a she. Miss Lavinia Crump of the University of Bologna if you want to check her out. And anyone less like a cop, well, you'll see when you meet her.' Cohen laughed out loud at the thought and then jotted down a few last details before the conversation ended. 'Bingo,' he said, smiling at Flora who tried without success to smile back. 'We've found Raymond. Ten o'clock tomorrow and it's only a couple of blocks from here. Everything I say on this phone is recorded and now all we have to do is hope like hell we can talk my supervisor into organising a backup team for the arrest at short notice.'

'Couldn't you delay it?' Flora asked.

'You heard,' he said. 'I tried. This Raymond guy knows what he's doing. He figures that if I'm a cop I won't have time to put together a sting in under twenty four hours and he won't meet in a public place which isn't a good sign either.'

'Can you put a team together in time?' she asked, her hand trembling as she put her glass down on the bar.

'They'll push back on budget but I'll give it my best shot. I feel happier having back-up just in case things go wrong.'

'You don't think they *will* go wrong, do you?'

'Not a chance. These guys are fences, middle-men, house cats. You'll be fine.'

'What do you want me to do?' she asked, hoping he'd say something like "stay in the bar until I come back".

'The next task for this evening is for you to take a look at some mug-shots to see if you recognise the guy who bumped me today. Let me take a shower and get the laptop set up and I'll give you a call.'

William Sunday University, Alabama

Donald Sumter strode down the corridor of William Sunday University's administrative block; head down, brows knitted, he made the perfect caricature of a rhino who has just spotted a particularly annoying Land Rover for the third time that day.

Without breaking stride he pushed open the door to Irvine's office and stormed in, slamming it behind him. 'Do come in, Donald,' said Irvine, looking up from behind his immaculately tidy desk. 'My door is always open so there's no need to knock.'

Sumter ignored him and threw himself down into one of the armchairs in Irvine's book-lined study. 'We've got a problem. Morley.'

'Who's Morley?'.

'The Reverend Morley. Remember?'

Irvine scratched his head. 'Vaguely. Remind me.'

Sumter rolled his eyes. 'The handover at the church. The shooting. He's the pastor. Remember?' Irvine's icy calm was starting to grate on his nerves. 'This is important, Andrew. Please look at me when I'm talking to you.'

With a sigh, Irvine took off his glasses. 'Go on, Donald, get it off your chest. I'm listening.'

Sumter ground his teeth. 'The wretched man's just spent the last hour in my office telling me about the terrible sin he's committed in not telling the police the truth about what he saw.'

Irvine sat bolt upright, the mask of indifference gone. 'Donald, if there's even a hint of scandal, the campaign's finished. We've taken enough risks already. If the police start nosing around again... well it doesn't even bear thinking about.'

'He's seen Raymond and his people face-to-face: if he picks them out of a police line-up, then what? He knows about the shooting. Now you understand why I say there's a problem.' Sumter thumped the arm of the chair, sending up a cloud of dust.

'Yes I do and the solution's simple. I take it you tried to reason with him?'

Sumter waved his arms in a gesture of exasperation. 'Of course I did. He's going to think about it over the weekend and come and see me on Monday.'

'Good, that at least gives us time,' said Irvine.

'Time for what?'

'Leave it with me. You don't need to know – *quod non videt oculus, cor non dolet.*' What the eye doesn't see, the heart doesn't grieve over.

'Andrew, too many people have been harmed already. This has to stop,' said Sumter.

'Thank you, Donald, for the lesson in morality,' he replied. 'Don't you worry, neither you nor I will be required to break the sixth commandment. Just let me handle it.'

Sumter sniffed condescendingly. 'And what about this wretched Israelite that your friend Raymond mentioned? Grossman, isn't it? What if he offers a better price?'

'Let me talk to Raymond again. If he's willing to be reasonable then Mr Grossman can huff and puff all the way back to Israel for all we care.'

Sumter made a snort. 'Raymond hasn't been very reasonable so far. What if he digs his heels in?'

'Then,' said Irvine, 'we make Mr Grossman go away. And not back to Israel either. We've got too much riding on this to let Jews, atheists and backsliders stand in the way of the Lord's will.'

Chapter Thirty-one

Judea AD 65

The voyage from Ostia along the coast of the eastern Mediterranean was tedious and punctuated by frequent stops to caulk a series of leaks in the *Demeter's* aging timbers. As days turned into interminable weeks under a baking sun and capricious winds, determined, or so it seemed, to prevent the ship ever reaching Herod's great port at Caesarea, so Josephus' anger and sense of injustice festered. Aware that Nero's support could never be taken for granted and that their mutual hatred of the *Chrestos* cult came from entirely different motivations, Josephus fumed at the irony of the emperor's own superstitions causing this sudden unwillingness to confront another far more dangerous one. Five of the Seven Stars were still at liberty and the cult was spreading like a cancer.

So much for Roman rationality, he thought, watching the *Demeter's* sail as it flopped in the barely perceptible air currents. Without oars, all they could do was wait and then wait some more. Somewhere to the east and lost in the haze lay the city of Ephesus.

On arrival in Caesarea Josephus found a city in chaos. In the taverns and the markets, truth mingled with half-truth and half-truth with rumour making it impossible for the traveller to know what to believe. Some blamed bandits while others spoke of fanatical *sicarii* behind every rock, waiting to pounce on the unwary, but more general consensus blamed first the Greeks and second the Romans for not keeping the Greeks in order. Whoever was to blame, tales of entire caravans disappearing without trace and of individual travellers meeting gruesome ends were enough to convince him not to risk the overland voyage across Samaria to Jerusalem but to continue by sea down the coast to Joppa.

Things were little better in Jerusalem. Tension between Jews and Greeks simmered just below boiling point, no thanks to a disinterested and undermanned garrison of third-rate Roman infantry. All his family could talk about, once the initial excitement of reunion died down, was the "fourth sect" or Zealots as they styled themselves. So far as Josephus could make out, the Zealots were nothing more than a bunch of young idiots whose religious fervour was being manipulated by their leader, Judas of Galilee, into a murderous cult that used the *sicarii* as its shock troops.

Word of his return spread quickly among Jerusalem's aristocratic families and everywhere he went Josephus was feted as a returning warrior prince. At first, he took pains to play down his achievements, crediting his success to the hand of the God and the help of others, but slowly, almost imperceptibly, he grew into the role, basking in the adulation, which, after a while, he convinced himself he did perhaps deserve after all. The source of these stories – tales which grew more fantastic with each telling – turned out to be Giora and when finally they met, for the first time since he'd left Rome, Josephus was overcome with delight at seeing his old friend.

As they walked in the cool of the evening along the walls of the city, Josephus told him of his expulsion from Rome and his fears that the current turmoil in Jerusalem would prevent him finding the remaining five apostles as they now called themselves.

Giora heard him out. 'Well, you've two less to worry about.'

Josephus' face lit up. 'Why? What's happened?'

'Yehudas and Simon Kananaios. I'll spare you the details, but the new governor of *Colonia Berytus* is a friend of my father's. I take it you got my letter?'

'I did: seems they were causing even more trouble than I'd feared.'

'Well they won't be causing any more,' said Giora. 'I went to *Berytus* in person and as luck would have it, the governor already knew all about what happened in Rome after the fire so he didn't take much persuading that Nero would look favourably on their disappearance.'

'So what did he do to them?'

'Had them sawn in half in the arena.' Josephus shuddered. 'And no, and I didn't stick around to watch, either,' said Giora.

'My family is forever in your debt, Giora,' Josephus said. 'Only three left to find, two if I'm honest because Didymus is in India from what I've heard. With any luck the barbarians will eat him. Philippos is somewhere in Anatolia and Matityahu seems to have disappeared altogether, I don't even know if he's still alive.'

'What worries me is the mob,' Giora said as they reached the towers guarding the Upper Gate.

'What? In Rome?'

'No. Here. Everything's up in the air. Just look around you: the old order is held in contempt and every servant knows better than his master. The Zealots are killing anyone who opposes them and the Romans do nothing. It can't end well.'

Josephus looked at the familiar western face of Herod's Temple. To him, its marble flanks, glowing in the last rays of the sun spoke of permanence and of God's covenant with his chosen people. 'It'll blow over. You'll see. If the Romans so much as stamp their feet, all these vermin will go scuttling back down their holes faster than you can blink.'

'I only hope you're right,' replied Giora.

Chapter Thirty-two

Manhattan, NY

Cohen swore and stuffed the cell-phone back into his pocket. 'Assholes couldn't get a fix on the phone. VOIP routed via a series of proxy servers. "Call us again in three weeks, we're kinda busy". I ask you. Fuck!'

Flora did her best to blank out the diatribe.

Cohen dialled again and within seconds of the conversation starting, Flora was treated to one side of a blazing row. 'Well find them, for Christ's sake,' he yelled into the receiver. 'I know it's late but you're not the one who's gonna get his ass shot off if we don't have cover. Call me back when you've got something.' He stabbed at the disconnect button. 'Assholes!'

'Who's going to get their arse shot off?' Flora asked as soon as the shouting match was over.

'It's a figure of speech,' he said, aiming a kick at the wall. I want the backup team in the offices on the same floor where we're meeting Raymond, but those idiots can't find anyone who works there to give us authority let alone a set of keys. None of the building's facilities numbers are answering either.'

Without a sound, Flora's patience snapped. She folded her arms and narrowed her eyes: anybody who knew her well could have told Cohen this wasn't a good sign. 'So, if I can summarise,' she said calmly. 'This has gone from a simple sting and arrest of a "minor player" as you called him to something requiring the seventh cavalry and all the king's horses just in case we're the ones walking into a trap –'

'Flora, please, you don't understand, I'm under a lot of pressure here.'

'Ben,' she said, raising her hand to silence him. 'Ben, will you listen to me a second? I really think you should.' Cohen stopped in mid-rant and took a nervous pace backwards as she walked towards him. 'Sit down, shut up and listen to me,' she said in that voice which Englishwomen normally reserve for recalcitrant children or badly-behaved Labradors. He obeyed straight away and she continued. 'You want your back-up or whoever they are in the next office, correct?'

'Correct.'

'And you can't find anyone to give you the keys?

'That's right.'

'Do you have an address?'

'Yes. Out in Hoboken,' he replied, avoiding eye-contact.

'So, Einstein, get the landline number.' Cohen said something she didn't catch. 'Say that again!' she shouted at him.

'I said it's an unlisted number. He's not in the goddam phonebook,' he shouted back.

'God, you're hopeless. Can you get a car or do we take a cab?'

'I'll get a car.' He reached for his phone once more

'Good. Now we're getting somewhere,' said Flora. 'You show your badge, you take the keys, his staff get the day off and your supervisor can square things after the event. Alternatively, you can meet Raymond on your own and I can get the next flight back to London.'

The trip to get the keys took just under an hour.

'What we just did was illegal. My supervisor will kill me for this,' said Cohen as they drove back to the hotel.

'I would have killed you far more painfully,' said Flora staring straight ahead from the passenger seat.

He swallowed and then blurted out, 'There is one more thing I forgot to mention.'

'Go on, I'm listening.'

'I'll need you to wear a wire.'

'Not on your nelly.'

'What?'

'It's English for no.'

'Look, Flora, there's something you need to know.'

'I'm listening.'

'The people we're meeting.'

'What about them?'

'How do I put this?' said Cohen. 'Without a definite on who we're meeting then there's a possibility they're likely to be... well...'

'They're likely to be armed. Please, Ben, if you try and patronise me once more, I'm not joking, I will stop trying to help you. Do you understand?'

'Yes, but –'

'Not "yes but". Do you understand?'

'Yes, Flora.'

'Good. Now shut up and listen. You're worried he thinks you're police, right?'

248

'Right.'

'So he's likely to search you. Therefore, you can't carry a weapon and you can't wear a wire. You're meeting on his ground and at short notice, so you haven't got time to put in cameras or microphones or whatever it is they do in the movies. Taken you for a bit of a mug, hasn't he?'

'I wouldn't put it like that,' replied Cohen.

'Wouldn't you? I bloody well would,' she replied. 'You want me to wear the wire because I can refuse to be searched.'

'Something like that.'

'What about your pistol?'

'You said it yourself, Flora. I'll have to go in unarmed. That's why we need the back-up.'

'And this famous back-up team, can they get across the room faster than the proverbial speeding bullet?' she asked.

'N-no, of course not.'

'Well then if things get rough, they'll be in time to find two dead bodies, won't they? At least we'll still be warm.'

They stopped at the next set of lights. 'What are you saying?' he asked.

'I'm saying one of us needs to be armed.'

Cohen turned towards her, his jaw practically on the steering wheel. The lights went red and the cars behind started hooting. 'You can't,' he said as they weaved away from the junction. 'You're a foreign national –'

'I'm not foreign, I'm British.'

'You know what I mean,' he spluttered. 'It's just not allowed. I'd be breaking the law.'

'I'd give it back to you afterwards,' she replied. 'Oh, and by the way, a short-barrelled .38 revolver should do the trick: none of that heavy artillery you people seem so attached to.'

He looked at her with a mixture of amazement and respect. As for Flora, her main concern was that she'd let him see too much of her training.

The alarm went at six thirty and Flora crawled her way unwillingly to the surface of the new day. Dressed once more as frumpy Lavinia she joined Cohen for breakfast. Choosing a table well away from the other early-risers he gave her an update.

'And the weapon?' she asked.

'Got that too. But for God's sake, if you have to use it, hand it to me

249

as soon as you can.'

'Don't worry,' she replied. 'I don't want to go to jail.'

'Oh, I couldn't care less about you getting locked up,' he said, laughing, treating her to a little of her own medicine. 'It's the paperwork I'm worried about.'

Uncomfortably aware of the transmitter pack digging into the small of her back and the tiny microphone rubbing against the skin of her neck at each movement, the previous night's bravado was miles away as she signed in with a "L. Crump" at reception. The elevator stopped on the eleventh floor and he gave her hand a reassuring squeeze. 'Knock 'em dead,' said Cohen.

'Not how I'd have put it, but thanks anyway.'

'Just remember, Grossman and Crump. Collectors of fine art.' he whispered as they approached the frosted glass door bearing the name "Sunlight International Trading Inc". The door on the other side of the landing showed it belonged to "Zeus Consulting Inc". Behind it, were seven armed FBI agents, waiting on Cohen's word to spring the trap.

He pressed the buzzer and a tinny voice from the intercom asked what they wanted. 'Mr Grossman and Miss Crump. We have a meeting at ten o'clock,' said Cohen in reply.

With a click, the door opened and they walked in. Waiting for them stood two men: one black and in his mid-forties; tall, slim, well-dressed and with just enough grey at the temples to add a touch of distinction. They shook hands and he introduced himself as Raymond. His colleague, Mr Luzzo, was half a head shorter but what caught her attention was the butt of a pistol protruding from his waistband. Raymond noticed her look of alarm. 'Don't worry, Miss Crump,' he said, with a disarming smile, 'just a sensible precaution until we get to know each other better.'

'I appreciate that, Mr Raymond,' she said, but is a gun really necessary for a simple transaction like this?' As she'd hoped, the FBI team leader, fifty feet away across the lobby heard her loud and clear in his headset.

While Luzzo bustled about in the kitchen making coffee the three chatted amiably. From the corner of her eye, Flora could see Raymond sizing his visitors up, and sat with her hands folded in her lap, hoping that their double-act was working.

Luzzo returned with the coffee: thin, bitter and watery, it left Flora wincing from the first sip. Still, she was supposed to be an uptight, humourless blue-stocking, so her reaction to the plastic cupful of unpleasantness fitted the image rather well she thought. 'Now,' said

Raymond, getting to his feet. 'First things first. I'm sure you know the score, Mr Grossman, Miss Crump, but I need to make sure you're who you say you are. Just a formality,' he added by way of reassurance. 'Wouldn't be the first time I'd met a collector who turned out to be a thief or a policeman down on his arrest numbers looking to put a hard-working member of my community in the frame. Could I ask you to stand up for a moment, Mr Grossman.'

Cohen grumbled and chuntered but complied none the less. Luzzo kept his hand on his pistol and watched carefully. 'Thank you, Mr Grossman,' said Raymond. 'Now, Miss Crump. Please don't take this the wrong way, but I need to search you.'

'You'll do no such thing,' Flora said.

'I really must insist —' she could feel his resolve beginning to show the first, tiny flicker of weakness.

'Insist all you like, Mr Raymond, you are not searching me, I am neither a common criminal nor a policewoman.' She stood up and turned to Cohen. 'Mr Grossman, I strongly suggest we leave at once.'

'OK, OK, I'm sorry,' said Raymond, nodding to Luzzo who disappeared into the next room. 'No offence, ma'am. Please sit down.'

Flora pursed her lips in a way she'd seen her mother do dozens of times when irritated with Flora's father. 'Your apology is accepted, Mr Raymond. Now please may we continue, neither Mr Grossman nor I have time to waste.'

Luzzo returned with a folder which he opened and placed on the table. 'Here are some copies of what we've got on offer,' said Raymond. First and second century Greek, Aramaic and Latin. A mixture of intact codices and scroll fragments. Also some pages from the *Devil's Codex* with which I'm sure you're familiar.'

Flora fought back the desire to leap on the copies but instead, drew out her reading glasses with a display of studied indifference and began reading. From the very first line, she felt sure they would notice her hand shaking, for in it she held what was without any doubt a photocopy of the original Aramaic copy of *Antiquities of the Jews*, lost since antiquity and stolen from the lab at Pompeii. 'Yes, quite interesting,' she said. 'Obviously I can't tell from a copy but given the calligraphy, sentence structure and grammar it looks genuine: I couldn't possibly date it from a copy of course.' Raymond smiled dutifully. Flora picked up the next copy. Again, Josephus' style was unmistakable. 'And how did you come by these documents?' she asked as nonchalantly as possible.

'I have contacts in Italy.' He watched her for a reaction but Flora

251

remained stony-faced.

'And do they have more where this came from?'

He smiled. The rapport was building nicely as both played the other. 'I'm led to believe so.'

'*Tombaroli*,' she said.

'I prefer the term "freelance archaeologist" myself,' said Raymond.

'Let's not argue over terminology,' Flora replied. 'We both know where these came from. They're from Pompeii, aren't they?'

Raymond leant forward in his chair. 'Yeah, but so what? Does it matter where they're from?' She'd got the admission he knew the finds were stolen, now came the hard part.

'Provenance is what interests me, that's all,' she replied. 'Now may I see the originals?'

The speed with which she pitched the question into the conversation caught Raymond off guard. 'Um, yeah, of course,' he hesitated for a moment. 'You must understand that some of these pieces are too fragile to be moved around, particularly in this weather. The more valuable pieces are being professionally conserved.'

'I'm very pleased to hear it,' She snapped her fingers. 'Now, the originals please. We haven't got all day.'

'No. No, of course not,' he replied and nodded once more to Luzzo who returned with a cardboard box which he set on the table. He reached in to take the top document from the pile and Flora delivered a slap to the back of his hand.

'Mr Luzzo,' she said in outraged tones. 'Do not even *think* of handling those pages with bare hands.' He immediately sprang back like a scolded child and Flora reached into her large, unfashionable handbag and drew on a pair of white cotton gloves. Taking a magnifying glass she gazed in wonder at the parchment in front of her. One side was written in Greek and on the other side was a jumble of Greek characters, many of them crossed out and replaced: clearly an early exercise in encryption, possibly done by one of Josephus' scribes. So lost in wonder was Flora that she almost forgot the role play. Luckily, she caught herself in time and said, 'These are wonderful. They're just the pieces we've been looking for.' An innocuous-sounding phrase, but one she and Cohen had pre-arranged as the signal that they'd found pages from the robbery in Italy.

Cohen in turn gave the code-word for the team to move in. Speaking loudly and in Grossman's version of English he said. 'Yes, this is the work from the dig at Pompeii. I am happy.'

His words crackled in the team leader's earpiece. On his sign the squad moved soundlessly to the door of Sunlight Trading where he took out the cloned swipe card. It didn't work. Precious seconds ebbed away. He stood aside and gestured towards the back of the group and two agents stepped forward with a door-breaking ram. The noise made by the team as they prepared to take out the door was audible inside. Luzzo shot a nervous glance at Raymond and pulled out his pistol, pointing it first at Flora and then at Cohen. 'Stay right where you are.' Cohen froze.

The outer door exploded into fragments, but before the team had taken more than three paces, they heard Luzzo shout from inside. 'Stop! One step further and they're dead. Now just back the fuck off.' A voice replied. 'Federal agents. Lay down your weapons and you will not be harmed.'

'Screw you!' Luzzo laughed and swung the pistol again. From outside, the team leader heard a gunshot and immediately, a woman's voice screaming.

Chapter Thirty-three

Judea AD 67

> *"Now Vespasian desired greatly to destroy Jotapata, for he had obtained intelligence that the major part of the enemy's army had retired there, and that the fortress was, so he was told, a place of great security to them."*
> — Flavius Josephus, *The Wars of the Jews, Book 3*

Vespasian's army showed no mercy to the defeated: the city of Gadara was razed and its male population butchered. The massacre of the Roman garrison at Jerusalem and the rout of *Legio XII Fulminata* under the indecisive Cestius Gallus, were fresh in his officers' minds, so no more chances were to be taken.

The rebel forces under Josephus had fortified nineteen towns, but one by one they fell as their inhabitants surrendered without a fight, desperate to avoid the fate of the thousands at Gadara who had paid the ultimate price for resisting the might of Rome's legions. When the citizens of Tiberias not only refused to fight but drove Josephus and his army out beyond the city walls, he had no option but to retreat to Jotapata, his supposedly impregnable headquarters. The weakness of Josephus' hilltop fastness against prolonged siege was its lack of water. However, that year the winter rains had filled the cisterns, grain was plentiful and the need for rationing was accepted by all with only minor grumbles. Furthermore, after the defeat of an initial attempt to take the city by the Roman commander, Placidus, morale was high.

Vespasian's army made camp outside the northern walls and almost immediately launched an assault. Not only was it beaten off, but sallies by the Jewish fighters caused him to withdraw to a safer distance.

The crushing heat of high summer beat down on the barren uplands around the city so now it was merely a question of which side would run out of water first. Advantage always lies with the besieger and despite a few successful attempts to bring supplies in by night across the Roman lines, Josephus and his lieutenants finally accepted that after six weeks of bombardment, defeat and death for the tens of thousands packed within the walls of Jotapata was only a matter of days away. The Romans would put civilians to the sword straight away, but as rebel commanders, suicide at the last moment of resistance was their only alternative to a slow, agonising death in front of the crowds in Nero's circus.

For the small group of men huddled round a table in the battered central redoubt, the news from the northern walls had just brought that last moment ever closer.

The messenger was bloodied, unshaven and exhausted by forty two days of manning the walls. His eyes seemed fixed on some point far in the distance as he spoke. 'Their ramp is nearly level with the top of the outer wall, sir. We've attacked and burned their battering ram twice but they've brought up a new one.'

'Then destroy it too,' said Josephus, his face set in an outward show of determination.

'We aim to, sir, but there's more. An envoy from Vespasian brought this. He said it could only be delivered into your hands because no one else would understand it.' The messenger passed Josephus a papyrus scroll bearing a seal that he recognised at once.

'Is the envoy still here?'

'Yes, sir. He awaits your reply. We've blindfolded him and given him food and water – I told him we've got so much he can take a goatskin-full back with him if he likes.'

'Good man,' said Josephus with a rare chuckle. 'That'll give them something to think about. Sit down and wait while I write a reply.' He spread the papyrus flat, holding it in place with his ink-stand. In the surface of the table, Josephus had scored a *tabula recta* formed by the twenty three letters of the Latin alphabet: the key he knew by heart.

The message to Josephus from Vespasian was stark in its awfulness. Deliver the city and its inhabitants or face a prolonged and very public death for the entertainment of the Roman mob. Josephus took out a wax tablet and began writing his reply. After twenty or so words he stopped, used the key to encrypt the Latin, wrote the encoded version on the unused side of Vespasian's message, double-checking each letter against the key and then wiping the wax tablet clean. When he'd finished, he rolled the papyrus into a cylinder and sealed it. Turning the wooden frame over the candle until every last trace of wax had melted, he turned to the others and said, '*Alea iacta est.*' The die is cast.

'What have you written?' the messenger asked.

'Vespasian wants us to surrender. I've told him my troops will fight to the last man. I also said that if it is God's will that Rome prevails, then I trust his honour as a fellow nobleman to spare our women, our children and the old. Now take it and go.'

Chapter Thirty-four

Manhattan, the East Side

A second gunshot rang out. For good effect, Flora screamed once more at the top of her voice. The arrest team burst into the office to see a fan of blood spattered against the wall and a dark, crimson pool spreading on the floor. Raymond stayed face down where he'd taken cover under the desk and Luzzo lay propped against the wall, clutching his arm and yelling at the top of his voice: the round from Flora's .38 had taken a ricochet off his fourth rib and shattered his left humerus just below the ball joint of his shoulder.

'Will he be all right?' Flora asked, her voice shrill and her bottom lip trembling.

'Sure, ma'am,' the team-leader said, lowering his automatic weapon and applying the safety catch. 'The noisy ones always do fine, it's the quiet ones who're hurt bad.'

Under the influence of a morphine shot, Luzzo calmed down and now sat upright below a small crater in the wall which showed where Cohen had loosed off a second round, aiming deliberately wide. The .38 was now in his pocket.

In all the mayhem following the shooting and arrests no one paid much attention to Flora whose face had turned an unhealthy shade of lime green and was swaying on her feet. 'I don't feel very well, Ben,' she said. 'Would anybody mind if I went and sat down?' Putting his arm around her shoulder Cohen led her to an empty office where, as soon as the door was closed, she burst into tears and threw herself into his arms. 'What have I done?' she sobbed. 'That poor man. I could have killed him.' The sound of a low-velocity round thudding into a human body had brought all the bad memories back.

'He could have killed us. You saved my life, you realise that? Mine, yours and possibly half the arrest team.' She shook her head and snivelled miserably, hiding her face against his chest while he stroked the top of her head.

'You don't understand,' replied Flora, her words muffled by his shirt front. 'All I could think of was the finds. I wanted to kill him... I hated him, both of them for what they've ruined. It was so easy. That's what's so awful. And all that blood...'

'Don't worry, he's going to be fine: you did brilliantly and we've still got two live suspects.'

'Then why did you try and finish him off?' she asked, staring up at him accusingly.

'I didn't. I had to fire a second round to make sure I had powder residue on me. There probably won't be any need for them to swab my hands or clothes, but just in case, it needs to look like I fired both rounds. Remember what I said about paperwork?' She nodded and he continued. 'Now, let's get you back to the hotel.'

Cohen collected her the following morning at ten and drove her to the FBI offices at Federal Plaza. 'Got some good news for you,' he said as they headed downtown through the gridlock. 'Your buddy Luzzo's gonna be fine – a few pins and stuff in his arm but that's it – and Raymond's agreed to co-operate.' Flora smiled weakly but said nothing. 'And you,' he said, 'get to play with the finds we took off them. We need to know what's still missing.'

At once, all her tiredness evaporated and she sat upright in her seat, turning a broad smile on him. 'Oh, Ben, that's fantastic. It makes yesterday almost seem worthwhile.'

'Only almost?' he teased.

'You know what I mean. Did you find anything more?'

'Yes and that's what I'm taking you to see. What Raymond brought to the meet was only a small sample of what he had tucked away. I spoke to your Carabinieri buddy Lombardi last night, and it looks like we may've recovered a significant part of what was stolen from Pompeii, but we need you to confirm it for us.'

'It'll be a pleasure,' beamed Flora. 'But hang on a minute. Shouldn't it all go back to Francesco Moretti's team in Pompeii? After all, that's where the finds belong.'

'Don't worry, everything will find its way back to the rightful owners. The Met Museum's looking after everything, but for now, the fewer people who know about the arrests the better, and that includes Moretti and his people.'

'But why? The poor man's worried sick.'

'Let's just say we don't want the news leaking in Italy and making the Carabinieri's job any harder.'

Flora spent the next five days in a room on the second level of the Metropolitan Museum of Art's Thomas J Watson Library, working on the finds retrieved after the raid. When she had finished the final edit of her report she called Cohen.

'Good news?' he asked.

'Not sure.' Flora had checked her results so many times she'd lost count, but they still didn't make sense.

'What do you mean?'

'I'll tell you when I see you. You in the office?'

Half an hour later Cohen showed her into a meeting room. 'So what's missing?' he asked before she'd even had chance to sit down.

'Quite a bit. Probably about seventy five percent.'

'That's bad.'

'It may be worse. There seem to be other sections missing that we didn't know about – well, according to Donald Sumter anyway.'

'What do you mean?'

'Remember we talked about Sumter going on TV and giving press interviews about photos of documents from the Pompeii dig?'

'Vaguely,' replied Cohen.

'He keeps going on about Aramaic texts which he says are eye-witness accounts of the New Testament period – the "Q document" to be precise. Thing is, I simply don't ever remember seeing them.'

'It's a big collection, you could've missed something.'

Flora shook her head. 'Possible but I don't think I did. Although Moretti's people hadn't finished cataloguing, anything in Aramaic would've jumped out at me, particularly something as important as the pages Sumter's on about.'

'So you're saying there's more missing than we thought?'

She thought for a moment. 'Well sort of… it looks that way. I suppose we ought to be grateful to Donald Sumter for being so meticulous. But I'm one hundred percent positive the texts he's copied weren't there when I looked at the collection.'

'So I can tell my supervisor we're onto a new development?'

'Well…'

'It'd be a great help, Flora.'

'OK, Ben. I'll keep my misgivings to myself if it helps.'

'It sure does,' he said, leaping to his feet. 'Stay here, I'll be back in five.' He returned in less than two minutes and this time his face wore a broad grin. 'My supervisor's pissed as hell but you just got me a reprieve. The word from on high is we have to be seen as co-operating with the Italians, and until we find out what happened to the whole collection, the ACT gets to stay on the case. He's gonna call Lombardi now.'

'If it's not a stupid question,' Flora said, wrinkling her brow. 'Had you thought of asking Raymond and his chum to double-check the list of what they've sold?'

'Not a stupid question, and yes we have. Says he doesn't remember anything in Aramaic.'

Flora looked at him scornfully. 'Like he'd recognise Aramaic.'

'Funnily enough, he might. He's an educated guy. Math and statistics major, former senior manager at Enron. Anyway, he lost everything: house, family, kids, the works. Couldn't even get a job in a 7-11 with that hanging over him, so he found another way of paying the bills as he puts it.'

She frowned. 'I wish he'd found some other way of making a living.'

'There's another thing. We know the buyer's still keen and we now know what happened at the first handover. The buyer's contacts tried to double-cross Raymond and he shot one of them. Couple of college kids he says, which ties in with the body the local police found.'

'College kids?'

'Yeah: from your buddy Sumter's Bible College – William Sunday University.'

'That's a weird coincidence,' Flora said.

'Yeah, that's what I thought at first, but when you think about it, if Sumter told his students what he'd been doing in Pompeii – no reason why he shouldn't – and somehow a couple of them got a line into Raymond, after all, he's been fencing artwork for the last ten years or so he says, then it kinda figures that they might want to get involved. Religious fervour and all. Don't forget, they've had stuff taken from their archives too.'

'Any other witnesses?'

Cohen nodded. 'Yeah, and this is where it gets weirder still. Raymond's told us both he and Luzzo were there, but in addition to the two kids, they ran into the local pastor – the Reverend Morley – who comes running into the middle of things, twelve gauge at the ready, all 'cause he thought someone was trying to break into the church. Raymond says he snowed him with some vigilante baloney about how they were going round checking on churches that'd been vandalised.'

'And?'

'Morley's wife reported him missing last Sunday evening. Local cops found him a couple of days later in the woods near their house.'

'Murdered?' asked Flora.

'No, looks like suicide. Full pathology report's not out yet but they're saying he took a big handful of painkillers and slashed his wrists with a box-cutter.'

'Seems rather a lot of coincidences.'

'Sure does. Anyway, after that, they arranged a second meet which involved Luzzo running half way round Alabama before he could make the deal.'

Flora perched on the edge of the table, tapping distractedly at the keyboard of her laptop as she scrolled through her report once more. 'I keep thinking I must've missed something, but I can't see where. Are you sure what we retrieved plus the pieces Raymond claims he sold tie up with the Carabinieri's list of missing finds?'

'Pretty much. Like you said, it hadn't been accurately catalogued but the Aramaic stuff Sumter photographed isn't on anybody's list. We've got to find who's got it.'

Flora looked at him sideways. 'I don't like it when you say "we" like that,' she said. 'Who did you have in mind?'

'Mr Grossman and Miss Crump.'

'I was afraid you were going to say that.'

Cohen smiled. 'Don't worry, it won't be anything like last time.'

'Good,' said Flora, keeping a straight face. 'Because if it is, I'll shoot you first, just in case.'

He threw back his head and laughed. 'OK, enough already,' he said, raising both hands in surrender. 'I've seen you in action. I promise it'll be safe.'

Chapter Thirty-five

Jotapata, Galilee, July AD 67

Inching forward under the cover of darkness, the small Roman force reached the foot of the wall. The officer in charge paused for a moment to make sure there were no stragglers, and then moved off to the left, feeling his way along the stonework, his mouth dry with anticipation. The opening was narrow and set into a deep recess. Heart pounding, he pushed against the door: as promised it was unlocked. Once inside he counted his soldiers through and then shut it behind them, taking the lead for the ascent of the narrow stairway which led into the heart of the fortress. Forty seven days without being able to breach the walls and now at last they were inside.

In the upper works of Jotapata a single figure, bent almost double to avoid detection by the sentries, scuttled away from the central redoubt. Sweating from a mixture of exertion and fear, he looked over his shoulder to ensure he'd not been seen and then dashed round the corner into the small courtyard. At first he thought he'd run into a wall, but as a rule, walls neither grunt nor swear and as an enormous hand reached down, he recognised the man immediately. 'What's the rush, sir?' asked the sentry, helping Josephus to his feet. 'The Romans are quiet as mice tonight. I don't think they'll try anything before morning.'

'Oh, you.... you know, just doing my rounds,' Josephus said. 'Making sure everyone's on their toes.'

The sentry made no reply and stared out into the darkness from where the night-time sounds of the Roman camp came softly on the breeze. 'Good job it was you, sir,' he said.

'Why's that?' Josephus asked, regaining a little of his composure.

'Well, at this time of night, if it was anyone else but you headed towards the breach, I'd have run them through on the spot for desertion. Wouldn't be the first time I've had to do it,' he added.

'Quite right too. Well done and keep it up.' Josephus marched off the way he'd come, trying to look as warlike as possible, all the while cursing under his breath. Now he was stuck. In the dark, Vespasian's troops wouldn't recognise him from the other defenders and he was likely to meet the same fate.

As predicted, the door to the upper courtyard was also unlocked. All around was quiet. From somewhere away to the south came the sound of snoring and the squad moved soundlessly forwards towards the first picket post. The two sentries were dead before they hit the ground, their throats slit by Roman steel. The detachment moved on leaving two men as rearguard while a third climbed onto the walls before letting down a long white streamer. At this signal, a dozen shadows came to life and stole through the night towards the outer door. The pass was sold.

By daybreak the bulk of the fighting was over and Vespasian's troops flooded into the city.

A runner skidded to a halt in front of the general and saluted. 'Well?' asked Vespasian. 'Have they found him?'

'Still nothing, sir.'

'Tell them to keep looking. As for the others, no prisoners.'

Twenty feet above his head the heat was unbearable, but in the cistern below the south-west tower Josephus shivered in the cool, green, dripping twilight. Shouts, battle-cries and oaths filtered down from above, but worst of all was the terrible screaming of the women and children. He tried to block his ears but to no avail. Occasionally, a Roman soldier would hurl a small child down through the grille above the cistern, the splash soaking him as he crouched in terror, not daring to move.

Towards the end of the afternoon the sounds of destruction seemed further off, no doubt the Romans' mopping-up operations had started and it was only a matter of time before every last hiding place, including his own, would be discovered.

In a few hours it would be dark – if he left it until after nightfall, he risked going unrecognised and being cut down like the thousands of others who had entrusted their lives to him; if he moved too soon, he might get caught up in the inevitable running battles between the Romans and those defenders making a last-ditch bid for freedom. Witnesses were the last thing he needed.

By the time Josephus moved, it was almost pitch dark in the cistern and he groped for the bottom rung of the series of iron hoops which led upwards towards the surface. Just below the grille he eased himself into the slimy darkness of the overflow pipe: ahead was a narrow sliver of light. Inching along the pipe on his back, pushing with his feet he stopped at the point where the light shone and, reaching above his head, pushed hard with both hands. At first the slab refused to move and panic rose in his throat. He tried again and this time, the slab moved, allowing him to lever it to one side and crawl out. He was just working it back into place when a voice came from behind. 'Halt, stand still, lay down your arms.' Raising his hands slowly above his head Josephus turned around to see the soldier thrust the point of his javelin to within two inches of his chest. 'Identify yourself,' he shouted.

'My name is Josephus. I wish to speak to Titus Vespasianus.'

The scene that met Josephus' eyes as he was marched across the shattered remains of Jotapata surpassed his worst fears. Everywhere he looked were corpses; soldiers, men, women, children and the old, some of them already turning black and swelling in the heat – the people who had followed him, the ones who'd trusted him and had come to Jotapata rather than trust their fortunes to the Romans. He stopped and gazed in disbelief, tears rolling down his cheeks: somewhere among the dead lay his friend Giora.

'They'd have died anyway.' Josephus turned and realised he was face-to-face with Vespasian. 'You did them a favour by not prolonging their suffering: dying of thirst is far worse, believe me.' He nodded for the soldier to return to his post.

'All I ask in return is a speedy and merciful death, sir.'

'We'll see about that,' said Vespasian. 'You're not exactly in any position to dictate terms.'

Chapter Thirty-six

'So what have you got?' Cohen's supervisor peered over Flora's shoulder at the unfamiliar symbols on the screen.

'I think it's what you'd call contradictory evidence.'

'You got evidence for us?' he asked, his features brightening for once.

'I've got extracts from what looks like a work from Josephus – a manuscript which was previously believed to have been destroyed in antiquity.'

'And that gets us a motive and the buyer, yes?'

'Not yet, but it'll get historians very excited,' she replied. The supervisor rolled his eyes, scowled at Cohen and marched out of the office.

'I said to try and be nice, Flora,' Cohen said.

'I *was* nice,' she protested. 'If he'd stayed I'd have told him all about it.'

'Tell him about how you'll help improve his clean-up numbers, then he'll stay and listen. Anyway, what *have* you got?'

'You know before you arrested Raymond and Luzzo we were talking about who would want this stuff badly enough to kill for it? Well, I didn't want to say anything in front of your supervisor, he thinks I'm a madwoman as it is, but I do have a hypothesis.'

'Go on. I'm listening.'

'OK, now please bear with me because I'm filling in a few gaps with assumptions here,' she said. 'Do you remember I told you the Pompeii finds included lots of writing with clear text on one side and an identical but encrypted version on the other?' He nodded and she continued. 'And we also found a mass of entirely encrypted fragments – what's commonly known as the Devil's Codex.'

'With you so far.'

'Well, I took a few samples at random and thanks to the copper grids plus some of the recto-verso texts all mixed in with a big handful of good luck, I can now decode all of them. I think Josephus was in the process of writing a sequel to *Wars* and *Antiquities* and he probably had one or more scribes helping him. That explains the different handwriting styles.'

'And?'

'The "and" is that I think we've found their first efforts at turning plain text into code – a bit like playing scales when you're learning the piano. Where things are entirely encrypted, it's the real thing. In other words, Josephus was writing it out in clear and passing it over to the scribes to encrypt. You see?'

Cohen frowned. 'I reckon. But so what?'

Flora smiled and tapped the screen with a fingernail. 'The so what is I'm almost entirely sure that what Francesco Moretti said before the robbery is correct. We've got fragments from *The Seven Stars*. Better still, I've got a reasonable idea what it's about. We've got a murderer on our hands.'

'In Alabama?'

Excitement was written all over Flora's face. 'No. At various points around the first-century Roman Empire.'

She could see that Cohen didn't share her enthusiasm. 'I'll file it under "cold cases", but thanks for the lead,' he said.

'No, listen. *The Seven Stars* were seven men – all Christians – and Josephus wanted them dead. I've got names for three of them and I'm working on the others. He obviously wanted to restrict the truth of what he'd done, hence the use of encryption. Each victim was assigned a different code: one to six were encrypted using the copper grids and the final one uses a *tabula recta* with a book key – Caesar's Gallic Wars, in this instance. The advantage of a book key, is that you don't have to schlep a lump of copper with you everywhere you go. It's an admission by Josephus that he was going around killing Christians two thousand years ago. He says the Seven Stars are the men who killed his father which explains why he hated Christians.'

Cohen laughed and slipped back into his Israeli accent. 'Hey, is this the face of concern already?'

She smiled back. 'Point taken. On the other hand if you take a look at "Republicans for Jesus dot com" –'

'At what?' asked Cohen, trying not to inhale his coffee. 'You gotta be shitting me.'

'Nope, it's a real web-site and Sumter's photos from Pompeii are on there together with translations from the Aramaic. And guess what? They're all eye-witness accounts of Jesus' life, saying what a great guy he was, son of God, miracles-r-us and so on.'

'I'm sure it's fascinating stuff,' he said. 'But a two thousand year old serial killer with a grudge against Christianity ain't the kinda stuff my supervisor wants to hear. None of this gets me any closer to an arrest.'

'It certainly explains why someone would kill for it though,' she said.

'Sure. It might do if anyone else knew about it. But apart from you, who does?'

'Raymond's clients?'

'In that case, we've definitely got to meet them,' Cohen replied. This time, Flora didn't even bother asking who "we" were and he picked up the phone and dialled. The conversation was brief and he turned to her once more. 'How d'you fancy a little conversation with our friend Raymond?'

She treated him to one of her looks. 'No guns?'

'No guns.'

The interview room was bleak and windowless: bare brick painted in a sickly pale green with neon tubes giving a harsh overhead light. Opposite sat Raymond, dressed in prison overalls, one wrist manacled to the desk. He looked pleased to see them, Flora thought.

The conversation was brief, one-sided and to the point. Raymond didn't need telling twice: co-operate or go to jail for a long time.

'There is one problem, though,' said Raymond. 'They don't like using the telephone,' he turned to Cohen. 'Like I told your people, most of the time these guys use the regular mail and we share a polyalphabetic cipher with a book key just in case the letters get seen by someone else.'

Cohen consulted his notes. 'Do you think you can set up a meeting?'

'I can try,' said Raymond. 'But I'm not wearing a wire. Every time we've met apart from that screw-up in the church with those stupid kids they've searched us and I don't mean no gentle pat-down neither, I'm talking one step short of latex gloves if you get my meaning.'

'Don't worry, I'd already thought of that,' said Cohen. 'We can set up a hotel room or someplace reasonably private with all the cameras and mikes we need. All you've got to do is get them there.'

Raymond shook his head. 'Won't work. When Luzzo did the last handover they moved him half-way round the county and we didn't know where the meet was till right at the end.'

'Can I have a word with you outside please, Ben?' asked Flora.

'Sure.' He nodded to one of the two guards who unlocked the door to let them out. 'So what've you got?'

Flora drew a deep breath. 'I can't believe I'm saying this, but you do realise what we've got to do?' He shook his head. 'If Raymond can't be the bait, then it'll have to be Grossman and Crump.'

Cohen looked at her with his head cocked to one side. 'So how does that work?' he asked.

'It might not but hear me out. Raymond tells the client he's sold a big chunk of the finds to Grossman. Now, if they're as desperate to get their hands on this stuff as we hope they are, they'll probably want to get it back and so –'

Cohen's face lit up with comprehension. 'And so Raymond puts them in touch with Grossman. That's clever,' he said.

'Insanity more like. I must be out of my tiny bloody mind,' replied Flora.

Birmingham, Alabama

Nothing, Flora thought, could be worse than the climate of New York in summer, but as she walked out of the aircraft door onto the jetway at Shuttlesworth airport, the first gasp of hot, wet air proved how wrong she'd been.

Once inside the terminal, breathing became a little easier. They were met by an agent from the Birmingham FBI Field Office who led them into the briefing room. Inside were twelve black-clad members of an FBI Special Weapons And Tactics team: at the back of the room sat two men wearing flight suits.

The briefing complete they set off, heading south west on Interstate 20 towards the rendezvous with the buyers. Cohen checked the mirror and was comforted to see the two small trucks. Both stayed several hundred yards back, and it was good to know that each held members of their back-up team. Somewhere out of sight and two thousand feet above them, a tactical response unit in an MD530 "Little Bird" helicopter was tracking the car's every move.

Turning south onto Alabama 5, they left the main road and entered a country of rolling pine-clad hills. 'Wouldn't take much to get lost round here,' said Flora, checking the map against the sat-nav.

'I think that's the idea,' replied Cohen, checking his watch and pulling off the side of the road onto a gravel hard-standing by the junction with Bear Lake Road. He picked up the radio's handset and broadcast to the other units. 'Stopping now. Next call due in three minutes.' Unseen, about a mile behind them, the two trucks pulled off the road and the helicopter turned in a lazy arc back towards the town of Centreville.

At exactly half past the hour, the call came into Cohen's mobile: number withheld. 'Grossman here,' he answered.

'Take County Thirty Eight, signposted Bear Lake Road and after six and one third miles pull into the turning on your right and wait. The line went dead. Cohen relayed the instructions and they set off once more.

As instructed, they stopped at the turning. The next call directed them down a metalled road with space, just, for two cars to pass. After less than a mile, the road narrowed and the surface went from paved, to loose stone, to truck-sized potholes in the space of only a few hundred yards. They jolted and bumped along, sending clouds of dust swirling into the air, the road now running beside a broad, meandering river. 'We're coming up to the bridge,' said Flora, eyes glued to the map, and Cohen slowed to manoeuvre the car onto the single-lane, steel swing-bridge which they crossed, tyres humming over the metal grating. 'Now right again,' she said as they reached dry land on the other side. 'Four hundred yards from here, stop for the next call.' The words were barely out of her mouth when the radio came to life.

'Abort, abort: Foxtrot One this is Hotel Alpha, I say again, abort, abort.' The urgent tone told them the helicopter crew had seen something. 'Foxtrot one, the bridge has just opened and Foxtrots Two and Three are still on the southern side. State your position.'

'Fuck, they can't see us,' shouted Cohen, stamping on the brakes. From above, the car was hidden from view by the canopy of trees covering the narrow road and the summer heat defeated any hopes of detection by the helicopter's infra-red sensors. 'Estimate three hundred yards from the bridge,' shouted Cohen, the fear in his voice audible to his helpless colleagues.

Flora glanced down at the map once more. 'I make it three-fifty,' she said and as Cohen transmitted the correction, from out of cover, about fifty yards in front of them, a red pickup emerged from the bushes and stopped broadside on across the road. Ramming the column shift into reverse, he accelerated hard, only to slam to a halt once more when another vehicle, closer this time, blocked their escape and three armed men piled out.

Chapter Thirty-seven

Galilee AD 67

Josephus had only met Titus, Vespasian's son, once before. Then, it had been in Rome under much happier circumstances, but now Josephus was a prisoner of war, his life dependent on Vespasian keeping his word and over-ruling Titus who wanted him sent to Nero.

After only one day, the stench of decay and the swarms of flies attracted by tens of thousands of rotting corpses became too much and the three Roman legions under Vespasian's command broke camp and returned north towards Caesarea. Josephus was kept under guard, travelling in a closed wagon near the front of the immense caravan as it snaked over a landscape shimmering under a pitiless sun. As Titus had pointed out, there was no need for shackles or close confinement: no-one could survive alone in such conditions and furthermore, once word of his treachery got out, he was far safer in Roman custody than with his own people.

For three days and nights he fretted alone in his cell until at last Vespasian's summons came.

Vespasian offered him a seat. 'I've been discussing you with Titus,' he said.

'Yes, sir.'

'We think you may be of use to us after all.'

Josephus brightened. If he'd had a tail he would have wagged it. 'I'm delighted to hear that.'

'You haven't heard what I've got in mind yet. The Jews in general, and you in particular, have made some very stupid decisions. We're losing supply ships to pirates from Joppa, the inhabitants of Tiberias and Taricheae have changed their mind about submitting to Roman rule and I'm losing count of the number of idiot factions in Jerusalem who're opposing us. Can you talk some sense into them before I lose patience?'

'I can try, sir.'

'Good. I want to get this wretched campaign finished and my troops home before the sailing season ends. The last thing I need is to be stuck here over winter with sixty thousand mouths to feed.'

Josephus swallowed. He knew this might be his last chance. 'There is one more thing, sir,' he said hesitantly.

'Go on.'

'After I sent you that message –'

Vespasian eyed him coldly. 'I've already told you I'm grateful, don't labour the point.'

'It's not that, sir. I started thinking – nothing more than a vague jumble of ideas really – but what you said just now about getting your army back to Rome made me see how it might work.'

'Stop talking in riddles, man, I haven't got all day.' The Roman got to his feet and headed for the door.

'I think you should stay here. You, Titus and the whole army. Going back to Rome would be a mistake.'

Vespasian spun round to face him. 'You dare to tell me how to manage my campaign? If you want me to send you back to Nero, just keep talking.'

'It's Nero I wanted to warn you about.' Vespasian looked at him, open-mouthed with stupefaction. Josephus continued. 'Piso won't be the last: there'll be other plots, we both know that. The emperor is fatally weakened. You saw what happened – he's executed so many of the people who were loyal to him he hasn't an ally to his name.'

The reply came accompanied by a contemptuous snort. 'So you're suggesting I throw my hat into the ring are you?'

'No, sir, not yet.'

'What do you mean, not yet? How dare you – ?'

'The senate, the army and yes, even the Praetorian Guard, have had enough. It's just a matter of time now.'

'You think I don't know?' shouted Vespasian. 'I'm a soldier, I'm loyal to my emperor... whoever he is.'

'That's the point, sir. There's no natural successor to Nero and when he falls, your loyalty to him will look like a threat to whoever comes after.'

Vespasian drew breath for another tirade but stopped short. 'Interesting conjecture,' he said. 'You know I could have you executed for talking treason?'

'I trust you won't interpret it as treason, sir, my intention was merely to suggest some options that might be to your benefit.'

'You dissemble like a lawyer, Josephus.'

'Thank you, sir.'

'Believe me it wasn't a compliment. So let's hear this "vague jumble of ideas" that's going to save my bacon.'

Josephus leaned towards him, speaking softly as though afraid of being overheard. 'Nero will fall: within a year at a guess. The result will be strife on a scale not seen since the days of Marcus Antonius. You stay out of it, you wait till the dust settles and then you decide –'

'Which horse to back?'

'No. Your happy dilemma will be whether to back the winner or to take the prize for yourself.'

'I don't see how that works,' said Vespasian.

'It works like this. With Nero gone, whoever comes out on top is likely to be backed by an army weakened by fighting professional Roman legions. He'll have made powerful enemies along the way. You have sixty-thousand men here: they're fighting rebels armed with sticks and stones. I can help you wrap this campaign up: at the end of it you'll be a victorious general, untainted by intrigue and the senate will jump at the chance to proclaim you as rightful emperor.'

'And you say you'll help me? Can I trust you, Josephus?'

'I think you know the answer to that, sir.'

Chapter Thirty-eight

Bibb County, Alabama

'Out, get out of the car and take cover!' screamed Cohen as the first round crashed through the rear window, showering them with glass. He kicked the door open and grabbed the microphone for the last time. 'All Foxtrot and Hotel units this is Foxtrot One, bring down rapid fire on my current position, I say again, rapid fire on my current position.' Rolling away from the car, partially hidden in the cloud of dust stirred up by their sudden halt, he fired three shots from his pistol at the nearest group, sending them diving for cover. Then, he fired at the group from the red pickup who were edging hesitantly forward and sprinted around the front of the car, nearly tripping over the reason for their slow progress: Flora was lying prone by the roadside and firing her .38 at them every time they came into view. 'Come on, we've got to move,' he yelled above the din of the approaching helicopter, and grabbing her by the scruff of the neck pulled her into the undergrowth.

'Now what?' she panted.

'Follow me,' he shouted back as rounds from their assailants' hunting rifles cracked around them. They sprinted along a deer path by the river bank. At a gap in the dense brush he stopped and pushed her forward. 'Get in!' he yelled and, kicking off his shoes, dived into the river. Flora hesitated for a split second but the decision was made for her when a 240 grain .44 inch hunting round slammed into a tree trunk inches from her head. As she flung herself into the water and surfaced for breath, two new sounds joined the deafening cacophony: first came the ominous hiss of bullets slicing through the water all around her; next came a low, purring rumble that seemed to accelerate in intensity for a second and then stop. Whatever this new sound was, the hissing stopped for a moment and she struck out for the far bank. Then a dark shadow blotted out the sun and the noise resumed. She looked up to see the underside of a small, black helicopter; a malignant tadpole spewing fire into the brush where they'd been standing just seconds ago. The sound she'd heard came from its twin 7.62mm miniguns and now a rain of spent casings cascaded into the water all around her. Suddenly, it banked away and sporadic firing, less accurate this time, resumed from somewhere on the far bank. Safety was now only twenty or so yards away but her strength was fading fast as the effects of trying to swim fully-clothed took their toll.

A bullet slapped into the water uncomfortably close and instinctively she ducked under the surface, swallowing a mouthful of water. Lungs bursting, she kicked towards the light but to her horror she realised something was holding her under. Fighting back the panic she tore at the side of her T-shirt which her scrabbling hands told her was snagged in branches. With the CO_2 level in her bloodstream rising to danger levels, her whole system screamed at her to breathe and she made one last desperate heave. The branch gave and her T-shirt ripped free, finally allowing her to butt her way to the surface against the lighter resistance from a mesh of twigs.

The saturated wood of the semi-submerged branch had just enough buoyancy to hold her up and so, gulping in delicious lungfuls of air, Flora allowed herself to be carried along by the current, oblivious to the continuing gunfire which now came from far away in a world that no longer had anything to do with her semi-delirious drift downstream. At last, a bend in the river brought her feet into contact with the bottom. Letting go of her makeshift life-raft she stumbled to the sandbar, pitching forward onto hands and knees as her legs gave way like a newborn foal's. She crawled forward a few feet and then collapsed on her face.

Whether she fell asleep or passed out, Flora never knew but at some point an uninvited stranger wandered into her dream and started shouting.

'She's alive!' A curtain seemed to open, allowing bright daylight into her eyes. She blinked again, levered herself up into a sitting position and stared angrily at the stranger. She meant to say, 'Of course I'm alive, just leave me alone,' but a mixture of early-stage hypothermia, exhaustion and shock turned her words into an incomprehensible babble, and she fell backwards into the arms of the FBI Agent who'd found her.

Near William Sunday University, Alabama

The man stopped for a moment and listened. The sounds of his pursuers crashing through the undergrowth had stopped but he knew they were near: twenty of them at least. Somewhere up ahead was the County road and maybe cars; somebody, anybody who might help or could call the cops: trouble was, in the confusion of his flight, his sense of direction had been scrambled. The man, archivist at William Sunday, knew the road was almost due north of the college – he'd driven along it plenty of times – but the two miles which seemed nothing on the map, were a trackless wilderness of winding creeks and viciously impenetrable undergrowth. So far as he could tell, the bugs hadn't eaten for months and were making the most of his arrival. With the sun almost directly overhead he tried to work it out: eleven AM; rises in the east; sets in the west, which means the road is...no, it must be that way... he had no idea.

Sweat ran down his brow and he tried to wipe the stinging drops from his eyes. At some stage during the initial struggle with his would-be executioners his glasses had gone and his horizon was now limited to a twenty-yard circle of forest, beyond which everything dissolved into a blur.

When the archivist of William Sunday University had arrived for work that morning nothing had seemed out of the ordinary. Certainly, the ongoing professional disagreement with Professor Sumter wasn't making life any easier and for the first time in over twenty years he thought of looking for a post somewhere else. It must have been just after ten – he knew that because he'd just made his second coffee of the day and unwrapped the last portion of his sister's home-made cake when they burst in. No fear at first, just indignation, because even in a world of plummeting standards, such behaviour had no place at William Sunday. He stood to remonstrate with them but they simply dragged him out of the office and into a ground-floor lecture room.

It had to be a joke, if these young punks were to be believed, he was on trial for his life. So great was his sense of outrage that a mist of undiluted fury came down between him and the young idiots, solemnly reading out charges of heresy, blasphemy and idolatry, such that the words failed even to register at first. It was only when one of them placed a piece of black cloth on his head and said something about "hanged by the neck till you be dead" that the archivist realised things had progressed beyond a macabre joke. 'Sentence to be carried out immediately,' said the same student and a group of young men, with fixed, almost ecstatic expressions moved towards him.

Prank or not, this was downright scary and so, with as much of his old agile self as his muscles could remember, the archivist turned, ran and vaulted over the sill of the open window into the flowerbed below. He'd report them and they'd all be expelled he thought as he puffed up the sloping lawn towards the admin block. A shout went up and, turning to look over his shoulder, he saw them giving chase. Then a second group, ten or more strong, rushed out of the very door he was headed for. He turned and headed for the parking lot.

He'd made it. With over one hundred yards' start on them, he reached his car. Scrabbling in his pockets for the keys, his relief turned to horror as he remembered that both they and his cell-phone were in his jacket, hanging on the back of his chair. The presence of his car, his safe, sensible, ten-year-old Volvo seemed to mock him as he sprinted towards the tree-line and plunged through a thicket of briars.

And now they were closing in. Mocking voices, calling his name came from all around. Heavy footfalls crashed through the undergrowth nearby and he tried to squirm under a bush but as he did so he caused its branches to move and with a yell they were on him. Despair lent him strength and he fought off the first one, but soon, ten pairs of hands pinned him down and shouting for the others they dragged him away.

US Navy Health Clinic, Quantico

On hearing the tap at the door Flora put down her book. The frosted glass slid aside to reveal her visitor as Cohen. 'The doc said you were well enough to see people. I thought I'd drop by and check you out.' He winked at her and smiled. 'Wanted to make sure you weren't malingering. So how're you doing?'

She looked up from the hospital bed and managed a passable attempt at smiling back, 'I'm feeling much better now, thanks. They've said I can leave tomorrow.'

'You did great, you realise that? If you hadn't held that first bunch up with that BB gun of yours, we'd have been in a lot of trouble.'

'If what you call "a lot of trouble" is worse than that, do please leave me at home next time you're out and about. Seriously though, is everyone all right?'

Cohen nodded. 'Yup, everyone's fine. The helicopter guys got a scare though: the "Little Bird" took a couple of rounds and they had to put down in a field before it shook itself to bits.'

'Any idea who was shooting at us?'

'None,' he replied. 'Both pickups had gone by the time we got people onto the other side of the river and the only clue's a big old heap of shell casings. Looks like our friend Raymond was partying with some heavyweight players.'

'I've been thinking about the motive,' Flora said. 'If Sumter's right, Josephus had documents, that if they can be authenticated, would add huge credence to the idea that the New Testament Jesus really existed. On the other hand, what we've got from *The Seven Stars* suggests Jesus was a charlatan and his disciples invented everything we know about him. It's potential dynamite to any number of major vested interests. I've got a theory but I need to take a closer look at what we've got.'

'Anything you can share?' he asked, perching on the corner of the bed.

'Not yet. I need a few more days.'

Cohen looked at her intently. 'So you don't want to go home after what happened?'

Flora shook her head. 'Not likely,' she said. 'I wouldn't miss this for the world.'

'Good, I was hoping you might say that. Looks like we might have a suspect.'

'That's fantastic.'

'Not really. He's dead. Bibb County seems to have a uniquely unhealthy climate. Another suicide: hanged himself. Guy called George Patterson.'

'Doesn't ring a bell,' she said.

'It wouldn't. He was the archivist at William Sunday university and guess what?'

Flora almost jumped out of bed at the news. 'Go on,' she said.

'Well,' said Cohen, 'He'd been with them for over twenty years and during that time he'd provided specialist consultancy services to museums, universities and libraries all over Europe.'

'And you think he was behind the thefts from the archives?'

'We don't know yet. He fits but the trouble is we don't have any evidence.'

Flora's smile faded. 'So no suicide note?'

'He left a note but it didn't say anything about archives; just a bunch of stuff about sins of the flesh. He was gay.'

'And?'

'And the Bible says it's a mortal sin.'

'But this is the twenty-first century,' she replied.

Cohen laughed. 'Not in Alabama it isn't. Anyway, according to the note – presuming he wrote it himself – he couldn't reconcile his faith with his sexuality: hanged himself in the woods by the college.'

'You say "presuming he wrote it". If he didn't who did?' she asked.

He shrugged. 'Who knows? The local police are keeping an open mind. He lived with an older sister and she says he seemed fine – she knew he was gay of course. The note was printed out from his PC, signed with a squiggle on the bottom and put in an envelope. Probably not foul play but someone at the college may be trying to cover something up. Anyway, they're checking it out.'

'So are you finally going to check out William Sunday?' Flora asked, savouring the thought of Sumter's outrage at FBI agents crawling all over his college.

'We can't yet. We've got to do a bunch more background work to find out if the dates of the thefts line up with the times Patterson was in those places: could take years.' He shrugged again. 'If we don't get the resourcing and budget, it won't get done at all.'

'But it's key to solving the case.'

Cohen shook his head. 'No it isn't. This case involves arresting the people who are buying and selling stolen document fragments from a dig in Pompeii, not in finding stuff that was taken from some dusty cupboard in Germany ten years ago.'

Flora was practically beside herself at this. 'But it's all linked. Can't your bosses see that?'

'Prove it's linked and they'll listen.'

'But it's obvious.'

'Not to them, it ain't,' he replied.

'So we're stuck,' she said, heaving a sigh of exasperation.

'Not entirely. The Director of the Agency doesn't like it when people shoot at his boys nor when they make holes in his expensive helicopters. Trouble is, right now he's got his ass in a sling.'

'Why's that?'

'It's the religious angle. He agrees with your theory that this is religiously-motivated, that's the good news.'

'And the bad news?' asked Flora.

'Whichever way he jumps, he's screwed. You start poking sticks at God in this country and just about every goddam crazy with a firearms permit and a grudge is gonna come crawling out the woodwork. Just look at that English guy, what's his name, Robert something?'

'Robert Darwin.'

'That's him. You know where he's living now?'

'I thought he was in hiding. Nobody knows where he is,' Flora replied.

'I do. Two doors down from Elvis and across the hall from Salman Rushdie. I mean, for fuck's sake; you call a book *The Paedophile of Mecca*, what do you expect?'

'Well,' said Flora. 'One of Mohammed's wives *was* six years old when he married her and nine when he…. well, you know, "consummated" the relationship. I think even the Mormons would draw the line at that.'

'Yeah, yeah, I know – free speech, First Amendment and all that good shit, but *Imaginary Friends: no Santa, no Fairies, no God* – you know how many death threats he got in this country after that came out? They're still holding book-burnings.'

Flora pulled a face. 'So you're going to back off rather than upset religious fanatics? Glad to know you've got your priorities right.'

'No. 'I'm just saying the word from on high is to tread carefully.'

'What does "carefully" mean in practice? For us, I mean?' she asked.

'It means we carry on what we started: we ramp up the media stuff. Anything to keep the texts and the robbery in the public arena. The more publicity we get the harder it's going to be for whoever's got the finds to shift them. The downside is that it'll scare the buyers – including the assholes who tried to kill us – back into the woodwork. The upside is that Grossman becomes the only buyer.'

William Sunday University, Alabama

'Calm down, Donald, there's no such thing as bad publicity,' Irvine said, waving a copy of The Washington Post under Sumter's nose.

Sumter shoved his hands deeper into the pockets of his jacket. 'There is when the press lumps us in with every other lunatic cult. This could turn us into a laughing stock – they're comparing us to the Scientologists, for Heaven's sake.'

Irvine spoke gently, like a mahout whispering in his elephant's ear. 'I told you, we're going to be fine. Just leave it with me.'

'I'm not sure I like what happens when I leave things to you, Andrew. There are limits – the end doesn't always justify the means, you know.'

'Not even when we're doing the Lord's work?'

Sumter rounded on him. 'Don't be glib.'

Irvine remained unruffled: not a hair out of place, not a speck of dust on his glistening shoes. 'Forgive me, Donald, but I disagree: this is different, you knew that when we started. Two unfortunate suicides –' Sumter scoffed but Irvine ignored him. 'I repeat, two unfortunate suicides and the loss of others who have fallen by the wayside – all regrettable but necessary.'

'And a stand-up gunfight between our students and the FBI – was that necessary?'

'Of course,' replied Irvine coldly. 'We need to recover the rest of the finds. Sooner or later someone else is going to decode *The Seven Stars*

278

and when they do...well, it doesn't bear thinking about.'

Sumter shook his head and began pacing the room. 'There's no independent corroboration of one single word in *The Seven Stars* and Josephus is a known liar. You're exaggerating the threat and you took an unnecessary risk.'

Irvine's mouth smiled but his eyes didn't. 'You've changed your tune, Donald. You forget you're the one who rang the fire bell when *The Seven Stars* turned up in the first place. And what about the risk you took in going live with the "Q document" extracts?'

'It's you who're forgetting, Andrew. If you want to consult the authority on Aramaic philology and epigraphy, you go where?'

Irvine bowed his head in mock deference. 'Yes, Donald, we all acknowledge your brilliance – the only reliable reference sources are your books on the subject, I know that –'

'So any academic who takes a closer look at the photographs will decide the "Q manuscripts" are genuine,' said Sumter. 'For goodness' sake, we've been over this a dozen times. There's a massive difference between minimal risks like that and a broad-daylight shoot-out with the FBI.'

'Yes, we took a risk. Had it succeeded we would have got rid of Grossman and recovered what he hoped to sell –'

Sumter gave a sigh of exasperation. 'Andrew, you know as well as I do, the FBI have either turned Raymond or they're using him without his knowledge: Grossman may even be co-operating with them for all we know. They'll be back.'

Irvine walked over to the window and waved his arm, indicating the broad sweep of the woods that ringed the college grounds. 'Back? Back where? Grossman and his friends are long-gone: Alabama's a big place. Nothing points our way, Donald. Nothing.'

Chapter Thirty-nine

Jerusalem, Summer AD 70

From the Roman camp which sprawled across the hills north of Jerusalem, the two men looked down on a sunlit vision of Hell. 'You've done well,' said Titus. 'Without your help we'd have been here another six months.'

Josephus mumbled a reply through his tears. From end-to-end the city was ablaze, the flames driven on by a hot south-westerly wind. About an hour earlier the inner sanctuary of the Temple, the Holy of Holies, had collapsed as the roof-timbers burned though. Although named for Herod the Great, it had stood inviolate for nearly six-hundred years but now, because of a stupid religious squabble and its inept handling by the Roman procurator, Gessius Florus, hundreds of thousands were dead and the Temple, the very sanctuary of the God of Israel, lay in ruins.

'I can't stay here,' he mumbled. 'This is God's punishment. Because of our wickedness, he has forsaken the tribes of Israel.'

'Then if your God has taken the wise decision to leave his temple and his city, you cannot be blamed for doing the same.'

'Where would I go? My own people don't understand what I've tried to do for them. They hate me.'

'They're wrong,' said Titus. 'If they'd listened to you two years ago, I wouldn't have had to do this.'

Josephus hung his head. 'They say I'm a traitor.'

'Then we'll have to make sure that history judges you otherwise. And as for the history of this wretched place, when I've finished here, no one will even know there were once walls around Jerusalem.'

'But where can I go?'

Titus clapped Josephus on the back in an attempt to cheer him up. 'Rome. My father has a long memory, as do I. You not only saved his life, but without your help, Vitellius would still be emperor and my father just another soldier with ambitions greater than his abilities. Go to Rome, Josephus, there's nothing more for you here.'

280

Chapter Forty

Washington DC

They stared at the TV screen in Flora's hotel room in abject disbelief. For three days the story had been raging without a break. 'Talk about "be careful what you wish for".' said Cohen. He zapped to another channel: it was there too. Three talking heads were all shouting at once, pitting the newly-found proof of Jesus' divinity against the premise that Christianity was an invented cult with just about every prophecy and conjuring trick known to the ancient world bolted onto the shadowy figure of an Essene preacher. Conspiracy theorists jammed the airwaves and the blogsphere, some blaming popular fiction baddies from the Jesuits to the Papacy itself, while others pointed the finger at government agencies or sinister cabals of bankers bent on world domination. All the news channels led with the Vatican's denial of any involvement with the theft and the anchors fell over themselves to come up with the most outspoken pundits to interview. Even the White House joined in: its Republican incumbent was known to favour laws based more literally on the Bible and since taking office had been doing his best, despite ferocious opposition from a Democrat-dominated House and an evenly-split Senate, to blur the line between church and state. His unguarded words in support of *Republicans for Jesus* to a news team as he was leaving church were now being dissected by commentators the world over.

Donald Sumter was ecstatic: seemingly never more than two feet from a TV camera or a microphone, his well-oiled evangelical operation wowed the faithful and gained a respectful hearing even from the sceptical.

'It's not all bad news,' said Cohen. 'You wouldn't believe the number of museums that've rechecked their archives and found stuff missing. I've got a job for life thanks to this shit.'

'So apart from hogging the front pages, has it done what you wanted?' she asked.

'Yeah, I reckon so.'

'Isn't there a risk they'll just dump everything and run?'

'There is but I don't think they will,' he replied. 'Anyone who's willing to kill to get their hands on this stuff isn't just going to roll over and give up. Remember, those guys in Alabama were trying to steal what we had, killing us was just a bonus.'

Flora shuddered at the memory. 'Not quite how I'd have put it.'

'Put it how you want. I reckon if we dangle the bait again, they'll bite.'

'They might do a better job next time. Find yourself some fresh bait.'

'No,' said Cohen. 'You're missing the point. When we got hit it was because they knew we had company.'

Flora wrinkled her brow, something she often did when something puzzled her. 'So if Grossman and Crump are compromised, who've you got left?'

'Raymond,' he replied.

'But surely they'd never trust him after what's happened would they?'

'I think they might,' said Cohen. 'I forgot to tell you, but the first thing I did after we'd fished you out of the river was to get back to my supervisor in New York. He got Raymond to phone the buyers with an urgent message saying "hope it isn't too late and all that good shit, but Grossman and Crump are possibly working with the Feds". Said he'd been running more background checks on us and there were holes in our résumés.'

'Did they buy it?' Flora asked.

'Impossible to tell. There was one development though.'

'What was that?'

'Don't know whether it tells us anything,' said Cohen. 'But on the call the buyer was much more specific about what he wanted. He mentioned the *Devil's Codex* and the *Seven Stars*'

'It shows the buyer knows his stuff. But where does that get us? If Grossman is compromised, the buyer won't come near him.'

'True, but if as a sign of good faith Raymond drops his price, carries out a clean sell with no wire, no one tailing him – leastways not as openly as last time – and offers to help track Grossman down with a view to a retrieving what he's already sold, then I think they might just have no choice but to trust him.'

'That's pretty flaky,' said Flora. 'It could get Raymond killed and we could lose priceless finds into the bargain.'

Cohen stood up and stretched. 'You got a better idea?' he asked.

'Matter of fact I think I have. Let's go and get something to eat. If I have another beer I won't be able to stand up.'

The hot, wet slap in the face that is the DC summer hit them between the eyes as they walked out the hotel. 'So what's this great idea of yours?' asked Cohen, forging ahead through the crowds.

'If you slow down and let me catch up I can tell you,' panted Flora. 'I wanted to ask you if your technical people could take a look at something for me.'

'Sure, what is it?'

'Some photos on the web. The ones Donald Sumter's crowing about – you know the Aramaic texts that were stolen from Pompeii but nobody else noticed were even there.'

'Sure. What do you want to know about them?'

'The resolution, what sort of camera they might've been taken with, any signs of cropping or Photoshopping, any hidden tags or references and most important of all, I want to see the text itself at maximum magnification consistent with sharpness.'

Cohen looked at his watch. 'Seven PM; should be someone around. I'll give them a call.' He dialled and after a short wait Flora heard him repeat her instructions. 'They'll e-mail me the details in a couple of hours. Now, how about you tell me what's on your mind.'

By the time they returned to the hotel the e-mail was sitting in Cohen's in-box. Flora read the details over his shoulder. 'Tell you anything you didn't know?' he asked.

'I'm not sure, I'll need to talk to Francesco.'

'You mean Moretti?'

'Yes.'

'No way. You can't. Any comms with Italy go through me and I'll talk direct to Lombardi.'

'Seems a bit melodramatic,' said Flora. 'But if it makes you happy, could you find out what sort of light-box equipment they've got at the Pompeii lab?'

'Sure. Am I allowed to ask what a light-box is and why you want to know?'

Flora tutted. 'A light-box is what you put things in when you want to photograph them. You make a box out of polystyrene, say, leave one side open, make a few holes in the top for lights and a camera lens and that's it. Means you can get high-quality images with a plain white background dead easily.'

'And why does this help us?'

'Because, as I suspected, the report says the pictures on Sumter's web-site were taken in a light-box using a high quality digital camera.' She tapped the screen. 'I mean, just look at the sharpness on these

283

enlargements. This is top-quality work.'

'Yeah, OK, I'm very happy for you. So what?' he said

'You haven't been listening, have you?' Flora would never have admitted it but she sounded just like her mother. 'No one at Pompeii remembers these fragments so the only logical conclusion is that, as he claims, Sumter took the photos himself.'

'Yeah, I'll buy that –'

'But Donald hates technology. He can barely send an e-mail or write a letter on a PC and I've seen his camera – it's an old, wet-film, twin-lens reflex. Look at the report, Ben, these images were done on a high-spec digital camera: Sumter wouldn't know where to start with one of those, let alone use it in a light-box.'

Cohen's eyebrows rose. 'So who did take the photos?'

'Sumter says he did. He's lying but I can't work out why. Can you get hold of Lombardi tomorrow? We need to know if any of Francesco Moretti's technicians remember Sumter taking the pictures or if he asked them to do it.'

'I'll send him a mail now,' said Cohen. 'They're six hours ahead so that'll give him a head start.'

At six the following morning, mid-day in Italy, Lombardi's call jolted Cohen awake. Neither Moretti nor any of his team at the Pompeii lab remembered Sumter taking any pictures and none of them had been approached by him for help.

Cohen broke the news over breakfast at Flora's hotel.

'Well that settles it,' she said. 'I need to pay a visit to William Sunday University.'

'Do you think Sumter would be happy about that? I thought you two couldn't stand one another.'

She laughed. 'We can't and if he *has* been up to something he shouldn't, then I'm the last person he'd let within ten miles of the place.'

'And those images on the web – you think he's got the original documents?'

'He says not but you're the detective, you tell me. No one at Pompeii has seen the originals but by a spooky coincidence Donald Sumter has not only seen them but managed to produce professional-standard photos of them. Come on, Ben, something's wrong here.'

Cohen thought for a moment. 'You're right. But it's still not enough for a search warrant. I need more.'

'That's why I need to go down there.'

'And you're just going to turn up at the door and ask them if they happen to have any stolen first-century documents on the premises and, if so, can you take a look? How many times do you think you'll bounce on your way down the steps, Flora?'

'Don't worry, I'll think of something. So long as Sumter's away I'll get in somehow.'

Cohen's expression was grave. 'You know you can't go down there as Lavinia Crump and you can't carry a gun either,' he said. 'Any trip you make is as a civilian and you won't get any protection from the law if you enter a building illegally.'

While their conversation was taking place another, yet more urgent, was happening in Italy. Moretti stood in the car park of the lab with his mobile clamped to his ear. 'We've got a problem. I said it was a risk and now the Carabinieri are asking about the photographs – Lombardi... you remember, the TPC guy from Naples?.... yeah him, well he just left. No. Fuck. Listen. I'm not saying "I told you so" I just thought, you know... whoever it is you talk to in the US might be interested.... no, I'm not telling you how to run your operation, I just thought you ought to know.' The line went dead as the other party hung up on him. 'Fuck you. Arrogant sons of bitches,' he said aloud and kicked at a fallen pine-cone, sending it skittering across the car-park.

Chapter Forty-one

Rome AD 70

'So how do you like it?' asked Vespasian.

'Well it's certainly big,' replied Josephus. 'It's just a little, well, overwhelming.'

'Vulgar, you mean?' said the emperor with a smile. 'Yes, the wretched thing takes up half the city and it'll all have to go.' They both gazed out over what to Josephus was a brand-new townscape, dominated by Nero's half-finished palace, the *Domus Aurea*, which sprawled from the Palatine to the Esquiline Hill. 'And what about you, young man? Titus tells me he's been keeping you busy.'

'I've done my best, sir, but it's good to be back,' Josephus replied, trying to force the memories of the revolt to the back of his mind. 'There are still three of the *Seven Stars* alive somewhere: my work's not done yet.'

'Would you like me to give you Alityros again?' Vespasian asked. 'I'm sure you could do with the help and I know he could do with the exercise – he's as fat as a barrel these days.'

Josephus' face lit up. 'You mean he's still alive?' he asked.

'Alive, well and eating four meals a day.'

'Well, I'm delighted he's all right and I don't wish to seem ungrateful –'

'But he's more of a hindrance than a help when it comes to chasing Christians?'

'Precisely, sir.'

'But that isn't why I asked Titus to send you here. I told you I had a long memory when you saved me from Nero all those years ago, and believe me, long memory or not I was sorely tempted to have you sent to him after Jotapata.'

'I'm glad you didn't.'

'So am I. Titus and his army would still be camped outside the walls of Jerusalem if it hadn't been for you. And before you say anything, yes, I do understand how you must feel, but Titus had no choice. Rebellion against Rome will not be tolerated.' Josephus swallowed hard. 'Sacrifice brings reward, Josephus: here's my offer. Accept me as your patron, take Roman citizenship and I'll see your talents don't go unrewarded. What do you say?'

Josephus stood rooted to the spot. 'I...I'd be deeply honoured, sir,' he said. 'The only problem is, you see I lost everything in the fighting and I don't even have anywhere permanent to live.'

The emperor smiled. 'You clearly don't understand what's involved. As my protégé you'll have an income, and as of today you are the owner and master of my old villa on the Pincian.' Josephus made to speak but Vespasian held up a hand to stop him. 'I haven't finished yet. Have you ever seen Pompeii?'

'Yes sir, but it was a long time ago, just after the earthquake.'

'And what did you think?'

'I thought it was wonderful.'

'Good,' said Vespasian, rubbing his hands together. 'One of the late emperor Vitellius' friends – the commander of *Legio XV Primigenia* to be precise – had a very nice villa down there, overlooking the coast. As you might suspect, it's now vacant: yours, complete with staff if you want it.'

'There's nothing I'd like more,' Josephus replied, barely able to believe his ears.

Chapter Forty-two

William Sunday University, Alabama

'After everything that's happened we're not really supposed to talk to journalists without Professor Sumter's permission, you do know that?' said the young man, sliding his thick glasses back up to the bridge of his nose.

'But surely, where a newspaper as well known as ours is concerned, those rules don't apply,' said Flora, leaning forward to read her notes and allowing him a view down the front of her blouse.

'The media have been saying horrible, blasphemous things about us,' he said, looking away as Flora caught his eye. 'It's too big a risk. I really can't.'

She pouted and tossed her hair. She caught him eyeing her breasts once more. 'Poor dear George said it would be fine, that's why I came all this way. I've known him, sorry, *had* known him for years: he was a wonderful man.'

He looked away, clearly embarrassed. 'We all had a great deal of respect for Mr Patterson. That he took his own life was a great shock to us all.'

Flora dabbed at the corner of her eye. 'And he spoke so highly of you. When he invited me over he sent a lovely e-mail with all his news about what Professor Sumter had found in Pompeii and how well you were coming on as his deputy –'

'He invited you? To see the archive?'

'Yes, of course, that's why I'm here. I know you won't let me down. Poor dear George. I can quite understand why he forgot to tell you with so much on his mind. And I'm very supportive of what you do here,' she added.

He hesitated. 'Well I suppose if Mr Patterson invited you, then –'

Flora saw the gap and was through. 'Oh thank you, you are such a total sweetheart. I knew you wouldn't let me down.' She reached forwards and flung her arms around his neck, planting a kiss on his cheek. 'When can we start?'

She noticed he'd gone bright red. 'Well, um, now I suppose. Look, if anyone asks, tell them you're a visiting grad student or something and for heaven's sake, when you write the article you mustn't mention you've seen the archives.'

'Of course not, silly,' cooed Flora. 'Just lead the way and I'll follow.' They set off with Flora's heels click-clacking on the highly polished wooden floor .

'This is just wonderful,' she said as she stopped to take pictures of the doors to the main library. 'It's like a film. Are they air-tight?'

'No,' he replied patiently, 'otherwise no one in there could breathe.'

'Oh, how silly of me,' said Flora with a giggle. 'You must think I'm totally stupid. Ever since dear George invited me over I've been doing so much research into museums and libraries and things that I think I've got a bit carried away.'

The archivist smiled, seemingly less intimidated for a moment. 'It does get you like that,' he said. 'Most people can't understand why I find my job so exciting –'

'Oh, I can,' said Flora. 'You're going to have trouble getting me out of here.'

'Well you can't stay too long,' he said, looking nervously at her as they walked through the research library. 'Firstly, I've got work to do and secondly, Professor Sumter's due back tomorrow and if he finds you here I'll be out of a job. And please don't mention what you've seen here in your article.'

'That's twice now: you don't trust me, do you?' she replied, doing her best to appear offended.

'No it's not that. It's just –'

She looked away and tilted her face slightly upwards. 'I've already told you, the piece is going to be about the evangelical movement and the finding of documentary proof supporting the New Testament. I can assure you it's not going to be critical of William Sunday University.'

He led her through a set of double swing doors. 'This is the archive itself,' he said. 'It's temperature and humidity controlled which is why we have triple-glazing on all the external windows, blackout curtains – even over the skylights – and those rubber baffles round the doors.'

'It's huge,' Flora said, genuinely impressed.

'What is it you want to see?'

'Anything relating to the New Testament would be wonderful.'

He handed her a pair of cotton gloves. 'If you wouldn't mind putting these on we can start.'

For the next hour, Flora had him scurrying around like a circus poodle, delighted to do anything he could for her. She put him at ease by deliberately confusing Coptic script with Greek and then flattered him for his cleverness when he treated her to a ten-minute lecture on the evolution from Egyptian demotic to the modern dialects of Coptic itself. As the visit wore on, she took every opportunity to follow him around and made annoyingly frequent trips to the water-cooler, coffee machine and, inevitably, the lavatory, each distraction yielding an opportunity for an uninterrupted look at doors, windows and locks.

After he'd described in detail yet another text supportive of the Jesus story, Flora took a deep breath and pounced. 'I know this is primarily a theological college and your collection of manuscripts is just fantastic, but are there any writings that, well, you know.... give a different point of view or are critical of what the Bible says.'

'Well there are, but most the items in the collection are just historical curiosities really. Not things anyone would take seriously.'

'What sort of things?' Flora asked.

'Oh, the usual. Fragments of apocryphal works, pieces from the *Devil's Codex*, that sort of thing. We call the collection "the Black Library". All harmless fun of course.'

'That sounds really sinister,' said Flora, clutching his arm. 'I've never heard of any of those books you mentioned. Do let me have a little look, I promise I won't keep you long.'

He hesitated but after a few minutes of Flora's wheedling, pouting and breathy admiration, agreed to show her the collection and led the way through yet another door into a room which formed the corner of the library block. The first few documents were written in Greek and much as she would have loved to spend the day poring over them, continued her act, asking the kind of questions she'd heard a thousand times from her own students. Then, clearly without any idea of the manuscripts' provenance, he placed two fragments down in front of her and Flora nearly choked. The last time she'd set eyes on them had been at Pompeii nearly a month ago. 'Oh, I recognise that writing,' she said, as nonchalantly as possible, placing her hands flat on the table so he wouldn't see they were shaking. 'It's the same as one you showed me just now. It's Hebrew, isn't it?'

'No. Very similar but it's actually Aramaic: same linguistic family as Hebrew of course – in the same way that German, Dutch and English are all related – but a distinct language with a slightly different character set. We believe it's the language Jesus spoke.'

And the one Josephus wrote them in, thought Flora. But how the hell did they end up here?

Watching carefully where the archivist replaced the Pompeii

fragments, Flora pretended to let her attention wander. While his back was turned she wandered towards an inner door. 'What's in here?' she asked.

'Oh just a store-room for technical stuff, nothing of any interest,' he said, steering her back towards the sloping table where the documents lay, gently weighted onto a padded cloth support. 'So, have you seen enough?' Clearly, the appeal of looking down her blouse had its limits and she detected an urgency in his voice, almost pleading with her to leave.

'I think I have thanks,' said Flora. 'That was utterly fascinating and so kind of you. I've got heaps of information and I'll send you a copy of the article when it's published. Promise.'

Almost bursting with excitement, Flora jumped back into the rental car, heading back across the sweeping grounds of the college and on to the Interstate. She drove for ten miles, breaking every speed limit, until she felt it was safe enough to pull over and phone Cohen.

'And are you sure you didn't do anything illegal?' he asked.

'Unless you count giving a geeky librarian the biggest erection of his life,' she replied.

'Uh, too much detail, Flora. But I don't think causing a hard-on in a built-up area is a felony so you should be OK. Look I'll go talk to my supervisor and we'll catch up when you get back.'

'And when are you going to arrest Donald Sumter?' she asked, glowing with pleasure at the thought.

She heard Cohen spluttering. 'Whoa, steady. First we'd have to prove that those documents are what you said they are, then there's the little matter of Sumter's complicity –'

'But he must know they're in his archive and he must know how they got there,' Flora said, raising her voice.

'I'm sure you're right, but I still don't have a case for busting down the doors at William Sunday and throwing the evangelical Right's blue-eyed-boy in a Paddy Wagon.'

'So what *are* you going to do?'

'I told you: talk to my supervisor, talk to my boss at the ACT to see what they say. Don't forget, we've only got your word to go on –'

'So you knew all along I was wasting my time coming down here? Thanks a bunch.'

'No, it's not that. Please listen –'

'And are you really suggesting you and your colleagues know more about first century Aramaic papyri than I do?'

'No, but it's not going to be easy to convince them and politically, given Sumter's profile, we'll have to approach this very sensitively. I need time and I need more evidence. Come back to DC and we'll talk.'

Another bucket of cold water hit white-hot enthusiasm and Flora's temper snapped. 'Well sod you then,' she said. 'You want more evidence, I'll bloody well go back and get it for you.'

'Flora, for Christ's sake listen to me. Don't go back there; you'll get yourself arrested –' She hung up and switched the phone to divert all calls to voicemail.

At just after eleven thirty that evening Flora turned the rental car off the main road and parked in a stand of trees, well screened from any passing traffic. She locked the door behind her and set out into the humid darkness with a small rucksack slung over her shoulder.

Chapter Forty-three

Hierapolis, Asia Minor AD 72

Josephus had never seen anything like it. The "holy" city of Hierapolis, entirely rebuilt after the earthquake of AD 60, was a cross between an infirmary and a retirement colony. In the early spring sunshine the streets thronged with invalids and the elderly. From all around came the relentless click, click of crutches and walking sticks against the flagstones. Now he understood why Vespasian had referred to it as "Hades' antechamber".

News had come that Matityahu and Philippos were both dead. However, on more detailed investigation they proved to be alive and well, enjoying the health-giving powers of Hierapolis' thermal spas and ministering to a growing community of aged Christian converts, anxious to secure a last-minute berth in the rapidly-approaching afterlife. Bribes, nudges and favours to the former governor of Ephesus, under whose control Hierapolis lay, had been enough to maintain the fiction of their demise, but Vespasian's new man not only offered Josephus his support, but also provided a detachment of soldiers to help track them down: two of the last three survivors of the group who brought about his father's death over thirty five years earlier.

It is said that the best place to hide a leaf is in a tree. The men he sought were in their sixties and instead of standing out in a world where few made it past fifty, it was the thirty-five-year-old Josephus who looked out of place in this necropolis of the living and he wasn't happy. The detachment of soldiers was nowhere to be seen. At first, he'd been overwhelmed by the kindness and diligence of the governor who had insisted on accompanying him all the way from Ephesus, showing him round the town and then making all the arrangements himself, until it dawned on him that he'd been played for a fool.

From every sweaty pore the city oozed wealth, a good proportion of it in the hands of the Christians and, much as the new man would never dream of disobeying his emperor, he had no personal responsibility for the success of Josephus' mission. Trying and executing the leaders of a cult considered dangerous by Vespasian would play well in far-off Rome, but would be catastrophic for business.

Of the seven soldiers allocated to him, one was deaf, the youngest spoke only an obscure Syrian dialect, another was morbidly obese and the other four were dug-out reservists all over fifty five. His instructions were simple and they had all claimed to understand so where in Jupiter's name were they?

Matityahu and Philippos had proved easy to find. The two Christians followed the same routine every day: preaching in the cool of the morning, two hours in the baths and then a gentle stroll into town before lunch. The witnesses had been well rehearsed and generously bribed, so all he had to do was arrange for the soldiers to arrest the two Christians on charges of sedition, the trial would be over in minutes and the governor's sentence of crucifixion would follow. But where were the soldiers? Josephus was alone, unarmed and in a city of which he knew little beyond his tour in the company of the governor.

Josephus spotted the two men leaving the baths and slotted in a few paces behind as they continued down the street. At the corner they stopped and fell into conversation with what Josephus assumed were friends or fellow-believers, so he busied himself inspecting the day's catch on a fishmonger's slab, all the while keeping one eye on his prey. Eventually, the one he'd identified as Matityahu continued on alone and Josephus followed, scouring the crowds for his missing soldiers. Then, as they rounded a corner, Josephus recognised where he was: just ahead lay the temple of Apollo and next to it the *Plutonium*, the sanctuary of the god of the underworld, Pluto. Drawing alongside the older man, Josephus addressed him in Aramaic, 'Master, can you spare me a moment of your time?' he asked.

Matityahu turned and smiled. For a fleeting moment, Josephus felt a pang of guilt. 'Yes of course, what is it, young man?'

'I was born a Jew, sir. I was present when God used the Romans to punish Jerusalem for its wickedness and I wish to know more about the teachings of the Christ.' He blurted it all out without pausing for breath. Matityahu smiled again. This isn't going to be easy, thought Josephus.

'But of course. Why don't you come along tomorrow morning? My friend Philippos and I give daily instruction to the faithful at the new theatre.'

'It's not that easy, sir. You see, I am a prominent citizen and open apostasy from the Jewish faith could see me ostracised. I want to know more before making the final decision – can we talk privately, just for a moment? I need to be sure I'm doing the right thing.'

'Of course,' he replied, placing a fatherly hand on Josephus' shoulder. 'Come to my house for lunch and I'll tell you the wonderful story of Christ's triumph over death and of the path to everlasting life.' As these words fell, any compassion Josephus may have harboured evaporated at the sound of this old fraud basking in the reflected glory of his father's murder.

Josephus swallowed hard. 'I don't wish to seem ungrateful, but until my decision is final, I'd prefer not to be seen in your company.'

Matityahu raised his snowy eyebrows. 'As you wish, young man. Shall we meet another time?' he asked.

Josephus pretended to think for a moment. 'Can't we just move from here? People are beginning to stare. Look, let's go in there.'

'But it's a pagan temple,' protested Matityahu.

Now it was Josephus' turn to smile, 'Surely, God is everywhere, even in the house of the pagans?'

'True. Lead on.' They continued up the dazzling marble steps into the cool dark silence within. 'Do you know what this place is, young man?'

Josephus feigned ignorance and pretended to study the image of the god on its plinth at the back of the sanctuary. He knew exactly what it was. 'A temple to Apollo, by the look of it,' he said casually.

Matityahu pointed out an open stone doorway with a set of steps leading down into the darkness. 'And this?'

'No idea,' replied Josephus.

'It's the *Plutonium*.'

'The what?'

'It's a sanctuary sacred to the god Pluto. The same underground forces that cause the springs to flow so hot also render the air at the bottom of the sanctuary unbreathable. The pagans say it's the entrance to the underworld.'

'How fascinating,' said Josephus, edging closer. He'd received the same guided tour from the governor three days earlier and although Roman science knew nothing of volcanology nor of the dense, odourless gas, carbon dioxide, a permanent seepage via a geological fault into the sanctuary created a pocket of it, lethal to any living creature.

'No, don't go any further.' He felt Matityahu's hand on his shoulder once more.

'But surely, it's just a superstition,' said Josephus.

'No, look, let me show you. See, there, at the bottom of the steps,' Matityahu said, pointing at a lighter patch in the gloom. 'That's a sacrificial offering: a ram by the look of it. The priests tie them to a ring and the animals are dead in seconds.'

Josephus smiled. It was just as the governor had told him, word for word. Matityahu bent forward to take a closer look at the dead animal and Josephus slammed his fist into the side of the unsuspecting old man's head. He drew his arm back to strike again, but Matityahu fell as though poleaxed, his temple crashing against the steps as he fell. Taking a deep breath, as he'd seen the temple priests do during his earlier visit, Josephus grabbed Matityahu by the wrists and dragged him to the very back of the sanctuary. With lungs bursting he half ran, half fell up the steps before daring to breathe. There he waited, watching for any movement from the darkness below and after five minutes he calmly walked out of the temple, down the steps and returned the way he'd come.

Rome AD 72

'And you've no idea where Philippos went?' asked Vespasian.

Josephus shook his head. 'The temple priests found Matityahu's body in the *Plutonium* and someone reported him having gone in there with a man of my description. I had to leave in a hurry: the governor would've had no choice but to arrest me. I presume Philippos left at the same time.'

'You will have another chance. We'll find him, just like we found Didymus.'

Josephus' face lit up. 'You found Didymus? Where?'

'Southern India of all places: in the kingdom of Chola. The word from the fleets has it the barbarians got bored with his nonsense and decided to eat him. Can't say eating one's enemies appeals, but it saves us having to chase him over the edge of the world.'

'One left,' said Josephus, shaking his head. 'Philippos. And I was as close to him as I am to you.'

'And when he's dead, then what are you going to do?' asked the emperor.

'I'll go back to Pompeii and carry on writing.'

'Poetry? Plays for your chum, Alityros?'

'No, sir. History. I've already started on a history of the Jews, including a detailed account of the revolt.'

'I'll look forward to reading it,' said Vespasian.

'And I've plans for another work,' said Josephus. 'You see I've kept detailed notes of what I learned about my father's life and the men who got him killed just so they could start that wretched cult. It's going to be called *The Seven Stars*.'

'Very apt. I hope it'll help reason prevail in men's minds, but you do realise what you're up against where superstition is concerned, don't you?'

'I do, sir.'

'I hope so. Pliny says man is a superstitious animal by his very nature. It's in our blood and there's only so much rationality we can take; even emperors.'

Chapter Forty-four

William Sunday University, Alabama

Flora glanced once more at the GPS display on her phone. Just as she began to think it was playing her false, she saw buildings through the trees: William Sunday University.

With the exception of a few chinks of light from the dormitory block, the place was in darkness and Flora stole from shadow to shadow across the grounds until pausing for a final check beneath the cover of an evergreen magnolia: fifty yards lay between her and the night's objective.

Waiting and listening until certain no one was around, she sprinted across the manicured turf and jumped over a row of shrubs where she crouched, panting, her face pressed against the brickwork of the library, still warm from the heat of the day. She peered right and left, counting the windows to make sure she'd got the right one, then stood up and pulled at the aluminium sill on the bottom glazing bar. Nothing. She tried again, but it refused to move. Earlier in the day, she'd identified the catch as worn and loose but now it wouldn't budge. Ducking back down she slipped off the rucksack and took out two of her earlier purchases: a small crowbar and a long-shafted screwdriver. With the former she levered the window up just enough to get the screwdriver into the catch. She pushed. Nothing happened. She tried tapping the screwdriver with the flat of her hand. Still nothing, so, reaching into the rucksack, she pulled out a rubber mallet and gave the screwdriver a thump. With a sound that she was sure must have been audible right across the State of Alabama, the catch turned and the window frame moved upwards. Then she posted the rucksack through the gap and slithered through after it, landing in a panting heap on the wooden floor.

After closing the window behind her she tiptoed towards the inner door. As she'd hoped, it was unlocked and she shut it behind her before daring to take out a pencil torch to find her way. Finding the box holding the Pompeii fragments was easy and she set it down on the bench. Next she tried the door to what the archivist had described as a store-room. At first glance it appeared he'd been telling the truth and Flora was about to leave when the torch beam flashed across something white: in the middle of a workbench stood a light-box. Again, nothing surprising – after all, she'd seen dozens like it – but her curiosity about Sumter's photographs made her look more closely. It was then that she noticed them: a series of three box files identical to those in the main archive next door.

Stretching up, Flora took one down and opened the lid. What she saw took her breath away. Fresh, clear and unmistakeable, she was looking at one of the documents whose photographs were all over the web.

Grabbing the boxes she ran back into the other room, opening the first one and gently laying the parchment fragment on the table. Then she stopped. Something wasn't right, something so obvious that she'd missed it in her excitement: unlike the other finds which were so delicate that even picking one up could cause it to fall into dust, none of these had any sort of protective covering and were as fresh and as pliable as new. She opened another box and shone the torch into it: more papyrus fragments but again, no protection. The colour was right but the page itself was flexible and robust. The answer was simple – they were modern fakes. And then another fact hit her: if she could see what they were by torchlight in the dark, then Donald Sumter must know too. And that meant the reason no one at Pompeii remembered seeing them was simple: the manuscript fragments had never left Alabama. The implications came as a cascade as Flora tried to work out the possible links between Sumter and the robbery. However, what she needed now was evidence so she ran back to collect the light-box and set it up on the table: no time to do all of them, but she got through the collection as quickly as possible and rolled up one of the suspected fakes, securing it with an elastic band before sliding it into the rucksack.

The first flash he took for the start of a summer storm and so paid it no heed but after the second and then more, each coming at regular intervals, the student got up from his desk and peered out of the window, resting his elbows on the sill and waiting. There it was again – it seemed to be coming from the direction of the library block and as he squinted into the humid darkness he realised that the source was inside rather than outside the building: one of the domed skylights. But what was it? An electrical short? – that meant fire and fire in the library would be a disaster so he pulled the window shut and turned to run downstairs. Then he stopped. The flashes were too regular and always of the same intensity: someone was taking photographs in the archive block, just like that idiot Patterson had done. There was no time to call Irvine, he had to act. Slamming the door behind him he sprinted to the other end of the corridor and hammered on the door. 'Mike, Mike. Wake up, we got a problem.'

Seconds later the door opened and a bleary-eyed face appeared round the door. 'Shit, man, you know what time it is? What's the matter with you –'

'Shut up and get dressed. Someone's taking photos in the archive block.'

'Shit!' The door closed and then moments later, Mike burst out clad in a T-shirt and a pair of shorts.

Three floors down Flora checked her watch. Ten minutes in the building was longer than she'd planned: a couple more photos then time to leave. She selected a battered codex: the back cover was in place but the front half of it was in a poor state. Skimming though the first few pages she was about to put it back in its box when something caught her eye. She read on but what she saw simply wasn't possible – right before her eyes was a fragment from the *Apocryphon of John*, a manuscript belonging to the University of Athens and reported as having been stolen from this very archive. This just didn't make sense. She thought about taking it with her but instead, used up another precious three minutes taking as many pictures as she could.

Time was running out and she'd already stayed longer than she'd planned. She scurried around, trying to hide all trace of her presence and putting everything back where she'd found it but as she replaced the last of the Pompeii boxes she stopped, frozen to the spot in terror. The muffled noise, whatever it was had come from the library, and then moments later her worst fears were realised as a light showed under the door, followed by the sound of two men's voices. She was trapped. Grabbing the rucksack she pulled aside one of the heavy, black curtains to leave via a window: triple-glazed, the archivist had said, but as long as they opened she couldn't have cared less.

Flora searched but there was no sign of a handle and the toughened glass would be proof against any of the tools she had with her. Heart pounding, she looked for somewhere to hide: the store-room was too small and the archive itself offered nothing better than row upon row of identical book-cases...the book cases, that was it, and so, using the shelves like rungs of a ladder climbed up and lay flat along the top. In the dark she misjudged the distance and cracked her head against something hard. Turning to see what it was, she noticed a faint glimmer of light: it was one of the skylights and its curtain was partially adrift, allowing her a tantalising view of a starlit Alabama night sky through the glass dome.

It was a risk, she knew, but a moment's illumination with the torch showed the skylight was opened and closed via a simple screw-jack with a hole in its base to take the hook of a winding handle. She fumbled in her rucksack and pulled out the screwdriver: using its blade in the hole, it was possible to turn the jack and, agonisingly slowly, the skylight began to lift. She turned off the torch and continued winding. The voices were coming closer but only a few more inches and there'd be enough room to squeeze through.

Then Flora's luck ran out.

Chapter Forty-five

Ephesus, AD 79

The governor of Ephesus shifted uneasily in his seat and glanced up at Josephus who remained standing in front of him, arms crossed. 'But you don't understand what's involved here,' said the governor. The wheedling voice was beginning to grate on Josephus' nerves.

'Not only do I understand what goes on in Hierapolis, the emperor does too and these orders are his, not mine. I'm just the messenger.' The fat, sweating Roman started blustering again. 'Very well,' Josephus said, making to leave. 'I'll tell Vespasian you're more interested in filling your personal coffers than doing his will. But if I were you I'd start spending fast because the way you're going, you've probably only got months to live –'

'No, don't go. Please, surely we can come to some arrangement. We're both men of the world –'

'Marcus Tullius, if you're offering me a bribe –'

'Oh, but of course not –'

'You're a lying old bastard, Tullius. You and I are going on a little trip,' said Josephus.

'Not to Rome. Please, not that.'

'That's up to you. Rome or Hierapolis: what's it to be?'

Hierapolis AD 79

The last witness delivered his lines with theatrical perfection and Tullius, sitting in his capacity as *magistratus* turned to look at Philippos. The old man could barely remain upright under the weight of the shackles and his face showed unmistakeable traces of a beating. 'Philippos, you have preached sedition and deliberately encouraged the credulous to turn their faces away from the natural justice and bounty that flow from Rome. I judge you guilty, therefore, of treason. Sentence of crucifixion to be carried out this day.' He rose and strode out of the audience chamber of the city's capitol, brushing aside the pleas of lawyers and Philippos' supporters.

'There, that wasn't so difficult, was it?' said Josephus.

'Maybe not for you. I on the other hand have to try and govern this province. Anyway, Josephus, you've got what you wanted so I won't detain you any longer. I'm sure you'll want to get back to Rome as quickly –'

'Nice try, Tullius. Get me off the premises and then as soon as my back's turned, cash changes hands and Philippos has a miraculous escape. No, I think I'll stick around: I've got a crucifixion to watch and then I think I'll visit these famous baths of yours.'

Rome, Summer AD 79

In his dream Josephus was back at sea and the storm flung them from one wave crest to the next. He heard a voice calling his name and made to reply but no sound came. The ship lurched once more, shaking his head from side to side. He snapped awake and the smoky yellow light from an oil lamp shone in his eyes. The slave was shaking his shoulder and a voice called his name again. 'Wake up, sir, you must wake up.'

Josephus blinked and propped himself up on one elbow. 'What's the matter, Felix? Is the house on fire?'

'No, sir. A messenger, from the palace. It's a summons from Vespasian.'

He swung his feet over the side of the bed and sat up. 'Vespasian's sick: what's he want with me in the middle of the night?'

'The messenger says the emperor is dying and he wants you to go to him.'

Outside in the pre-dawn chill stood the messenger accompanied by three men from the Praetorian guard. The little group hurried through the empty streets and within half an hour Josephus was climbing the familiar steps to the royal apartments.

The doctor looked up and shook his head as Josephus edged into the emperor's bed chamber. Yet another hazard of Roman life which stubbornly refused to respect rank was the typhoid bacillus and, because of a single cup of contaminated water from the *Aquae Cutiliae* spa, the emperor Vespasian lay dying. Dehydrated and wracked with agonising spasms in his gut, he turned his filmy eyes towards the new arrival and stretched out a hand. Josephus knelt and gently took the old man's hand between his own: tears filled his eyes but no words came. In spite of everything, Vespasian forced his parched lips into a smile – even at the last his cynical wit remained undimmed. 'You've timed your arrival well, Josephus. Damn it, I think I'm turning into a god!'

Josephus remained in Rome during the period of public mourning for his patron and delayed his departure to Pompeii until the final week of August. Keen to resume his writing, he planned to stay there until he'd finished the first draft of *The Seven Stars*. A feeling of pride came over him when he thought of what he'd written so far. *The Great History of the Jewish People*, as he called it, was complete as was *The Great Jewish War*: the latter in particular was a work intended to resonate down the years. In reality, *The Wars of the Jews*, as it became known, was a massive exercise in self-justification and spin, seamlessly interwoven with hard fact, although its author had long ago convinced himself that his version of history was the truth.

Sending his slaves on ahead by land, Titus Flavius Josephus, as he now styled himself, took ship from Ostia for a leisurely cruise along the coast to Pompeii.

As the vessel entered the bay of Naples, passing between the mainland and the island of Prochyta, the weather changed abruptly for the worse. Visibility dropped to under a mile, an overpowering stench of sulphur filled the air and the surface of the water was covered by an oily scum. They pressed on but after an hour, the captain announced that he was making for port at Puteoli. As they neared land, the colour of the water turned to a sickly grey-green, covered by a floating carpet of what looked like ash. Here and there, bloated corpses of animals, and, worse, still, people, bobbed in the long flat swell while seabirds feasted on the unexpected bounty.

Under an ashen sky Puteoli loomed out of the sulphurous fog to show a town enveloped by a choking blanket of grey dust: rooftops, streets, even the people themselves were covered in it.

Once ashore, accurate reports of what had happened were impossible to come by. Some blamed the wrath of Vulcan, others said it was the Christians. The one consistent strand in all the accounts was the continuous stream of refugees heading north from further round the bay. Josephus accosted one of the stragglers in the street. 'What do you mean it's gone?' he raged.

The old man wouldn't make eye contact, his focus seemed fixed on a point, far off in the smog. 'Go and see for yourself, boy. Pompeii's gone and so's Herculaneum. Half the mountain's missing and all.'

'But that's not possible.'

'I know it isn't,' said the old man. 'But it still happened. We all got out upwind and we've been back twice looking for our house... but where it was isn't there any more.'

'You're drunk, you old fool,' Josephus replied, shoving him away. With a face like thunder he stormed back to the inn and yelled at the inn-keeper to find him slaves and transport to take him to Pompeii.

304

Chapter Forty-six

William Sunday University, Alabama

The lights snapped on leaving Flora temporarily blinded. For a moment, the two students remained glued to the spot, unable to believe their eyes. 'Just come down nice and slow. Don't make us come up there and get you,' said the one called Mike. Flora ignored him and cranked the screwdriver, the frame of the skylight inching upwards but painfully slowly. 'Call the police,' he shouted.

'I wouldn't do that if I were you,' replied Flora. 'This archive is full of stolen and forged documents. You call the police and it won't be me they'll arrest.'

'You're full of it. Don't say we didn't warn you.' He ran to the bookshelf and jumped, his hands reaching for the highest shelf just below her feet. Luckily for her, the force of his arrival tipped the shelves forwards and he slithered down to the floor, cursing, under a pile of boxes and papers, but Flora's reprieve was momentary. The other student joined him and from each side they began to climb, more carefully this time. A pair of hands appeared at the top of the bookshelf and Flora stamped as hard as she could on the fingers and the hands disappeared: another couple of seconds gained.

A warm breeze flooded through the widening gap and she was about to try and force herself through when from the other side of the bookshelf she felt a hand clamp round her ankle. She pulled the screwdriver out of the hole and stabbed downwards. With a scream the student let go and Flora threw the rucksack out onto the roof, then forced herself through the gap. Memories of being trapped underwater by the branch flooded back as she struggled, scrabbling desperately for any purchase she could find. She was almost out when an unseen hand held her back once more, but kicking hard with one foot and slipping out of the shoe her assailant held, she knocked him off balance and at last rolled out onto the flat roof of the library, gasping with exertion and fear. Ignoring the sharp gravel underfoot, she grabbed the rucksack and ran towards the point where the flat roof met the main building and where the rising ground gave her the shortest drop. Flora swung herself round so she was hanging from the gutter by her hands, aimed for what she hoped was a bush in the border below and let go.

305

With a thump that left her winded she hit the ground and fell back, coming to rest in the soft earth of a flower bed. For a moment, she lay still, looking up at the stars and hoping nothing was broken. From its silhouette against the night sky, she recognised the evergreen magnolia and got up, running towards it. Ahead lay the safety of the treeline and as she ran, lights went on all over the accommodation block accompanied by shouting. Crashing blindly through the dense undergrowth, Flora made sure she was well out of sight before risking a look at her GPS display: two hundred yards lay between her and the car. By the time she reached it the sounds of pursuit had faded into the distance.

'You realise I should fire you for this?' bellowed Sumter, causing the archivist to flinch as though the Professor were about to hit him.

'But she said she was a journalist. From *The Times*, not the *New York Times*, the one in London –'

'I know what *The Times* is, you fool. Did you ask to see her press pass? Did she give you a business card?'

'N-no, sir. She said Mr Patterson had invited her over to see the archives. She'd come all the way from England and I couldn't really send her away, could I?'

'And how many pieces by "Charlotte Drewry" have you read in *The Times*, pray?'

'Well, not many… in fact I've never read it.'

Sumter brought a hand crashing down on the desk causing Irvine, who was sitting quietly in an armchair, to flinch. 'Well I have and it took me precisely five minutes and one phone call to find out that no such person has ever worked for *The Times*. And did it ever enter your head to wonder why a journalist would want to see manuscripts written in languages most of the fourth estate wouldn't know from Chinese?' He paused. 'Of course, that's it. Get Holmes and Watson back in here, there's something I need to ask all of you.'

The archivist returned to Sumter's office a few minutes later followed by the two students who had almost caught Flora, one of whom sported a heavily-bandaged hand. 'Right,' said Sumter, 'take a look at this and tell me if that's her. He handed them a magazine open at a page showing a group photograph of a conference he'd chaired in Berlin two years earlier. Seated in the centre of the line-up was Sumter himself accompanied by about fifteen other people. The image was small but the attractive, dark-haired woman who stared back at them from the middle row was certainly familiar.

'I think that's her,' said the archivist. Her hair's different but I'm pretty sure.'

'What about you two?' Sumter asked.

'That's her all right,' said the one called Mike.

'I didn't get a good enough look,' said the other. 'But I reckon it could be.'

'Thank you, gentlemen,' said Sumter. 'It may interest you to know that we've just had a visit from Doctor Flora Kemble who happens to be a palaeographer from Oxford University. I've often had doubts about her sanity and now they've been confirmed. Thank you gentlemen, you may go and I shall now call the police.'

'Just a minute,' said Irvine, getting up from his chair. 'You two go,' he indicated to the students. 'You,' Irvine pointed to the archivist, 'can stay.' Once they'd left, Irvine resumed. 'All we ask, young man, is diligence and loyalty. Your loyalty is not in doubt – that, after all, as I'm sure you recall, was your predecessor's undoing – kindly prove yourself worthy of keeping your job, help us find Charlotte Drewry, or whatever her name is, and you won't share the same fate.'

Once the archivist had gone, Irvine picked up the telephone on Sumter's desk. Before phoning the police he made an international call to Italy.

FBI Headquarters, Washington DC

'Are you out of your tiny fucking mind?' yelled Cohen. 'Hundreds of man-hours and Christ knows how many tens of thousands of dollars down the can.'

Flora's bottom lip trembled. 'But I got you the evidence you wanted,' she said, fighting back the tears.

'No,' said Cohen, brandishing a sheaf of papers at her. 'You didn't. This is the report from the local sheriff's department. I'll paraphrase.' He turned to the second page. 'An unidentified woman, answering the description of Flora Kemble, a British national, gained entry to William Sunday university by falsely claiming to be a journalist, broke into private property causing criminal damage to a window frame and a skylight, carried out an assault using a deadly weapon – a screwdriver as it happens – and stole a piece of papyrus which may or may not date from the first century. And you know why I got a copy of the report?'

'No,' she replied, too ashamed to meet his gaze.

'Because – and I know you Brits think we can't do irony – they sent it to me hoping it would help with the ACT's investigations.'

'But the *Apocryphon of John*, the evidence –'

307

'Worthless. It is now anyway. You've got a bunch of photos that could've been taken anywhere – yes I know they show stolen documents but how's a court to know you didn't steal them in the first place?'

'But you know that's not true,' protested Flora.

'Yes, I know it's not true but it wouldn't take five minutes to make you look like the prime suspect. And,' he added, slapping the papers down in front of her, 'it would bump my clear-up rate and get my goddam supervisor off my back, so don't fucking tempt me, Flora. Just don't.'

'I suppose it's no good asking about the forged papyrus…'

'You mean the one you stole? To explain the many ways in which it's now useless would take all day. Believe me, this case is in deep shit because of you and the amount of ass I'm going to have to kiss to save it does not leave a nice taste in my mouth.'

'I'm sorry,' said Flora, still looking down at the floor. 'I was only trying to help.'

He walked over to where she sat and laid a hand on her shoulder. 'Yeah, I know,' he said. 'So next time maybe you'll listen to me, eh? I do this stuff for a living. Sumter and his buddies are involved in some bad shit: your visit confirmed that. Trouble is, at the same time you've just made it a whole bunch harder to prove in court. Still, it's not all bad news though.'

'It isn't?' she said, looking up and trying to smile.

'No, while you were playing at Catwoman in Alabama, we got lucky with Raymond. He called his contacts again to say Grossman and the FBI had a big falling-out after their unplanned swim. Grossman reckons the Feds set him up to get whacked at the last meet and he's not playing ball any more. What's more, he wants to sell everything he's got.'

'That's even flakier than the last call. Sumter'll never buy that.'

'Course he won't,' said Cohen. 'It's his chance to double-bluff us and he's gone for it. He wants to get his hands on the whole collection – the pieces that Raymond's still got plus the ones he sold to Grossman – and he's willing to take risks which suggests he wants it real bad. Now, here's how we hooked him: Sumter wants to rob Grossman and ideally whack him too; he wants to do the same to Raymond so when Raymond offered to bring Grossman along to a meet with a guarantee that he'd use his New York guys to make sure the FBI weren't following; Sumter, or whoever's acting for him, jumped at it.'

'So we're the bait in the trap again?' asked Flora.

''Fraid so,' said Cohen.

FBI Field Office. Birmingham, Alabama.

Cohen looked up from the lectern and flicked to the last slide of the briefing. In front of him sat two civilians, Raymond and Flora, and fifteen FBI agents. 'OK, are there any questions so far?' he asked. None came so he continued. 'Right, let's recap the stuff that's going to keep us alive. Any Foxtrot callsign can call the abort at any time. I guarantee no recriminations and no Monday morning quarterbacking if it turns out to be a false alarm. Safety is paramount, especially as it's my own pasty white butt that's gonna be first in the firing-line if things go wrong.' A ripple of nervous laughter went round the room. 'Also, if you lose the signal from the tracker on my vehicle for more than a couple of minutes, get on the radio and I'll make the go/no-go call depending on the tactical situation as I see it. I retain operational control throughout. If I go down, opcon passes to the leader of team Foxtrot 1. All clear? Good. We move in one hour, fourteen minutes.'

The teams' radio net was up and working and the direction finders, designed to take a GPS feed from a unit fitted underneath the car that Cohen would be driving, all checked out to the foot. It was time to go.

Flora turned round to Raymond who was sitting in the back seat. 'Nervous?' she asked.

He shrugged and gazed out of the window at the panorama of everyday southern Birmingham street scenes as it unrolled past them. 'More fatalistic than anything,' he replied. 'If I don't play ball with Special Agent Cohen here and his buddies, I'll end up copping for every homicide from JFK to Jimmy Hoffa.'

Cohen smiled and looked at Raymond in the rear-view mirror. 'Got a couple of unsolved wire frauds too if you wouldn't mind wearing those,' he said.

'Be delighted to help, officer. Always a pleasure.' The nervous banter and strained humour went back and forth, helping to take their minds off what lay ahead less than forty five minutes down the road. No following vehicles this time, just them, heading into the countryside and looking for all the world like any another car on the interstate. Suddenly, the radio burst into like. 'All Foxtrot units this is Foxtrot control, abort, abort, abort. All units acknowledge.'

Cohen swore and picked up the hand-mike. 'Foxtrot zero, acknowledged.' The others callsigns all followed suit.

'What's happened?' asked Flora, trying to mask the relief in her voice.

309

'Dunno. We'll find out when we get back,' said Cohen, pulling into the parking lot of a truck stop to turn round.

Flora and Raymond waited in Cohen's office while he went to talk to the Field Office commander. It seemed odd to be alone with a man whom she'd looked at down the sights of .38 revolver just over a week earlier but who now made engaging small-talk as though nothing had happened. He explained the insidious process by which he'd become caught up in the Enron scandal. It started with creative accounting, moved almost imperceptibly to deliberate oversights and then rapidly to outright fraud. Everything about it was wrong, he freely admitted: ethically, professionally, morally, you name it, but by the time he decided to get out, it was too late and had it not been for a good lawyer and a plea bargain he'd have spent at least five years in jail. As it was, the fine ruined him financially and the public dissection of his conduct did the same for his career. 'Then I met a guy who knew a guy who knew someone else, and I just kinda took to it,' he explained. 'I was always interested in history, art and the like, I got to meet some interesting people, never had anything to do with guns –'

'Until I came along,' said Flora.

'Yeah, well, occupational hazard when you start working cross-border I guess. No hard feelings though.'

'And the man I shot, he was your link to Italy, right?'

'Yeah, it was supposed to be pretty simple. Luzzo dealt with the Italians, I was the cut-out between them and the end buyer.'

'And do you know who the end buyer is?'

He looked at her with a half-smile on his face. 'You shouldn't go asking questions like that,' he said. 'But yeah, I met some guys, they gave me names but they're all John Does. Doesn't pay to ask too many questions: makes folk nervous.'

'And the man who was murdered in prison?'

Raymond held up both hands, palm outwards. 'Whoa there, you're way out of your pay-grade, Flora. That's police shit. Like I told your buddy Cohen, I didn't know anything about that.'

'Do you know, I think I believe you,' she replied.

He laughed. 'Well, even though it's the truth, you'd make a lousy cop going around believing what people say.'

The conversation was interrupted by Cohen's return. One look at his face told Flora all she needed to know. 'The operation's suspended until further orders, the ACT's been stood down and the casework's going back to the Birmingham Field Office to wrap up for handover to the local sheriff's department.'

'But why?' asked Flora, aghast.

'Word from on high. Your buddy Sumter's kicked up hell and the Director of the FBI has had to go down on his knees and grovel just to avoid an official complaint. Sumter wants charges brought against you so the sooner you leave the country the better.'

'What you been up to, Flora?' asked Raymond, winking at her.

'None of your business,' said Cohen. 'We're off the case until I hear otherwise. Raymond, can you please step outside.'

As soon as the door closed Flora stood up and gesticulated angrily at Cohen. 'After all we've done. This is ridiculous,' she shouted.

'Wait. It gets worse. The reason the Director's involved is that he got it in the ass direct from "senior White House staffers" which in case you didn't know, means this has come from the President.' Flora stared at him in disbelief and Cohen continued. 'Sumter is a major fund-raiser for the Republican Party, a personal friend of the President and has a lot of contacts in the Senate too. The GOP stands to get it's ass kicked in the mid-terms and the President doesn't want to make things worse.'

Flora shook her head. 'I can't believe I'm hearing this. Sumter's a crook, a forger, a liar and he tried to get us killed –'

Cohen slapped his leg in mock exasperation. 'Yeah, darn it, now you tell me. If only I'd remembered to mention it... Listen Flora, I know all that, the supervisor here and my boss at the ACT know too, but when shit like this comes down from on high, we have no choice.'

'But that's –'

'Let me finish. The evidence for Sumter's involvement with the robberies is circumstantial, there's no proof he's harmed anybody and, within reason, he's free to put anything he wants on the web. There's too much political downside if we take him on. This is a local matter now and for the moment it's out of our hands.'

'What about Raymond?'

'Oh, he's not going anywhere, the sheriff's office have got plenty for him to do.'

She perked up at this. 'Could I help too?'

'Flora, you show your nose in Bibb County and you'll be arrested. Everything's on hold so for the moment you're not going anywhere. You're going back to the hotel and I want you to stay there.'

It was mid-afternoon when Cohen dropped her off: an awkward time of day, too late to start anything and too early for the first drink. To hell with it, she thought, and picked up her mobile phone to call Lombardi in

Naples. He listened without interrupting as she ran through the latest developments.

Flora heard him swear. 'So after all our efforts the case is on ice?'

'Afraid so. Is there anything you can do?'

'If I tried it would only cause problems. The last thing we want is a row with our American friends: it was hard enough to get them onside in the first place. I can ask Colonel Andretti but I don't think he'll be able to do anything.'

'So we just give up?' said Flora. 'An hour down the road from here, Donald Sumter is sitting on a pile of stolen manuscripts and using faked ones to hoodwink millions of people. Why can't you come over and help?'

'Flora, I'd be out of my jurisdiction and so would any of my TPC guys. I don't want to cause a diplomatic incident and I certainly don't want to lose my job.'

'So what do you suggest? I'm within touching distance but if I try and do it on my own –'

'Do what on your own?'

'Get proof that Sumter is behind the robbery of course.'

'What if the police arrest you?'

'I'll cross that bridge when I come to it. I need expert help and I need it now.'

Lombardi paused for thought. 'You've just given me an idea,' he said. 'I'll have to square it with Rome, but do you think Francesco Moretti would be willing to help?'

'I think he'd jump at the chance,' said Flora. 'The robbery was personal for him – like someone burgled his house.' She hesitated, half-afraid to say the words. 'You know the FBI don't trust him?'

'I do, they've told me as much. I'm not even sure they trust me. To them, anything south of Lombardy equals Mafia. Moretti's fine. I'll make some calls then let you know how I get on.'

Pompeii

The three men met in their usual restaurant and Elvis did most of the talking. 'Alabama, who'd have thought it? Seems we only just missed her in England, she did go to Washington after all and now we know she's helping the FBI.'

'But why me?' Pleaded Moretti, his face the colour of putty.

'Because she knows and trusts you. Lombardi's paying your air-fare and she'll be expecting you: it couldn't have worked out better.'

312

Chapter Forty-seven

Pompeii, AD 79

Josephus couldn't believe his eyes. From horizon to horizon stretched a grey, undulating moonscape. In places it was pockmarked by craters where scavengers and desperate householders had tried to dig down to the buildings below. The tattered stump of Vesuvius loomed over them like a malformed ash-heap. 'So you think it should be right here?' Josephus said to the slave accompanying him.

'That's what I reckon, sir.' He looked up from the scroll of papyrus and pointed to the north east. 'If those pillars sticking up are the capitol and assuming that lump is the circus, then we're in the right place.'

'But my house was only a hundred paces from the shore. The sea's a quarter of a mile away so we can't be.'

The slave kicked at a lump of pumice, sending up a little cloud of dust. 'No accounting for sorcery, sir.'

'Sorcery, my arse,' said Josephus, snatching the map away from him. 'My life's work is somewhere underneath this slag-pile and I want it back.'

'Should've brought a pick and shovel then, shouldn't you, sir?

'And my scribes. It took me years to train them. Where they hell have they gone? How am I supposed to find them?'

'Like I said, sir. Pick and shovel.' Josephus considered hitting him but thought better of it. He'd just have to start again from scratch.

Chapter Forty-eight

Birmingham, Alabama

When Francesco Moretti came through the barrier into the arrivals hall Flora threw herself into his arms. Physically, he returned her greeting but a sixth sense told her there was something wrong, something missing. Trying to push it to the back of her mind she chattered excitedly all the way back to the car park.

'Your hotel's only a couple of blocks from mine,' she said as they drove through the downtown traffic. 'They're supposed to be watching me to make sure I don't leave mine but as you can tell, they're pretty hopeless. I could come over later.'

He gazed out of the rental car window at nothing in particular. 'Sure, that would be nice.'

'Nice!?' said Flora turning to look at him. '"Nice" is for chocolate cake. What's the matter with you? Not your conscience I hope – it certainly didn't bother you when we were in Italy.'

'I'm sorry, Flora. I shouldn't have done that. It was a mistake.'

Flora gave a snort. 'That's not what you said at the time. And kindly don't dismiss fucking me as a mistake –'

'I'm sorry, Flora, that's not what I meant.'

With a smile she reached over and put a hand on his knee. 'No, it's my fault. I'm the one who should apologise, not you. Let's not row.'

'I'll just be glad when all this is over,' he replied, staring at the streams of traffic ahead of them.

'But you've only just got here. Don't you want to see Sumter behind bars?'

'You should be Italian,' he replied. 'Vendettas are our thing.'

'It's not a vendetta. He's a crook. And anyway, don't you want the finds back?'

'Of course I do, I just don't see how we're going to do it without getting killed or arrested.'

'Don't worry, I'll think of something,' she replied.

Moretti turned to her, his face contracted into a worried frown. 'But Lombardi said you had a plan.'

'I do...well I did but I've decided it was rubbish. I'll take you to meet Raymond. He'll help us think of something.'

Linn Park, Birmingham, Alabama

Flora, Moretti and Raymond sat on a low wall under the shade of a tree. 'No, no, no,' said Raymond. 'That is the dumbest idea I ever heard in my goddam life.'

'So do you have a better one?' asked Flora.

'Yeah, I walk away, I call Agent Cohen and tell him you're a dangerous lunatic and will he please lock you up. And anyway, what's in it for me?'

'You said it yourself,' she replied. 'If the FBI drop this case and the local guys file it under "whatever" your usefulness goes from being an informer to a clean-up statistic.'

'I'm beginning to think jail's not such a bad idea. Listen, Flora, why don't we try something like this.' Flora listened attentively while Raymond spelled out his idea. 'So what do you reckon?' he said at last.

'It's complicated, but I think it might just work,' she replied, looking down at the notes she'd taken while he was talking.

'And safer for you. Sumter's not afraid to use force.'

'Tell me about it,' she replied. 'So why should it be any different this time? They could just shoot me.'

'I told you, because of Francesco here. If he takes both of you out, it'll be obvious he's trying to hide evidence –'

'That'll be a great consolation when I'm six feet under.'

'You wont be, don't worry. Now listen, both of you, here's what we do.'

William Sunday University, Alabama

'Good news,' said Irvine, shutting the door behind him. 'Moretti's found the girl.'

'Why, that's wonderful news.' Sumter's face said differently. 'Where?'

'Birmingham.'

'And has he, you know –'

'Killed her? No, not yet. She's under FBI protection at the hotel. We have to think laterally about this.'

'How so?'

'Moretti's English isn't very good and he's not completely sure what she's up to but it sounds like she and that nigger friend of ours, Raymond, will shortly do us the honour of a social call.'

'Where? Here?'

'Yes, Donald, here.' He paused. 'Are you all right?' You've gone pale.'

'N-no, I'm fine, just feeling a little bilious, that's all.'

'Irvine treated him to a reptilian smile. 'Not getting cold feet are you, Donald?'

'No, it's just that –'

'It's just that you don't mind inconvenient people disappearing so long as you can convince yourself you had nothing to do with it. Correct?'

'No, Andrew, it's more complicated.'

'Hypocrisy usually is.'

Sumter ignored the barb and sighed deeply. 'Do what you must. I'm not sure allowing the student body their head on such matters is a good idea.'

'Surely you're not questioning the authority of Exodus 22:18, Donald?'

'No, Andrew, I'm not, it just seems a little excessive that's all. If they must kill people at least they could do it quickly.'

Irvine left the room leaving Sumter slumped with his elbows on the desk, head in hands and fighting a losing battle with the remains of his conscience. He was interrupted by a bang on the door. 'Come in,' he boomed and the archivist almost fell through the door, panting with excitement.

'I've found her,' he said.

'Well done,' Sumter replied in a world-weary tone.

'She's got a message for you.' The young man was positively bursting.

'Go on, I'm listening.'

'She says she'll give you back the modern manuscript in return for all the Pompeii finds and the *Apocryphon of John*.'

'Was that it?'

'No, sir, and this was the bit I didn't quite understand. Here's what she said,' he pulled out a scrap of paper from his pocket and read: '"Francesco has corroborated the age and origin of your "Q" fragment. If you try to back out I'll expose you". Those were her exact words, sir,' he added quickly.

Sumter's expression remained impassive. 'Tell her tomorrow at three. I'll meet her here in my office.'

The car drew to a halt at the side of the narrow road and Flora switched off the engine. 'Now, Francesco, this is vitally important. I will

316

check in with both of you at half past three. If you don't hear from me, you must assume something's gone wrong. Raymond will call for help and you are to drive back here to collect him. If he's not here, then wait, do not go off without him. Have you got that?'

'Yes.' Flora could see that, like her, Raymond was trying to hide his nerves but Moretti spoke in a dull monotone as though he simply wasn't interested.

Raymond took up the briefing. 'As soon as I'm in place, Flora, I'll text you with "See you tomorrow at ten" if I've got good line of sight into Sumter's office. "Can't make it tomorrow" means I can't see anything –'

Flora brought her hand down hard on the top of the dashboard, causing them both to jump. 'Francesco, are you listening?' she shouted.

He stopped gazing out of the window and turned to look at her. 'Y-yes, Flora, of course.'

'Good, now pay attention,' she said. 'If everything goes to plan, I'll call to let you know. Francesco, you drive to the front gate, collect me from there and then we come back here for Raymond. Everyone happy?' They both nodded and Raymond slung a pair of binoculars round his neck and opened the passenger door. Flora leant over and gave him a peck on the cheek. 'Good luck,' she said.

'You too. Take it easy now, babe.'

In five minutes they arrived at the front gate: the college buildings lay about a quarter of a mile away and Flora jumped out. She kissed Moretti too and, in return, received a few mumbled words she didn't catch, and a wan smile. Closing the car door, she set off towards the administration block. The sudden buzzing of her phone made Flora jump. She checked the text: Raymond had good line of sight and she began to breathe a little more easily. In an hour it would all be over; Sumter would have his forgery back, she would leave with the finds from Pompeii and, if things went to plan, a recording of a conversation that would convict the professor out of his own mouth.

The receptionist was all smiles and southern charm. She led Flora through to a waiting room and a few minutes later, two students, tall, well-dressed men in their early twenties, greeted her by name.

They walked either side of her chatting amiably. This was going to be easier than she thought. 'Professor Sumter's really looking forward to seeing you,' said the first. 'Please step this way.' He stood aside and gestured her forward while the other student held open the door. 'After you, please –'

She took a step forward and froze, her briefcase hitting the floor with a thump. Whatever it was, this wasn't Sumter's office.

Someone shoved her in the small of the back, propelling her into the arms of another two young men who secured her hands behind her back with cable ties and pushed her forward once more. What she saw next almost caused her to retch: also bound, but bloodied and dishevelled, Raymond sat on a plain wooden chair. She realised they were in a lecture theatre with a stage at the front and rows of seating rising in a series of tiered quarter circles to the back: about fifty of the seats were taken and the occupants were male. On the stage was a row of a dozen single chairs, all empty.

On the stage next to Raymond stood Moretti, also with his hands behind his back. 'Did you have chance to call?' she asked him in Italian as they led her forward.

He shook his head. 'No calls, Flora, sorry. You see, it's Anna,' he said, opening his arms in front of himself in a gesture of apology. He wasn't bound and she couldn't understand why at first. Then she noticed that, unlike Raymond, he showed no signs of having been in a struggle.

'What's Anna got to do with this?'

'They said they'd hurt her.'

'Who would? What are you talking about?'

'People I know in Italy. You know, the –'

'That's enough,' said the student who had tied her wrists, we haven't got all day. Put the prisoners in the dock.'

Flora ignored him. 'You betrayed us? Francesco, not you, please say it's not true.' Tears coursed down her face as she was manhandled into the makeshift dock and forced to sit down next to Raymond.

'Sorry,' said Moretti, also in tears, but no one heard him in the clamour of voices.

One of the students moved in behind the lectern and stood facing them. He shouted, 'All rise.' Folding seat-backs clattered as the students came to their feet.

Raymond stayed where he was. 'Fuck you,' he said.

'On your feet, boy,' said the student. 'This is my court, I am its president and you will do as I say.'

'Go fuck yourself –'

He nodded and Raymond was hauled, cursing, to his feet. 'Gentlemen of the jury, please take your seats.' Twelve young men trooped silently forward and sat on the chairs set out on the stage.

'These clowns should be on *Saturday Night Live*,' said Raymond.

'Silence,' shouted the president, banging his wooden gavel down on the lectern in front of him. 'Or you will face charges of contempt of court.'

'Contempt?' replied Raymond, 'Believe me, motherfucker, contempt ain't the half of what I think of this crap.'

'Sergeant-at-Arms, make the prisoner be quiet.' The burly student who had manhandled Flora strode over and punched the helpless Raymond in the kidneys, causing him to double up on the floor in agony. 'Very well, we will continue. Flora Kemble, you are charged with theft, blasphemy and the bearing of false witness. Are you guilty or not guilty?'

'Look, you've had your fun, you've got the manuscript back and now if you don't mind –'

'I will take that as a plea of not guilty.'

Raymond was hauled to his feet once more. 'Prisoner at the bar, state your name.'

'Most people call me Raymond.'

'State your full name.'

'I told you, my name's Raymond. That *is* my full name, asshole.'

'Sergeant-at-Arms –'

'Yeah, OK, sorry. Asshole, sir.' Flora winced as a fist smashed into the side of Raymond's head, almost knocking him clean out of the dock. He staggered back to his feet.

'Don't antagonise them,' hissed Flora. 'Try and play for time.'

The president began once more. 'Flora Kemble –'

'Just hang on a minute,' she said. 'If this is supposed to be a court, where's the prosecuting counsel and more to the point, where's my lawyer. I want representation –'

'Miss Kemble, as president of this court I act in the capacity of examining magistrate. I shall place the facts affecting this case before the jury and they will decide whether you are innocent or guilty.'

'Have you read Alice Through the Looking Glass?' asked Flora.

'Silence,' he shouted, going red in the face. 'One more outburst like that and I'll have you flogged.'

The witty comeback was on the tip of her tongue when rather late in the day, a ghastly reality dawned: he wasn't joking.

The archivist was chivvied out of his seat and made to take an oath on the Bible. He gave a scripted and heavily embellished version of his encounter with Flora's journalist alter-ego and every time she caught his eye, he looked away. 'Thank you,' said the president. 'Gentlemen of the jury –'

'Hold on, that's not fair,' said Flora. 'Don't I get to question the witness?'

'No. The testimony was given on oath and therefore is the entire truth.'

Next it was Raymond's turn to answer the same charges. To every question he replied "no comment".

The president then addressed them both. 'Do you realise what you could have done, what you could have put at risk?'

'Nope, but I've a feeling you're about to tell us,' said Raymond. Flora shushed him.

'We are approaching the End of Days,' he said, a beatific smile spreading across his features. 'The prophecy will shortly be fulfilled. We are building the House of the Mountain of the Lord and all nations shall flow unto it.'

'This guy's been skipping his medication,' whispered Raymond.

'The Temple of Jerusalem will be rebuilt and then the Great Tribulation of mankind will begin; but those who are saved will meet in the air on the day of Rapture –'

'Not so fast,' said Flora, cutting him off in mid-stream. 'Can I ask a question?'

'You may,' said the president. 'But it won't affect the verdict.'

She looked at him with contempt. 'Are you really saying that if you can pack enough people into the churches on a Sunday then it'll help hurry the Second Coming along?'

'Isaiah, chapter two, verses one to five: when the people of the earth flow unto his house, the Lord will return.'

'Even if you've tricked them into turning up by using a dodgy website and forged manuscripts? I don't think Jesus will be very happy if he turns up and finds you've done that –'

'Gentlemen of the jury,' he shouted over the top of her. 'In the case of Flora Kemble, have you reached a verdict?'

'Yes, sir. Guilty on all counts.'

'And in the case of Raymond Doe, have you reached a verdict?'

'Yes, sir. Guilty on all counts.'

'Very funny, but would you mind untying us now?' asked Flora. 'My wrists are hurting.'

'Silence,' said the president. 'You'll have a chance to speak later. I will now pass sentence. Isaiah, chapter forty seven, verses thirteen to fourteen shall be my guide: "Let now the evil men stand up, and save thee from these things that shall come upon thee. Behold, they shall be as stubble; the fire shall burn them; they shall not deliver themselves from the power of the flame."'

Raymond and Flora exchanged bemused glances. However, the young man's next pronouncement left them in no doubt of the horror in store: the joke was well and truly over. 'The sentence of this court is that both prisoners be burned at the stake until their bodies be entirely consumed by the cleansing flames. May the Lord have mercy on their souls.'

'You've gotta be shitting me,' said Raymond, although Flora could see that his cocky swagger had gone.

'Show them,' said the president. Flora and Raymond were forced to turn round to where one of the floor-to-ceiling blinds was being raised. On a patch of ground just before the sports fields, three solid metal poles stood embedded in the ground: each showed signs of charring and around two of them other students were stacking bundles of faggots. Flora felt her knees giving way and she slumped to the floor.

Chapter Forty-nine

Rome AD 80

The emperor Titus choked in disbelief at what he'd just heard. 'You want me to do what?' He put down his drinking cup and wiped away the wine that had reappeared down his nose.

'To rebuild the Temple of Jerusalem,' said Josephus.

'Have you gone mad? My army of Alexandria spent six months flattening Jerusalem and now you want me to rebuild it?'

'Yes, because if you don't, very soon this Christ cult will be too big to stop.'

'So how does rebuilding the Temple help and what am I supposed to do with the treasures my army paraded through Rome? Have another parade in the opposite direction?'

'I've explained it before, sir,' said Josephus. 'The men responsible for my father's death perverted our law, the teachings of the prophets, even the law of God as handed down to Moses.'

'I know all this,' Titus replied. 'But they're all dead. What use is continuing a family squabble beyond the grave?'

Josephus became agitated. 'No. It's more than that – much more. The only way to get people to realise it's all false is to show them that the prophecies of the Jews are the only true ones.'

'My prophecy's bigger than yours. Lacks a certain philosophical sophistication, doesn't it, Josephus?'

'Please, listen, sir. The prophet Daniel speaks of a desolation, an abomination. For us, that was the destruction of the temple.'

Titus snorted derisively. Josephus could see he was losing interest. 'You brought that on yourselves, prophets or no prophets.'

'But it's what comes afterwards, after the desolation. Once the temple is restored then the true Messiah – not the one Peter and his cronies invented – will come and bring about the end of days. All will be united in the bosom of the Lord.'

The emperor looked at him pityingly. 'So not only is my prophecy bigger than yours, you get to say "I told you so". Listen, even Rome's resources have their limits. Face it: your God deserted you. Why else did he allow us to defeat you? Finish writing your histories and let posterity be the judge of who was right.'

322

Chapter Fifty

William Sunday University, Alabama

'Pick her up,' the president of the court ordered and Flora was hauled, sobbing, to her feet. 'Raymond Doe,' he said. 'I will start with you. Do you have anything to say?'

'Yeah. Go fuck yourself, asshole.'

This time he ignored the insult. 'Flora Kemble, do you have anything to say?'

She swallowed hard, choking back the tears and a rising tide of panic. 'Yes I do but I want to say it to Donald Sumter.'

'Very well, but you do realise it won't change anything?'

Two chairs were brought and the prisoners allowed to sit down while one of the students ran off to fetch Sumter. Outside, the last of the faggots were packed into place. Flora and Raymond watched in terrified disbelief as two young men began drenching the firewood in what could only be gasoline.

A door opened at the back of the auditorium. The students in the tiered seats turned round to look and the president banged his gavel for silence. Sumter, accompanied by Irvine, looked down on the impromptu court and its prisoners. 'Mr Moretti, would you come here please,' said Sumter. 'There's no need for you to watch this.' Moretti walked up the central aisle, head down, looking neither right nor left. Sumter continued. 'I understand you have something to say to me, Flora?' he said.

Despite all Flora's efforts her tears flowed anew and the halting words came out punctuated by sobs. 'Donald, for pity's sake, stop this and let us go. The FBI have given up, you've got your manuscript back. I admit it, you've won. Please don't let them do this.'

He made to speak but she saw Irvine say something to him behind his hand and then grip the Professor's arm. In Irvine's eyes she could see nothing, no emotion, no pity, not even a scrap of understanding: the cold, dead eyes of a shark. Sumter shot an anxious glance at Irvine, looked down and said quietly, 'Let the Lord's will be done.' Irvine led Moretti out through the door and after a final backward glance Sumter, with Flora's briefcase in his hand, made to leave.

Before he had taken a single pace Flora felt rather than heard the explosion. The blind took some of the impact but a shower of safety

323

glass flew across the lecture theatre like hail. A second detonation, more muffled this time, was immediately followed by a crackle of automatic fire, punctuated by the high-pitched cracks of single-shot weapons firing in reply. Instinctively, Raymond and Flora dived to the floor amidst a chaos of shouting, clouds of acrid smoke and running feet.

Black-clad figures in gas-masks swarmed in through the shattered windows. Cries of "Federal Agents: get down, don't move," filled the air. Lying on her side half in, half out of the makeshift dock, Flora saw the student president aim a handgun at the intruders, but he was flung backwards by a burst of high-velocity, rounds, the pistol flying out of his hands and sliding off the back of the stage. Most of the other students bolted for the exits: others were already pinned to the floor, their wrists and ankles tightly bound. Suddenly, she was aware of someone kneeling beside her, calling her name, muffled almost to incomprehension by his gas-mask. Ducking down, he removed first his Kevlar helmet and then the mask. 'You OK, Flora?' It was Cohen.

'No I'm not,' was all she could think of saying as he cut the cable ties holding their wrists.

'Keep down and don't move or you'll get shot,' he said, getting to his feet.

'But Sumter, what about −' but he was on his feet and gone before she'd finished the sentence.

She crawled forward a couple of feet. Raymond, who'd also been freed by Cohen, caught her by the ankle, 'Are you out of your fucking mind? You heard what the man said.'

'Don't worry, I'll be fine, just let me go.'

'Have it your own way,' he said, releasing his grip.

From what she could see, the FBI agents seemed occupied with securing the building and no one noticed her as she inched across to the back of the stage. Fumbling in the gap her fingers closed round the butt of the student president's pistol and she tucked it into the waistband of her skirt. She looked around to make sure no one had seen, and then, with as much calm as she could muster, walked briskly out of the door through which they'd been led not fifteen minutes earlier.

The air in the corridors was heavy with smoke, and the sound of nearby gunfire made her flinch with each burst. 'Flora, where the hell are you going?' She spun round to see Cohen: no gas mask this time, but clad in body armour and topped with a protective helmet he seemed twice his normal size. 'I told you to stay put.'

'Sorry, Ben. This is important. There's an archive full of stolen

324

manuscripts downstairs and I want to make sure nothing else happens to them.'

'Not a chance. Go back to the lecture room or I'll arrest you for your own safety.'

Cohen's personal radio crackled into life. 'Agent down, reception area, western side. Nearest unit identify yourself.'

'That's you, Ben,' she said pointing towards the end of the corridor. 'Up there, turn left then straight on.'

He moved the mike up towards his mouth. 'Foxtrot Bravo three responding. I'm thirty seconds out,' he said and then turned to Flora, releasing the transmit button and wagging a gloved finger in her face. 'And you. Do as you're damn well told.'

'Yes, Ben,' she said meekly and turned to retrace her steps as he charged off. Waiting till he was out of sight, Flora continued towards the library. Twice she had to step over the motionless forms of students cut down by the FBI's weapons.

Flora took the pistol from her waistband and moved gingerly down the steps. The library was in darkness; the curtains were drawn with only the glow of the emergency lighting to show the way. The electricity had been cut.

She tiptoed inside but had only gone a few feet when from ahead in the gloom she heard men's voices, one of them unpleasantly familiar: Sumter.

Using the cover of a bookshelf she inched closer, crouching down as low as she could get. Ten feet in front of her, Moretti, Sumter and Irvine were hurriedly piling archive files into cardboard boxes.

Flora hesitated. The sensible thing to do would be to go for help. On the other hand, there might not be time. She decided to stay. Trouble was, each man kept ducking in and out of the archive room meaning she never had clear sight of all three at the same time. Moretti won't be armed, she thought, but as for the other two, that was anybody's guess. Standing up to get a better view between the rows of books she came up onto tiptoe, pistol in one hand, the other steadying herself against a shelf, watching and waiting. Then, she strained just a little too hard to get a better view and her left hand slipped, sending her clattering sideways, grasping helplessly at thin air and tumbling books. As she hit the ground, the pistol jolted out of her hand.

The three men spun round and Irvine pulled out a pistol, pointing it at Flora who was now sprawled on the ground between the bookcases. 'You don't learn, do you?' he said, taking careful aim. She closed her

eyes, flinching for the impact, and heard the gun fire. There was no pain
and for a moment Flora assumed she was dead. Then she heard the all
too real sounds of a struggle and a man cursing in Italian. Irvine broke
free from Moretti's grasp and with the sole of his foot, pushed him hard
in the stomach, sending him sprawling against the opposite wall. Irvine
levelled the weapon and fired twice into Moretti's chest, the blood
spraying high up the wall. The moment's reprieve was just enough. Flora
lunged forward, grabbed the pistol and as Irvine swung towards her, fired
a single shot that hit him just above the right eyebrow, removing the top
of his skull and toppling him backwards towards the lifeless form of
Moretti. By the time she'd recovered from the recoil, Sumter had gone
and the doors to the archive slammed shut. Her first instinct was to
follow him but the thought that he might be armed made her pause. Then
she looked down at Moretti and the pool of blood forming around him.
Whatever he may have been blackmailed into doing, he hadn't deserved
this and a red mist of hatred rose up, driving her on. Now it was like old
times and a cocktail of training and adrenalin pushed her old demons into
the background. Barging the door open with her shoulder, she dashed out
of the library.

In the thick smoke filling the corridor, she almost ran head-first into
a squad of FBI agents coming the other way. 'He's in there,' she panted.
'In the archive room. I think he's armed.' Without a word they pushed
her aside and clattered down the steps: a phalanx of alien beings. She
called after them. 'Be careful with anything in cardboard boxes. It's
fragile....'

Flora began to choke. With no doorway in sight, she opened one of
the sash windows and dropped down into the flowerbed. In front of her
stood the familiar evergreen magnolia. As she bent over, coughing and
retching to clear her lungs, a squad of black-clad figures doubled past
and were lost to sight behind the end wall of the library. Seconds later
came a warning shouted through a loud-hailer, ordering Sumter to
surrender. She took a couple of paces towards the tree when at once the
air seemed to disappear from her lungs, followed instantly by a deafening
concussion. When her ears stopped ringing she heard gunfire and then a
series of smaller explosions. Smoke poured from the shattered library
windows and then tongues of flame.

This was too much and she backed away up the slope, trying to get
as far away as possible. A sudden movement caught her eye and at first
she couldn't work out what it was. Something was moving the curtain
under one of the skylights – the very same one she'd used as a makeshift

exit – and then she saw the face of Donald Sumter, red and panic-stricken as he pushed and beat at the unyielding toughened glass dome above his head. Little threads of smoke began to appear around him. Another bang ripped through the air, accompanied by a flash and she saw him look down as a bright red glow blossomed through all four skylights of the archive. It was on fire. She watched, helplessly as he beat against the glass, the flames now shooting up around him, but it was too much to bear and as he opened his mouth to scream she turned away.

'Christ, you're still alive,' said Cohen as Flora walked back into the Art Crime Team's offices.

'Alive? Why shouldn't I be? The man's a poppet.' Her hair shone, she was wearing a new dress and her old bounce and self-confidence were back.

He shook his head in disbelief. 'I've heard the Director called many things but "a poppet" isn't one of them.'

She put her head on one side and looked at him. 'Well, he seemed a bit grumpy at first but after I explained a few things to him, he was fine.'

'I wish somebody would explain them to me. The first thing I knew was when your friend Moretti called saying someone was about to kill you and Raymond. His English was lousy, by the way.'

'True, but thank goodness he discovered his conscience when he did,' said Flora, her voice catching at the thought of the man of whom she'd once been so fond. 'Have you heard from Lombardi yet?'

'Yeah, I got off the phone with him about ten minutes ago. He's embarrassed as hell – I mean, after all, he tried to short-circuit every procedure in the book and ended up sending us the very man the Camorra wanted to get next to you. He made their job a hell of a lot easier.'

'What's going to happen to him? Lombardi, I mean.'

Cohen shrugged. 'Probably get his ass kicked, that's all. Moretti was never here officially and I'm sure both the State Department and the Italians will want to punt the whole thing into the long grass. The press are all over the religious angle to the exclusion of anything else which suits everyone just fine.'

'Yes, I saw that,' said Flora. 'You've got crazies out there comparing it to Waco – Sumter's being treated as a martyr for Christ's sake, and church attendance has gone up even more since the fire.' She paused for a moment, deep in thought. 'We didn't win this one, did we, Ben?'

'Dunno about that. On balance I think we did. Sumter and Irvine were up to a bunch of nasty shit – some of the witness statements we've got from the students would make your hair curl – you wouldn't have been the first people they'd burnt either.'

'I suppose I define winning differently to you,' she said.

'Officially of course, you're right – all the stolen archive material's gone and we didn't get to arrest any of the key players,' he slid a thick sheaf of papers across the desk to her. 'Take a look at this. The kid who took over as archivist from George Patterson gave us a full list of the manuscripts that were in there. I'll bet half of it hasn't even been missed yet.'

Flora thumbed through the first pages. 'And so priceless manuscripts are lost forever, a few students get locked up and the religious slanging match goes on. Wasn't quite what I had in mind when I said I'd help.'

'Not everybody sees it that way. They believed what they wanted to and the stuff Sumter faked up just helped reinforce it. The fact your buddy Josephus said it was all a crock won't mean a thing to them.'

'It frightened some of them enough to make sure *The Seven Stars* never saw the light of day though,' she replied.

'Do you reckon there's enough of it left to work with?' he asked.

'I hope so, for Francesco's sake, even after everything he did. Trouble is, even if we can piece it all back together it'll be Josephus' word against the Christians' and the result of *that* fight was decided nearly two thousand years ago by the likes of Eusebius.'

'True.'

'By the way, what's going to happen to Raymond?' asked Flora. 'You're not going to arrest him are you?'

'Nah. He's one of the good guys now. I can't go into detail but let's just say Raymond's agreed to help us. He'll be fine.' He stopped midstream and looked at her intently. 'More importantly, what about you? You got any plans for this evening?'

'Packing,' she replied. 'My flight leaves for London tomorrow evening. Giles Smith and his chums want to debrief me too according to the Director.'

'So how long's it take you to pack a case?'

'I don't know. Hour or so maybe.'

He looked at her with the makings of a smile creasing his face. 'Why don't we go and get drunk?'

Flora bounced across the room and gave him a kiss on the cheek. 'That's the best offer I've had in weeks.'

THE END

The Seven Stars – Author's Note

Although this is a work of fiction, the first-century background to *The Seven Stars* is based on real events, places and people. That said, I've taken quite a few liberties in filling in history's gaps so it's only fair that I should take a little time, now you've been so kind as to read this far, to add a bit more detail.

I'll start with Titus Flavius Josephus, born into an aristocratic Judean family around 37 AD and originally known as Joseph son of Matthew (Yosef Bar Matityahu or Yosef Ben Matityahu, both terms for "son of" being pretty much interchangeable between Aramaic and Hebrew). He took the surname (Flavius) of his imperial patron, Vespasian, after the Jewish Revolt which ended in 70 AD with the sack of Jerusalem and the burning of Herod's Temple by the Roman army of Alexandria, commanded by Vespasian's son, Titus. However, to avoid confusion, I've used the name "Josephus" throughout the narrative.

Despite Josephus' obvious intellect it's difficult to find any redeeming features in his character, but his value to us lies in his two major works of history: *The Wars of the Jews* (written c.75-79 AD), an eye-witness account of the disastrous uprising against Rome; and his twenty-volume monster, *The Antiquities of the Jews* (c. 93-94 AD), also written for a Roman audience and designed to show Jewish culture and religion as resting on ancient foundations, thus making it comparable to those of Rome and Greece. As with much of his writing, both works represent a selectively edited version of history – I'm almost tempted to use the word "spin" – and are riddled with self-justification, but nonetheless they give the modern reader an invaluable insight to the period and to the Jewish world view prevailing at the time. In *The Wars*, Josephus takes this self-justification to new heights when he tries, not that successfully, to explain why he was one of only a handful of Jewish defenders to survive the siege of Yodfat (also known as Jotapata) in 67 AD. Not only did Vespasian spare his life but immediately took Josephus under the Flavian wing, all – according to Josephus – on the basis of a last-minute and utterly contrived religious prophecy that he persuaded the cynical and pragmatic old Roman warrior to swallow. My version of events, where Josephus betrays the fortress and its defenders in return for his life, is pure fiction, but so I suspect is his.

The Seven Stars is my own invention too, as is the whole idea of Josephus as the son of the Biblical Jesus – so before reaching for the green ink, please remember; it's just fiction, a load of old fibs that I made

330

up. The same applies to his quest to track down and kill the surviving apostles. However, some of the events recounted by Josephus in his autobiography (or *Vita*) (c. 99 AD) do have uncanny parallels with stories in the Gospels. For example, Josephus was such a prodigious scholar that at fourteen he was consulted on the Law by Jerusalem's chief priests: an almost identical story is told of the twelve-year-old Jesus in chapter two of Luke's Gospel, written at around the same time as the *Vita*. The shipwreck of St Paul recounted in the Acts of the Apostles (again, contemporary with Josephus' writings) is remarkably similar to Josephus' account of his own misfortune, also on the way to Rome, which I've adapted in chapter 3. Whether or not the writers of the Gospels cribbed ideas from Josephus is a debate for far wiser heads than mine: all I would say is that I've taken the liberty of moving the shipwreck from the Adriatic to the coast of Sicily in order to introduce two real characters; Alityros the actor and Proculus the naval commander.

Alityros, also of Jewish birth, was a favourite of Poppaea Sabina, Nero's wife, and through Alityros Josephus gained an introduction to the Imperial court: that said, there's absolutely no evidence to suggest he was on the ship with Josephus and I apologise to his shade for dunking him.

Proculus is brought into the narrative as a patron of Josephus although nothing suggests they ever met: the Admiral was one of the key players in the unmasking of Piso's unsuccessful coup against Nero via his friendship with Epicharis, a woman who was horribly tortured to make her reveal details of the conspiracy.

Gubs, steersman and all-round good egg, is fictional too but the Roman fleets must have abounded with stalwarts like him – good men to have on your side in a crisis. As for *Lamia*, the child-eating demon of Greek mythology, she was a daughter of *Poseidon* and often appeared to mortals as a shark. Even today, Great Whites are common in the Mediterranean (apologies to anyone who's reading this on holiday but maybe going for a last swim isn't such a good idea after all...) and in ancient times were far more numerous. *Lamia* was known for turning up whenever sea battles took place, attracted by the noise and by blood in the water, so Gubs' concerns about her having a liking for shipwrecks weren't far off the mark.

Josephus' writings tell us he eventually reached Rome via Puteoli but for some reason he omits to mention that I waylaid him, sending him for a scenic tour along the bay of Naples and its villas.

Thanks to Poppaea's intervention, Josephus achieved the aim of his trip, to persuade Nero to release his friends: three Jewish priests sent to Rome under arrest by Governor Festus. Before they can make it home, I admit to kidnapping them, giving them new names and setting them to work with Josephus in his hunt for Paul and Peter. In the process of helping my narrative, two of them are killed and a third, Giora, is with Josephus when they inadvertently start the Great Fire of Rome in 64 AD. The wooden grandstands of the original Circus Maximus would have been an ideal spot for the fire to break out.

Not only had fiddles not been invented in Nero's day but he probably wasn't even in the city when the blaze started. However, the legend of fiddling while Rome burned stuck, and the fire did a very convenient urban clearance job, giving him just the space he needed to build his vast palace complex, the *Domus Aurea* or "golden house", subsequently demolished by the Flavians.

Nero gets a deservedly bad press but I've given him the benefit of the doubt when it comes to the death of Poppaea – no angel herself and implicated in a number of dynastic murders. I've shown her as dying in childbirth rather than following the versions offered by three men who disliked Nero: Suetonius, Cassius Dio and Tacitus, all of whom blame some kind of domestic violence, meted out by the emperor in the last weeks of her pregnancy, as the cause of death. Although in fairness to these august gentlemen, given that Nero had his own mother murdered, adding wife-beating to the charge sheet is hardly stretching credibility.

Nero considered himself a great musician, actor and poet and forced audiences to sit through agonisingly long and dreadful recitals. Men did indeed feign illness, sometimes even death, as an excuse to leave these performances and women pretended to go into labour. If the emperor was in a particularly bad mood, the penalty for falling asleep could, on rare occasions, be death. Vespasian, as a repeat offender, was banished from Nero's court but this happened in Greece, not Rome, and the story of Josephus interceding to save the senator from execution is a convenient invention to fit the plot and to provide a reason for his sparing Josephus' life after Jotapata.

By 66 AD Josephus was back in Judea where the first stirrings of revolt were in the air – for a highly readable account of the collision between the Roman and Jewish worlds I recommend Martin Goodman's excellent book, *Rome & Jerusalem – the Clash of Ancient Civilizations*. Josephus subsequent claim that he was forced against his will to become a leader of the revolt reads very much like an after-the-event, "a big boy made me do it and then ran away," excuse. Whatever the truth, he was a poor general and, as we've seen, may well have changed sides in order to save his own skin: his own people certainly thought so at the time and they also blamed him for helping Titus' army to take Jerusalem three years later while supposedly acting as a negotiator. Nice guy.

Vespasian and his sons, Titus and Domitian, were highly generous to Josephus throughout his remaining years – again, no one's entirely sure when he died but the range 100-102 AD seems to get the most votes – but there's no evidence of this generosity extending to the gift of a villa in Pompeii. It seems that he remained in Rome, living in what had been Vespasian's villa, granted to him when his patron became emperor.

As for the fate of the apostles, with few exceptions, nobody seems to be very sure how, when or where they died – such vagueness is a great help to writers of fiction; with no pun intended, an absolute godsend. Even for Peter and Paul, both martyred in Rome, there seems to be no agreement over when the executions took place so once again I've picked dates, places and events to suit the narrative of my fictionalised Josephus' quest for vengeance. One thing that isn't fictionalised is the *Plutonium* at Hierapolis where a lethal concentration of CO_2 from a volcanic fissure gathered in a hollow over which the shrine to the god was built. Given that nobody seems to know what happened to the Apostle Matthew, I thought it convenient to have Josephus kill him there.

Finally, William Sunday University isn't real either, although it's named after William Ashley Sunday, a baseball player turned evangelist who lived from 1862-1935 and it bears no resemblance to any US Bible college whether alive or dead (just in case any lawyers are reading – one never knows).

Now, if anything in this book causes offence, please remember that it's only a novel: I made it up.

Simon Leighton-Porter
August 2012

Lightning Source UK Ltd.
Milton Keynes UK
UKOW031238221012

200977UK00005B/12/P